Chapter One

Goddess Epona arrived at the iron gates of the Otherworld bearing in her tender arms the spirits of one hundred thousand slain warriors. She deposited the spirits at the gates, and rang a bronze bell to signify the imminent approach of midnight. The goddess informed the spirits that the sacred festival of Sowain was at hand and inserted a key in the lock, which she kept on a twig of white roses about her graceful neck. Then she opened the heavy iron gates.

She granted the hundred thousand spirits one full day in the world of the living, the sacred festival day of Sowain. Before allowing the spirits to depart however, she informed them that they were required to return by midnight before the echo of the bronze bell faded away, or the heavy iron gates would be closed permanently against them. Then their deathly spirits would forever roam over lonely hills and valleys in search of a new home, but destined never to find one.

As the spirits readied to depart, Epona opened a silver casket. In this she kept the earthly memories of the slain warriors. She returned the memories to the spirits, each in turn; but warned each in turn to use it carefully, and not to cause trouble in the land of the living. Soon all the spirits were fled, and she locked the iron gates again.

Early morning dawned in drifting cloud-fogs on the bleak westerly and windswept province of Connaught, where King Ailill prepared for the sacred festival. His servants placed a round slab of pine resin from Gaul in an earthen bowl. They heated the solid dark resin, and when it changed to liquid they massaged it into the king's red hair. Then they piled his hair on the top of his head and allowed it to harden. On top of this they placed his kingly crown, and held a mirror to his face. The crown signified his importance, and the resin added to his height.

Through the wet and clinging fog, thirty Connaught chiefs journeyed over bogs and heather to celebrate the sacred festival in the craggy hilltop fort at Knocknashee, the residence of King Ailill and Queen Maeve. The fires – which had been allowed to die out with the ending of the old year – were rekindled for the New Year, and the servants huddled around to get some warmth back into their bodies.

Meanwhile, male servants of the king selected and cut out the weakest sheep in the flocks, and slaughtered them to celebrate the New Year feast. The slaughter also served another purpose: it saved precious fodder for the coming winter. The meat was stripped, rolled, and salted; and placed in a huge bronze cauldron of fresh water. Onions were halved and carrots sliced, and put in the cauldron with the meat. Then the bones of the slaughtered sheep were stacked on top of the burning turf fire.

As the bones burned heating the water, the servants selected six of the fattest turnips, cutting off the heads and scooping out the insides. They put balls of yellow pulp into the cauldron where it simmered with the meat. Into this mixture they put handfuls of ripened blackberries, filled with juice.

4

John Henry Rainsford

Queen Maeve

AUSTIN MACAULEY PUBLISHERS™

LONDON • CAMBRIDGE • NEW YORK • SHARJAH

A CIP catalogue record for this title is available from the British Library.

ISBN 9781786298829 (Paperback)
ISBN 9781786298836 (Hardback)
ISBN 9781786298843 (E-Book)

www.austinmacauley.com

First Published (2018)
Austin Macauley Publishers Ltd.
25 Canada Square
Canary Wharf
London
E14 5LQ

One of the servants – an old woman – greased two pieces of string with the fat of a slaughtered sheep. She took the string to the gate where two skulls were hanging. These were the heads of two enemies hanging at the entrance as a warning. The flesh had long since decayed, and only the white bones remained. She placed a greased string in each skull and set it alight. The lighted skulls grimaced in the fog, warning evil spirits they were not welcome.

The sacred festival of Sowain was the most important of the year, heralding the end of one year and the beginning of another. A period of one day elapsed between the ending of the old and the beginning of the new. This was the day when the spirits of the dead returned to the land of the living. On this most important day, the three iron gates of the Otherworld were thrown open and the spirits of the warriors were free to return to the lands of their birth, and of their death. The servants were careful when preparing the feast to leave out food for the roaming spirits. The servants and chiefs were fully aware that if the spirits were not made welcome in this world, they would not be made welcome in the next. Seats were left empty to greet the visiting spirits to the feast, and fires rekindled to warm them in the land of the living.

When the chiefs arrived, the servants stoked up the turf fires until the hot flames danced, and handed out tankards of dark brown ale. The chiefs drank the ale and warmed their hands, commenting on the foggy weather. They wore their hair long but groomed well, falling to their shoulders and turning inside. Universally they wore their hair this way, except one chief who was bald. They wore long drooping moustaches, combed and smooth, but otherwise they were clean-shaven.

They were dressed in woollen leggings, bound in strips of hide, and their upper garments were also made of wool, held by ornamental clasps. A few of the chiefs wore white wool, teased and spun from the raw fleece, and knitted by their wives and daughters. These garments were ideal for the wet climate because they resisted the rain. However, most of the chiefs considered white too common to wear, and instead wore rich garments of maroons and blues and yellows. They took great pride in their clothes, and in their appearance.

The dyes were obtained by selecting flowers and herbs, the colours required, and boiling them in a pot with the wool. This was done in layers, the wool below a layer of flowers and herbs until the pot was ready for the fire. Then it was boiled for a day and a night, and left to cool for a second day and night. The wool was then dried and spun in strings, and knitted into garments by the wives and daughters. However, these dyed garments did not resist the rain since the boiling process removed the protection. Yet the chiefs were not bothered about getting a soaking as long as they looked good in company, choosing outer display over inner comfort.

A game of little children played out by grown men began the festivities in the stone hilltop fort. This childish game concealed a serious intent. A wooden vat was filled with ice-cold water and the servants floated a huge apple on the surface. Fifteen young chiefs were blindfolded by the servants and hands tied behind their backs. The purpose of the game was to seize the floating apple between the teeth and lift it from the vat. The chief who accomplished this task had the privilege of sitting nearest the royal couple during the feast.

Fifteen bound and blindfolded young chiefs knelt around the vat and a servant clapped hands. As one they plunged their heads into the ice-cold water. Like stags meeting in challenge, heads butted in deadly combat as each man fought for the privilege of sitting nearest the royal couple, and to demonstrate his strength. The older chiefs refrained from the contest of the heads, choosing instead to view the butting young chiefs in the churning water. Blood from their wounds turned the water red, and it churned like a sea in storm. The older chiefs sagely shook their heads and passed comments about the rash impetuosity of youth, and recalled in fond remembrance the times they too had fought for the apple.

It was the chief of the O'Malley clan who won the apple, a man of nineteen summers wearing a red moustache and long turning hair. His fine yellow woollen jacket was drenched in foaming water, and bright blood gushed from a wound in his forehead. He was determined to prove his strength however, and ignored the wound. He pushed the ripe red fruit to the bottom of the vat and held it there. None could hold their breath as long as O'Malley as each chief in turn was forced to give up. His victory did not sit modestly on his broad shoulders, for his tribe was much given to boasting.

"O'Malley is the best man here!" he declared.

The waiting servants unbound his hands and removed the wet blindfold, drying his face and cleaning the head wound. He glanced around the assembled chiefs, daring any to challenge his claim, and pushing away the servants. The older chiefs grinned at his foolish words, and wisely held their tongues. The O'Malleys were much given to boasting at festivals. The older chiefs grinned even wider when they observed the young chief carefully preening his long hair and moustache, and shaking the water from his yellow cloak, asking the servants for a polished mirror.

Knocknashee, in Sligo, was the ancestral home of the Kings of Connaught, a hilltop fort standing on a craggy mountain-top overlooking a wide sea of frequent storms. Violent gusts of wind shrieked over the fort from the sea, and such was their ferocity that no trees grew in its vicinity. The most westerly and desolate, Connaught was also the poorest of the five provinces in the land. This rocky province was ruled by King Ailill and Queen Maeve, a couple wed in law though not in mind. To the east, across the broad River Shannon, the verdant and fruitful fields of Meath produced yearly abundant crops. Further east were the rolling hills and many forests of Leinster, and to the south were the lush clovered meadows of Munster. The richest province lay to the north in Ulster, and riches always attract envy.

King Ailill joined the visiting Connaught chiefs and they celebrated the sacred festival, drinking dark brown ale from large copper tankards. The waiting servants announced the arrival of the queen, who came alone to the dining hall. Maeve had flaxen hair and she wore it braided, looping down her back. Over her shoulders was a rich woollen cloak dyed deep purple, and secured at the neck by a gold brooch inlaid with gems. Her crown was larger and more ornate than the crown of her husband, and in the glow of a dozen burning torches the heavy gold crown sparkled with precious rubies and lapis lazuli.

The king was visibly angry, but kept it under control. Holding his tongue, he gestured to a harpist who plucked the strings of his tall standing harp. Sweet strains of music wafted across the dining room, finding favour in the ears of the listeners. Servants moved amongst the chiefs filling their copper tankards, and the dark brown ale flowed freely. A great fire burned in the stone grate, stacked with black burning turf.

Now a bard stepped forward and recited verse. Bards were most respected, for they could enhance the reputation of a warrior, and of a king. They could also destroy a reputation. So they were liberally fed and housed wherever they travelled. The bard recited the past glories of Connaught, and the feats of its proud warriors. In this oral way, the history of the province was preserved, and passed down to the next generation.

When the bard ended the recitation, the king spoke to O'Malley, "Come, Fintan, come join us at the head of the table. Tonight we welcome into our hilltop fort the spirits from the Otherworld. We have lighted the skulls of our enemies at our gate to deter evil spirits, for the iron gates of the next world remain open until midnight, and not all who come from that place are good." He closed his eyes and called out, "Spirits, how many have come to join us at the feast?"

In silence the chiefs awaited the reply.

"One," a voice replied.

"Unseen spirit, I bid you a hundred thousand welcomes to Knocknashee, the Mount of the Fairies," said Ailill. "What was your name when you dwelt here?"

"Soon I shall appear," replied the voice.

"I bid you a hundred thousand welcomes to my home this day whoever you are," said Ailill. "We have set out a table and we have prepared thick mutton stew to sate your hunger. We have left vacant seats at our table, and we have filled tankards of dark brown ale from Munster. We have lit turf fires and bones to warm you on this cold day, for no fires burn in the Otherworld."

Fintan O'Malley swaggered to the top of the long table and sat near the king and queen. King Ailill held up a copper tankard and spoke to the empty seat. All thirty chiefs stood up and held their tankards to welcome the visiting spirit to Knocknashee, their heads bowed in reverence.

"Spirit, show yourself," said the king.

A wispy spirit appeared in the hall, and though the chiefs feared no mortal they withdrew in horror at the sight of the spirit. The older chiefs recognised the spirit of the slain warrior. It was Talteann, former King of Connaught, slain in battle against the forces of Ulster. The spirit did not sit down, but floated around the hall, staring at each chief in turn. It had no bodily substance and resembled a grey puff of smoke in the form of a man. Now the spirit removed its head and held it aloft for all to see. A line of red circled the neck, in stark contrast to the universal greyness of the spirit.

"King Connor of Ulster slew me in gory battle," the head said. "I fought well that hard day, for I was a king strong in arms. But the gods threw their dice, and they turned against me. It is the fate of kings to kill in battle, or be killed. Such is the destiny of a man who wears the crown. Yet when I fell on that bloody field not one chief protected my dead body. Connor cut off my head and tied it to his war-chariot. My courage became his, for he took it from my severed head. I see some chiefs gathered here who let that happen. They left me on that bloody field."

Some of the older chiefs dropped their eyes in utter shame, for the disgrace still hung over them like a heavy chain. They had not fought over the dead body of their slain king, and they had allowed Connor to steal his courage.

"My brother, we fought well that bloody day but we were outnumbered," replied Ailill. "I was but a mere boy when you fell fighting at my side, a stripling youth of fourteen summers. At that moment, in the white heat of battle, I had to make a decision. We had a choice to die on the field, or retreat. I chose the latter, and I do not regret my decision. Ours is a poor province, short of men. I did not see the point of throwing away good lives to recover the body of a dead king."

"Retreat?" spat the angry spirit. "No warrior retreats with honour intact. Better to die than take a backward step. Connaught has never turned its back on an enemy. We fight and we die, but we do not run. Our enemies fear us as much in death as in life!"

"Brother," answered Ailill, "each king must make his own way in the world, and his own decisions. I grieved long over your death, for you were my older brother whom I regarded no less than the immortal gods. When we made peace with Ulster, did I not afford you all the honour due to a dead king? Did I not build a tomb for you of white granite and cover it in soft earth? Did I not fill a wagon with golden objects and place it in the tomb though ours is a poor province? Did I not put your ceremonial sword and shield in the tomb? Did the gods not know by my worthy actions that you were a king in this world? Come, my brother, come and sit down with the chiefs. Your time here is short, and time must be enjoyed, not wasted."

"Maeve was sent by her father from clovered Munster to wed me," said the spirit. "She wed you after my death. Ailill rules Connaught now, but Maeve rules Ailill. That is why she wears a bigger crown. A king who cannot rule his own wife cannot hope to rule his kingdom. Connaught has come to a sorry state when it is ruled by a woman."

Under the impact of these words, Ailill blushed furiously.

"Such base utterances are not worthy of a king, living or dead!" he exclaimed. "This day is our most sacred festival, and we have gathered in Knocknashee to celebrate. Brother, either withdraw the wounding words or depart from my home at once. Connaught is now my kingdom, not yours. It passed to me on your death."

"What chief here has the courage to avenge my death?" asked the head, staring at each chief in turn, its grey eyes blazing red in fury. "I count thirty chiefs here, but I do not count one who dares look me in the eye. At least your shame has not gone the same way as your courage! I speak to ye as your former king. Did courage die in Connaught with me?"

"Brother, we have made peace with Ulster since your death on the field of battle," replied Ailill. "A treaty was signed, witnessed by the immortal gods, and the treaty stands. You have insulted me in my own home, though I prepared a place at our table for you. Our old and sacred laws of hospitality extend both to host and to guest. Withdraw the insult, or depart."

"I depart, but I shall return again and again until I am avenged," vowed the spirit. "We shall meet again next Sowain."

"No, we shall not meet, for you are not welcome," said Ailill.

"This is my home, to come and go as I please," the head said.

King Ailill's temper broke, and he seized his sword from its scabbard. The iron sword was short, the length of his forearm. This was the sword most favoured by the men of Connaught, for fighting the enemy up close. With reddened cheeks the angry king lunged at the spirit. The spirit disappeared as quickly as it had arrived.

When the spirit departed, the king sought to limit his shame by a plea to the gathered chiefs. Yet his cheeks could not conceal the hurt caused by his brother, for they were redder than O'Malley's blood. "It is fully twenty years since Talteann was killed in battle against Ulster," he began. "Ye who come here yearly since that time know I have never neglected to leave a seat for him at our table. I have always honoured him as a king and a brother. But since his death he has not once paid his home a visit, until now. And when he did come he sought to stir up trouble for his brother. No guest should behave in an evil manner in the home of his host, living or dead. Well, that spirit is not welcome here next Sowain. Come, my friends, let us eat and drink and enjoy this feast."

The harpist pulled on his strings and sweet music wafted across the great dining hall. The servants removed the empty seats and piled black turf on the fire. The chiefs ate the thick stew and drank dark brown ale from Munster; but they ate and drank in silence.

Seated at the table was Bricriu, a chief of the O'Kelly tribe. Now this chief was not happy unless he was causing mischief.

"The deathly spirit of Talteann spoke the truth," he said. "Our king turned his back that day and fled from the field of battle."

Malachi Mac Carthy looked up and spoke. "No, Bricriu, he used his head. His retreat saved us. Many men alive here now would be dead but for the king. We were outnumbered that day and surrounded on three sides. The king made the only choice available to him. Do not confuse bravery with stupidity."

"It was nothing but the spineless act of the basest coward, and it brought disgrace on our province," replied Bricriu. "Better to die with honour than live as we do in shame."

This Malachi Mac Carthy was a proud and honourable man who was upset by the words of Bricriu. He made an instant reply, "Sowain is a sacred festival to welcome the spirits from the Otherworld, and though Talteann uttered rude words to the king there is no need to add insult to his hurt pride. He is our king and must be treated with due respect. Your vile words are not fitting for this sacred occasion. Remember always that the gods are listening, though we cannot see them. If your tongue is unable to speak good words this night, let it speak no words at all."

Rebuffed by Mac Carthy, Bricriu turned to Rory Guinan, a chief from Leitrim. "I have heard it told that our king is not the father of his own daughter," he said. "They say that the father of Grainne is not live Ailill but dead Talteann. Connaught has come to a sorry state that we are ruled by a king who is weak of mind and of body."

"It is nothing but base rumour," Guinan replied.

"Our law proclaims that the king must wed his province before he weds his bride," Bricriu said. "He married Connaught, but what dowry did he bring to our land? Our sheep are skinny and our fields bear no harvests. Even the crows find it hard to live here, and that is the king's fault. The gods do not smile on Ailill."

In the early morning hours, the king stood and instructed the servants to bring his druid to the hall. The servants departed, and the king spoke to the chiefs. "Turnod has studied in the arts of vision. He drinks from the sacred chalice of the gods, and Brigid opens the door to the future and allows him enter. Turnod is ready to tell us of the coming year and what it holds for us and for our beloved province."

The druid Turnod was a man of three score and ten years. He wore his white hair braided in three strands, and his long beard was parted down the middle. His linen gown was dyed green, the colour of Connaught. On the front of the gown, stitched in white wool, were three red-eyed salmon coiled in winding loops, symbols of wisdom.

Old Turnod spoke to the royal couple and to the assembled chiefs, "I am but a medium, and it is my task to tell the things Brigid pours in my ears. At this time of year, the gates of the Otherworld are thrown open by Epona, the goddess beloved of spirits. My undead spirit flies there and Brigid welcomes me with her wisdom. That loveliest of goddesses does not lie and therefore I do not lie. The things I see shall come to pass as certain as night follows day."

A servant brought the druid a chalice of oakwood carved with figures of sacred spiral symbols. From a leather pouch tied around his waist, the druid took three toadstools, and ground them into the chalice using his thumb. Next he ground in three mistletoe berries, and added red wine. Turnod drank the sour brew, and the king waited.

The druid went into a trance, and his features changed. His voice became harsh and loud, like the keening of old women after the death of a chief. "Wise Goddess Brigid has spoken to me with a broken heart," he said. "She foresees death stalking the land with a bloody sword. She foresees the old men of peace shouted down and the young men of war heard." His voice rose to fever pitch.

"She foresees brother waging terrible war against brother. She foresees the invincible son of a god destroying the chiefs and bravest warriors of our province. She foresees evil Morrigan, the goddess of war, feasting on their dead flesh. She foresees funeral pyres of burning wood turning the grassy and verdant slopes of Meath into burnt ashes, and their black pyre-smoke blocking out the sun and turning the land to darkness. She foresees the keening of wives and mothers in every desolate district of Connaught. She foresees the death of a wise king. She foresees a dead warrior slaying a queen. This is the vision and the prophecy of Brigid."

After the terrifying prophecy, the undead spirit of the druid returned from the Otherworld, and he fell into a disturbed sleep, his eyes rolling beneath closed eyelids. The man-servants of the king carried him from the great hall of feasting, holding his old trembling body in their arms. The foreboding prophecy of the druid was received in many different ways by the thirty assembled chiefs. Some did not believe the prophecy and closed their ears to the words. The young chiefs welcomed the prophecy, and cheered loudly at the prospect of gaining glory on the field of battle, and avenging the defeat Connaught had suffered at the hands of Ulster. The old chiefs were appalled by the prospect of war and shook their heads. A number of chiefs clamoured to speak, but Ailill held up a hand and silenced them.

"The words of my druid have always found truth, and yet perhaps his vision is clouded this time," he said. "For it seems to me that druids always predict evil events in the future and neglect good events. Let him come back when he awakes and give us another prophecy. Perhaps his vision will map out a different future."

It was eminent Mac Carthy who replied to his king. He was two score and ten years old and his bald head bore the scars of past battles. He did not speak often and when he did men listened.

"Good king," he said in a voice of gravel, "we have heard the prophecy once. Brigid does not repeat herself."

"The prophecy is foolish," said Fintan O'Malley. "For how can a dead warrior slay a queen?"

"Brigid does not lie," Mac Carthy said.

Now the queen spoke to the chiefs, "The vision of Turnod has fallen on many ears. Some do not believe his words, though they have not lied in the past. Some desire war, for they can win riches and glory in battle, and women to warm their cold beds when the snows fall. Some do not desire war, for they fear the loss of their lands and their wives. Such are the ways of wars since the beginning of the world. The losers give, and the victors take. In the distant land of the Mesopotamians, they teach that the stars guide our destiny; and yet in the lands of the Argives the old and wise philosophers preach that men have free will. The druid of my father was learned in their ways. He told me that free men have free will, and that they can choose their own destiny in this world. Which is right?"

Eminent Mac Carthy replied to the question, "Maeve, we are but untaught warriors, not philosophers. All we know is that when Brigid speaks through our druid, we must listen."

After the feast, the chiefs settled down to rest for the night, lying on the floor in the heat of the burning turf fire. The king and queen left the hall of feasting and retired to bed. The king sat on the rowan bed with his back to the queen, and undressed in darkness and silence. He pulled back the sheephide covers and drunkenly fell into the bed. The ale had loosed his tongue, and the large crown of the queen weighed heavily on his mind. The words of the spirit added to his discomfort and would not allow him sleep. He tossed and turned in the rowan bed seeking peace in sleep.

Lying awake on his back, he fatefully uttered the words that insulted a queen and started a war. "Happy is the wife wed to a rich husband," he complained.

The queen turned in anger to her husband in the darkness of the room. "What did my lord say?" she asked.

The king repeated his words, and added some more, "My wife came to Connaught with nothing but a holed black shawl to cover her nakedness. She was betrothed to Talteann, but when he was killed in battle she fixed her gaze on me for she desired my kingdom. That is why she wed me, for my riches and for my high title. Now she walks around in a weighty crown of gold and lapis lazuli, and clothes of linen and silk, though we are but a poor province. Has she no shame?"

Proud Maeve replied instantly to the insult, "Some men can hold drink and some cannot, my lord. My husband is a man who is unable to drink without feeling sorry for himself. Such men should learn to keep their stupid gobs closed, or stop drinking altogether."

The great quantity of consumed ale did not allow the king to curb his loosened tongue, and he spoke again to the queen in an angrier tone, "My wife can find faults in her husband but not in herself. A woman who marries a man for his riches alone cannot afford to criticize anyone."

The haughty queen responded in a flash: "Poor windswept Connaught was never rich, not in your time or not in any time in the past. It is a sinking land without trees and filled with bogs. Nothing grows in the soil except stones. A crow finds it hard to scrape out a living in this place! If my lord must find fault, he should try at least to be truthful. Now, I wish to sleep."

But the spirit of his dead brother gnawed like a rat at the king, and banished sleep from his body. And though the wispy spirit of Talteann had returned to the Otherworld, it remained inside the head of his brother. So Ailill spilled his wrath on his wife. "My wife came here with nothing but the clothes on her back!"

"My lord lies again," replied the haughty queen. "I came from my father King Cormac of Munster where the sweetly tall grassy meadows hum with winging bees and butterflies. I was his firstborn, and he lavished on me the finest dowry. I brought to this poor place three bars of yellow gold and a herd of ninety fat cattle, most of which died due to lack of grazing in this poor land. I brought to this desolate place a running flock of three hundred clover-ripened white sheep. I brought to this poor place a basket of sparkling sky blue lapis lazuli from the other side of the world. I brought to this poor place three bolts of fine silk. My father traded one hundred hides of sheep for each bolt from distant Cathay. The clothes and the crown my lord wears came from me. Now, I wish to sleep."

The king sat up in the bed and raised his voice to such a pitch that he wakened the servants. "Why did my wife wed me?"

"Because I thought I was marrying a king," replied the queen, her voice calm in contrast to her husband. "Too late I discovered my lord was not even a man. Now, I wish to sleep."

The sharp barbs of the queen angered the king. "I was rich, but my wife stole away my riches and my life! She is the cause of all my woes!"

"How quickly the sweet words of the lover turn into the bitter words of the husband," replied the haughty queen sharply. "When my lord was seeking my rich hand in wedlock, he told me that my falling hair was more golden than ripened fields of buttercups in springtime. When he was seeking my fair hand in wedlock, he told me that my eyes were bluer than bluebells in the shaded woodland. It was my gold that glittered in my lord, not my hair. It was my lapis lazuli that was blue in my lord, not my eyes. Now, I wish to sleep. I suggest that my lord does the same lest he say something he might later regret."

Yet the ale was too high in the king, and he did not relent. The ale and the spirit, and his wife's crown would not permit him to sleep, or to forget the insults.

"We can settle this once and for all!" he exclaimed. "Let us send the herald Cathal to count our possessions! Let us put our wealth on the ground for all to see! I am rich in my own right! My goods will prove that I did not marry Maeve for her dowry!"

"My lord, the words of a man high in dark brown ale are confused and make no sense," replied the queen. "Let us wait until the pale winter sun rises over our windswept province, and then order the herald to count our goods. Let him give the count before the chiefs depart, and let them witness whether the king has the wealth, or the queen. Though he shall not include my dowry, for we both can lay claim to that! Let him count the numbers of cattle and sheep we each have, and bring his report."

"Let him count! King Ailill is not a kept man!"

There can be no hidden secrets where open-eared servants are present. Woken by the raised voice of the king, the servants put their ears to the door, and in glee listened to the royal argument. The news spread faster than a million tongues of fire in a dry forest.

Chapter Two

Surrounded by a high wall of grey and black stones, Knocknashee ascended from the treeless mountain to enclose the royal palace and protect the royal couple. The huge stones were shaped and fitted closely to deprive an attacking force of a foothold. The royal palace was wooden, and six pillars of oak supported the structure. Separate conical wooden quarters housed the royal servants and the craftsmen of the royal couple.

Outside the confines of the round hillfort of Knocknashee, another wall of stones was constructed enclosing nine bleak acres where the flocks were wintered and fed until the coming of spring, protected against marauding wolves. This area was sectioned into separate holding pens for sheep, goats, and cattle. The frontal approaches to the hilltop fort were protected by sharp jutting stones, rammed into the ground to break down attacking or raiding formations. The sharp jutting stones were densely packed, and covered more than thirty acres. A narrow road wound from the fort to a wooden road across the bogs and marshes.

A pale winter sun cast shafts of dull light over the ringtop fort, and over the stone compounds of sheep and goats and the few cattle. The young herald picked his way under a dark sky to the compounds and began counting the flocks. He used coloured stone beads strung on woollen threads to count the animals. He was finished before noon, and he reported the count to the royal couple and the assembled chiefs. The numbers were written with charcoal on a roll of parchment, and he assured them that the count was correct. He had counted the animals of the king by their red signs, and the animals of the queen by their blue signs. Ailill and Maeve owned the same number of sheep and goats, but he had found a difference in the cattle.

"My king and queen," he continued, "I have counted the numbers of cattle on my fingers, for ours is a poor land that does not support very many. Sheep and goats can live on sparse scraps of grass and nettles; but cattle require much fodder, especially in winter when snows lie on the ground and the grass does not grow. The king has eighteen cows, and the queen has the same amount. The herd of the queen does not have a bull, but the herd of the king has a white bull."

The queen was quick to query the count, "A white bull? That is my bull, Cathal."

"My queen, it appears that your bull leaped over the wall and challenged the king's bull," replied the herald. "In the fight the king's bull was slain. Then the white bull remained with the herd of the king. That is how I took the count."

"You have done well, young herald," said the king. "The white bull is mine since it has killed my bull. Our ancient Brehon Laws ordain that compensation must be paid in kind for loss, and our laws are just. My wealth is greater than the wealth of the queen. The matter is ended."

"The white bull leaped the wall and fought because he refused to be ruled by a woman," said Bricriu to the chiefs. "It seems a dull beast has more sense than our king."

King Ailill supped mulled hot mead with the chiefs before they departed, and they discussed the prophecy of the druid. Queen Maeve left the hall and the drinking chiefs, and hurried to the wooden house of Turnod near the gates of the hillfort. She woke the sleeping druid and explained her position to him, telling him that her husband had humiliated her honour before the chiefs.

The old druid listened patiently, letting the queen exhaust her anger. "My queen, it is a matter of little importance," he said. "A small cut on the arm if left untouched soon heals, and that is my observation. However, if it is scratched the small cut becomes a deep wound, and the whole arm becomes infected. Soon the body too falls prey to the poison. Maeve, do not scratch the small cut."

"The rich crown he wears he owes to my dowry, and the clothes he wears were paid for by my gold," she said, her anger gathering as the storm outside. "Yet he insulted me before the chiefs, and I demand revenge."

The druid nodded sagely and replied: "My queen, sometimes we must take a blow to our pride for the common good. I did not reveal all the vision since it was too terrible. However, I shall reveal it now. I saw a vision of Newgrange at Tara burning in flames on the summer solstice. I saw the solar road to the Otherworld cut off so that no spirits could reach there. That is what you risk by going to war."

But Queen Maeve was not listening to the wise advice. She paced up and down in the cramped wooden house.

"Why do you take sides for my husband against me, Turnod?" she demanded. "Is a queen not worthy of the same respect as a king? I came to you for assistance to right a wrong, and you give me none. Very well, give me your knowledge. Where is the best bull in the land? On whose rich grass does it graze?"

The druid was reluctant to give a reply, but he recognised that the anger of a queen is dangerous. "There is such a bull in Ulster, but it is sacred to the goddess Morrigan," he informed her. "It is known as the brown bull of Cooley for that was the place of its birth. The great beast has three horns, having an extra one on its forehead. Connor will not part with the beast, though requested by a queen."

"He dare not refuse the request of a queen," she said. "Let us speak now of another matter, my daughter, Grainne. She was happy here at Knocknashee learning under your wise teaching. Suddenly she decided to go away to distant Gaul, sailing from Galway on a trading ship. Why did she go?"

"Maeve, when a chick grows feathers in the nest, it flies the nest," Turnod replied. "She went to seek how others live and that is good. She is your only child, and is destined to rule in your place. May that not be for a hundred years! Grainne shall return wiser than when she left. Now, heed the warnings of Brigid, the wisest of the gods. Do not take our province to war."

At noon, on the day after the sacred festival of Sowain, thirty Connaught chiefs departed from Knocknashee under a grey and overcast sky of brooding clouds. A violent storm was driving in from the heaving ocean, and grey, dark clouds scudded over the hilltop fort.

Wild winds whipped up and battered against the outer wall, and large hailstones fell in white flurries.

Turnod threw a few sods of black turf on the fire, huddling down to sit out the storm. The wild winds grew in fierce intensity, dislodging a plank from the roof. The shrieking winds crowded into the room and whipped a burning ember from the fire. The old druid tried to stamp out the flames but the winds were too strong, and he fled the burning house.

"This storm is an evil portent of things to come," he said, in the shadow of a brooding sky. "A war is coming."

Speckled starlings and nightblack crows fell from the sky like stones and sought shelter from the storm. No birds dared fly in the storm, except a raven. On silent wings the dark bird drifted, unmoved by the shrieking winds as if untouched by their power. It hovered for a moment over the hilltop fort and flapped its wings in descent. It flew to the bedroom of the queen, and then changed shape. The bird became a young woman, dressed in a scarlet robe. She had long black hair, and might have been beautiful but for her stark eyes, which had triple irises. The outer iris was white, the colour of battle. The centre iris was red, the colour of the blood of slain warriors. The inner iris was black, the colour of the flesh of the dead.

"Do you know who I am, Maeve?" she asked, her voice as the harsh call of the raven.

"We have not met before," replied the queen, "but I suspect that you are Morrigan, the god of war. Why do you come to my home in Knocknashee? We are at peace with our neighbours."

"Turnod the druid spoke to you in prophecy, but he did not tell you everything for he is fearful of war," said

26

the goddess. "Some druids cut the message to suit their own purpose, as a bolt of cloth is cut to make a cloak. He is one of those careful old men. The goldenhide bull of Ulster has been blessed by me for mighty deeds. The great beast has three horns that signify its holy purpose. Its bright hide is the colour of beaten gold, and it stands taller than river saplings in summer bloom. Seize the bull, Maeve, and grasp what every woman desires."

The queen combed her hair in a polished mirror. "I have my beauty and I have my position. What more does a queen desire?"

"Revenge," replied the goddess. "Unbound riches too. This poor province is not worthy of your beauty or your intelligence. Your husband the king is content to live here in royal poverty; but you desire more, and you deserve more. You were made for greater glory than this, Maeve. You were made to live in a rich palace and to have everything your heart desires."

The queen stopped combing her hair. "How can the Ulster bull help me achieve riches and revenge, Morrigan?"

The god of war took the ivory comb from the queen's hand and combed her flaxen hair, teasing out the long tresses slowly and with care. "There is a legend told by old men about the coming of a goldenhide bull bearing on its broad forehead three sharp horns and blessed in mighty strength by the eternal gods of the Otherworld," related the god of war. "The legend states that the lone person who sleeps in its hide for three days and three nights shall gain its strength. On the anointed day, the person destined to be king shall emerge from the hide and approach the Stone of Destiny at Tara. The stone shall call out three times, and proclaim the person, High King of Ireland."

"Person?" asked Maeve. "So, it can be a woman?"

"It can be the Queen of Connaught," replied Morrigan.

"We already have a High King in Tara," said the queen.

"In name, not in power or prestige," Morrigan replied. "The Stone of Destiny has been silent for many decades now. Long ago it was all very different. Then the screams of the stone could be heard from the hills of Donegal to the high mountains of Kerry, and from the glens of Antrim to the beaches of Cork. The stone screamed like a thousand banshees when kings met to fight for the title, High King of Ireland. Now kings have grown soft, and the title passes down unchallenged from father to son. No wonder the crown has lost its former prestige! No wonder Diarmuid is High King in name only! But you can change everything, Maeve."

The queen braided her long tresses and tied them on her head, viewing her reflection in a polished mirror held by the war goddess.

"You say the stone shall call out three times and proclaim the person who sleeps in the hide as High King," she said. "Will the kings accept the verdict of the stone?"

"Yes, Maeve, for when the Stone of Destiny speaks, kings obey," replied the dark god of war. "That is the right reward for your courage. The title has lost its allure and prestige. Seize this ripe opportunity with both hands. I promise to give you every assistance."

"Yesterday was the feast of Sowain when we gather to welcome the spirits from the isles of the Otherworld," Maeve replied. "The grey spirit of Talteann turned up at the feast. I was betrothed to him by my father, and he was a strong king. He died in battle, though he did not die in my heart. I married his younger brother who prefers to die in his bed rather than on the field of battle! My shame is too heavy to carry."

"Every queen must make her own destiny in this short life," replied the war-god. "The destiny of Maeve lies in that northern rich province. Seize the triple-horned bull and you seize the future. What is your desire for the coming year? Do you wish to remain the wife of a minor and poor king, or do you wish to become the supreme ruler of the whole island? The choice is in your own hands."

"Words are easy, but actions more difficult," said the queen.

The war-god held up the mirror to the queen. "The opportunity lies before you, Maeve," she said. "Send your herald to Ulster and ask to borrow the goldenhide bull. In this manner you can gain revenge on your husband, and also become High King of Ireland. Deliver two blows with one strike."

"Borrow the bull, and then slay the beast?" asked Maeve. "For how can I sleep in the hide of the bull without slaying the beast? No, that is against our laws."

"The weak make the laws and the strong break the laws," said Morrigan. "Nothing is ever gained in this world except by bold actions. Nobody remembers the weak, but nobody forgets the strong."

The seed of ambition sown by the goddess in the mind of the queen had, by morning, blossomed and flowered into a spreading forest of burning ambition. On awakening, she sent for her herald and swore the young man to strict secrecy. The herald came to her bedchamber, his eyes fixed on the floor. Humble Cathal was eighteen summers old, with dark hair and a pale complexion, displaying in his youthful features his utter devotion to Maeve.

The queen took his hand in hers, and spoke to him. "Young Cathal, the mission I seek from you is of the utmost importance. The king has basely insulted me. He has stolen my prize bull and he has used the beast to rub my womanly heart in the dirt. Take fast horse to the court of King Connor in Ulster. He is a very noble king, and I wish to borrow the goldenhide bull that dwells in his province. Then I shall demand another count from my husband. When the count is complete, I shall return the bull on the feast of Brigid."

"The word of my queen is a command," Cathal said.

"Take the chief Bricriu with you."

A look of puzzlement crept over the features of the young man, and he made the reply, "Bricriu, my queen? I am young, not versed in the ways of easy diplomacy, but he is not worthy of the honour. His tongue is unfit for the court of a king, and fit only for the company of drunkards."

The queen dismissed his concerns, and replied: "He is strong in battle, and I fear for your safety on the road. Take him, but do not let mead pass his lips."

As Cathal readied his horse for departure, he was approached by the chief of the Mac Carthy clan, his bald head dripping in rain.

"Young man," said the old chief, "do not for a moment forget that you go to represent Connaught at the palace of Connor. He is a wise king, so journey as a supplicant and not to make demands. Use honey on your tongue and do not permit Bricriu to speak in drink. Drunken words have caused more trouble than you can ever imagine."

Chapter Three

The laws of hospitality ruled the land as effectively as the laws of kings. Bards travelled from court to court and sang the praises of generous hosts. Bards could also destroy the reputation of a host by accusing him of miserly behaviour. Since no host wished to be branded a miser in the palaces of kings, travelling bards and guests were liberally treated with food and drink, and lodgings. Thus when Cathal and Bricriu arrived at the court of King Connor at Emain Macha, his servants heated water and prepared a wooden bath for the cold and hungry guests. A change of clothes was provided for them, and meats and bread served on silver dishes.

A society that lives in peace seldom makes preparations for war. Emain Macha was such a society, bathed in the calm blessings of peace. The circular wooden palace of the royal family and the round buildings of the king's officials stood atop a green hill overlooking sweeping plains and ordered fields, in full view of the people. A wide sandy road swept up to the palace, winding its way past groves of holly trees and stately oaks. The oak trees were now dormant and leafless, awaiting the arrival of spring. The dark green branches of the holly trees bowed heavy with red berries in clusters of ripe fruit.

Their bellies filled and the cold banished from their bones, Cathal and Bricriu took a stroll behind the wooden palace and went into an orchard. Below them stretched the green and fertile fields of Ulster, sectioned by brown winter hedgerows, resting fallow until the coming of spring. Cathal stooped and picked up a ball of clay, teasing it in his hands.

"Look at this fine soil, Bricriu," he said. "It is not sodden with water as the soil of our province." He squeezed the soil in his hand and went to a bare apple tree. "Look, Bricriu, mistletoe, the food of the gods. Here it is abundant, but we rarely see it at home. Here it grows thicker than the nests of crows on tall trees."

"Connor is wed to Ulster, and he found favour with the gods," Bricriu said, closing his eyes. "Connaught is cursed by the gods because we are ruled by a weak king."

"There must be another explanation why we are poor and they are rich," replied Cathal. "Look at this ball of clay."

The chief did not observe the clay or the mistletoe, but regarded instead the rich buildings of Ulster. "The servants told me the king is holding a feast in our honour tonight," he said.

"That is so," answered the herald. "The queen has instructed me to do the talking. She gave instructions not to let mead past your lips. Obey her."

Bricriu shot back an angry reply, "That haughty woman might rule her husband, but she does not rule me!"

The magnificent feast King Connor gave for the two visitors from Connaught reflected his status as the richest king in the land. The hall of feasting held thrice one hundred guests. The wooden floor was smooth and polished in honey wax, and the walls were adorned with the hides and antlers of stags. Two log fires, one at each end of the hall, welcomed the guests to the feast. When Cathal and Bricriu arrived in the hall, servants poured goblets of red wine from a wooden barrel, and plunged two redhot bands of iron into the wine. This was called mulling the wine, and it warmed the cockles of the heart. The wooden tables groaned under the weight of venison, roast boar, ribs of beef, boiled fowl, and sliced sides of salmon.

Bricriu sat down at the table and drank a goblet of mead in one gulp. "Queer fish these Ulstermen," he said, filling another goblet. "They bring their women to a feast of men. That is a sure sign of weakness."

King Connor and Queen Rosheen sat at the head of the tables. They did not wear crowns, and their clothes were no richer than the garments of the chiefs and their wives. They wore cloaks of white linen, the colour of their province, and adorned with a red hand, its emblem. To the right of the queen sat Ferdia, the firstborn and heir to the throne of Ulster. To the left of the king sat Lorcan, the second son. Seated at his side was Nolan, druid to the royal family.

When the noble king stood to speak, the assembled chiefs and guests gave him their full attention. "Friends and guests," he began, "tonight we welcome the messengers from Connaught. We grant them both a hundred thousand welcomes to Ulster. They come in peace and we accept them with open arms. Our sacred laws of hospitality are stronger than ties of blood. Whilst they remain under my roof, they are in my care, and under my protection. Let no man raise hand or voice against them or he will answer to me."

Now Cathal stood up to speak, and his wise words belied his young years. He spoke in a clear voice so that all heard. "Good and noble king, your fame and your generosity are renowned throughout the land. No beggar coming to your door naked goes home without a cloak. Queen Maeve sends her regards and begs a request. There is a triple-horned bull in your kingdom and she seeks it on loan. It is known as the brown bull of Cooley. The bull will be returned at the feast of Brigid."

"What of her husband, the king?" asked Connor.

"Noble lord," replied the young herald, "when a king asks a question it must be treated with respect and an answer provided. But on this occasion I beg your forgiveness if I cannot answer for my lord the king. We are here under the orders of the queen and here we have made her request."

Now Nolan the druid to the royal family stood up to speak. He wore a long linen gown of white, the colour of his province. On the breast of the tunic he bore a red hand, the symbol of his province.

"Bad news travels faster than the swiftest hawk," he said. "It has reached my ears that an argument took place between the western king and the queen. That is an internal matter for that province and is of no concern to us. If we loan the queen the goldenhide bull, are we not interfering in the affairs of another province? This matter should be settled where it belongs, in Connaught."

"What of the request of a queen, Nolan?" asked Connor.

"The wise king puts the security of his province and of his people before all other matters, my lord," replied the druid.

Noble Connor thanked the druid for his advice, and made reply to Cathal. He announced that he would sleep on the matter for three days, and then give his answer to the request.

After the great feast, when the guests were departing, Cathal approached the king and secretly asked to speak with him in private. Connor invited the herald outside, and under the pale moonlight the herald walked with the king. Clouds drifted over the moon and snow began to fall, drifting lazily like the falling leaves of autumn.

"Noble king, I beg of you to give us the bull," he said. "Once we were enemies, but now we live in peace. Such an act would demonstrate that our provinces have left the past behind, and can journey into the future in peace."

"Wise words indeed for one so young," said the king. "Speak to me of the conflict between Maeve and Ailill."

"The king was goaded by the spirit of Talteann, his brother," related the herald. "I do not know why spirits stir up trouble, except that they do. The spirit should have enjoyed the day with its former friends. It should have sat with us and drank dark brown ale, but it caused mischief instead. After it departed, the king turned his wrath on the queen and accused her of marrying him for his wealth. That is why she sent us here to borrow the goldenhide bull."

The young herald left the king alone with his thoughts, the snow falling gently and resting on his grey beard.

Meanwhile, Lorcan approached Bricriu and sat beside him on the wooden bench. The younger son of King Connor mistrusted Connaughtmen, and regarded them as the natural enemies of his province. He suspected they were seeking any excuse to break the peace treaty. He poured more mead into Bricriu in an effort to loosen his tongue.

"I have heard the men of Connaught are the best drinkers in the whole of Ireland," he said.

Bricriu nodded his head, his eyes bulging. "Ireland?" he said. "We are the best drinkers in the whole wide world! Why, our women can drink any Ulsterman under the table!"

"My father is a very generous king," said Lorcan. "He gives readily and expects nothing in return. He intends to loan the bull to your queen for that is his nature, and no man goes against his nature. Unfortunately as you know, my friend, some gods delight in causing mischief. What happens if a god urges him not to part with the bull?"

Bricriu filled a goblet with mead, and drank it down. "If he refuses, it is our aim to seize the beast by force of arms," he said. He removed his short sword from its scabbard and plunged it in the table. The sword swayed from side to side. "This is how we act in Connaught. Now, I ask you a question. Where is your brother, Cuchulainn? Why has he insulted us by not attending the feast in our honour?"

"It was no insult," replied Lorcan. "As we speak here, he is out guarding the borders of our province. Though we are at peace, my brother is always prepared for war. He took a solemn vow to protect Ulster from its enemies, and such men do not take vows lightly. You shall meet with him tomorrow morning."

"I cannot wait," slurred Bricriu.

When Cathal returned to the hall of feasting, he found Bricriu lying over the table, drunk and sleeping. Aided by a strong servant, the herald carried the drunken chief to their quarters. As they undressed the chief for bed, he woke up and demanded more mead, abusing the servant.

"No more mead, or no bull for Connaught," Bricriu slurred. "What sort of hospitality is that? Ulstermen have no respect for the sacred Brehon Laws. This is a province rich in land, but poor in manners. Ye have no honour. Our aim is to take the bull by force if your king refuses. The men of Ulster are weak and have no heart for a fight."

Secrets are impossible to keep hidden where servants are present. The servant aided Cathal to undress Bricriu and helped the drunken chief to bed, biding his time. Then he hurried on fleet legs to the palace of the king with the news and related the uncouth words of Bricriu to the bedroom servants. They promised to tell the king at his breakfast next morning.

As Queen Rosheen slept, her husband slipped out of bed, pulled on his cloak, and passed unnoticed by his servants into the night. A full moon turned night into day, and pockets of snow rested on the ground. The king walked down the sandy road, beneath the leafless oaks and bowing holly trees. He was deep in thought, considering the request of Connaught.

A tall god appeared at his side, and he resembled a mortal man. He carried a nine-stringed gold harp on his back, and he spoke to the king in the moonlight: "Do you know who I am?"

"Yes, we have met before," answered the king. "Aengus, you are as the bats, coming out by night. This is the time when your spells bind the strongest. Why have you come here? Have you come to cast your spell on Ferdia, who is not wed? That boy is more a poet than a warrior, and I fear he shall never wed a wife."

"No, noble Connor, that is not why I am at Emain Macha," replied the god. "Evil Morrigan is abroad seeking to foment a war. Men who go to war do not make offerings to the god of love. The god who is not given offerings is quickly forgotten. Make your ears deaf to her calls."

"We have signed a peace treaty with Connaught and I am a king of his word," Connor said. "As we speak here, two envoys from that poor province are awaiting my response to the request of their queen. Should I refuse, I break our sacred laws of hospitality. Should I agree, I fear no good will come of the matter. Yet the duties of a king require hard decisions."

"Epona, who otherwise has a kind heart, has slammed the iron gates on Morrigan," said Aengus, walking at the side of the king. "She fears that war-loving goddess would cause the same chaos and suffering in the Otherworld as she does on Earth. She fears that the spirits of the dead warriors would follow the siren goddess of war again."

"Is not Dagda the king of the gods?" asked Connor. "Surely he can put a stop to her malice?"

The god of love shook his handsome head. "That god is seldom in the Otherworld," said Aengus. "He spends most of his time living hidden in this realm. When he is away, the gods are at each other's throat. Each god, and indeed each goddess, seeks to rule in his stead. Perhaps Dagda does not understand the nature of power because no palace remains empty for long."

"I thought no conflicts flared in the Otherworld," said Connor.

"Violence is not permitted, but fierce conflicts of the mind are fought there," explained the god of love. "Connor, let me tell you of the struggle for power in the

Otherworld since Dagda went missing. Lugh is the god of light who believes he is entitled to rule because he makes the sun shine. Morrigan is the goddess of war who believes that she is entitled to rule because men follow her blindly. Brigid is the goddess of rebirth who believes she is entitled to rule because she brings forth new life every year, and inspires wisdom in bards and druids. Manannan Mac Lir is the god of the seas who believes he is entitled to rule because he can raise the oceans to white frenzy. Ogma believes he is entitled to rule because his words are compelling."

"What about the other gods?" asked Connor.

"Some gods are important, and some are not," said Aengus. "In that respect, we are much the same as you. I deserve to rule, because I alone can grant men and women the gift of eternal youth. Let me demonstrate, Connor, and render you young again."

The god took the golden stringed harp in his hands and he began to play. "The harp is the instrument of love," said Aengus, "for it banishes the cares of this world and sends the feet in flights of fancy." In the blink of an eye, the old king was transported to a past land of his youth. In the journey, he shook countless passed summers from the wheel of his life, and he took brief flight on the happy wings of memory. He was not old now but young. In the blink of an eye, he was no longer in Emain Macha, but in the lush and verdant meadows of Meath.

He walked through a birdloud woodland of dappled light and shade, and emerged into a meadow of flowers and spotted looping butterflies in flight. The sap of flowing youth coursed hot in his legs, and his body was lean again and filled with strength. The sounds of gurgling water reached his ears, and his pace quickened. His young legs raced through the swarming bees and supping butterflies to the waters. He reached the River Boyne and knelt on the bank, and scooped the crystal waters in his hands, sating his thirst. Rainbowed trout darted under the mossy banks, flashing sparkling hues to the sun. The settled water reflected a young man of twenty years with blue eyes, long hair, and drooping moustache. At a deep pool in the river he undressed and cast his clothes aside. His headlong plunge sent a column of water into the sky, falling in bright cascades of glistening light. He swam a few fast strokes beneath the water, surfaced, and tossed back his long blonde hair. Emerging from the stream, he stretched on the grass to bathe in the sun.

Rosheen strolled slowly over the brow of a flowering hill, looping daisies in a chain, yellow and white flowered links. He leaped into the stream as she approached, sending spouts of foam into the afternoon sky. She sat on the bank of the river, making a point of ignoring him, threading daisies on a chain. He reached under the bank, found and tickled a brown trout, and raised the fish triumphantly.

She completed the daisy chain, saying: "Childish games."

He kicked under the river and surfaced near her. "Come in, Rosheen, the water is freezing," he teased. "Or are you afraid?"

She looped the daisy chain over his neck, and replied: "My modesty forbids it."

He removed the flowers from his neck and watched them float away on the calm water surface. "We are betrothed," he said.

She undressed and leaped into the stream, and the water erupted. She swam to him and ducked his head beneath the surface of the placid waters. Her young laughter rang over the rolling meadow and forests, over the buttercups and daisies, and echoed back in his ears.

The hoot of a night-hunting owl rang out over the palace. The king opened his eyes, and he was old and stiff again, and standing beside the humanlike god at Emain Macha. The god had stopped playing, and the harp was idle in his hands. It was night again, and the moon was in full bloom. And the old king had the same problems, and the same decision to make.

"The god of love is right," he confessed. "For a brief moment I was young again, happy and without a care in the world. I was a youth back then, when Rosheen and I ran through yellowed meadows, deeper hued than bog butter. Once we were young, but now we are old. Once I did not have to make decisions, but now I do. I fear the decision I must make will start a war."

Chapter Four

On the morning of the third day, Cathal and Bricriu went to the palace of the king to receive an answer. To his dismay, Cathal saw that Bricriu had been drinking, though the hour was early. A servant took them to the king, who invited them to join him at breakfast. His two sons were with him, the princes Ferdia and Lorcan. Another young man sat near the king. He had shoulder- length black hair and dark eyes, and was slightly built. Cathal thanked the king for the invitation, and they joined Connor for breakfast.

"My sons Ferdia and Lorcan you have already met," said the noble king, breaking an egg and eating. "This young man seated at my right hand is Cuchulainn. He is my foster-son. Have you have heard of him?"

Bricriu stared at him with hostility. "I have heard of him."

They dined on boiled eggs and brown breads, and strips of sliced pears dipped in honey. Cathal thanked the king for the breakfast and discussed the weather, in the manner of a good herald. "Dark clouds to the east," he said. "I do believe we will have snow soon. Let us hope we do not get heavy winter snows before we reach home. The roads will be impassable, not to mention the ford of the Shannon."

The king nodded gently, though his mind was on other matters, not on the weather. "Much thought has been given to the request of your queen," he said. "I have reached my decision, and I will give you my reasons for that decision. The worldly duties of a man and the worldly duties of a king are two separate things. Were I only a man, I would with all my heart loan the goldenhide bull to your queen. Yet I am also a king, and in that respect the safety and welfare of my people come first. I must decline your request."

Bricriu leapt to his feet. "That is an insult to Connaught!"

Cathal turned his head and told the drunken chief to keep quiet. Then he turned to the king and said: "Please forgive him, my lord, for he is high in mead though the day is young. It is not the place of a herald to lecture to a king, but I should point out the request of a queen must be treated as a command, even by a king. Noble Connor, if I am to return empty-handed to my queen, what do I tell her?"

"The good of a province must come first, tell her that," the king replied.

Now Cuchulainn spoke in hard words: "My father is too noble to speak plain words, but I am a warrior, not a diplomat or a king. He received ye into our home with courtesy and respect according to our sacred laws of hospitality. His servants bathed and clothed ye, and my father gave a feast in your honour. He promised to consider your request for the goldenhide bull. I do believe he would have given the bull to your queen, except our servant brought disturbing news to his ears. The servant reported that ye were ready to take the bull by force. So it was ye who broke the sacred laws of hospitality, not my father."

Lorcan added his voice to the debate. "I too heard that Connaught chief make the boast with my own ears. He spoke in mead, and that does not lie. He drew his sword in a hall of pleasure. Such actions are not worthy of civilised men. "

Bricriu's anger rose to his cheeks. His eyes bulged, and his breath gasped in short bursts. "We did not journey from our windy western province to be insulted by two mere boys who should be still at their mother's breast!" he charged. "Lorcan is not worthy of my contempt, or my sword. As for this skinny Cuchulainn and his bloated reputation as a warrior in battle, all I can say is that fools are easily impressed. He must have made it against soft Ulstermen who were grown fat and sloppy from easy living. He has not met a Connaughtman in battle. Let him come back in three years when his puny body has filled out and his beard has growed, and I will teach him what real fighting is all about."

Cuchulainn leaped up in anger, drawing his sword, and spoke in hostility to the chief, "I am ready now!"

Bricriu jumped from his chair sword in hand. The two warriors were bent on confrontation. Lorcan and Cathal sought to restrain them and keep them apart. Insults were traded freely. Cuchulainn accused the chief of loud drunkenness, and of insulting his father's hospitality. Bricriu accused Cuchulainn of hiding behind his reputation.

"Let us step outside and settle this!" Bricriu shouted.

The king held up his hand. "My son, sit down and put away your sword," he said. "This man is under my protection and no harm shall come to him in my home.

The gods frown on such base actions. Having said that, he and Cathal have outstayed their welcome. They must leave immediately."

Cathal dragged the angry chief to the door. Before leaving, Bricriu jabbed a finger at Cuchulainn. "We will meet again!" he stormed. "Then you shall die!"

"We will meet again," replied Cuchulainn.

Grey clouds scudded across the sky as they prepared to mount their horses. Then King Connor appeared leading a pair of horses. They were fit and lean stallions, bred for racing. "Accept this gift of friendship from Ulster to Connaught," he said. "This white stallion is called Dawn for his coat resembles the dew on the flowers in early summer. This brown stallion is called Chestnut, for he resembles the nuts of that tree in late autumn. Present one to Ailill and one to Maeve so that there is no animosity between them."

They mounted their horses and huddled up against the biting cold, pulling their cloaks above their heads. Cathal took the reins of the stallions in his hand. A servant of the king readied an ass, and tied six bundles of hay across its back for the journey. Cathal and Bricriu trotted the horses and ass down the sandy road, and set out for Connaught to bring the bad news to the queen.

In dim silence, they journeyed to the west, and the only sound was the clopping hooves on the road. As daylight gave way to darkness, they dismounted and prepared to rest for the night. Cathal fed the horses, and using a flint and some straw, started a fire. They dried the wet cloaks before the fire, and sat warming their hands. The anger had not departed the breast of the chief.

"Not only did the king insult us, but also his two brats," he said. "Lorcan does not drink to get drunk, but merely to get others drunk. Is that any way to treat a guest? He used mead to trip me up, a dirty trick. As for skinny Cuchulainn, well, we will meet again, mark my words." Cathal warmed his freezing hands, tears streaming down his cheeks. "How can I return empty-handed to my queen?"

"The concerns of that haughty woman do not bother me a bit," Bricriu said. "Cuchulainn is the son of a god. Warriors meeting him in combat were already beaten because the fools believed he was invincible. No man born of woman is invincible. Next time we meet, my aim is to kill him. Next time he will die. Let Morrigan hear my words."

The young herald yawned and pulled the dried cloak over his slim shoulders. "Go to sleep, Bricriu. I shall sit here and keep the fire going."

"Watch out for wolves, and roaming spirits," Bricriu warned.

Cold dawn broke over the misty fields and muddy road, bringing pale light to the land. Bricriu awoke and yawned, rising and stretching. The fire had gone out, its ashes greyer than the rising dawn over the distant hills. Cathal was lying beside the fire, his legs tucked into his chest. Bricriu nudged him with his foot. "Time to go." There was no movement from the young herald. He nudged him again. "Come on, boy, time to go." Again there was no movement. Bricriu stooped and turned him over. A dagger protruded from the chest of the young man, lodged in his heart. The hand of the young herald clutched the dagger in a deathly grip. Bricriu knelt over the body of the dead youth, and wept.

Overhead in the grey sky, a raven observed the chief weeping over the body of the dead herald. On silent wings the raven descended, and changed into a young woman carrying a shepherd's crook.

"Who are you and what happened to the young man lying dead at your feet?" Morrigan asked. "Did he die at your hands? I was out tending my flocks of woolly sheep when I heard your sobs. You certainly do not look like a murderer to me, so there must be some other reason for his death."

Bricriu wiped his tear-filled eyes with the back of his hand, and replied, "Young lady, your kind words are more than welcome in this time of sorrow. Cathal was my friend and that is why I weep. He died by his own hand, for he could not stand the dishonour he received in Ulster. We were sent on an errand to King Connor to borrow the goldenhide bull. That king refused the request, and his two sons rubbed salt into our wounds by insulting us. One is named Lorcan, a mere boy. The other is named Cuchulainn, and I would have killed him except Cathal stayed my arm."

A tear rolled from the eye of Morrigan. "I hear your sad words, and let me tell you that right is definitely on your side," she replied, wiping away the tear. "Every wrong must be avenged, otherwise a warrior earns a reputation for cowardice, and no man worth his salt can live with that stain. It does not require the wisdom of a druid to see that King Connor and his sons are at fault here. Our ancient laws of hospitality are sacred, and they who break them are worthy of nothing but contempt. If they had not refused the reasonable request of your queen, then this young man would not have killed himself."

Bricriu thanked the young woman for the advice. He put the body of the dead herald on the back of his horse, tying it down. Morrigan, who had the power of transformation, now changed into a wolf and howled. The horses became frightened, bucking and kicking. The ass was the first to break free. Bricriu struggled to hold the horses, but the stallions tore the reins from his grasp and galloped back to Emain Macha. Bricriu managed to calm his horse by placing his cloak over its eyes. He removed Cathal's cloak and also calmed his horse. Then he led the horses to the ford of the Boyne. Before crossing the ford, he stopped and shook his fist to the north, vowing to have his revenge. He entered the province of Meath, and set the horses on the road to Connaught.

The burning midnight funeral pyre lit up the land and the darkened night, and the high keening of the women rent the silence. They were keening over the dead body of the herald. The parents of Cathal cried openly as the leaping fire consumed his mortal remains. Dancing flames reflected in the faces of the chiefs and the royal couple. The fire burned fiercely and sparks showered the night sky. When the fire had consumed the body and the wooden pyre, the servants used iron tongs to remove the bones, overseen by Turnod the druid. They placed the bones on a large stone dish, and carried it into the passage tomb. Turnod instructed them to leave the tomb, and he remained.

The royal servants poured water on the dying embers, and carefully extinguished the remaining fires since darkness was essential for the ceremony. In darkness the chiefs and the royal couple awaited the rising of the sun. Turnod had assured them that the mid-winter sun would rise for all to see, and that no mists would dim its early light.

On the dawn of the winter solstice, the winter sun emerged from the mountains of Knocknarea and bathed the land in golden shafts of pale yellow sunlight. Turnod knelt at the burnt bones and watched the shaft of sunlight enter the passage tomb. If the light embraced the dish, the spirit of Cathal would journey to the Otherworld. If the light did not embrace the dish, his spirit would roam the world and find no home. Turnod watched the shaft of light slowly creep along the earthen floor of the passage tomb. The shaft reached the round dish and embraced it in brilliant light.

Outside the tomb, Turnod approached the weeping parents of Cathal, and he poured words of solace and comfort in their willing ears: "The light came into the tomb to take your son to the Otherworld. His spirit ascended from the bones, and walked in peace along the solar path. His spirit journeyed to the west, and now resides in the Isles of the Otherworld."

At the mouth of the massive passage tomb of Carrowmore in the west, in the diminishing shadows of the mountains of Knocknarea to the east, Queen Maeve gave a speech to the chiefs and to the parents of Cathal. She instructed the royal servants to lift her on top of a stone boulder, and the servants lifted her up.

"My people, this ancient stone passage tomb of Carrowmore has sent the royal spirits of your great ancestors on the solar path to the Isles of the Otherworld for nine hundred generations," she said. "My herald Cathal was not royal, yet I held the youth in such high esteem that I now break with tradition and allow his spirit to journey from here. My people, I sent my young friend and herald Cathal to the court of King Connor to seek a favour. Not only was my request turned down, but my herald came back dead. He could not live with the insult of Ulster. By insulting your queen, King Connor also insulted you, my chiefs."

In the clear blue sky a black raven appeared, wheeling in lazy circles over the passage tomb of Carrowmore, and drifting down on silent wings. The dark bird landed on the tomb and folded its wings, unseen by the people, cocking its black head, and listened to the speech of the queen.

The chiefs, roused by the speech of Maeve, thrust their spears to the sky in an angry mood. They shouted as one: "War! War!"

One chief alone did not call out or raise his spear for war. Old and eminent Malachi Mac Carthy walked amongst the chiefs, his head bald and scarred, mute testament to many battles.

"It is true good Cathal is dead and his spirit on the solar path to the Otherworld," he said. "He lived a good life, and I pray that the gods treat his spirit with respect and courtesy. He is no longer involved in the affairs of this world, but we are. We must not let his death blind us to doing what is right for Connaught, or allow revenge to cloud our judgement. Cathal was sent to Ulster to seek the goldenhide bull. I am proud to call King Connor my friend, and he is a man of honour. He would have gladly given the bull to the herald, but something must have happened. We are not getting the whole story."

Bricriu stepped forward, hand on sword. "Whose side are you on, old man?" he asked, his voice raised. "You are either with us or against us."

Eminent Mac Carthy responded to the jibe. "King Connor would not allow the sacred laws of hospitality to be abused. What happened at Emain Macha? That is the question. We should not like fools rush madly to war. Let us send Turnod to the court of noble Connor to determine the truth when the snows leave the ground. This matter must wait."

"We wait, but we must we prepare for war," Maeve declared. "For if we do not respond to the death of my herald, we shall be seen by the other provinces as weak. If we are seen as weak, we are certain to be attacked. Let us prepare for war. Let the smiths bend their brawny arms and let their hammers sing like robins."

Mac Carthy waited until the cheering died down, and then spoke, "If our smiths make weapons of war, we will be regarded by the four provinces as the aggressor. If we have to wage war on Ulster, let it be with great reluctance. Let the lumps of iron lie idle until dialogue is exhausted. If this matter cannot be resolved by talk, then let the smiths turn the lumps of iron into swords. If Connaught must go to war, let it not only be just but also seen to be just. We must have right on our side. That is why we must uncover the truth about what happened at Emain Macha."

"Ulster refused the reasonable request of our queen," said Bricriu. "Nothing happened at Emain Macha except that rich province sent us packing like beaten dogs with our tails between our legs. He who says otherwise is a liar. I challenge him to step outside."

"If the naked sword or the threat of violence can silence debate amongst men, we cannot call ourselves rational," eminent Mac Carthy said. "I am older than you, Bricriu, and I have fought many wars, terrible wars. They should be avoided at all costs. War can be likened to a heavy boulder atop a mountain. A single pair of hands can send it crashing down headlong, but a million pairs of hands cannot stop its momentum once started. It crushes everything in its path."

"He that is not with us is against us," Bricriu charged.

"What about gifts?" asked Mac Carthy. "You took home a dead herald from Ulster but no gifts. Connor is renowned for hospitality. That is why the gods smiled on Ulster and made it rich. No beggar leaves Emain Macha without a full belly and a rich cloak. Yet you have returned empty-handed."

"There were no gifts but insults," replied Bricriu.

Turnod the druid spoke out, "Mac Carthy speaks wise words and they come from experience. Right now we grieve over our herald and the blood is up in the chiefs. But a war should be given much thought by cool heads. Once started, there is no going back. When the goddess comes and releases the iron grip of winter from the land, we celebrate the festival of Imbolg at Tara. The five kings will attend the games. Let them discuss with Connor the manner of Cathal's death, and perhaps avoid a war."

Mac Carthy glanced over the assembled chiefs. "I do not see my friend Dara O'Brien here," he said. "Why is that? It is unlike that chief to miss a gathering such as this, for he always honours the dead. Perhaps he realised that some would use the gathering to speak of war."

"He lies sick in his bed," Bricriu said. "This is the time of year for such maladies. O'Brien is one chief who has not lost his courage, unlike some I could mention."

Standing on a boulder at the passage tomb of Carrowmore, Maeve spoke to the assembled chiefs, "It was never my intention to start a war with Ulster. It was my intention to send out a message that we are not weak. I have honoured my herald by sending his spirit to the Otherworld from the royal tomb. I am also willing to listen to Turnod. The advice of a druid is not taken lightly, since he is in contact with the gods. We wait until the festival of Imbolg."

The chiefs and the royal couple departed, and they left the passage tomb of Carrowmore behind, and they left the mountains of Knocknarea behind, and the bones of Cathal. King Ailill returned to Knocknashee, and the chiefs departed for their ringforts. But Maeve did not return to Knocknashee. She told her charioteer to take her to Lough Corrib.

The queen instructed her charioteer to stop in a forest near the lake. On foot she approached the lake carrying a ceremonial shield, walking through the tufted snows. The shield had been part of her dowry and she bore it in pride. Patches of ice clung to the edges of the lake. The main body of water was free, rippling in the pale sunlight. She waded into the lake bearing the shield above her head. The oblong shield was made from bronze and intricately carved in flowing circles. It had three bosses, carved in exquisite detail of interlinking swirls, each inlaid with red glass.

The queen threw the precious shield in the water in votive offering to the goddess of the lake. It bounced three times on the surface and came to rest. "Goddess Corrib, accept my humble offering and grant Connaught victory in the coming war," she prayed. The shield did not sink but remained on the surface. "Goddess of the lake, accept my offering and grant Connaught victory in the coming war," she prayed. The shield remained floating on the surface of the dark blue lake, like a currach riding the waves.

From the sky a raven descended and alighted on the floating shield. Water rippled over the bronze edges of the shield, and it sank beneath the waves. The raven flew to the land, and Morrigan stood beside the queen at the edge of the lake. "The goddess of the lake has accepted the offering," Morrigan said. "The voices for war far outnumber the few voices for peace. The omens are good."

"Rich Ulster has insulted us too many times," said Maeve. "Connor is responsible for the death of Talteann and for the death of Cathal. He killed Talteann on the field of battle and he killed Cathal by refusing my request. Does he think he can rub our faces in the dirt and suffer no retribution? I hunger to avenge Talteann and Cathal."

"War solves all hungers, Maeve," said the war-god.

"Morrigan, at the beginning of spring we celebrate the festival of Imbolg at Tara," the queen said. "The five kings will be there to view the games. What if they demand we remain at peace with Ulster?"

Morrigan put her white hand on the shoulder of the queen. "War has as momentum of its own," she said. "The grinding wheels of war are in motion and nothing kings say can stop them. They are already rolling thunder in the hearts of the warriors. The fever is gathering in their minds. There is no going back now, Maeve."

Chapter Five

Goddess Brigid left the Otherworld and confronted the Winter Crone in mortal combat. The lovely goddess smiled, and the snowy body of the Winter Crone began to retreat from the land. The lovely goddess blessed the waters, and the old crone released her icy fingers. Soon she was in full retreat, deserting the lands and the lakes. Then the goddess bade the old crone depart from the frozen land and lakes, for she had caused much suffering to the people and their flocks. She had starved them and she had killed them. The Winter Crone had no defence against the radiant smile of Brigid, and she departed the land and the lakes. She vowed however before departing that she would return again next year. The lovely goddess vowed that she too would return again next year and defeat her again.

From on high Brigid poured soft and gentle words on the waking land, and on the waking people, "I am Brigid, the only daughter of Danu, Mother Earth, whom I now awaken from her winter sleep. She is the natural mother of all things, mistress and governess of all the elements. She is the initial progeny of worlds, the giver of life. Arise, dear mother, and put on your greenest leaves and shoots. The Winter Crone has held you in shackles of ice for three months, but your daughter has defeated her. I have set you free again."

Then Brigid unfurled her cloak of red and white and blue, and set spring free. New life entered the land and the animals, and the goddess of rebirth strode across the land banishing the small pockets of remaining snow and ice. Where her lovely feet fell, snowdrops and primroses sprouted in her footsteps.

The annual festival of Imbolg at Royal Tara celebrated the coming of Brigid to the land. She was more than the goddess of rebirth; she also brought healing, poetry, smithcraft, and inspired wisdom to the people. She was the bright goddess of spring and the blossoming of new life, the only god or goddess who could defeat the Winter Crone.

King Diarmuid ruled the province of Meath at Tara under the Title: High King of Ireland. However, it was a title in name not in power, since the four remaining kings did not recognise his authority. The arrogant and powerful king of Leinster, Marbery, regarded his own royal person as the rightful High King. Leinster was by far the most populous province and its king could field the strongest army in the land. Yet although Marbery was arrogant and powerful, he was also a pragmatic king. He did not attempt to take control of the whole island for a very powerful reason. That was the prospect of an alliance of four provinces arrayed against Leinster, surrounding it on three sides with its back to the sea.

The four independent kings paid titular lip-service to Tara, but they did not pay tribute. Tribute equated with authority. They were willing to live in peaceful co-existence with the High King and to recognise his right to rule his own province. They were not prepared to recognise his right to rule a country. As long as Diarmuid confined his affairs of state to the province of Meath, there would be no conflict. If he attempted to interfere in the affairs of a province outside Meath, he faced the prospect of war on all sides. The rules were not written down, but each king fully understood the rules, especially Diarmuid.

The four kings arrived at Royal Tara with their wives and their bards to celebrate the festival of Imbolg, and to take part in the festival of games and competitions. The royal families were resplendent, wearing fine clothes and jewellery. The kings wore torcs of twisted gold about their necks and the queens wore pendants of dangling golden birds and boats. Their pale arms and wrists were covered in gold bands, symbols of their high position. They wore clothes of royal status and bright colours, dyed wools brighter than the rainbow. The kings wore tunics of fine embroidery, intricate circles needled in threads of many hues. Their cloaks were trimmed in dyed wools, running at the edges. The queens were dressed in long gowns and woollen cloaks, held by brooches of fine craftsmanship. The brooches were carved in gold, circular to signify the nature of life, and clasped by a heavy pin. The pins too were gold, shaped, and bearing the heads of animals.

The smiling druid of Diarmuid welcomed the royal families to Tara with golden chalices of warm ewes' milk, sacred to the goddess. Ingall wore a woollen tunic, dyed gold the colour of his province, and adorned with three linen salmon, formed in a circle, the symbols of wisdom in the province of Meath. Then he sprinkled their heads with spring water in an act of purification, so that they could take Brigid into their hearts.

Watched by the five kings and their queens, he lit the sacred fire on the Hill of Tara in a bronze cauldron, muttering incantations. The athletes were required to jump over the cauldron and through the flames to purify their bodies before taking part in the games.

King Cormac of Munster spoke with his fellow kings in the royal tent of the High King before the games commenced, "My friends, I have nine daughters and no sons. Eight of my daughters are married, and one alone remains at my palace in Cashel. She is named Emer, and she could not be named better. The princess is gentle and kind, and her beauty and modesty bear no comparison. She should be married to a king, as Maeve is, but there are no kings in search of a wife. My duties as a father compel me to seek a good husband for Emer, for I am growing old and desire to settle my affairs before I die and journey to the isles in the western sea. We are gathered here today to celebrate the festival of Imbolg, and to take part in the games. We have brought our best athletes to compete at Royal Tara. I propose to offer the fair hand of Emer to the athlete who wins the games."

The four kings pondered on the words of Cormac, and each in turn gave his assent. "What dowry does the princess carry?" asked Marbery. "My firstborn son, Tagdah, is fleet of foot, and can hurl a spear above the tallest oak. He has taken after his father, and has a burning desire to win. I have no doubt he will top the games."

"That is in the lap of the gods," replied Cormac. "I give Emer the same dowry as I gave to Maeve. No father who calls himself good can give less to the lastborn as he gave to the firstborn. The athlete who wins her hand will find me generous. After all, I am a Munsterman."

"Cormac is a man of his word," agreed Diarmuid.

"I look forward to welcoming the princess to my palace at high Leighlin in the eastern province of Leinster when Tagdah brings her home," said Marbery.

Below the hill at Royal Tara, in the sweeping plain rolling down to the River Boyne, the field of the athletes was marked out with stripped sapling poles and dyed strands of wool. The carpenters had constructed seats of carved oak for the five kings and their wives, raised above the competition field, from where they could watch the games and encourage their athletes. Young maidens crowded into the field to view the athletes, and to seek out good husbands. They carried white snowdrops in their hair as testament that they were both chaste and unwed.

Ingall dedicated the sacred games to Brigid by throwing a handful of incense on the fire in the bronze cauldron. Blue sparks leaped from the cauldron and crackled, indicating that the goddess was pleased with the offering. Then the druid announced the first event of the morning.

Four stripped young men from each province, numbering twenty in all, gathered for the first race. The eyes of the crowd focused on two loin-clothed athletes. One was Tagdah, son of Marbery, and the other was Cuchulainn, son of the god Lugh, and foster-son of King Connor. Twenty athletes watched Diarmuid, who started the race by dropping a ball of white wool from his outstretched hand. When it hit the thawed ground, the athletes began to race.

After thirty paces, Tagdah and Cuchulainn surged ahead, and left the rest of the field behind. At sixty paces, they could not be separated, their legs and arms pumping together. They raced towards the finishing posts at three hundred paces, and there Tagdah increased his pace. He pulled ahead, beating Cuchulainn.

Marbery leaped triumphantly from his seat. "That is my son!"

"Our son is out of sorts this day," observed Queen Rosheen.

"He is a true warrior, not a true athlete," replied her husband. "When the games of the warrior are played, look for a different Cuchulainn."

The servants of Diarmuid constructed a wall of stones for the next event. The athletes were required to leap over the tall stones without touching them. Twenty athletes formed into a line and ran to the wall. The stones were raised again and again, eliminating all but two athletes, Tagdah and Cuchulainn. The son of Marbery went first and leaped over the stones, but Cuchulainn's heel clipped one of the stones and knocked it from the wall.

Marbery leaped triumphantly. "Two down and four to go!"

The third event required feats of great skill and accuracy. The purpose of this event was to guide a speeding chariot between six sets of gates without touching them. The athlete had to achieve this task with one hand, holding a spear in his free hand. Having negotiated the six gates without touching any, he had to unleash the spear at the head of a boar tied to a tree. The head of the boar was thirty paces from the last gate.

Again, all but two contestants were eliminated. Some struck the gates, others missed with the spear. The son of Marbery guided his two horses between the gates and flung his spear from the racing chariot. It grazed the boar's head but did not penetrate the skull, glancing to one side. Cuchulainn guided his chariot through the gates and flung his spear. It penetrated the boar's head, straight between the eyes.

The fourth event was a simple contest of brute strength. A line of nine boulders confronted the athletes, each one heavier than its companion. The contestants were required to move up the boulders, lifting each one in turn. After the eighth lift, three contestants were left. Tagdah put his arms around the ninth boulder, but could not lift it. Cuchulainn too tried without success to budge the huge rock. Maol, a son of Mac Carthy, put his heavy arms around the huge boulder. Sweat pumped from his red face, and veins stood out like twisted ropes on his forehead. He succeeded in lifting the boulder, and was declared the winner of the event.

The fifth event appeared simple and easily accomplished, but it was the most difficult and required great skill. Eighteen fresh branches of the blackberry bush were bound and placed on two poles. The purpose of this event was to slice through the bundle with a sword, cleaving it in two. Contestant after contestant tried to cut the bundle with the sword, and failed. The new sap in the branches rendered them supple, and they bounced from the swords. Cuchulainn alone succeeded, slicing the bundle into two pieces with a single swift blow.

The sixth event excited the crowd far more than the preceding five, especially the young maidens. This was the contest of the osser, pitting man against man in single combat in a test of skill and endurance, and raw courage. The osser was shaped like a bone crafted in iron, with a heavy knob on each end. Each athlete was given two, one for each hand. This event gave the athletes the opportunity to display their courage and bravery before the seated kings, and also before the watching maidens. It was a contest of skill and intricate dance, requiring deft footwork, the feet of a dancer. The winner gained much honour on the tongues of bards, and in the hearts of maidens.

In the early afternoon the contest started, man against man. Blows were dealt and received in silence. No shouts or cries of pain uttered from the lips of the athletes, only the sounds of iron thudding on flesh, and the cracking of bones under the dull sun. Two stripped and bloodied athletes were heading on a collision course, standing upright in a mangle of twisted and broken bodies lying on the field. One was Maol Mac Carthy of Connaught, and the second was Cuchulainn of Ulster.

Ingall gave the two standing athletes time to take water and to recover their wind. They rested on the grass and drank cool water served by the druid. He whispered encouragement in their ears as he held the water to their lips, and informed them that the watching gods were pleased. Maeve left her seat and strode to Maol, his face and torso bloodied and beaten.

"You have fought with the sure courage of a Connaughtman, Maol," she said. "One more effort and my sister is yours. Let your victory be the victory of our province. Look yonder at Cuchulainn seated on the grass. They say he is the son of a god, yet does he not bleed as a mortal man? Is his blood not red too? Defeat him for our beloved province."

Maol landed the first blow and caught Cuchulainn on the head, opening a gaping would. Blood rushed from the wound into his eyes, blinding his sight. Maol stood back and allowed Ingall clean the blood from Cuchulainn's eyes. There was no honour in fighting a man who could not see, and winning with honour was the purpose of the contest. The duel resumed, and Cuchulainn landed the second blow, and the third. They traded blows, their sweat and their blood mingling, and their feet moving in harmony. Cuchulainn tried to dance away from a heavy blow, but the osser hit his wrist. The crack echoed in the still afternoon air. The heavy osser fell from Cuchulainn's left hand, his wrist broken. He rallied for a final effort, fighting with his right hand. He hit the chin of his adversary an upright blow, putting his whole body into the strike. Like a tall oak brought low by an axe, Maol fell to the ground. Alone, Cuchulainn stood in the midst of the fallen and broken bodies.

Young maidens rushed to him, touching his sweat and blood with adoring hands. Diarmuid issued instructions, and his servants carried Cuchulainn from the field, and took him to the palace of the king. There they bathed his body, washing his wounds and pouring honey on the cuts. King Cormac went to his bedside and announced that Emer would be his bride. Then the exhausted athlete fell into deep sleep.

That night the kings and their wives gathered in the great wooden palace at Royal Tara before departure next morning. Diarmuid warmly embraced them and bade them welcome to his royal home, according to the sacred laws of hospitality that were handed down from their forefathers. They feasted well on venison and wild boar, and they drank mead and wine from golden goblets. The kings and their wives discussed the games of the warriors, and all agreed that Cuchulainn was a worthy winner, except Marbery and his wife Fiona.

"Lugh favoured his son today," said Fiona, the wife of Marbery, who was as arrogant as her husband. "That cunning god guided the hand of his son in the contest of the osser and struck down my son. In the contest of the boar's head, the aim of Tagdah was true, and his spear would have pierced the boar's head, but the hand of Lugh turned it aside so that his son won."

"I have consulted with Ingall my druid and he assured me that the gods did not interfere in the games," Diarmuid replied. "The games are over now and the athletes departed from the field, and kings or queens should not look back. They should make plans for the future to ensure their people are happy. Fellow kings, it is my duty as High King that I bring up a painful subject. Bad news travels faster than an eagle, and news has reached my ears that a dispute has arisen between Connaught and Ulster. Tell me, is the rumour true?"

"A herald of Connaught went alive to Ulster and came back dead," came the swift reply from Maeve. "Our herald could not live with the shame Ulster put on his youthful shoulders. Men of Connaught do not take insults lightly. They would prefer the cutting edge of the sword on their necks."

"Two men came alive to my court at Emain Macha and two men departed from my court alive," said Connor. "The gods do punish the king who breaks our sacred laws of hospitality. I am a king who obeys the laws, not a king who breaks the laws. Cathal did not die at my hands but at his own. The gods in their infinite wisdom grant men free will. A man can choose to live or he can choose to die. Cathal chose to die."

"Men of Ulster can live easily without honour but not men of Connaught," said the queen. "My herald chose death before dishonour. Does King Connor think he can insult us because we are poor and he is rich? Or does he think we are without feelings? He is responsible for the death of the king I was to marry, and also for the death of my herald."

"Bad news has also reached me that treeless Connaught makes keen preparations for war," continued Diarmuid. "If one province prepares for war, the rest are certain to follow. This matter must be resolved by men of words and not by men of action. We must not put the flaming torch of war to the dry forest or we are all consumed."

"Let the women be removed from here before we speak more of this matter," Marbery said. "Men speak more easily and more truthfully when they are not present. We can use words man to man that we dare not use with women in the room for they take offence too easily, and they do not forget a grudge. Diarmuid, tell them to leave."

Diarmuid bowed to the request of Marbery, and the five queens departed. The five kings drank more wine and mead to fortify their minds for the harsh words that were coming. In silence they drank the wine and mead, each king preparing his words. Marbery spoke first, his grey curls shaking in disbelief.

"Domestic rows should be kept at home and dealt with at home," he began. "Words of common men do not travel far, but words of kings reach every corner of the land. The harsh words of Connaught have reached my ears, and now a domestic row between a weak husband and his strong wife threatens to end in bloody war. If it were not so serious we could laugh in our cups and make jokes. Ailill, I am married to Fiona. If I tell her to fetch wine she fetches wine though she is a queen. If I am drunk and tell her to remove my boots, she removes my boots though she is a queen. If she shows dissent, she feels the weight of my hand on her face! Fiona knows that she is a queen, but she has not forgotten she is first a wife. Maeve has never learned to be a wife, and you have not learned to be her master. If you cannot rule your own wife, how can you rule your province?"

Ailill was stung by the sharp words of the Leinster king, and his cheeks flushed in anger. The king was smaller than Marbery and his lack of stature added to his anger.

"Do not interfere in my province, and I will not interfere in yours!" he sharply replied.

Marbery filled his goblet and spoke again: "I do not understand your position in this stupid argument, Ailill. It was in your interest to stop Cathal going to Ulster, yet you did nothing. If Connor had loaned Maeve the bull she would have rubbed your nose in the dirt. Unless, of course, there is another reason why you did not stop him."

"What reason?" the Connaught king demanded.

"Why was Bricriu sent to Ulster?" asked Marbery. "He has not the honeyed words necessary for an envoy, or the temperament. That man is a hothead and a loudmouth. I bet that fool would insult the gods in the Otherworld given a chance! It is my belief that Maeve sent him in the knowledge he would create mischief. She seeks an excuse to start a war."

Ailill was still smarting under the barbed insults of Marbery, and responded, "The wine has infected your tongue, Marbery. Why should my queen wish to start a war?"

"Have you no ears to listen, or are you ignoring the evidence?" said Marbery. "Did not Connor kill her betrothed in battle? Women are not the same as men and queens are not the same as kings. They do not think as we do. They take offence very easily and they do not readily forgive. They carry a grudge to their grave and cause wars on the way. Women are the cause of wars, but it is men who die in wars. Beware the wrath of a woman!"

"I killed Talteann, and that is true," said Connor. "If any king deserved killing, he did, though it grieves me to say such a thing. He invaded my province in search of booty. What is booty but theft by another name? Every king has a right to defend his province, and I did. Now Connaught is using his death to start a war. There is no doubt that Ulster is in the right here."

"A proud and haughty queen in that vengeful frame of mind is more dangerous than a wounded boar!" Marbery told the assembled kings. "A woman in her frame of mind needs to feel the fist, not the gloved hand! Perhaps the heart of the queen's problem lies closer to her bedroom. Her husband is insecure as a king and he is insecure as a man. He should take his manly rod to the queen more often! The woman who gets the manly rod three times a week seldom complains!" He drank the blood-red wine and poured another, laughing as he supped. "A woman who does not get the rod often finds other things to complain about!"

Ailill flushed angrily. "I take insults from none, be he man or king!" He moved with menace towards Marbery, his fists twisted into two hard lumps. Marbery put down his goblet and readied for the fight, his fists held high.

"Let us not trade insults here, but wise words," said Diarmuid with a smile, intervening to stop the row before it came to blows. Neither of the angry kings was prepared to unclench his fists first. "How do we resolve this problem and prevent a war?"

"It is a problem for the palace of Ailill, not for mine," said Marbery, unclenching his fist and picking up his goblet. His dark eyes were filled with mocking venom, and were fixed on Ailill. "I certainly would not tolerate a wilful queen for a moment. He should have put his foot down with Maeve from the start of their marriage. He should have laid down the rules of his house and his bed. Now it is too late. Let him sort out his own house."

"I am prepared to give Maeve a bull, though not the goldenhide bull," said noble Connor. "That is the solution I propose here. If Ailill agrees, I can arrange to have the beast sent immediately."

Marbery put down his empty goblet and left the room. He called for his druid, Owen. The old druid rushed to his king, pulling on his garment and wiping the sleep from his eyes. The garment he wore was dyed blue, the colour of Leinster. It had three red-eyed salmon woven into the fabric, the eternal symbols of wisdom. The king put a goblet into the hands of the druid and filled it with dark mead. The druid drank the sweet mead, and Marbery asked him to repeat the legend.

Owen wiped his lips and repeated the legend: "It has been handed down from generation to generation by old men at night fires. A legend, not a prophecy, but often legends come true. The legend says that a bull with three horns is destined to be born in Ulster and blessed by the gods. Such a beast now exists in the rich province of Ulster. The legend says that the person who sleeps in the hide of the bull for three days and three nights is destined to acquire the strength of the bull, and be invincible in battle. The legend says that the grey Stone of Destiny at Tara shall call out three times to proclaim that person High King of Ireland."

Marbery thanked his druid and sent him back to his bed. Then he looked at the four kings, each in turn, his grey locks shaking.

"What we have here is the kernel of the problem," he told them. "This foolish queen desires to be High King."

The words of Marbery were greeted in silence by the gathered kings. Diarmuid moved among them, offering to fill their goblets. Finally, he broke the silence, and the tension.

"My brothers," he said, "long ago, in the misty dawn of our forefathers, the Stone of Destiny shrieked like a thousand banshees when the High King was challenged to defend his crown. Its shrieks were heard in every corner of the five provinces, by princes and by herders, by the old and by the young. Its voice was not silenced until a new High King waded through blood to claim the throne. The Stone of Destiny has been silent for a very long time, and that silence has been of great benefit to our provinces. Our forefathers realised that fighting for the crown was not only uncivilised, but also led to instability. That is why they came up with the present arrangement. The High King sits at Tara, which is in the province of Meath. The title passes down from father to son because Tara passes down from father to son. Having said that, Tara does not belong to Meath alone, but to all five provinces."

"It is a simple case of naked ambition," continued Marbery. "Maeve desires to rule, not only in Connaught but the whole island. Here is what happens when a queen is allowed to rule her husband! She gets ambitions beyond her province! Your gift is not acceptable to her, Connor, because no other bull can grant invincibility. Does that silly woman really believe I would accept her dominion over Leinster? I could smash her puny army in a week!"

"We came here to discuss peace, not war," Diarmuid said. "I fear that the goddess of war is behind this mischief. She desires to feast on the flesh of dead warriors. The gates of the Otherworld are shut against her so that she roams here, and that is why war has never departed from this world. That foul goddess is never sated, no matter how much flesh she devours. We, as wise kings, must ensure she remains hungry. We, as peaceful kings, must make every effort to avoid war."

"We must make sacrifices for peace," Connor said.

Cormac of Munster now spoke, "Send the bull to Connaught, and in that way war is avoided."

"I cannot do that under threat," replied Connor.

"The problem is beyond our human minds to solve," said Diarmuid. "What I propose is that we let the gods decide. I propose they send us a sign. Let us wait for that sign. It is in their lap now."

The five kings raised their goblets of wine, and spoke: "Let the immortal gods decide."

The kings slept in beds at Royal Tara with their queens, and Lugh the god of light left the Underworld with lovely Brigid, and journeyed to the palace. The god and goddess went to the room where Cuchulainn lay sleeping. Lugh was moved to pity and tears by the broken and bloodied body of his son. Brigid knelt at the bed and administered medicines. She knitted the broken wrist bones, using a golden needle and a strand of her golden hair. In an instant Cuchulainn recovered, and sat up in bed. He arose from the bed and embraced his father. Then he knelt before Brigid on one knee, and the goddess blessed his head, and departed.

Cuchulainn left the room and walked with his father to the Stone of Destiny standing tall on the Hill of Tara.

The footprints of the god burned into the grass, and wisps of smoke curled into the night sky. Father and son stood before the Stone of Destiny, and Cuchulainn spoke to Lugh. "Father, I am a warrior skilled in arms, but unskilled in reason. The druids are wise and reason spills from their mouths, and yet they differ on destiny. Is the destiny of a man written on his forehead at birth, or can a man forge his own?"

The god replied to his son, saying, "Each man has free will but each man must follow his destiny."

"Father, I do not understand," said Cuchulainn.

"None but the immortal gods understand," replied Lugh. "My son, twice I have offered you the protective shield of invincibility and twice you have refused. I came here to offer the gift for a third and final time." Lugh held a bunch of mistletoe in his hands. "This is the food of the gods. When I eat of this white fruit, my spittle becomes the liquid of invincibility. Rub my spittle on your broken body, and no sword can wound your flesh. Rub the spittle over your body, and no spear can penetrate your defences."

"Father, there can be no honour in invincibility or no virtue," Cuchulainn replied. "How can the warrior display his courage and skill in battle if he is immune to the spear and the sword? How can the warrior live if he has to live without honour? No, I refuse your gift for a third and final time."

Chapter Six

At the first light of breaking day, the servants of Connor prepared the four-wheeled wagon for the journey from Emain Macha to the wooden palace of King Cormac at Cashel in Munster. They provisioned it with food and water, and loaded hay for the horses. They stacked woollen blankets in the wagon to keep the princess warm, and hides of sheep. Then they shackled two horses to the wagon, and tied a spare horse at the back.

Connor breakfasted early with his three sons, for he looked on Cuchulainn in no less regard than his two natural sons. They breakfasted early on boiled eggs and brown bread. Cuchulainn's face was completely healed, and he bore no scars from the games. After eating, Connor and Ferdia left the palace and went outdoors, the king glancing up at the sky.

"Son, return quickly with the princess Emer for Cuchulainn! There can be no peace of mind amongst the married men in my kingdom until he is married off, for they fear their wives shall run away with him! As for the unwed maidens, they bang down the doors of my palace nightly! The sooner he is tied in wedlock to Emer, the better I can sleep in my bed at night!"

"I journey to lush Cashel to fetch the princess, father, since your wish is my command. But I would prefer if

Cuchulainn went in my place. After all, Emer is his future bride."

"Ferdia, evil Morrigan is abroad in the land determined to stir up mischief," said the king. "She seeks an incident to start a war. I am equally determined to stop war at all costs. Cuchulainn serves Ulster best here. He is our safeguard against her warlike wiles. Ulster is safe whilst he remains here as its hound."

Connor and his eldest son walked to the waiting wagon. Before he mounted the wagon, Ferdia embraced his father. Then Cuchulainn and Lorcan emerged from the palace to say their farewells. Lorcan shook his brother's hand and wished him a safe journey and speedy return to Emain Macha. Cuchulainn clasped Ferdia, and they held each other in fond embrace for a long time under the clouded sky.

"You are my oldest brother and I trust you with my life. More, I trust you with my future wife. Journey fast to clovered Munster and bring her to Emain Macha. I know in my heart that the princess will be safe in your hands. I know in my heart that you will honour her as you honour me."

The wagon was ready for departure, and two piebald horses tugged on the restraining ropes, hoofing at the sandy road. Ferdia sat on the four-wheeled wagon and took up the reins, pulling his cloak over his head against the biting cold. Lorcan and Cuchulainn returned to the palace; but the king followed the wagon down the sandy road, walking beside the horses. The king gave parting words to Ferdia.

"The rivers are in fast flood, so be careful using the fords. Be very vigilant on the roads and be prepared always to use your sword if you are attacked by bandits.

Tell Cormac I shall send an armed guard to collect the dowry in the summer when the roads are better. Heed my advice, my son, and be careful on the journey."

"Father, behind your concern for my safety I sense you are trying to tell me something."

"These are worrying times, my son, and I must make provision for the future. You are my firstborn, and the crown passes to you on my death. That is the way of kings. I have arranged for you to take a wife. She is called Devlina, and she lives on an island with her father."

The journey was uneventful, and after eighteen days on the roads Ferdia reached his destination, the wooden palace of King Cormac at Cashel. It stood on a large outcrop of rock rising vertically from the green honeyed pastures of Munster, towering over the adjoining fields and forests. There was no need for defences because the towering vertical rock could not be scaled. The wooden palace of the king was accessed by a single narrow road, winding to the top like the coils of a great serpent. A small band of warriors holding this road could withstand an army of thousands.

The servants heated water and bathed Ferdia, and supplied a change of clothes according to the sacred laws of hospitality. They took him to Cormac who was dining with his queen, Ashling. The king welcomed Ferdia to his palace and invited him to join them for dinner. The servants brought him a goblet of hot mead; and when he had supped the mead, they brought him a dish of hot venison stew.

"My father sends his greetings, my lord. He promises to send an armed guard in the summer for the dowry. He has sent me to bring the princess to his palace at Emain Macha. Cuchulainn did not come because my father fears for the safety of his province. I promise to defend the princess on the journey."

"Ashling and I thank you for your concern, and we feel certain that Emer shall reach Emain Macha unharmed. We are indeed very honoured that Connor has sent his firstborn to take my daughter to his palace. Your sense of duty is renowned throughout the land. As we speak, the young princess is in her room preparing for the journey. She dines with us at supper tonight, and there you can meet with her. Ferdia, you are welcome to remain here for as long as you wish."

"If it pleases the king, I intend to depart in the morning."

Morrigan was not the only god intent on causing mischief to mortal men and women. Aengus caused as much mischief, but the gates of the Otherworld were not closed to him because the gods could not live without the god of love. As night's darkness fell, Aengus journeyed from the Otherworld to Cashel, and entered the palace of Cormac. He had not been able to ensnare Ferdia, and he could not resist this challenge to his authority. He sat unseen beside Ferdia at the supper table and readied his snare. As a result, when Emer entered the room Ferdia fell instantly in love with her beauty.

"I have heard you are a poet, Ferdia."

"A bad one, good king."

"What do you think of these rumours about war?"

"Let us hope that is all they are, rumours."

The morning return to Emain Macha took place under a light drizzle, the rain falling gently in hazy waves. Ferdia placed a cloak over Emer and walked the piebald horses forward down the steep road, grasping the reins tightly. He led the horses carefully down the steep incline, slowly leading them down the rocky road. The wagon left Cashel behind and rolled between the honeyed fields of Munster, and the herds of cattle and sheep now grazing in lush meadows after the visit of the lovely goddess.

They journeyed until night fell on the land before stopping to eat. Ferdia put out hay for the horses, and cut slices of meat and bread for Emer. He lifted her gently from the wagon, and they sat beside the wagon to eat.

"Tell me of your brother in Emain Macha, the one I am to wed. Is the warrior as handsome as everyone says? I have heard there is none more handsome in the whole land. I cannot wait to meet with him. How is his hair?"

"Black, princess."

"How is his face?"

"Noble, princess."

"Is he brave in battle?"

"The bravest."

"Not a man of many words, are you? My father told me that you are a man of books and of much reading. Such men tend to talk a lot in the company of a woman, for they love to display how wise they are to impress her. Either my father is wrong, or you are not read in books. I think my father is wrong."

"Princess, we have a very long and difficult road ahead of us. We should try to make the journey as easy as possible."

"My father had to drag the words from you, as a team of men have to drag a cow from a boghole. Very strange behaviour for a man who is supposed to be a poet."

Emer went to sleep in the wagon, and he covered her over with blankets of wool and sheepskins on top. Afterwards he lit a fire and fed the horses. Then he sat beside the wagon, his sword drawn, rising only to throw branches on the flames. From the surrounding forest came the deep baying of wolves, coming closer. He piled more wood on the fire, and the flames soared in the night sky.

"Are you awake?"

"Yes, princess."

"I hear wolves, but I do not fear them. Ferdia, if I have to spend many days and nights on the road with you, I do not wish to spend them in silence. There is nothing so boring to a woman than a silent man. A woman loves to hear a man talk, even lies! In fact, given the choice between a man of silence and a man of lies, every woman would choose the latter... Do you find my manner offensive?"

"No, princess."

"Ah, indeed, I think I know what the problem is. My father the king told your father the king that Emer is modest and gentle. Every father says that about his unwed daughter, for what man wishes to wed a woman with a mind of her own and a tongue to use it? I have a mind of my own, and a tongue of my own. Neither am I afraid to use either."

"Go to sleep, princess. We resume the journey early."

At dawn's first light, Ferdia prepared the horses for departure and shackled them to the wagon, tying the spare horse at the rear. He poured water on the dying embers of the fire, and covered them in wet soil to prevent the forest catching fire. He awakened the sleeping princess, and served her dried meats and breads on a copper plate. Having eaten, they mounted the four-wheeled wagon and resumed the journey to Emain Macha.

As the journey progressed, Emer expressed a desire to bathe, telling him that a lake was nearby. Lough Derg nestled in the dusk of falling day, its waters dark and soundless. He wheeled the wagon and guided the horses down a track of budding oak and hazel trees leading to the lake. He lifted her from the wagon and went into the nearby forest to collect wood.

Aengus appeared to him in the falling darkness, took him by the hand, and led him to the lake. Though he attempted to resist, his legs disobeyed, for no mortal can resist a god. The finger of the god of love pointed to Emer splashing in the cold waters in the dusky light. She resembled a seal in a bay, diving beneath the surface, and emerging sleek and glistening.

"Ferdia, Emer surpasses every woman in beauty, does she not? Even the fairest goddesses in the Otherworld are jealous of her loveliness. Beauty belongs to the man who seizes it. A man gets but one chance in life for happiness and this is yours. Every man is equipped in his own way to win beauty. The warrior uses his sword to win a woman and the poet uses his tongue. Use your words and she is yours."

"She is promised to my brother."

"Do not talk foolish words, Ferdia. No mortal man who gives away the woman he desires most can live a happy life. Pour into her willing ears the seductive words of the poet. That is how the best women are won, by the power of men's words. Compose a poem for her, and you can make her your queen."

"I am under the orders of my father, and my honour."

Though Aengus persisted, the prince did not waver or bend to his snaring entreaties. He struck a flint and lit a fire, ignoring the temptations of god of love, who disappeared into the night. From the surrounding forest came the dying cry of a deer, crying in the darkness like a child in distress. The chasing wolves had made a kill. He piled the fire higher, building it up.

"Look how brightly the stars shine tonight above the trees," Emer said. "The druid of my father told me that men who believe in the stars are fools. He said they are too distant and remote to influence our lives. How can stars that far away influence our lives? No, we must cut our own way through the forests of the future...Speak to me now of Cuchulainn in battle, Ferdia, and I command you to speak to me in more than a single word."

"In peace he is handsome, none more so in the whole land. In battle however he changes so totally that not even his mother recognises him. It is called a battle-warp. During his transformation, he kills without pity."

"How can a handsome youth turn into a demon?"

"It happens only during battle, princess. His handsome head develops ugly horns and his hair stands up like jagged thorns on a rosebush. I have seen it just once and he frightened me, his own brother. During the battle-warp he did not know me, or recognise me as his brother. Afterwards he embraced me as if seeing me for the first time in years."

"How can this be?"

"I know not how or why he changes in battle, except that he does. He kills men in battle without a thought, as a woman kills flies in her home. After the battle has ended, he would not kill a lamb for dinner. Perhaps a druid can tell you why, a wise man who speaks to Brigid, but I am not able to find a reason."

"Are you jealous of your brother?"

"No, princess. Why should I be?"

"He is the son of a god and he is handsome. You are the son of a mortal and you are not. Your ears are too large and your nose is not pleasing to look upon. As for your hair, it is neither dark nor fair, but resembles the coat of a mouse."

"Go to sleep, princess. We start early tomorrow morning."

Aengus travelled unseen with the wagon along the road, and he was determined to cause mischief. At the end of another day, before moonless darkness departed the land, he confronted Ferdia, who was rubbing down the horses as Emer slept. The god of love sought to ensnare Ferdia and Emer, and to bind them in his spell. This was a personal challenge to him and he was fully determined to succeed, not considering the consequences for a moment should he succeed.

"The wagon rolls mile by steady mile towards Emain Macha, and each mile brings the princess closer to Cuchulainn. Each day brings her farther away from you. Act before it is too late, Ferdia. Women love men who act, not men who do nothing! Why do you avoid her eyes when you talk? Leap into their green pools and bathe in their warming and loving glow."

"Why do you tempt me with base thoughts? Do you not realise how hard I must fight every waking day against her eyes? I would prefer to confront a pack of hungry wolves than battle against her beauty. Aengus, you are strong, but honour is stronger, and loyalty, and family. She goes to Emain Macha to meet her future husband. That is how it is, and that is how it remains."

The god took the hand of Ferdia and led him to the wagon where Emer slept, and pulled back the sheepskins and blankets. The princess slept quietly on a bed of straw, her breasts rising and falling. "Does not her unbearable beauty inspire you to eternal poetry? Ten thousand poets long dead would give up their spirits in the Otherworld to be here in your sandals at this time. Speak to her when she awakes, and let her skip over the horizons of your mind."

Ferdia was determined to resist the will of the god and to take the princess to his brother. With this in mind, he did not sit beside her on the four-wheeled wagon, but continued the journey on foot, leading the horses by hand. As he walked along the road, he noticed movement in the forest on both sides, and heard twigs breaking. They were being followed. His ears pricked and listened to the sounds. They were not the padding paws of wolves, but the footfalls of men. He surmised there were at least four of them stalking the wagon, waiting for the right opportunity to pounce.

He halted the wagon in the forests of Edenderry, selecting a wide clearing with little cover for attackers. The nearest trees were more than thirty paces from the wagon.

"We rest here, princess. The weather is changing."

"The signs of a change in the sky are not seen by me. There is plenty of daylight left, Ferdia. Let us continue the journey, for each passing hour brings me closer to Cuchulainn. Why are your ears deaf to the command of a princess? Continue the journey at once!"

She was not pleased that he disobeyed her loud command, and continued to ignore her shouted instructions. He collected firewood, and closed his ears to her scalding words. When the flames were leaping, he took a ball of wool from the wagon and began to spin a thread.

"You have the manners of a sow! How dare you close your ears to my commands! Now you play with a coarse ball of wool like a kitten! A growed man! We could have made six more miles before nightfall, but no, you would prefer to play childish games! I thought you were a prince, but now I see you are a fool!"

He spun out the coarse thread and walked around the clearing, tying it to the trees on the perimeter at the height of his knees. He completed a circle with the wool around the wagon. Taking a sheepskin hide from the wagon, he placed it beside the leaping fire, and stuffed leaves and mosses underneath to resemble a sleeping body. Then he returned to the wagon, crept underneath, and tied the string around his wrist. Drawing his sword, he settled down to wait.

The attack came as clouds passed slowly over the moon and it came suddenly. The string tugged on his wrist indicating that the perimeter was breached. A dark figure sprinted from the forest and fell on the sheepskin hide, plunging a dagger into the sheepskin again and again. The figure was silhouetted against the fire. Ferdia crawled from beneath the wagon and rushed at the intruder, parrying a blow from the knife. His sword cleaved the man from shoulder to stomach. There were more intruders in the clearing, moving in the shadows. Emer screamed loudly, her plea for help echoing through the forest. Two intruders barred his path to the princess. He killed the man with the club first. The other intruder was armed with a sword and he knew how to use the weapon.

A glancing blow caught Ferdia on the side of the head. Hot blood coursed down his left cheek. The intruder swung the sword to finish him off. The prince ducked the blow and plunged his sword into the belly of the man. Staggering to the wagon, Ferdia saw a fourth intruder grappling with Emer. He brought the hilt of the sword down on the man's head and knocked him out. Weakened from the open wound and loss of blood, he collapsed beside the wagon.

He awakened in late daylight, his head resting on her lap. She was bathing his wound, her hand stained with his blood. Ignoring the pain, he raised his head from her lap and surveyed the scene. Four bodies were lying dead in the clearing.

"If you are not the strangest man I have ever met. Why did you not kill the man who attacked me? Was it because his back was turned and that was against your honour? Honour be cursed by the gods! He escaped your vengeance, but not mine! I killed him with your sword. He would have done the same to me, or worse."

"I should not have worried about you, princess. It seems you can take care of yourself."

"No man has ever fought for me, Ferdia, or put his own life in harm's way to protect me. I owe you my life, and much more. I owe you an apology too. How does a princess who has not apologised before know where to begin? I said foolish things and behaved worse than a spoiled child. I am the fool, Ferdia, not you."

He lapsed into listless sleep, and she was unable to revive him. She tore a strip of cloth from a blanket and tied it over his wound. Then she shackled the horses and led them from the clearing.

For three days and nights she continued on the journey to Emain Macha, bathing his wounds by night when she rested the horses. He did not awaken from sleep, even when she poured water between his lips. Not until the fourth day did his eyes open. Then he discovered a changed princess. Before the attack, her tone had been brash and filled with the certainty of youth. Now her personality had changed and there was a new maturity in her voice.

"One night has turned me from girl to woman. Before we continue the journey, there is something I must or surely die of wanting. I have no control over my feelings. I think I have fallen victim to the nightly wiles of Aengus."

She leaned down and kissed him on the lips; not in the manner of a girl but in the way of a woman, strong and with passion. His weakness did not permit him to pull away, or fight for his senses against her beauty. Her kiss banished all thoughts of honour and duty from his mind. Yet when she pulled away, his honour returned, and his duty lay before him like a straight road.

"Forgive me, Ferdia. How foolish I was to think you were playing games with the ball of wool. It was used for my protection. It warned you of their approach. Forgive me too for my unbridled tongue. I am the youngest of my father's daughters, and he did not curb my tongue, allowing it to run free as a wild horse. That is no excuse, but it is the only one I have."

The days and nights passed quickly, mostly in silence; and on the morning of the eighteenth day Emain Macha came into view, standing on a hill less than a mile ahead. Ferdia pulled the wagon to a halt and rested the horses before the final journey. She gazed at the wooden palace on the hill without speaking.

"There is the palace of my father. Soon you will meet your future husband."

"I no longer wish to meet him, Ferdia. I do not care if he is the most handsome man in the world. The journey has taught me that the beauty inside a man is more important than the beauty outside. You have that inner beauty unseen to careless eyes. That palace up there on the hill is not the start of a new life for me, but the end of my brief happiness. Have you no feelings for me? It is not too late."

"For what, princess?"

"To turn back, Ferdia, to find a cave somewhere, or a greening forest. To build a cabin in the forest and live together as man and wife. Let me be your muse and your love, and you can write of me poetry to stun the world. Once I set foot in the wooden palace of your father, I can never turn back."

"Princess, I am under obligation to your father, to my father, and to my brother, your future husband. A man has to honour his obligations or he is not a man. I cannot fall out with my father, my brother, and all that I believe in. Neither can you fall out with your parents. That is the way of the world."

"I would fall out with the whole world for you. I would give up my place in the Otherworld to be at your side. I would insult the immortal gods to wake up at your side. Do you not feel the same for me?"

"No, I do not. I was a messenger, nothing else. I was tasked to bring you here, and I have accomplished that task. Your hand is promised to Cuchulainn. That is how it must be."

"It is not, Ferdia. You are a man and I am a woman. We both have free minds, have we not? We can turn this wagon and never be found again. We can live happy lives together."

"Happiness cannot exist without honour, princess."

Chapter Seven

The black-feathered raven flew into the bedroom of the queen at Knocknashee, and transformed into Morrigan. Maeve combed her flaxen hair and related the news from Royal Tara. The kings required a sign from the gods. The kings were not prepared to break the truce.

"How can the fools call themselves kings if they are incapable of making one simple decision?" asked the war-god. "Why do they always have to put the responsibility on the gods? Why do kings fear to fight when their warriors clamour for the fever of battle? Kings should lead in affairs of war, not gods."

"Morrigan, send them a sign," Maeve said. "Cast your sleeping cloak over that too-rich province. Let their juicy and fat people sleep the deep slumber of unwaking dreams. Let their bulky cattle and sheep die from burst udders for lack of milking hands. Let their unripe crops rot in the untouched fields. Let the weeds grow wild and choke the land. Let the deep rivers stop running and fill with reeds and mosses. Go, Morrigan, and do the work you do best."

The goddess transformed into a raven and took flight. The raven flew to the north and started the terrible work. It hovered above milking girls milking cows, and they soon fell into deep slumber. It hovered above men working in the fields, and they fell on the ground and slept. All across the rich province men and women slept in the fields and in the homes. Soon the cattle began to die in the fields from lack of milking. Ravenous packs of ribbed wolves emerged from the forests and fell on the flocks of sheep, devouring them. The starving dogs too joined in the easy feast, returning to the wild and forming roaming packs.

The rivers and lakes clogged with reeds and mosses, and the fish began to die. The stench of death hung in black clouds over the unhappy province. Black flies swarmed on the carcasses like plagues of locusts. The sleeping sickness was laying waste the richest province in the land, and everyone slept except Cuchulainn, who was under the protection of Lugh.

King Ailill of Connaught was still bruising over the insults of Marbery at the games and approached Maeve in the ringfort.

"Arrogant Marbery insulted me at Royal Tara and you are the reason," he charged. "Why was I not informed that you were sending Bricriu and Cathal to Emain Macha? Why did you want the bull, to rub my nose in the dirt? Or do you believe the legend?"

Haughty Maeve replied in an instant, "If you were a man, you would have given Marbery a box in the gob! If you were a king, you would have declared war on him! Of the five provinces, we are the poorest and that is why we are insulted at the gathering of kings. That goldenhide can raise up our province because it grants invincibility to the person who sleeps inside for three days and three nights. Let me tell you, Ailill, none dare insult a victorious province."

"We are at peace with Ulster," the king reminded the queen.

"Nobody remembers the province that breaks a truce, and nobody forgets the province that wins a war," Maeve said. "We are invading Ulster and you can join the chiefs or remain behind in your bed, to your eternal shame. Once you left your brother's body on the field of battle. Connor gained his courage by cutting off Talteann's head and tying it to his chariot. This is a chance to redeem yourself. You might never get another. Do not be a dwarf in mind as you are in body."

Queen Maeve called a council of war at Knocknashee and invited the chiefs of the thirty tribes to attend. She put to them her intention to invade Ulster and seize the goldenhide bull by force. There would be no resistance, for the warriors of Ulster were asleep. It was no longer a matter of personal pride or an argument between Ailill and Maeve. The seizure of the bull would be conducted for the pride of a province insulted by Connor, and to avenge the deaths of Cathal and Talteann. The assembled chiefs cheered loudly, eager for the punitive raid. One chief did not cheer however, and he was Malachi Mac Carthy.

"So, now our proud province intends to become as the thief who steals the property of others," he said to the queen. "So, now our proud province intends to fall on the sick province of Ulster like vultures. We should be helping noble Connor and his people in their hour of need, not preying on them. Good queen, when we are long dead, this incident will be long remembered to the lasting and eternal shame of Connaught."

The harsh words of Mac Carthy cut Maeve to the bone, and she replied in an instant: "You are the leader of a clan, Malachi, but King Ailill and I are the leaders of a province. We have to respond to an insult. If we do not respond others will regard us as weak, and weakness is always attacked. We must send out a strong warning to the four provinces that we are prepared to fight."

"Fight?" asked Mac Carthy, walking through the assembled chiefs and eyeing each in turn. "Against what warriors do we fight? Against sleeping men? We are warriors who win glory in combat. Where is the glory in a cattle raid?"

"Cuchulainn has not fallen asleep," Maeve said.

"One man or I should say, one boy whose beard is not yet growed," the old chief said. "This is a foolish move you make, Maeve. Consider the consequences for our province, for the wives and children. I urge you to step back from the brink and abandon thoughts of invasion."

Bricriu stepped forward in haste from the crowd and spoke to Mac Carthy, "Do you ignore the evidence of the gods? The sleeping sickness is a sure sign that Ulster is in the wrong. Four kings look north from their wooden palaces and see that the gods do not smile on that sorry province. They see that the gods punish Ulster because that province has broken the peace treaty by abusing our sacred laws of hospitality. We have a crow to pluck with Ulster, and the sooner the better."

"There is a marked difference between fighting for its own sake and fighting in a good cause," replied the eminent chief. "How can a cattle raid against a weak province be called a good cause? If the kings and armies of the four provinces combined to attack Connaught, my sons and I would be in the vanguard of the fray. We would fight until we had driven every one of the invaders

89

from our lands. This venture is different. I will not go to Ulster, and where I do not go my warriors do not go."

"In our province the tribal chiefs can go their own way, for that is our long tradition," said Maeve, raising her hand to silence the voices raised against the chief. "Mac Carthy does not wish to fight Ulster. Very well, let him return to his lands and to his own clan. There is strength in numbers and clans should be united, but our traditions of independence go back for many generations. Yet I ask how would Malachi react if the arrogant curly-headed King of Leinster attacked his lands? Would he not come running to the clans to seek assistance? Would he not demand we unite and throw back the forces of Leinster? I think he would."

Alone, Mac Carthy stood amongst the hostile chiefs. Bricriu had sword in hand, and was threatening to use it. The mood was angry, the chiefs calling him a traitor.

"The fever of impending war has infected your minds and bodies," he said to them. "Remember, before the first blow is struck that all wars start in fever, and end in death. I will have no part of this venture. As for the gods giving a sign to us, it is my belief that Morrigan is responsible for the sleeping sickness. That goddess is never sated no matter how many warriors she devours."

"We march tomorrow morning," declared Maeve.

"Then you break the truce that morning," warned the chief.

After Mac Carthy walked out on the assembly, the remaining chiefs planned for the raid into Ulster. Queen Maeve called for a count of the warriors. Twenty-nine chiefs each pledged three hundred armed warriors and one chariot. The queen instructed them to assemble the warriors and the war chariots.

Now Morrigan appeared in the midst of the chiefs, displayed in her full regalia as goddess of war. On her head she wore a helmet of bronze, antlered as a stag. On her neck was a gold torc, gleaming in three twisted and interwoven strands, and meeting at the ends in the heads of boars. The armour on her body was carved in the image of a warrior; ribbed and tautly muscled, so that she no longer resembled a woman but a man. Her sandals were made of iron, and her fingers were ringed in gold. She stood in the circle of chief with a bow and six arrows in her ringed hands.

"I have cast the dice and sided with Connaught in this conflict," she said, "and come to offer the queen assistance in this war because she has been insulted. In lands across the sea, men use this weapon to win wars. I can supply as many bows and arrows as ye desire. Use this weapon to avenge the wrongs that Ulster has inflicted on your queen."

"Nothing but playthings for women," Bricriu murmured in discontent to O'Brien. "Does that foolish goddess forget that the men of Connaught are warriors who fight their enemies close at hand? We are not as others across the sea who hide behind ditches and kill from afar. No, we love to look into the eyes of our enemies as we kill them."

Bricriu moved to seize the bow and arrows from the goddess and break them in his calloused hands. However, O'Brien clasped his hand over the mouth of Bricriu and pushed him into the arms of two chiefs, instructing them to hold him and keep him quiet. Good soothing diplomacy was required at this time, since insulting the goddess of war was very foolish. His province would need all the help it could get in the coming war, and there was no better ally than Morrigan, or no greater foe. He stepped out from the ranks and examined the bow carefully and with pride. The chief of the O'Briens had ruddy cheeks and greying brown hair, none braver in battle.

"It is indeed a thing of rare beauty," he commented, pulling the bowstring and releasing it. "We are honoured that the goddess has offered us such a weapon. Her generosity shall not be forgotten when the bards write the annals of our time. How does this weapon work?"

Morrigan arrowed the bow, pulling the bowstring, the shaft between her ringed fingers. The feathered arrow sped from the bow and lodged in the wooden pillar supporting the roof.

"I speak for myself, not for other chiefs, and I must decline the kind and generous offer of the goddess," he said. "Neither do I desire to cause offence to Morrigan, for I am a man who respects the gods. Let me give my reason for declining her gift. We are warriors of Connaught who go to war to win honour and glory, so that the bards may sing our praises in the palaces of kings. I see no honour in this weapon, or in waging war against my enemy from a distance."

The goddess offered the bow to the other chiefs, and each one in turn declined the offer. They would fight the war with swords and lances, man to man, warrior against warrior, face to face. That was the way of their forefathers and it was their way too.

When the goddess of war left the assembly of chiefs, O'Brien spoke to them. "I pleaded ignorance of the weapon because I did not wish to insult the goddess of war. No man in his right mind dare do that, except Bricriu! That chief should learn to use his brain before unbridling his unruly tongue! Of course I have seen such weapons used in distant Bohemia as a young man. It seems to me that each society chooses its own way of fighting and its own weapons."

The gods dared not interfere in the work of Morrigan. Earth was her realm, and they gave her a free hand. The gates of the Otherworld were closed against her because they feared she would bring war to their realm. Thus when Lugh heard his son calling out to him in despair, he closed his ears.

Returning from a hunt, Cuchulainn ran on sandalled feet through the silent halls of Emain Macha in anguish. His father and mother lay asleep in their bed, and he could not rouse them. He bathed their foreheads with cold water and lifted their eyelids, but he could not waken them. Their eyelids slipped back into deep slumber. His brother Lorcan was lying on the ground beside his young wife and two children. Cuchulainn lifted them and carried them to their room. He found Emer and his brother Ferdia slumped over a table in the fruit cellar. He tried to revive Ferdia by slapping his face, but his brother did not awaken. Emer slept beside him, her head resting on his shoulder.

He called out to Lugh, "Father, help me!"

Lugh closed his ears to the many entreaties of his son. He had already interfered once in the realm of Morrigan by arming Cuchulainn against the sleeping sickness. To interfere a second time risked bringing the wrath of Morrigan down on his head. The god of light picked up his uilleann pipes and played a tune.

Cuchulainn lifted the sleeping Emer in his arms and carried her to a bubbling stream running near the palace. He placed her in the stream, and the cold waters rushed over her; but the cold waters did not revive her. He removed her and dried her dark hair in his cloak, and wrapped her body. Then he carried her back to the palace and lit a fire. The servants too were sleeping, and all the fires at Emain Macha had died. He removed the wet clothes from the sleeping princess and put her in bed.

The black-feathered raven hovered in the night sky above the wooden palace at Emain Macha, and descended in silent flight. Inside the palace, the bird transformed and became Morrigan, walking the silent corridors in search of Cuchulainn. The goddess of war was not the only immortal in the sleeping palace. Aengus was there too, and a bitter rivalry existed between them. Morrigan desired to rule the Otherworld, but Aengus too coveted that highest title. He decided to teach her a lesson, and to give the goddess a demonstration of his remarkable powers.

The stone-hard heart of the cold and ruthless goddess of war was turned to flesh and blood when she saw Cuchulainn stooping over the sleeping princess. Though not tall, his muscled body was proportioned well, and his chest broad. Though his youthful face was hairless, it was strong and determined. He had long black hair to the shoulders, and his dark eyes indicated clarity and courage. The goddess of war fell instantly in love with the warrior.

"Do you know me?" asked Morrigan.

"Yes, we have met many times."

"Princess Emer is very beautiful, but she is mortal doomed to death," said the goddess. "I too am beautiful, but I am immortal. I do not grow old, and my dark hair does not taint by silver strands. My flesh does not wrinkle and puff out, and my hands do not rust in patches like winter leaves."

Cuchulainn bathed the forehead of Emer, and replied: "Why do you say these things to me in the palace of my father?"

"Come with me and be my love," pleaded the war-god. "Forsake this foolish young girl and be my husband. I can grant you the gift of the gods which all men desire, and that is called immortality. Every human in this world craves above all else to live for ever. Together we can rule the minds of men and mould them in our hands as pieces of clay."

He did not look up but continued bathing the forehead of the princess. "I am betrothed to Emer."

"I can lift the sleeping curse from this drowsy land," she promised. "My power can return your parents to moving life and the servants who care for their needs. Your brothers too and the sleeping princess can be restored. The servants can relight the fires and the herders gather up the scattered flocks and herds. Be my husband, and the province of Ulster can be awakened again."

"The sleeping curse should not have been placed on Ulster," replied Cuchulainn. "No god who inflicts punishment on innocent people is worthy of respect."

Aengus, having given a demonstration of his powers over men and gods alike, lifted the binding spell and departed into the night. The heart of the goddess of war returned to cold stone, and anger appeared in her triple irises.

"The foolish man who rejects the gift of a goddess rejects the protection of that goddess," she said coldly. "No man should make an enemy of a goddess, especially one as powerful as I. From this day forward, you will find in me an implacable enemy."

He pulled the covers over the sleeping princess and left the room. The goddess of war walked behind in his footsteps. He stopped and spoke to her, "I have fought enemies before and won. I have fought and have never been defeated. None has bettered me in battle."

"You have not fought one such as I," she sharply replied.

"If I am fated to fight you, so be it," he said.

Cuchulainn went to the kitchen followed by Morrigan and lifted the sleeping Ferdia on his shoulder.

"The druids speak of the future but they have not been given the eyes of gods," Morrigan said. "Your future is already mapped out step by step, and none can change its course. The war will go badly for Ulster. The final battle will be fought beneath the Stone of Destiny. There you will meet your doom, and I will devour your flesh. That is your future. What do you say to my prophecy?"

"I am a warrior," he said. "To die in battle is my greatest wish."

As the people of Ulster slept under the downy spell of Morrigan, the army of Connaught moved to the Shannon ford. The broad river was in flood, the ford impassable. Maeve called on her druid to offer blood sacrifice to the goddess of the river. The warriors captured an antlered stag and took the animal to Turnod. He pointed the animal's head at the river and cut its throat. "Goddess Shannon, accept our sacrifice," he chanted.

The warriors cut the head from the dead stag, and lit a fire on the bank of the river. They roasted the body on a pyramid of leaping fire, offering the first slices of meat to the goddess. Under the glow of the rising flames, they cut a tree from a nearby forest, stripping its branches and sharpening its end with their swords. Then they stuck the tree in the ground and placed the head of the stag on top, its lifeless eyes staring across the river. Sitting on the grassy bank, they waited for a sign. From the sky a raven flew and landed on the antlers. The omen was good.

Goddess Shannon accepted the sacrifice, and the swollen waters subsided. The army of Connaught crossed the broad river into the verdant province of Meath. The invading army was not opposed by King Diarmuid since he believed that the immortal gods had cursed Ulster. He allowed the army pass unhindered across the rich pastures of his province, and through the budding forests of oak and rowan and beech, taking on new life again. They were astonished at the richness of the land and the numbers of cattle grazing on the lush meadows. The cattle had more fat on their bones than the skinny cattle of their province, and they were more numerous than sands on the shore.

Maeve issued strict instructions to the chiefs of the tribes against plunder, and vowed that any warrior caught stealing or violating the goods or property of the province would be dealt with severely. The army swung north and marched towards the borders of Ulster, reaching the banks of the River Boyne, and following the broad sweep of the rushing river.

Nine miles from the ford of the Boyne, Maeve halted her men and set up camp. She ordered riders to scout the ford, who reported back that there was no activity. She sent for Maol, the son of Mac Carthy. Now this young man had deserted the tribe of his father because he wished to fight and gain glory. He considered his father a coward who had sullied the proud Mac Carthy name, and he desired to restore its honour and its famous reputation in battle.

"Your courage at the games endowed us with much honour in Connaught," she said to the young warrior. "You would have won too, except Lugh intervened on behalf of his son. I have a special mission for you this day. Take fast horse and ride to the wooden palace at Emain Macha. I foresee no resistance. Seek out the field of the goldenhide bull that lies behind the palace. Report to my ears alone about the beast and its condition."

Maol selected a horse and rode north towards the ford nine miles distant from the camp. He stopped at the swollen ford and allowed the horse drink before fording the river. The stench of death assaulted his nostrils. Pulling his cloak over his mouth, he trotted the horse along the road to Emain Macha. On every side of the road, carcasses were rotting in the fields, covered in swarms of buzzing flies and squabbling crows. Packs of wolves watched his progress, fat and not afraid. They had left the forests and were now living openly in the fields.

At silent Emain Macha he dismounted, and tied the horse to a holly tree. He skirted around the hill and the palace, and sought out the field of the goldenhide bull. The triple-horned beast stood alone in the field, chewing on the lush grass. Around the grazing bull thirty grey wolves lay dead, their gored entrails black and rotting.

"The beast is an animal of power and magic," he muttered.

Returning to the horse, a creature confronted him, standing beneath the holly tree where the horse was tethered. The creature had the body of a man; but its head was horned, and its hair stood up like thorns on a rose bush. The creature was armed with a sword, and was clearly ready for combat.

Maol drew his iron sword, and spoke to the creature: "Are you a man or a demon? Let me warn you, I am afraid of neither. My name is Maol Mac Carthy and I come from a long line of proud warriors."

"We have met before," replied the creature. "We met at the games in Royal Tara, competing with muscled legs and arms. I am Cuchulainn, and what you see is my battle-warp. You were a worthy opponent at the games, but this is something quite different. This is not a game, but life and death."

"Death it is to you," said Maol, rushing at Cuchulainn sword in hand. He had not learned from his previous encounter, or learned that games are a preparation for war. Cuchulainn parried the blow as he had parried the ossers at Royal Tara. He struck at the heart of Maol and the legs of the young warrior crumpled. He was dead before he hit the soft earth.

Cuchulainn knelt at the side of the slain warrior and cut off his lifeless head, braiding the long hair, and tying the head to the chariot. He made a vow in the darkness, and spoke to the severed head. "Maol, do not feel lonely, for the heads of any Connaughtman who violates the borders of Ulster will soon join you."

When Maol did not return from the mission, Maeve moved her men to the ford of the River Boyne, the border with Ulster, and halted. Nine standing stones lined the banks on the other side of the rushing river, with symbols etched in the grey granite. She called for her druid Turnod, and asked the meaning of the symbols.

"My queen, the strange writing is called Ogham," he explained. "The language is the invention of Ogma, god of rhetoric and speech. This god has taken rich Ulster under his protection, for in that province across the river the bards compose songs in his honour. They call this god of speech Honey-Mouth because he can persuade men to act against their will, and women to abandon their modesty. He is a very powerful and jealous deity who must not be offended."

"What do the symbols say?" enquired the queen.

Turnod crossed the ford and read the symbols, reporting back to the queen. "The stones say that the peace-loving province of Ulster is protected by the greatest warrior in the land," he explained. "They who cross the border armed in search of conflict shall not live to see their homes and families again. Cold death shall strike them without warning. Cold death shall fall on them swiftly as a falcon swoops on a pigeon."

The queen spoke to the chiefs: "We cross tomorrow morning."

In the dark green marble halls of the Otherworld, on the Island of Gods, Ogma looked on with disgust. He was deeply upset by the total disregard of his words by the brazen queen. He called for a conference with the gods and goddesses. When they assembled, Ogma stood on a green marble table and spoke in an angry voice.

"Do not forget that it was I who improved men and lifted their base thoughts to a higher level of existence," he declared. "It was I who bestowed on them the gift of rhetoric and fine speech, so that they could live peaceful and honourable lives, and forsake their savage nature. I can sway the inner minds of men, and move the soft hearts of women. Without me, men would still be living in caves and clubbing each other over the head! Now brazen Maeve has insulted me by ignoring my symbols. I demand that she is punished."

"Do not forget that the land of the living is the sole realm of Morrigan, and none can interfere in her affairs, not even the immortal gods," Lugh replied. "If Queen Maeve is to be punished, she will bring it down on her own head. The gods measure out a piece of life's rope to queens and humans alike. They can use it to make a skipping rope, or a noose."

Ogma was not pleased with the answer. "Then what may I ask is the purpose of the gods?" he asked. "Why do we give them advice if they ignore us? What is the purpose of our existence?"

"Because we gave them free will too," replied Lugh.

"Dagda should be here to put manners on that brazen queen," said Ogma. "Why is our king always missing in times of crisis?"

Aengus now offered his opinion. "It is obvious that Dagda has relinquished his authority by his absence. For if a ruler is not at hand to deal with a crisis, what is the point of his existence?"

At Emain Macha, Cuchulainn attempted to wake his charioteer, but Begmore was under the influence of the sleeping sickness. The warrior broke two twigs from an oak tree, and used them to keep his eyelids open. Then he told Begmore to take the chariot to the river. Begmore whipped the horses, and the chariot sped to confront the invading army of Connaught.

Heavy rains greeted the waiting men of Connaught, and the wheels of the chariots lodged in the mucky ground. Clinging mud covered the legs and cloaks of the warriors. They huddled for cover beneath trees, and uttered loud curses at the dark and brooding sky. Lightning flashed in darting branches across the sky and drums of thunder rolled. It was a bad omen.

Turnod hurried on frail legs to the wooden shelter of Maeve and Ailill. Water cascaded from the roof of the shelter and dripped on the floor. Shaking the rain from his white head, he spoke to the royal couple in a trembling voice, "My king and queen, Ogma is angry that we ignore his warnings. It is bad enough that we fight Ulster and break the peace treaty, but we must not take on the gods as well, else we are heading for disaster."

"What do you suggest we do?" asked the queen.

"Turn back now before it is too late," Turnod replied.

"No, we have taken too many insults from rich Ulster to turn back now," replied the queen. "Ogma is the god of rhetoric, and he can be ignored in a time of war. Taranis controls the sky. He is the god who should be appeased, not Ogma. How long must we suffer his rains and bolts of lightning before we have to make the sacrifice of the triple death?"

"Do not make enemies of the gods," warned Turnod.

"Answer my question, druid," said the impatient queen.

"My queen, the triple death is reserved only for the king who fails to bring prosperity to his province," explained Turnod. "If the harvest fails for three years in a row, then the king must be sacrificed by his people to appease the anger of that god. His back is broken, his throat is cut, and he is drowned in a bog. The triple death does not apply here."

A drenched messenger arrived at the shelter and interrupted the conversation between the queen and her druid, saying it was important. The charioteer of Cuchulainn was seeking an audience. Maeve issued instructions to feed him and to supply a change of clothes. Begmore was bathed, but his hands protected his face and the twigs. If they fell out he would fall asleep again. The royal servants clothed and fed the charioteer, and took him to the queen.

Begmore spoke to the royal couple, "Royal Ailill and Maeve, I come here under the instructions of invincible Cuchulainn who guards the ford with a request. The warriors of Ulster are now asleep and none knows when they wake except the gods. Ye are many and he is but one. He proposes one warrior to step outside the ranks and fight him until the warriors of Ulster awake and take the field."

"Why should we give up the advantage of numbers?" said Maeve. "That is foolish talk. Advantages in war must be pursued, not thrown away. Connaught intends to win, not lose as we did before."

"Our ancient laws of combat demand it," replied the charioteer.

"The messenger has the laws on his side," Turnod reminded the queen. "A request of honour cannot be denied. Our actions in this sorry endeavour will be judged, not only by the four watching kings, but also by posterity. We dare not refuse the request of the hound of Ulster."

Maeve and Ailill consulted and came to an agreement. Then the king gave his answer to Begmore: "Go tell your terrible master that his terms are agreed. Single combat at the river it is. If he is killed, we ride over his dead body to Emain Macha and seize the goldenhide bull. If the warriors awake before he is killed, we attack in full force."

The rains did not cease until evening came, and the ford had turned into a quagmire. When the driving rains eventually ceased, the warriors shook the water from their sodden clothes and hair and looked across the wild river. On the other side of the muddy ford, rain-soaked Cuchulainn stood upright in his bronze chariot with Begmore at his side. He spoke to them across the rushing Boyne waters. "Who is the first amongst ye who desires to join the gods in the Otherworld?"

One of the O'Nally tribe of Galway, a warrior called Declan, took up his long spear and walked to the river. He spoke to Cuchulainn: "The warrior you challenge has already killed three Ulstermen by the strength of his spear when last our provinces met. Though my hair and beard are grey, my arm is strong. Many youths desired me to remain at home on windy mountains tending skinny sheep, since I am forty years old. Yet I came here to prove that I am as good a man today as I was twenty years ago. This is the manner of man you challenge."

The two warriors stripped to the waist and ran into the rushing waters of the river. O'Nally flung his spear first. Cuchulainn evaded the swift spear, and it passed above his head. He flung his spear at O'Nally, though none saw his arm move such was its speed. The spear struck the warrior in the chest and hurled him into the river. Cuchulainn waded to the slain warrior and pulled out the bloody spear. He cut off the head of the slain warrior, braiding the hair, and tying it on the chariot beside the head of Maol.

Chapter Eight

Kind-hearted Epona heard the plaintive cry of O'Nally's spirit and made fast preparations to leave the Otherworld. She went to the rose-garlanded stable where the magical horse rested. The horse was called Capall, and its flowing mane and coat were whiter than snow. Epona placed a halter of red roses over the white neck of Capall and sat on its back.

Epona held the key to the gates of the Otherworld. She carried the iron key around her neck on a twig of white roses. She went about her work quietly and efficiently, rescuing the wispy spirits of warriors slain in battle, and taking them to the many Isles of the Otherworld. Epona lacked ambition, and as a consequence she had the ear of every god and goddess, since they did not consider her a threat to their own ambitions.

However, her own lack of ambition had its drawbacks because she tended to be overlooked. Her voice did not carry much weight at the conferences of the gods. She never questioned any god or goddess who came to her for the key to the gates of the Otherworld, believing that they were leaving to create good on Earth, not to cause mischief.

On the fleeting silver hooves of Capall, Goddess Epona raced over the wave-tossed western ocean, and over the land until she came to the River Boyne. There she played her golden harp over the slain warrior, and the spirit responded and left the body. She washed and purified the spirit in the rushing ford, readying it for departure. Then she wound the spirit in a garland of red roses, and galloped across the land and the wave-tossed blue ocean to the Otherworld.

Epona asked for a conference to discuss the state of Ulster, but the gods were not interested. They had other more important matters on their minds. They were engaged in a battle for the succession of the crown, in the belief that Dagda had lost the right to rule by his many absences. It was not a battle fought with arms, since violence was not permitted to pass the gates. The battle for kingship was fought with strong godly minds and stronger godly wills. Cunning too was employed to achieve the highest position. They ignored her call for a conference. Besides, Ulster was in the realm of Morrigan, and no god dared interfere.

Now, even the lowliest member of a group can cause problems for the highest, and even the mildest member can rise to anger when a reasonable request is refused. The mild-mannered goddess reacted to the refusal in her own way. When Lugh came to her seeking the key to the gates, she refused. Lugh was severely shocked because the mild-mannered goddess had never said no before. The key was also refused to Ogma, and to Aengus. The god of love tried his many charms to get the key, but Epona remained steadfast. She would keep the gates locked until she had her conference. They had no choice but to grant her wish.

Epona spoke to the gods, "I have rescued the spirit of a slain warrior at the ford of River Boyne and taken it home. The immortal gods should be ashamed of themselves for giving Morrigan a free hand on Earth. No god or goddess should have that much power. If the gods had a cup of courage, they would stop this conflict before I am over-burdened with work. It is not too late to stop this war. Yet none here dares confront Morrigan who feasts on the flesh of slain warriors. Why do the gods treat her with respect and deference, but ignore me? To my way of thinking, the god who does evil should be banished from society, and the god who does good should be elevated in society."

Lugh stood and spoke to Epona, "We hear the words you say, but this is the way of our worlds. It has always been thus, and shall always be. Tell us of your concerns, Epona. Tell us why you have called the conference."

"Lugh says it has always been thus, but that does not make it right," replied the kind-hearted goddess. "If the all-knowing gods are unable to recognise the difference between right and wrong, how do they expect humans to know? I will tell you why I called this conference and why I have withheld the key. But before I do, tell me why I had to keep the gates locked to get a response?"

Brigid stood and spoke to Epona, "Kind-hearted goddess, let me speak for myself and not for others. I am concerned with life and all its aspects. I defeat the Winter Crone every year who strangles the land in ice and snow. I restore the land to growing life and the people to life and the animals to living life. I mean no disrespect to you, but you deal in death. I am not comfortable with death in any of its aspects."

"Who is to rescue the spirits of the slain warriors if I do not perform the task?" Epona asked. "As for death, it too is part of life and all its diverse and wonderful aspects.

Every human born on Earth is fated to die and turning your face against that truth does not make it go away. Brigid, you are wise, but you are also subtle in the manner of they who seek to rule. I am ignored because I do not seek to rule, and I am overlooked because I do not raise my meek voice or make outrageous demands. If the Otherworld seeks to set an example for men on Earth, the words of every god and goddess must carry the same weight."

Aengus stood and spoke to Epona: "I give you my solemn oath that I will in future listen to your meek voice. Give us the reason why we are assembled here."

"Your promise is as that of a base man who desires to violate the body of a woman," replied Epona. "The promise is used for effect and to get your own way. Whilst you are locked up here, you cannot cause mischief on Earth. You would be better served binding the heart of one man to one woman for life. But no, you cannot do that task, because you prefer to cause mischief. Yet you are regarded more highly than me."

"Goddess of the kind heart, I beseech you to inform us of your mind," said Lugh. "Why are we assembled here?"

"Even you, god of light, even you have not heard my wise words," Epona said, replying to Lugh. "They have gone in your right ear, and gone out your left ear. What is the purpose if speech if you do not listen? Let me tell you why we are here and please do not fall asleep. Ulster and Connaught are engaged in mortal combat, but it is an uneven struggle. Cuchulainn is holding the ford of the Boyne alone against the forces of Maeve. Is that just or fair?"

"The gods are neutral in war and we do not take sides," Brigid said. "We leave conflicts to Morrigan."

"He cannot hold out forever," Epona told them. "The curse must be lifted from the sleeping land. Let me give my reasons why the curse must be lifted and if that means confronting Morrigan, so be it. For if we do not confront evil, how can we call ourselves good gods? How can we set an example for mortals to follow? Fleet Capall of the silver hooves took me to the ford of the Boyne to retrieve the spirit of the slain warrior. I witnessed the carcasses of horses lying in the barren fields, savaged by wolves. Fellow gods and goddesses, horses are sacred to these people. If the horses die, the people will never forgive the gods."

"We all promise to look into the matter as soon as possible," Aengus said. "Give me the key."

"Do you think that I am a foolish young girl who is readily swayed by the honeyed promises of a god who does his business by night as the bats?" said Epona. "Action, not words, is required. The key remains in my possession until Morrigan is confronted and the curse lifted from Ulster. I urge you not to underestimate the determination of a meek goddess."

The goddess of the spirits departed, and the remaining gods decided to approach her separately, believing her meek nature could not hold out. The god of light tried first, and failed. He found in Epona reserves of inner strength that he had not noticed before. Lovely Brigid tried next, and also failed. She found the kind and meek goddess immovable. When Aengus approached, the goddess refused to listen to his words, and sent him away. The honeyed words of the god of rhetoric also fell on deaf ears.

The Otherworld was not a happy place because the gods were caged behind the gates. No entreaty could move Epona to unlock the gates, or no promise. Meanwhile, the spirits of warriors slain by Cuchulainn were roaming Earth in search of a home, crying out by night. The people were terrified by the cries and offered sacrifices to the gods, but their entreaties were not answered. Epona refused to collect them. She kept Capall in the rose-garlanded stables, and the key to the gates around her neck.

The gods and goddesses were forced to bow before the sheer determination of Epona. She opened the iron gates, and arranged a meeting beside the passage grave at Carrowmore. Epona arrived late, having collected the roaming spirits of the slain warriors and taken them to the Otherworld. The sight that she saw roused her meek nature. The gods and goddesses were fighting over the highest boulder.

Epona spoke to them, "Brave warriors are dying daily under the swift spear-arm of Cuchulainn, and ye are playing king of the castle! Have ye no shame? Have ye no concern for the lives of the warriors? Come down here and sit on the hard ground, though I doubt if the stones could grant ye humility! Put the petty squabbling aside, and think of the brave warriors who are dying for a change. Already Cuchulainn has sent the spirits of nine brave men to the Otherworld."

They did as she requested, though under protest. Even on the hard ground they craned their heads to appear taller. Epona led the white horse into their midst, and Capall towered over the gods. The message was not lost on them, and they quietened.

"Your shoulders alone carry the blame for this mad conflict," Epona said, accusing Morrigan. "You sowed the warring seed of impossible ambition in Maeve, and it took root in the fertile mind of that brazen queen. Blind ambition has caused more deaths than love or hate. The others here dare not speak lest they offend you, but I have demonstrated that you have no power over me. Was it not I who slammed the gates in your face? I urge you not to confuse my meek nature for cowardice. That would be a costly mistake. Lift the curse."

"Who are you to change the rules?" demanded Morrigan.

"I have to pick up the broken spirits of the slain warriors caused by your mischief," Epona replied. "I have never complained, and the happy spirits thank me for taking them across the western ocean. No mortal ever speaks badly of me, which is more than can be said for you! It is bad enough that you have started this accursed war and sown an evil seed in the mind of the queen; but to curse a peaceful province with the sleeping sickness is unforgivable."

"Do not dare speak of things you do not understand," Morrigan said. "Warriors love war, and it is my function to see they are not disappointed. How can they prove their courage otherwise? By herding mooing cows down dreary lanes? Mind your own business and allow me to mind mine."

"In hot Libya live vultures that feed on the carcasses of dead animals, but even they get sated and fat so that they can eat no more," Epona responded. "Yet you are never sated, and the more flesh you consume the greater your appetite becomes. Here is my promise to you and to the other gods. Unless the curse is lifted from Ulster, the iron gates of the Otherworld remain closed."

"This is intolerable! How dare a meek goddess speak in those terms to one as powerful as I! Fellow gods and goddesses, who is this Epona who would change the laws of the Otherworld? Who listens to the meek voice, or pays attention when it is raised? She has no importance. She is bluffing, and we must call her bluff."

"The dice have been thrown," Epona told them. "Either we play by my rules or the gates remain closed."

From midnight until dawn they debated the problem, and tried to get Epona to change her mind. The kind-hearted goddess refused to bend. She gave the gods and goddesses the final ultimatum: either the curse was lifted, or the iron gates of the Otherworld would stay closed. Then she mounted Capall, and the fleet-hooved horse sped over the land, and over the western ocean.

"Do not ask us to explain what has happened to Epona because we are in the dark," Ogma said to Morrigan. "We all took her for granted, and she behaved as we expected her to behave. Suddenly she began to act out of character and to refuse the key to us. We recognise your authority on Earth and that goes without saying. Having said that, we all have the same problem here. Epona has slammed the gates shut in your face and now she threatens us with the same punishment. If she were human, I would say she has gone quite mad! Morrigan, this is your realm, not ours. I beseech you to lift the sleeping curse and let us return to the Otherworld."

"God of rhetoric and overblown speech, the sound of your own voice makes you deaf to reason," Morrigan replied. "Let us discuss the problem we have with Epona. If we allow her to bully us over this matter, where does she stop? Does her meek nature conceal another desire? Does she seek the high kingship of the Otherworld in the absence of Dagda? Mark well my words for that is her purpose."

"No, she does not desire the crown, for she does not associate with the powerful," Lugh said. "That is the way of they who desire to rule. Epona treats the weak and the powerful in the same manner. The slain spirit of the chief is treated in the same way as the slain spirit of the warrior. Capall is her pride and joy, and she spends all her time in the rose-garlanded stables where he is tethered. I went to the goddess and tried to persuade her to give me the key. She replied that Capall had shed tears of silver because the carcasses of dead horses were lying on the barren fields of Ulster. Horses are sacred to the meek goddess, and she regards their deaths as a great sacrilege."

"Ulster and Connaught are at war," Brigid said to Morrigan. "It shall end, for all wars that begin must end sometime. Old warriors shall gather around fires and talk of battles fought. Old enemies shall become new friends in time. Enmity shall be forgotten, and friendship remembered. But neither side will forgive or forget the destruction of the horses. Lift the curse."

"Goddess of rebirth, try to understand my feelings, and walk in my iron sandals for a mile or two," Morrigan said. "The heavy gates of the Otherworld, the home of the gods, my home, were slammed shut in my face. Did you speak up on my behalf? No, you did not. Earth is my realm and theatre of responsibility, but the Otherworld is my only home. Let me propose a bargain here at Carrowmore of the large stones. I promise to lift the curse if the gates are thrown open to my return."

"Epona will not agree, and she holds the key," Lugh said.

"The dice are thrown on the ground," Morrigan said. "We play by my rules, or not at all."

Next morning the swift-hooved Capall galloped over the western ocean, and the sounding silver hooves echoed in the ears of the gods and goddesses at Carrowmore. Epona halted the horse, dismounted, and led Capall into their midst.

"No agreement yet, I see," she said. "If the knowing gods themselves cannot solve a simple problem, what hope is there for mankind? Let me guess what Morrigan has proposed. She has suggested a trade, is that not right? If she lifts the curse from the unhappy province, in return she desires to return to the Otherworld. That is completely out of the question! What she is doing is wrong. What I am doing is right. If ye cannot see that, ye do not deserve the high title of gods, or the respect of men."

"The conditions are set and the dice thrown." Morrigan said. "Pick them up and accept my terms, or leave them there and the curse remains."

"The gods trade words here whilst warriors trade spears and shed their young red blood in the torrented salmon waters of the Boyne," Epona countered. "As we speak here, Maeve is losing her patience and threatens to break the promise of single combat. Her brave warriors are men of extreme honour, but they will not stand by idly and watch the hound of Ulster killing their comrades in single combat at the bloody ford. They are certain to avenge their friends and slay Cuchulainn by rushing him in a body."

"He will not die, but live on the tongues of bards and in the hearts of brave men for all time," Morrigan said. "That is his reward. No warrior could ask for more."

Epona mounted Capall and spoke to them, "Once again I return to the rose-garlanded stables with Capall. The gates are locked, and they remain locked until the evil

114

curse is lifted. These are my final words on the matter. I urge you not to underestimate the will of a meek goddess. Let me give you some advice, though I doubt if your ears are open to good advice. Forget your petty squabbling over the leadership. Think of the dying warriors and not your blind ambitions."

"We shall meet again, meek goddess," Morrigan called out.

The voice of Epona replied, "We shall meet again."

Daylight in mists dawned on the gods and goddesses seated at the passage tomb at Carrowmore on the high boulders. They were unable to reach a decision, or persuade Morrigan to lift the curse. They expressed a desire to return home, but the iron gates were locked. They were powerless.

Mist-laden cold dawn frayed their fragile tempers, and they started arguing with each other. Brigid made a threat, declaring she would not confront the Winter Crone next year. The land would be bound eternally in ice and snow, bound in unbreakable shackles. Then Ogma threated to withdraw the gift of rhetoric, and Lugh to withdraw the great gift of light, the source of life itself. Morrigan suspected they were bluffing and refused to lift the curse.

A heavy downpour concentrated their minds, and their thoughts. The rains sleeted in from the grey western ocean and drenched them. Lugh was soaked to the skin and thoroughly fed up with his condition. He was a god who detested the rain, choosing only sunny days to visit the land of the living. Now he decided to carry out his threat, and withdrew the gift of light from the land. Dawn receded, and darkness enveloped the land. Lugh held his hand close to his face, and could not see it.

At the ford of the Boyne, the warriors were alarmed by the loss of light from the land, and both sides regarded it as a bad omen. Cuchulainn returned to his chariot, and in darkness guarded the ford. The warriors lit fires and made sacrifice to the gods. Turnod lit a torch and sought out the wooden shelter of the royal couple. Urgently he spoke to Ailill and Maeve, "Here is another sign from the gods showing their utter displeasure. They have withdrawn the light, and without light nothing can live. We are doomed to die unless this madness stops. Call off the war and let us go home."

"Of course the gods are angry, and this is a sign from them," Maeve replied to her druid. "Are they are not angry with too-rich Ulster? Have they not laid waste that province? This is a sign for Ulster, not for us. The gods are telling that province to give up the goldenhide bull."

For three days and three nights the land was held in darkness, without the sun and without heat. The fighting at the ford ceased and the wet warriors huddled around campfires warming their hands, and muttering about their sufferings. Rain-sodden Cuchulainn stood in his chariot and called out to his father for the return of the light. Lugh did not reply to his son because he was engaged in a battle of wits with Morrigan. The goddess of war was not willing to bow to the god of light, but no warriors were being killed and she was getting hungry.

On the morning of the fourth day, she reluctantly agreed to lift the sleeping curse from Ulster, and Lugh agreed to return the light. The killing resumed again, and Morrigan once more feasted on the flesh of slain warriors.

Chapter Nine

Slowly, the wasted province of Ulster woke up from its deep slumber. The herders of the herds and flocks piled high the dead carcasses of cattle and sheep, and set them alight. Some went in search of the scattered herds, whilst others organised hunting groups to hunt down and kill the ravaging wolves.

King Connor too awakened from the downy sleep and instructed the waking servants to light the fires. He went outside, and wept at the utter devastation in the fields. Walking to the rear of the palace, he counted the dead bodies of sixty grey wolves gored to death by the goldenhide bull. The king returned to the palace much saddened by the loss of his herds and flocks.

The chariot of Cuchulainn raced up to Emain Macha along the sandy road, driven by Begmore. He had removed the twigs from his eyes, and no longer felt the desire to sleep. Without waiting to tether the horses, he ran into the wooden palace. The servants took him to the king, and he spoke to Connor, "My lord, I have hurried here to report the army of Maeve at the ford." His chest heaved before continuing, "I fear the horses will die from the effort. Your son holds the ford of the Boyne against the hard warriors of Maeve, and he is exhausted.

Assemble the warriors quickly, and send them to his relief, or he is doomed. I beg of you not to delay."

"You have indeed done well, Begmore," replied the king. "So, the war has started. I did not desire this war, and I forgot the golden rule of a king. A province that desires to live in the blessings of peace must always be prepared for war. I will assemble the warriors and send them to the relief of Cuchulainn as quickly as possible. I can only pray that we are in time to save his life."

Princess Emer awakened in bed, and was most surprised at her nakedness, for she had no memory of undressing. She called the servants and asked for her clothes, and went in search of Ferdia. The servants related the news about the war at the ford of the Boyne, and that her future husband was standing alone against the forces of Maeve. They added that the king was gathering the tribes to relieve Cuchulainn as soon as possible.

She spoke to Ferdia in the cellar, where large vats of ripened apples and pears were stored in straw baskets: "Was it a dream I had in my unexplained slumber or did we travel from high Cashel to Emain Macha? Was it a dream that in my foolish youth I caused you insult, but that overnight I changed from a girl to a woman? Such things seem strange now, as if they happened many years ago."

"Princess, this is not a time for discussion about the events that have passed," Ferdia replied. "As we speak, my brave brother fights for the very survival of Ulster, and you are his promised bride. That is how it is, and how it must be."

"My father promised my body to the winner of the games at Royal Tara, but my mind is my very own," she said. "It is not the property of my father or the property of

Cuchulainn. It is yours, Ferdia. I love you and none other. It is not too late for us."

"Princess, you are young, and young hearts fall easily to the wiles of Aengus," he said. "Wed Cuchulainn, and soon you will grow to love him, and forget me."

"The druid of my father spoke to me about love, but words alone do not adequately express the intense feelings for you in my heart," she confessed. "I wish to be with you for eternity. I wish to go to bed with you, and wake beside your warm body. Do not try to tell me you think otherwise! I have seen how you looked at me during the journey. Looks such as yours do not lie."

"Emer, our lives are on different paths," he said.

King Connor assembled ninety warriors, including his youngest son Lorcan, and made preparations to ride to the ford of the Boyne. It was his keen intention to relieve Cuchulainn, and to engage the forces of Maeve until reinforcements arrived. He sent messengers to the chiefs of the sixty Ulster tribes, and asked them to come with three hundred men each. Before leaving for the ford, he called Ferdia to his side.

"We ride to relieve Cuchulainn at the ford of the Boyne," he said. "If I am killed, the crown of Ulster passes to your head. The duties of a prince are not the same as the duties of a king. A prince may think for himself, since he has no responsibilities; but a king must think for his province and the welfare of his people. I detest war, but I must fight this one. Every king and every province has the right of defence against an aggressor. I will try to talk reason to the men of Connaught, but if they do not listen I will fight. If I am killed in battle, wear my crown."

"I do not desire the crown, not in this way, father," Ferdia said. "Come home safely. We are in the right, and the gods smile on the righteous."

The forces of King Connor reached the ford of the Boyne as night was falling on the rushing river, and took up position on its trampled banks. Cuchulainn was exhausted, and the warriors lifted him from the chariot. The king issued instructions, and the warriors tied him to a horse. Two horsemen took the horse and the exhausted Cuchulainn with all haste to Emain Macha. Then Connor walked to the bank of the river and sent his voice ringing to the other side. King Ailill and Queen Maeve appeared with their forces on the other side under a forest of torches.

"For eighteen days and nights my brave son has held this ford, and in that time many of your bravest warriors have been slain," Connor said. "The goddess Epona has worked tirelessly to bring their spirits to the Otherworld. I did not desire the deaths of your brave warriors and my heart grieves for them though they are not from our province. Too many have already died. Let me propose a compromise so that no more need die. This flowing river carves out the borders of Ulster. As yet the borders have not been violated. Return home now, and I promise to withdraw my army from this bloody ford."

"We do not stand here for personal glory or because Connaught is by nature warlike," replied Maeve, under the dancing light of one hundred burning torches. "We stand here at the ford because the sacred laws of hospitality were abused and the burnt bones of Cathal lie in the tomb at Carrowmore. The gods have shown their utter displeasure with Ulster for abusing the sacred laws of hospitality. They have cast a downy sleeping sickness on the land and poisoned the rivers and lakes. We are in the right and that is why we stand here. Connor can easily settle this dispute, for it is in his hands to do so. Hand over the goldenhide bull, and we depart."

"Ulster is prepared to avoid war at all costs, but not at the base cost of dishonour," replied noble Connor. "How would the King of Ulster be regarded across Ireland if he were seen to hand over by the threat of force that which he denied by request? He would be seen as a weak king, and weakness in this world is always punished. I have the authority to hand over the goldenhide bull, but not the will to cast Ulster in a cowardly light. Therefore, I must decline."

"Then we must proceed across the ford and seize the bull," said the queen. "This war is your fault, not mine. The deaths of your brave warriors will lie heavily on your breast, not on mine. We attack tomorrow."

"We are determined to defend by force of arms our territory," said noble Connor. "But ponder before you attack. I feel in my bones that evil Morrigan is behind his death, and that she entered Cathal's mind and sowed the seeds of his destruction. She desires this war. The borders have not yet been breached. If you choose to breach them tomorrow, if one of your warriors sets a single foot on our sacred soil, there can be no going back."

"The spirit of my dead brother cries out for vengeance against Ulster," Ailill said. "He was killed by your hand, and his head tied to your chariot. The business between us is not finished, and it is a business that requires war to end it."

"What is it ye seek from Ulster?" challenged Connor. "Is it the bull, or is it revenge? I killed your brother in single combat, Ailill, though I did my best to avoid conflict. It is true I tied his head to my chariot for that is how we wage war. His courage became mine and rendered me stronger on the field of battle. Yet I did not kill Talteann on the soil of Connaught, but on the sacred soil of Ulster. I thought I could avoid war by dialogue, but it takes two willing kings to hold a conference. He desired to conquer my province and I as the king could not permit that."

At Emain Macha, Ferdia took the exhausted body of Cuchulainn from the horse and carried the sleeping warrior to his room, followed by Emer. They bathed the body and rubbed in oils of snowdrop and primrose. They poured honey into his wounds and bound them in linen strips. Then they applied dried and crushed oak leaves to the skin to protect him from evil spirits.

"The brave hound of Ulster sleeps, exhausted from eighteen days of savage fighting," Ferdia said to Emer. "There lies your future husband. My father has plans to build a wooden palace for you both, and grant you many lands. That is your future, and there can be none other."

"We shape our own futures, Ferdia," she said. "We can find a hidden cave or a forest somewhere and live as man and wife. I have not yet lived, but I know one thing, and that is nothing matters in this world except a man and a woman. This war does not matter, this land does not matter, and this life does not matter if we live apart."

"No, princess, we cannot run away from life," said the prince. "There is much more at stake here than a man and a woman. Your destiny is to marry Cuchulainn. My destiny? I take it as it comes. Remain here and take care of him. I have work to do elsewhere."

Dusk fell on the ford of the Boyne, and in secret Turnod called a meeting with two chiefs. One was Rory

Guinan, a redfaced man of one score and fifteen years from Leitrim. The other was Dara O'Brien, ten years older and from Sligo. The two chiefs walked in the footsteps of the druid into the evening forest near the ford, under a clouded moon.

"As your druid, my friends, I have your ears, and I can speak plainly," Turnod said, shaking his old head. "I fear our queen has gone quite mad! If she crosses the ford of the Boyne tomorrow, war most terrible is bound to follow. Thus far eighteen of our bravest warriors have fallen under the swift spear-arm of Cuchulainn. The object of her quest is the triple-horned bull that patrols the green field behind Emain Macha. Here is what I propose. Let a fast raiding party ride from here under cover of darkness and take a detour, and seize the bull. Emain Macha has no defences because Connor guards the ford. We can achieve the quest, and avoid a full-scale war."

Red anger spread over on the face of Dara O'Brien, and he spoke to Turnod: "We came here to fight, not to steal! There is no honour in a raid. I have no intention of doing anything to bring disgrace on my name, and where I do not go my warriors do not go."

Rory Guinan too was angry. "I came here to fight and to gain honour in combat, not to become a thief in the night," he said. "I pray there is fighting because that is why we are here. I have lost two brave warriors to the swift spear-arm of Cuchulainn, and I burn to avenge them."

Though disappointed, the druid did not cease in his efforts. He went from campfire to campfire speaking to the warriors. He told them they could gain much honour in the raid, and that bards would sing their praises in the palaces of kings. When the first shaft of dawn reached the ford, sixty warriors moved silently through the forest, leading their horses by hand. They tied cloths over the hooves of the horses, and walked for three miles before mounting them and riding along the banks of the river seeking another ford.

Dawn awakened the sleeping armies, and they lined up along the banks of the rushing Boyne. Maeve and Ailill appeared on their chariots ready to do battle, and Connor appeared on the other side. The warriors on both sides were eager for the fray, and their loud voices silenced the birds and the rushing waters.

Before the warriors forded the stream, Bricriu's voice rang across the river and found the ears of Connor and his warriors: "Noble king, I had wished to meet Cuchulainn today in combat, though it does me no honour to kill a hairless boy. I am willing and ready to fight your bravest warrior to demonstrate just what you are up against. Connaught is a harsh place of sinking bogs and stony soil, and such places produce the hardiest warriors. We fear nothing, except Taranis throwing the sky on our heads! Ye in Ulster have grown fat and lazy from easy living."

Lorcan leaped from his chariot and rushed to the riverbank. "We in Ulster live in peace, but it does not follow we are weak or afraid to fight an enemy," he said. "They who think otherwise are in for a big shock! My name is Lorcan, second-born son of King Connor, and we have met before in the palace of my father. Let us see if you can live up to your boasting."

"Another hairless boy!" exclaimed Bricriu. "I know not whether to fight him, or to spank him! Or perhaps he is a girl in the clothes of a man. Go home to your mother, boy, and seek her unripe breast in comfort. This ford is a place of warriors, and you do not match that description."

Stung by the taunting words, Lorcan smeared mud on his chin. Then he gathered clumps of mosses and stuck them to the mud. In this manner he constructed a beard, so that he looked older than his years.

"The boy has become a man!" he shouted across the ford.

The weapons of the two warriors were similar. Both carried heavy swords of iron, straight as a sapling in the heat of summer, although the sword of Lorcan was longer. Their long spears were straight and trim, made from the wood of the ash tree, and tipped in fire-hardened iron. The iron tip was hammered and shaped as the leaf of the birch tree by their brawny smiths. Their shields were made for fighting, not ceremony, light but strong. Triple layers of bullhide were soaked in brine and stretched over a frame of alderwood. The handles were made from oak, durable and strong. The bosses were constructed by strips of toughened leather, bound in balls, and sewed in the centre of the shields.

Bricriu removed his cloak and tunic before fighting, and laid them on the grass. They were his pride and joy, and he was fearful they might become torn or dirtied in the fighting. The cloak was deerskin, dyed in the yellow colours of buttercups in summer. His tunic was woollen, dyed as brown as the heart of the sunflower, and kept in place by gold pins. He placed his golden fastening pins and bracelets neatly on the clothes. Stripped to the waist, his upper body was powerful and muscled.

Lorcan wore a linen tunic, pleated on his chest, tufted in many layers for protection. Seeing that his opponent was bare-chested, Lorcan removed the shirt.

"Lorcan, the bold warrior you face has more experience than you," Connor told his son. "The tunic makes the fight more matched, yet you throw it away to fight bare-chested. I beseech you to put it on again."

"Father, it is too heavy for my honour," he replied. "This is not about who has more experience in battle. This is a message to these warmongers that we are not gone soft from easy living. They need to know that. They think we will roll over without a fight. Well, I intend to prove them wrong. If I die here at the ford of the Boyne, take care of my young wife and two children."

The two warriors flung their spears at the same moment. Both evaded the deadly throws. They drew swords, rushing into the waters, and clashing in mid-stream. Like two evenly matched stags meeting in a frosty clearing, neither was prepared to yield, and steam rose from their bodies. The waters churned in boiling torrents, and their swords sang the strident song of battle. The warriors on both banks watched the battle, unsure who was winning. The two bodies writhed and became as one, squirming and slashing in the white- sprayed foam. The spray turned from white to red, and the waters turned to blood.

A headless body floated in the river, and one warrior raised a severed head. A tumultuous roar echoed in the throats of the men from Connaught and they raised their shields and spears aloft. They beat their shields in loud rolls of triumph. Bricriu was victorious, and Lorcan was dead.

"My son is dead, and soon Epona rides to take his rose-bound spirit to the Otherworld," tearful Connor said. "I request six days of peace to mourn my slain son, in accordance to the sacred laws handed down by our forefathers. We must return to Emain Macha to conduct our rites, so that his mother and his wife can participate.

Afterwards, we shall place his bones in our passage tomb at Navan. Let us meet again at this bloody ford when we have conducted our rites, and our mourning."

"The mourning request is granted in accordance to the laws of our forefathers," Ailill replied. "Noble Connor, you can be proud of your son. He fought with the grace of the eagle and the strength of the bull. The bards will sing his praises in the palaces of kings."

At the first shaft of light over the ford, sixty warriors had set out to detour Connor and seize the goldenhide bull. As dusk fell, thirty reached Emain Macha. Thirty warriors and their horses had been lost crossing the rushing waters, and washed out to the ocean. There were no guards at the wooden palace, and the surviving warriors broke down the wooden fence and entered the field of the bull. The beast bellowed three times as the silent warriors drove it through the broken fence.

Cuchulainn was awakened by the bellows and called for his weapons. The servants told him that Ferdia was away in the forests searching for the scattered herds and flocks. Running from the wooden palace on bare feet, he engaged the warriors in combat, and slew the man holding the torch. It fell with the dead warrior to the ground. He snuffed out the torch, and in darkness fought the warriors. Holding his breath, he listened in the darkness for the breathing warriors. One by one he struck them down in the night. When dawn came, thirty men lay dead, and the bull grazed in the field again.

Black rising smoke from the funeral pyre ascended to the sky accompanied by the keening of the women. The parents of Lorcan wept bitterly over their dead son. Ferdia held the sobbing young daughter of Lorcan in his arms and Cuchulainn held his young son. Fidelma, widow of the slain warrior, stood closest to the burning pyre, and threw crushed and dried oak leaves on the reaching flames to ward off evil spirits.

The young widow was not weeping, and pride glowed in her happy face. Lorcan had died an honourable death. He had displayed boundless courage at the ford of the Boyne, and the bards would sing his praises for all time in the palaces of kings. The glory of the warrior reflected well on his wife and granted her great honour. She was the widow of a hero.

Chapter Ten

The strong and bearded god of the sea, Manannan Mac Lir, did not visit the Otherworld very often. The gods and goddesses whispered amongst themselves and asked each other why he was visiting them now, and whether he would be in a good or a bad mood. The problem with the broad god of the sea was his utter unpredictability. One moment he was calm and placid, and the next moment he flew into a violent rage. He was respected in the Otherworld because of his vast sphere of influence, but he was not loved.

Goddess Epona opened the iron gates and allowed the god of the sea enter the Otherworld. Lugh, Brigid, and Ogma were seated at a high marble table in the palace, and looked up when the broad god of the sea entered, trying to anticipate his mood. The omens were not good. His face was grey with anger and his eyes blazed like storm-tossed waves. Brigid was by far the most diplomatic of the gods, the most skilled at pouring oil on troubled waters. She said that he looked tired and hungry, suggesting he should eat before saying what he had to say. "Words are expressed better on a full stomach than on an empty one," she said. "The laws of hospitality rule in the Isles of the Otherworld, as they rule in the land of the living. Pull up a chair and sit down, my dear friend. Let me order some food and drink for you. Then we can discuss the reason why you left your wide realm to come here."

The sister who appeared in the room under the summons of Brigid was one of three, triplets born of an encounter between Aengus and a mortal woman named Meera. No mortal woman was safe from the sweet words of the god of love by night, and Meera had succumbed to his words. The three sisters born of the encounter were deaf and dumb. To compensate them for their lack of speech and hearing, Dagda had endowed them with scorching breath.

The triplets were the keepers of the Cauldron of Plenty. This was a cooking pot of precious silver engraved with sacred symbols. They were required to keep the pot filled with hot food, filling it up again after the gods had eaten. Since no fires burned in the Otherworld, they kept the food hot with their hot breath, so that it never was allowed to cool.

The sisters divided the day into three periods. Maidin served the gods in the morning, bringing them the first meal of the day. Meanlae served them in the afternoon, before they took their daily nap. The last meal of the day was served by Nocht. The gods never knew which of the sisters served them, since they were identical. Neither did they ask the name of the sister serving them, because she was a servant.

All gods except Epona, who knew each of the sisters intimately, and addressed them by name. She always thanked them when they brought the meals, and was not afraid of getting her hands dirty, often helping them clean the great feasting pot. In return, the three sisters placed themselves under her protection, recognising her kindness; but also recognising that, although meek, she had a mind of her own, and was not afraid to stand her ground. Most of all, they saw that she had the good of the Otherworld at heart, and the spirits of the slain warriors were always uppermost in her mind.

Dagda had acquired kingship of the Isles of the Otherworld by sheer strength. He carried a club and was not afraid to use it. The gods recognised that none could match him for brutal physical strength, or no enemy stand against the power of his right arm.

However, times had changed, even in the Isles of the Otherworld. Brute strength alone was frowned upon. The gods and goddesses alike required something more substantial in their king. They required the gifts of wisdom and understanding. Above all, they required the gift of wise judgement. Time had moved on, but Dagda had been unable to move with the changing time.

Then, one night, he left the Otherworld, leaving aside the kingship to find peace in the land of mortals. He slipped out unseen and unheard, leaving behind his crown and the vacant throne. He went to live alone on Inishmore, an island in the stormy western ocean. There, in a cave overlooking the wild sea, he contemplated on the life of a king. He could not come to terms with the changing times, or why the gods and goddesses had lost respect for him.

Maidin silently served up engraved silver dishes of mistletoe stew and goblets of rosehip wine, and departed as quietly as she had arrived. Before the meal was finished, Manannan Mac Lir spoke to them, "My visit here is brief because I have left my two sons in charge of the wide oceans. Who can tell what sort of mischief sons get up to when their father is away? Let me tell you why I have come here at this time. Sixty men and sixty horses approached the wide mouth of the Boyne seeking a ford to cross. They did not seek my permission to cross the estuary, and they did not offer sacrifice. These ignorant men showed no respect for my authority, and wickedly began the crossing. I sent a tidal surge to punish them and killed thirty men and horses. I do not regret killing the men because they should have known better, but I do regret killing the horses. Men have free will, but horses do not; and blindly follow where men lead them. The blame lies on their breasts, not on mine. I have come here to find out why armed warriors from Connaught forded the Boyne into Ulster, and why they showed utter contempt for me by not offering sacrifice."

"Manannan, a war has broken out between Connaught and Ulster," replied Lugh. "The warriors were on a clandestine mission to seize the goldenhide bull. As for not showing proper respect to you, I can only assume that in times of war men forget their duties and responsibilities to the gods."

"Where is our great king when he is needed?" asked Manannan. "Gone to ground, as usual! Very well, let us conduct matters in his absence and discuss mortals. They are more in need of us in times of war than in times of peace. Let me tell you why men are losing respect for gods, and why they no longer listen to your words or to your advice. Ye allow humans to transgress against your realm without punishment. I do not. They do not lightly treat me with contempt because I punish every transgression. If they set out on a voyage by ship and do not offer me sacrifice, I smash that ship against the rocks to teach them a lesson. Let me assure you that they do not repeat the mistake!"

Nervously the gods glanced in each other's direction. They sensed a row brewing up, and they wished to avoid it. Brigid attempted to steer the conversation in another direction, but the god of the sea would not be swayed. Lugh began to talk idly about the weather. Manannan Mac Lir was not interested. He focused his mind on the topic of respect, and he banged home his point.

"Ye are weaklings and I am strong," he said. "That is what mortals desire most in a god, brute strength. They do not bow the knee to the god who loves them, they bow the knee to the god who punishes them severely. Which brings me to the reason for my visit here: Dagda Og has forfeited the crown by his long absence. Place the crown on my head and that will send out a strong message to foolish mortals who pay no attention at present to the gods. They really fear my wrath, and when I am declared king they will fear you too."

"My dear friend, I agree wholeheartedly with your sentiments, and in my humble opinion you should be declared king," Ogma nodded. "Strength in a leader is always respected by friend and foe alike. However, we are on the horns of an ethical dilemma here. Speaking for myself, I have no objection to your proposal; but we must consider not only the ruler, but also the ruled."

"Your flowing rhetoric is used as a fisherman uses his net, to catch the unsuspecting in its mesh," said Manannan, not concealing his utter disdain for Ogma. "I believe in plain speaking, but you, Ogma, you use words that say one thing but spell out the opposite. Of all the gods and goddesses, I trust you the least. I would not turn my back on you, not for an instant! I do not understand why you are held in such high regard by mortals. Nevertheless, I am prepared to listen to your words because today is one of my better days. Speak, but remember to whom you are talking."

Ogma responded to the god of the sea as if he had not heard his comments, or if he had, was ignoring them: "Friend, where there is rule there must also be ruled, just as day does not exist without night, or left exist without right. Let us examine what that entails. They who would be ruled must give their consent, otherwise they cannot be governed. That fact speaks for itself. Given the crown, how would you rule us? Would you allow us to exercise our own powers, or would you usurp those powers to yourself?"

"I should prefer to fight the ravenous creatures of the oceans than engage you in words!" the god of the sea shot back. "But since you asked the question, I will give the answer. My rule would be strong, but fair. I certainly would not usurp your powers or your own theatres of responsibility. On the other hand, I would not tolerate any god or goddess who acts without my express authority."

The god of rhetoric responded to the god of the sea: "My good friend, I speak not for myself but for the others. Take lovely Brigid, for instance. Each year she journeys from here to engage and defeat the Winter Crone, and release the land from its ice-bound shackles. If she were forced to seek your permission before she departs, she would feel very offended indeed. Would she not feel as the small child who must seek permission from the knee of her father to go outdoors?"

The features of the god of the sea clearly showed his displeasure, and his contempt for Ogma. "How you twist my words!" he shouted. "I use them to speak, but you use them as weapons. Brigid can leave without my permission to perform her tasks. I merely implied that no god or goddess should act against the common good."

Ogma, smiling, responded to Manannan Mac Lir: "My friend, I believe your words, though I am unable to speak for the others. As for not tolerating any god or goddess who acts without your express authority, I know it was a slip of your tongue. Even gods are prone to that error! Look across the marble table to Lugh who seems concerned. How would you allay his fears that your rule would be one of gold, and not one of iron?"

Now Manannan Mac Lir's rage exploded in full fury, and he picked up the marble table. Ogma, with a smile, reminded the god of the sea that violence was not permitted in the Otherworld. The god put down the marble table, and replied to Ogma, "I intend to use luring gold where it is required, and hard iron when it is required! That is the very essence of good rule, to use the carrot when it is appropriate, and to use the stick where it is appropriate!"

With these words he stormed out of the hall. However, he was unable to leave because the gates were locked. He was forced to sit tight until Epona returned, which did not help his dark mood. When the goddess returned and unlocked the gates, he stormed out and returned to the grey ocean. Rolling waves tossed high on the ocean and battered against the shore, displaying his anger for all to see.

Ogma smiled and spoke to the gods, "He has a vile temper, has he not? A wise ruler must not be prone to random acts of violence, for that demonstrates he is irrational. A good ruler must have a calm head at all times, and to express his thoughts in clear and concise words. Speaking for myself for a change, I sincerely hope he does not attain the crown."

At dusky Emain Macha, when the burning fires of the funeral pyre died down, King Connor gathered the chiefs in his wooden palace.

"After these days of deep mourning, we return to do battle at the ford of the Boyne," he said. "This is a time of mourning, but in the midst of this accursed war life must go on. Let us take this brief opportunity to bring a little joy into our lives at this time of sadness. I propose that my son Cuchulainn be married to Emer. The wedding ceremony of course must be simple, for her parents cannot travel to Ulster whilst this war rages at the ford. Afterwards, if the gods allow us to survive this ordeal, we will celebrate the marriage with much feasting and drinking."

On the third day of the truce, the royal servants dressed Emer in a marriage gown of white linen. They braided her hair in white sprigs of hawthorn, the plant beloved of Brigid, and wound it over her head in strands of interwoven plaits. Then they held up a polished plate, but Emer did not look at her reflection in the mirror. She left the room in search of Ferdia. She found him near the field of the bull preparing his chariot for war.

"What do my eyes see in the morning's early light?" she asked. "Do not tell me the madness has seized you too! You are a man of books, not a man of spears. No, do not answer. I require but one answer. Were you driving to the ford of the Boyne without coming to see me?"

"Princess, I was trained in the arts of war before peaceful books stole me away," Ferdia said. "To answer your question, yes, I was going away without saying farewell."

"I understand fully, and I will speak on your behalf at the wedding ceremony," she said. "I will tell your parents and your brother that you have driven to the ford of the Boyne to keep watch. I pray that the gods forgive the lie. I know why you do not attend my wedding. Your eyes refuse to look on your love marrying your brother. Ferdia, it is not too late for us."

"Princess," he said, "it was always too late."

He mounted the war chariot and urged the horses down the sandy road towards the ford of the Boyne, and did not look back. The king ran after him, waving and calling out to his son, puffing for breath. Ferdia brought the chariot to a halt, and his father spoke to him: "Our province is at war, and only the immortal gods know how it is destined to end, my son. I spoke before of Devlina, daughter of Art Maguire in Fermanagh of the many lakes. She is alone in the world with no brother or sister, and when her father dies she inherits his lands. I have proposed a match, and Maguire has agreed. After all, you are a firstborn prince and the kingdom passes to you when I die. The alliance will make us stronger."

"Father, I will answer the call to my duty," Ferdia said.

As Emer wed Cuchulainn, Ferdia drove his chariot through the day, and when night fell he unshackled and watered the horses. He lit a fire to keep away prowling wolves. Aengus was abroad that night, for he was a god whose business required the night. He sat beside Ferdia beneath the stars.

"So, you stood aside and did nothing whilst your brother wed the woman you love," he said. "Ferdia, men make more mistakes in love that they do in any other endeavour. When you are old, when your hair whitens and

137

your legs creak, you shall ponder at your decision, and curse your lack of courage."

"I did my duty, Aengus. That is what I shall remember when my hair whitens and my legs creak."

"Duty?" asked the god. "What is that in comparison to waking on a summer's morning beside the woman you love? Or strolling with her hand in hand through flowered meadows of rainbow colours with the music of larks in your ears? Or swimming in the waters of the Boyne at midnight in the image of the moon, and lying naked beneath the stars with her on the grassy bank?"

"How do you think a man can stroll with a woman through the rainbowed meadows of summer in peace, Aengus?" he queried. "It is because some other man elsewhere has done his duty."

When dawn broke he shackled the horses, and drove to the ford that marked the boundary of Meath and Ulster, reaching it as night fell on the river. At the ford, Ferdia's words rang over the rushing river. The royal couple went to the bank to listen to the words.

"Royal Maeve and Ailill, my name is Ferdia, firstborn son of Connor," he called out. "I do not come here to break the truce or to cause mischief. I intend to observe the truce fully until it ends."

"I give you my word that we will not break the truce either," Ailill called over the rushing waters. "Rest peacefully tonight beside your chariot and your horses, good Ferdia. Neither do we attack until your father arrives. Then we cross into Ulster to end this war."

King Connor, having marched for three days at the head of a large army, reached the ford of the Boyne in the late afternoon. His army was no in way inferior to the forces of Ailill and Maeve, though Cuchulainn was not at his side. The army of Ulster numbered eighteen thousand iron-armed warriors and ninety chariots. The king deployed his forces along the green bank, ready to repel the invasion of his province.

At dawn's first light, nine youths stepped from the massed ranks of Connaught. They bore bronze trumpets on their shoulders. The trumpets ascended high above them, the mouths pointed at the enemy. The heads were shaped in the form of wild beasts and birds. One was shaped as the head of a boar, another shape of a wolf, and another the shape of an eagle. When the youths blew the trumpets, they sang the dreadful cries of war. The fearful cries sowed terror in the ranks of Ulster, for Cuchulainn was not in the ranks to bolster their courage.

Bricriu led the attack in his war-chariot, whipping the horses into the river. The rushing waters covered the axles and wheels. The lined army of Connaught watched the two horses struggling against the rushing torrent. Bricriu controlled them with his left hand, holding the spear in his right. He flung the spear at a warrior in the first rank and killed him. Another warrior took his place immediately.

Now Ferdia saw the blackened head of his younger brother Lorcan dangling from the chariot of Bricriu. The Connaught chief was adding the courage and strength of Lorcan to his own, and gaining strength from its display. Ferdia told the warriors to stand aside and urged his warhorses into the river. The wheels of the twin-wheeled chariots locked, and iron swords clashed in deadly purpose. The horses too were locked in combat, biting at the rumps of their adversaries. The two armies remained in position watching the duel in the river. Bricriu and Ferdia fought in silence, and in silence Bricriu died. Ferdia's sword cleaved open his shoulder, and Bricriu toppled into the flowing river. Ferdia cut his brother's head from the chariot and took it to Connor. Then he retrieved the body of Bricriu in his arms, and carried it to Maeve and Ailill.

"He was a hothead and a loudmouth, that is true," the prince said. "He insulted my father, and that also is true. Yet he was also a good warrior and we must admire him for that quality. We hold that quality above all others, and that is remembered when all else fades into dust. He deserves to be honoured for his courage in battle. Prepare a funeral pyre for him, and have your women keen over him."

In vain King Connor tried to stop his army advancing across the river; but the blood of the warriors was up, and they were eager for battle. Horses and chariots and men surged headlong into the rushing river, and turned the clear waters into a sea of mud. The clashing impetus broke the front ranks of the Connaughtmen, and fierce hand-to-hand fighting broke out. Neither side was prepared to give way and warriors died where they stood. They fought until darkness put an end to the fighting, and the exhausted warriors fell on the ground. When night fell, the sky was lit up by the burning shelters of Maeve's army.

Connor called a war conference beside the burning shelters. He spoke to the chiefs, "We have inflicted many casualties on the enemy, and fully six hundred lie dead beside the Boyne. I know little about war, but I do know Morrigan is a fickle mistress, and the victory she granted us today could be reversed tomorrow. The time to make peace is in the midst of victory, not in the midst of defeat. I propose to seek a treaty of peace with Connaught to end this conflict before more warriors are killed."

The wise words of Connor were met with wails of dismay by the chiefs of Ulster. They had defeated Connaught once and they were convinced they could do it again. They argued that the army of Maeve was broken and on the run, and that it should be destroyed before it could escape across the broad Shannon.

One young chief expressed the concerns of the others: "My lord, my father is sick and could not come. My brother and I came in his stead. My name is Hugh Mac Neill and I fight alongside my brother Desmond. Forgive me if my words do not fall gently on your ears, and I intend no disrespect to the king or to the name of the king. No leader can consider hasty peace in times of war, not until the threat to his existence is removed. My lord, the time is right to press home the total advantage of our victory. If we destroy their army now, we remove the threat to our province. If we allow their army to regroup, they will surely attack us again to our disadvantage."

Noble Connor listened to the pressing words of the young chief. He turned and spoke with Ferdia, who was standing at his side: "I value the words of Hugh, but a second opinion is always useful. What is your opinion, my son?"

"We have crossed the boundary of the Boyne and are now in the realm of Diarmuid, our High King," the prince pointed out. "We have violated the border and that puts us in the wrong. We should withdraw across the Boyne and resume our defensive positions. If they attack again, we have the river for a barrier. Let us not forget that Cuchulainn is absent from our ranks."

The assembled chiefs closed their ears and raised their dissenting voices. They were intent on crushing the fleeing forces of Maeve before they could escape across the broad Shannon. The king and his son could retreat behind the Boyne, but they were going on the attack at first light. Connor was fully aware that the warriors followed their chiefs, not their king. If he did not lead, he would be regarded as weak, and replaced by another king selected by a council of chiefs from their own ranks. This was the law of the tribes, and Connor had no doubt that his position was in jeopardy. He was left with no choice but to lead the army against the forces of Connaught when morning came.

In late conference with Ailill and her chiefs, Maeve considered her options. The defeat at the Boyne had drained the confidence of some, but not one considered the thought of going home. They had to recover their lost honour, and the only way to achieve that task was in battle.

Maeve spoke to her chiefs, "Our brave warriors are bruised by this setback, but I know they are eager to avenge the losses of their friends and relations at the ford. Ulster attacked when we were not ready. Next time we will be ready. They pursue us now with the smell of success in their nostrils and the eagerness of an easy victory in their bursting hearts. They have too much confidence. Let us deal them a blow they will not forget in a hurry!"

Now Ailill spoke to his men, "Once before I ordered a retreat from the field of battle. It brought great shame on me as a man and as a king. Yet that retreat saved our province from destruction. Today I ordered another retreat, though ye were all willing to stand and die where ye stood. In times of war bravery is a great quality, but bravery must bow before clear thinking. That is the best quality in a king, to keep a cool head in the midst of carnage. When his province and his men are collapsing all about him, a king must not lose his head but think of a way to retrieve the situation."

The men listened with bowed heads. Now the king put his arm over the shoulders of Rory Guinan, saying: "My friend, I ask your forgiveness for dragging you by the hair from the forefront of battle. Connaught needs men of your courage, and your death would have cut off my right arm. The day was already lost when I called the retreat, and further deaths could have lost us this war."

But Guinan replied, "I prefer death before dishonour."

At first light, Connor led his army in pursuit. The warriors were in high spirits, and with light steps walked behind the chariots. They talked about the honour they would achieve in crushing the men of Connaught, and how their wives and family would welcome them home in glory.

The men of Ulster were in high confidence of a great victory, and readily advanced with light feet. They saw victory over the next hill, over the horizon. Such was their confidence that they did not notice the narrowing of the road, or the rising hills on each side.

The attack came suddenly in a clash of blaring trumpets and rolling chariot wheels. The queen led the attack, flanked on each side by Guinan of Leitrim and O'Brien of Sligo. She hurled a swift spear at Connor. His charioteer reacted to the speeding weapon pursuing its deadly course and put his body before the king. The spear toppled him from the chariot. Guinan flung his spear at Hugh Mac Neill. It cut past the gold torc and pierced the neck of the young chief. The warriors of Connaught now flung their bodies into the fray, screaming war cries. Connor tried to rally his forces, but confusion was sown wild in their ranks. The warriors in the rear could not advance because the chariots were blocking their path. The chariots could not advance because they were locked in combat with the enemy. Too late, Connor realised that he had marched the army onto the horns of a trap.

The skirmish soon turned into a total rout and former thoughts of glory were abandoned as warriors fled for their lives. Ferdia called to the chiefs above the screams of the dying: "Do not give way! We must hold this ground until night falls! Then we can retreat under cover of darkness!"

His pleas fell on deaf ears as men abandoned their weapons and fled for their lives. When black night fell, nine chiefs of Ulster lay dead in the narrow pass, and more than nine hundred warriors. King Connor led the remaining chiefs back towards the ford of the Boyne. Ferdia brought up the rear, urging on the stragglers, and offering kind words to the dejected warriors.

Maeve called her chiefs in conference, and spoke to them, "We have with one strong blow avenged our reverse at the ford, and our warriors have regained their lost honour and pride. They have shown their courage in battle for all to see. Connor should be dead, except his charioteer took my spear in his heart. He expects us to wait until light before attacking. The secret of success in war is to do what the enemy least expects. We pursue his army tonight, and we destroy it utterly tonight. Here is my plan. Gather dried sods of turf, two for each chariot. Mount the turf and set it alight. Send for the bards and have them bring their bagpipes."

When the bards answered the call, the queen instructed them to blow the bagpipes. She was not happy with them. "This is war, not a festival!" she exclaimed.

"Play them like the wailing of banshees! Play them like the demons of the night! Play them to strike terror into the hearts of Ulster!"

In silence the shattered and demoralised army of Ulster rested, and no warrior dared look another in the eye. They had not only lost a battle, they had also lost their courage. Shame bowed their shoulders and hanged their heavy heads. Ferdia sought out his father, and spoke: "Peace terms were acceptable before this defeat, but not now. Now we must fight to the death. I suggest we retire immediately beyond the Boyne and prepare our defences. Let us move quickly before they pursue their advantage."

"It was my fault," said the unhappy king. "Had I been a king of war, I would not have led the army into a trap. Yet I am a king of peace, unused to the wiles of battle, and unable to anticipate the enemy. The shame hangs on my breast heavier than the stones of a dolmen. Let the men rest, for they have earned it."

A sense of foreboding haunted the warriors and portents of evil were seen in the dark night. They huddled in groups and spoke in hushed terror of hearing the piercing wails of the banshee proclaiming their imminent deaths. Wraiths were seen everywhere in the sky, dark and terrible harbingers of evil rolling in shadows. The wraiths took the form of eerie mists and swirled about them in human form. A lone warrior stood up and pointed into the darkness, his face frozen in a mask of fear. His companions looked into the darkness, and watched in horror as pinpricks of burning fires advanced on them in columns. Screeching high-pitched wails resounded in the night and were borne to their ears. The terrified warriors watched in horror as the columns advanced, and listened to the unearthly wails in frozen fear.

"The banshee leads the demons of the night!" they cried.

Blind panic ran like wildfire through the demoralised ranks of Ulster and removed the senses of the terrified warriors. Hope was abandoned as they fled headlong into the dark night. Some were trampled underfoot as each man sought his own personal safety. Many ran to the rushing river and threw themselves into the swirling waters. Few managed to make the safety of the other side, and their drowned bodies drifted to the ford. Even the chiefs were afraid of the advancing demons and fled in their chariots from the approaching ranks of flickering flames.

The victorious army of Maeve arrived in triumph at the debris of abandoned weapons and discarded shields. The chiefs approached a lone warrior standing in his chariot. This was Prince Ferdia, whose charioteer had also fled.

"We have met before at the games in Royal Tara," Rory Guinan said. On his chariot was tied the head of Hugh Mac Neill, dripping blood. "You are Ferdia, son of Connor. I am Rory Guinan of Leitrim, where dolmens grow as daisies in the field. My courage is boundless. I did not retreat from battle when our forces last met, but was pulled away by Ailill. He seized my yellow hair and tore out a great tuft."

"Yes, I remember you at the games, and I saw you in the forefront of the fighting," Ferdia replied.

"Why do you stand alone in your chariot when the army has fled? Do you desire to fight me?"

"I desire to speak with the royal couple, but if you desire to fight let us begin. I am the son of a king and I have not forgotten my duties and responsibilities. I stand here alone, but I stand for Ulster."

"Dismount, brave warrior and put down your bloodied sword," the queen told the prince. "Your courage is rewarded and now you speak to the queen. My husband, Ailill, was wounded in the leg by your hurled spear, and he has gained much honour by the blow. Now when he rises to speak in conference, men listen."

Ferdia dismounted and walked to the chariot of Maeve, and stood beside her. Two burning sods of turf danced flickering jigs of light on her chariot, mounted on two spears. In another chariot, stood three bards with bagpipes under their arms.

"Bagpipes," the queen said, gesturing to the instruments in the arms of the bards. "Your men thought it was the wail of the banshee calling for their spirits. The spirits that the banshee harvests never reach the Isles of the Otherworld. Ferdia, men speak of honour in war when they should speak of winning in war. Maeve knows how to win wars."

"It was a battle we lost, not the war," Ferdia said.

"My firstborn could have been you and I should have been as proud as a peacock to have a son of your courage," she said. "The gods gave me a daughter who lives across the sea. One day, perhaps, she will marry a warrior of honour like you. Grainne is her name. Ferdia, your father is responsible for this war, not I. He refused the request of a queen. Our ancient laws of hospitality state that the desire of a queen is a command. He brought this war down on his own people."

"Good queen, I stand here as the son of a noble king who does not desire this war," replied Ferdia. "It was Bricriu who insulted the sacred laws of hospitality by threatening to seize the goldenhide bull by force. No envoy should use threatening words in the palace of his host. Call off this war."

"It is within the powers of your father to stop this war, Ferdia. He has the goldenhide bull. If he hands it over, I withdraw the army across the broad Shannon and declare peace. Is the safety of your province not worth that price?"

"My father cannot bend the knee to force," Ferdia replied.

"Very well," said the queen. "Force it is. We make haste to the ford, for speed is the essence of war."

The warriors of Connaught cleared the dead bodies from the ford, and the army crossed into Ulster. When dawn broke it advanced, meeting with no resistance. The warriors had respected the lives and property of the Meathmen, but they regarded the province of Ulster as booty of war. Cattle were taken from the fields and slaughtered. They were roasted on spits, and the warriors fed well. After feasting, the army moved to Emain Macha.

Three chariots of Connaught drove up the sandy road to the palace. Maeve strode up the sandy road to the wooden palace accompanied by her two chiefs, Guinan and O'Brien. The royal servants took them to the chambers of Rosheen, who invited them to sit. She gave instructions to bring mead and bread for the queen and her chiefs.

"My husband is meeting with the scattered chiefs as we speak, and he is gathering reinforcements," Rosheen declared. "Soon you will be driven from our province."

"Pray, good queen, that he does not meet me on the field, or your husband will ride with Epona," Guinan said.

Maeve told her chief to curb his tongue, and spoke to Rosheen: "Forgive my chief, good queen, for he is hot in words as he is in battle. We, as women, know how men are! This war was not my fault."

"I have lost my son Lorcan to your naked ambition and unbridled pride," Rosheen flashed. "You have no son, Maeve, and therefore have no concept of the searing pain the loss causes. A son is most special to a mother. May Epona garland your spirit in nettles for the pain and anguish you have caused to my family!"

"Your attitude as a mother is understandable, but your attitude as a queen is quite astonishing!" angry Maeve responded. "Lorcan died a brave and courageous warrior. The bards are already singing his name proudly in the palaces of kings. Would you prefer he had died unheard and unsung? Would you have him walk down the lonely road to death leaning on a stick? Or his young body shrinking in old age? That is not the way of the warrior, and your attitude is not the way of the queen."

Sounds of laughter drifted from the field of the bull into the palace. Maeve and her two battle chiefs recognised the raised voices of their laughing men and went out to investigate. They found the warriors in the field teasing the goldenhide bull, holding the tail of the beast. Some were attempting to mount the savage animal and ride it as a horse. Three gored warriors rested against the wooden rails surrounding the field, their wounds being treated by wet bog mosses.

Maeve spoke to her men: "My chariot to the man who mounts that brown-eyed monster and rides it three times around the field!"

Chapter Eleven

Sulking in his palace in the sky because he was being ignored by the warriors, the bearded god of thunder, Taranis, decided to act. Like Morrigan, he did not dwell in the Otherworld. His permanent home was the sky. If there was one god the warriors feared, it was Taranis. He could drop the sky on their heads at any time. He was no respecter of seasons either, and could destroy the harvests of Lughnasa at his pleasure. It was essential to keep him happy.

Taranis had suffered the insults of men for far too long. He went to his stables and opened the doors. He did not keep horses in the stables, but his wheels of thunder. These had six spokes, and when he rolled them across the sky the noise was deafening. That's how he showed his anger. Then he picked up his bolts of lightning, and acted.

The warriors at Emain Macha stopped in their attempts to ride the bull, and their eyes scanned the sky. Black clouds made the day dark, and thunder roared. Clearly Taranis was angry.

The noise stampeded the horses, and they bolted in all directions. Warriors sought shelter where they could find it from the driving rains. Now he fired his bolts of lightning. They flashed and flared across the sky. A tall oak cracked and broke like a twig from a strike.

For three days and three nights the dark storm continued and showed no sign of letting up. Maeve called a meeting of her chiefs. They all knew what Taranis demanded: blood sacrifice. However, unlike other gods he would not accept the sacrifice of a stag or boar. Taranis demanded the sacrifice of a noble with no blemish of body or mind.

"Not honouring a peaceful god brings no revenge, but not honouring an angry god is a grave mistake," reported the queen. "I blame Turnod the druid. It was his duty to appease Taranis, and he failed in his duty. Now the queen must do his job for him."

The chiefs were silent. There was but one way to appease the angry god. It was Eoin O'Callaghan who stepped forward. The sacrifice demanded royal blood, and he was the son of a chief. Eoin was nineteen summers old, with blond hair and blue eyes. His youthful body bore no blemish, and his hands were not calloused from hard work.

"No warrior can do more for his home than lay down his life for it," said Eoin. "I shall appease Taranis for Connaught. Let my friends act quickly and send my spirit to the Otherworld. We shall meet there and enjoy our friendship again."

His two best friends cut his head from his body with swift blows from their swords. Then they called on Epona to carry his spirit to the Otherworld. Soon the gentle goddess appeared in the sky on the back of Capall. The human sacrifice appeased Taranis, who reined in his wheels of thunder. Soon the dark clouds left the sky, and the sun returned.

The smoke from the dying embers drifted over two horses trotting in the surfing waves ridden by a young man and a young woman. The surf lapped at the legs of the horses and rolled to the white sands of the Antrim coast. The horses and riders emerged from the waters and walked along the white beach, leaving hoofprints in the sand.

"Tell me of your birth," Emer said.

"One day a handsome young man came on a gold chariot to Ulster," Cuchulainn replied. "My mother, Deichtine, was so taken by his youth and beauty that she ran away with him. Together they journeyed in his chariot to Newgrange near Royal Tara, and there I was born. At the tomb of Newgrange my father revealed his true form to my mother. She had eloped with Lugh, the god of light. He is my father."

"How did you get your name?"

"My mother gave me the name, Setanta and I held that name until I was nine summers old. When she died, I journeyed to Ulster to find my relatives. I took a hurley stick and ball to make short the journey. King Connor was holding a feast for his smith, who was called Culainn. The wooden palace was protected by a savage hound owned by Culainn. The dog attacked at my approach, and I hit the ball with such force that it killed the dog. The king made me his son and gave me the name Cuchulainn, or the Hound of Culainn. I promised the king that I would take the place of the hound and defend Ulster against its enemies."

"No matter who they are?"

"No matter who they are, I will defend Ulster to the death," he said. "That is the promise I made to Connor, and that is the promise I made to my father. It cannot be broken."

"Forgive me if my tongue is loose, my husband, but I believe in saying what the heart holds," Emer said. "The servants who dressed me for the wedding spoke of you. They said you gad about in the moonless night and that you meet ladies underneath the stars. That was acceptable when you were unwed, but not now. I wish you to understand that I expect to be the only woman in your life."

In the distance, wheeling fast across the white sands, a chariot appeared driven by an armed man. Cuchulainn kicked the flanks of his horse and sped to the chariot. Emer too kicked hard on the horse's flanks. Ferdia dismounted and embraced his brother beside the surfing waves. Emer watched them speak, and she saw the face of her husband change from happiness to gloom. Ferdia had brought bad news.

He walked along the beach and spoke to her: "Princess, the news is not good, and I offer my apologies for interfering in your happiness. The army of Maeve is in Ulster and living off the land. We are gathering our forces to make an attack on them, and we need your husband."

"Why do men have to make war?" she demanded. "Lorcan is dead, and only the gods know who dies next. War is nothing but dour madness. Ferdia, have you been fighting?"

"Yes, princess, I have seen battle," he said. "We are in the right. We have been invaded by Connaught, and they must be driven out."

He helped her down from the horse, and she clung tightly to him. Ferdia unlocked her arms from his neck. "Who cares if they are right or you are right?" she said. "Let my mad sister have the bull if it means that much to her. Why do so many men have to die over a four-legged beast? It makes no sense to me."

"Princess, if she can seize with impunity the bull, where does she stop?" he told her. "Does she come next time to seize our herds and our crops too? Do her warriors return to seize our women? No kingdom can be held to ransom that way. We must fight."

At Emain Macha Connor readied his warriors to attack and drive out the marauding army of Connaught. His men were eager to recover their lost honour, but ashamed that they had lost their courage. A great roar erupted from the men when they saw Cuchulainn and Ferdia driving up the sandy road to the palace in the chariot. Emer stood between them and two horses trotted behind, tethered to the chariot. Connor embraced his two sons, tears in his eyes. Cuchulainn ran into the wooden palace to retrieve his weapons, and Begmore readied his chariot.

The army of Connaught had set out with a single purpose in mind: to seize the goldenhide bull. That single unity of purpose had maintained them in the field, and had held the tribes together. The objective had focused their collective minds and kept their unruly discipline in check. Having achieved their objective, the coherence and discipline of the force relaxed, and the chiefs went their own way. Plunder was now on their minds, the booty of war. The army split into raiding parties, rounding up herds of cattle and sheep and driving them towards the ford of the Boyne. Flocks of geese too were driven off, and houses raided for valuables. Riches blinded the chiefs to the fact that the enemy was bound to regroup, and that they were far from home.

The army of Ulster, led by Cuchulainn, fell on the marauding and looting bands like hungry wolves on a flock of feeding sheep. Hundreds of the invaders fell before the fury and the sword of the avengers. The advancing army swept with irresistible force in full pursuit of the stolen bull and the loot-laden wagons. An advance party, led by Cuchulainn, caught up with bull. The beast was in the midst of a large herd being driven to the ford by Rory Guinan in a chariot of oak and inlaid ivory.

"Take the beast to the ford and drive it across the dividing waters," Guinan told his men. "I will remain here to make time."

He turned the chariot and wheeled it against the advancing Ulster warriors. Guinan spoke to Cuchulainn: "My name is Rory, battle chief of the Guinans of Leitrim, where the dolmens grow as thick as daisies in summer. We are a hardy tribe, living off the rocks and the sparse vegetation. The Guinans of Leitrim have never turned their back on an enemy. Indeed, if the immortal gods faced us on the field of battle we would fight them to the death! I challenge you to step outside."

Cuchulainn dismounted from his chariot and left the ranks of the men of Ulster. "Rory, you now face an enemy who is more skilled in fighting than any you have faced before," he warned.

"Before we fight, let me tell you how I won this chariot from my queen," said the Connaught chieftain. "Others tried to grasp the beast by the horns, but they were gored. The maddened bull chased me across the field. I leaped over the fence, and the bull thrust its mighty bellowing head through the wooden stakes in an attempt to gore me. In an instant, I stuck a rope into the nose of the beast. Then I mounted the beast, and it bucked and kicked, but it could not dislodge me. This is the man who challenges you to combat. I have fought many foes and none has survived to tell their tale."

Cuchulainn suspected that Guinan was fighting not only for glory but also for time. He accepted the challenge of the chief, determined to finish it before the bull crossed the ford. They fought on foot without shields, circling each other, seeking an opening. Cuchulainn flung his swift ashen spear in quick and deadly earnest. Guinan had a dancer's feet, and danced away from the onrushing spear. It missed the dancing body of the warrior and embedded in the ground sixty paces behind. Now Guinan flung his spear in deadly earnest. Though not as powerful as the throw of his opponent, it was accurate, and would have pierced the heart of Cuchulainn but for his swift feet. He too moved as a dancer, as if dancing a jig at a wedding and not fighting for his life. The spear missed the target.

They circled each other again. Cuchulainn swung his sword and sliced a blow at Guinan which the warrior evaded. Blow for blow was given, neither warrior prepared to retreat or yield a blade of grass. They fought at midday under a burning sun, their bodies caked in dust like a second skin, and beads of sweat rolled down their cheeks. Neither man rested to catch a breath and the contest continued as fiercely as it had begun. It was Guinan who made the first mistake, and that mistake was punished severely. Tiredness overcame his body, and his feet hesitated to dance. Cuchulainn took full advantage and moved in for the kill. A swift thrust ended the life of Guinan. Cuchulainn cut the head off the brave warrior, braided the hair, and tied the head to his chariot.

The advance guard rushed to the ford, but they were too late. The bull was on the other side, and the warriors of Connaught lined the bank, their spears bristling.

Epona journeyed to scene and garlanded in roses the spirit of the slain warrior; and on the swift back of Capall galloped over the western ocean to the Otherworld. She took the horse to the stables, and using a silver comb removed the salt spray from the flowing mane and coat. She took a silken cloth to the silver hooves and brushed away the layers of sea salt. Next she washed the white horse in fresh spring water, and dried the coat and the flowing mane. She fed the magical steed with honeyed oats and barley, and gave it sweet rosewater to drink in a silver bucket.

As Capall ate and drank, she cleaned out the stables and brought in sweet-smelling hay, and spread it on the floor. Then she tended the roses growing in the stables, cutting the stems to promote their growth. The war was showing no signs of ending, and she would need every red rose in her stables.

That night lovely Brigid went to the stables to request the key to the gates. She found Epona sleeping in the hay beside Capall, her head lying on the belly of the steed. Compassion filled the heart of Brigid at the sight. Both goddess and horse were exhausted, and her presence did not awaken them. She decided to act on her own accord, and gently removed the key from the neck of the sleeping goddess. She opened the gates and flew on the wings of night to Royal Tara.

Diarmuid was in bed with his wife, though he could not sleep. The war was being fought on his borders, and he was fearful that it would spread. His warriors were restless, and clamouring to join in the fray. Diarmuid was aware that young men are always eager for battle and his dreams reflected his concern. Vivid and terrible images of Royal Tara in flames haunted him.

The goddess came to his room and closed his eyes in sleep. She entered his dream and spoke to the king, "Do not be alarmed by my presence in your dream, Diarmuid of Tara. Though I carry the key to the gates of the Otherworld about my neck on a twig of roses, I am Brigid and not Epona. I have not come to take your spirit to the Otherworld but to seek your help. The heartless goddess of war has no concern for the lives of the warriors. The wails of keening women across two provinces are as the plucked strings of the harp to her wicked ears. Knock the heads of Ailill and Connor together, and demand a truce. I have come here on wings of the quiet night from the stables of the Otherworld. There I saw tired Epona sleeping beside Capall, exhausted from their endless work, her head resting on the neck of her horse. They who care for horses, as we do, must care for their welfare, for horses never complain. They work until they drop. Speak to me in your dream."

The king replied to the goddess in his dream, "Brigid, wisest of the gods, your dreamy words are music to my ears; but unlike most words in dreams, they make sense. It is about time that someone uttered wise counsel, for we are all living in the midst of madness. The bloody war has infected two provinces with violence and I fear it will spread to mine soon. I will do as you command. Pour the wise words in my ears so that I know what to say."

"Insist on a truce of nine days and nine nights," Brigid said in the dream. "That is ample time to allow warlike minds to recover their lost senses. Send fast envoys to the four provinces, and call a council of peace at Royal Tara.

Knock heads together, and bolt the doors if you must, but do not allow them to leave your palace until a permanent treaty of peace is achieved."

"I can speak with them, but will they listen? They call me High King to my face, and ignore me behind my back. They pay obeisance to me in public, and scorn me in private. I have no authority over them, since each province is independent. That is how we are made, and that is how it has always been."

"Diarmuid, what was the real cause of this misjudged war?" asked the lovely goddess. "None seems to understand why it started. Two armies struggle over the ownership of a bull, but the beast is only an excuse for the conflict. Where does the bull now reside? It lives now on your lands and it eats your grass. According to your laws, the bull is your property, though you are too honourable to seize the beast and hide behind the law. You can, however, use its presence to force the warring parties to the peace table."

"The gods are wiser in their ways of thought than mortals, and you are the wisest by far," Diarmuid murmured in his dream. "When you depart, I will arise from the bed and ride hard to the ford of the Boyne, and knock some sense into their heads. A king who ignores the advice of the gods is a fool."

"The authority of kingship is not driving men, but leading men," the lovely goddess confided. "Morrigan believes kings are made on the field of battle, but I know true kings are made around the tables of debate. It is not the strongest arm that wins the kingly crown, but the strongest mind."

King Diarmuid awoke suddenly in the night and looked around his bedroom. The dream was so vivid and real that he expected to find the goddess standing in the room. He was alone except for his wife, who was lying beside him breathing gently. The king called for his servants and issued quick instructions. He ordered them to send messages to King Marbery and King Cormac, requesting them to attend Royal Tara. He then gave instructions to the servants to ready six horses.

At first light he rode to the ford of the Boyne with a small band of warriors. He arrived at the camp of the Connaught army and went to the conical wooden shelter of the royal couple. Columns of smoke rose into the sky from a dozen funeral pyres, and the smell of burning flesh filled the air. The king was appalled, and pulled his cloak over his nose to shut out the foul smell. Ailill and Maeve were accustomed to death and ignored the foul smell of burning flesh. The servants too behaved normally in the midst of death, bringing bowls of meat and goblets of beer, and placing them on the table.

Diarmuid ignored the food and drink placed before him, and his stomach churned over. He scurried out of sight and threw the contents of his stomach up on the grassy mound. Afterwards he wiped his lips and returned to speak with the king and queen. Ailill and Maeve did not notice his ashen features and tucked into the food, both king and queen eating heartily.

"Last night I had a dream in which lovely Brigid poured wise words into my ears," he said. "There is none wiser than her in the Otherworld. She requested a truce of nine days, and a conference of peace at Royal Tara. This is the wise message I bring from the goddess."

"We thank you for your visit to our camp, and we throw ourselves on your open hospitality," Maeve replied. "You have permitted us to camp on your lands because we both know Connaught is in the right. The wise words of Brigid are indeed difficult to ignore; but war has its own momentum, and it must be pursued until one side triumphs. Our warriors are getting ready for the final battle. Connor must attack us here at the ford and that is why we wait. Better at the ford where we have the advantage than fighting him on open ground. One battle will decide this war, and after we defeat him we intend to return home"

"I must insist that we obey the wise words of Brigid, for only a fool ignores the advice of the gods," Diarmuid said. "Think of the terrible consequences of disobedience. Every year the goddess journeys to free our land from ice and snow; but if we ignore her she shall not come next year, and the land shall die. As for finishing this war in a matter of days, Ulster has Cuchulainn on its side. As long as he lives, that rich province cannot be defeated, for he is invincible."

"How this war started is now not important," Ailill said to Diarmuid. "What is important is the honour of my province. Ulster is on its knees. Their warriors fled from us before and they will do so again because they are too fat from easy living. Cuchulainn is but one man. I faced his brother in battle, Ferdia, and I took his spear in my thigh. Next time we meet he will feel my spear."

"Ailill, do not let the fever of war infect your head as the spear has infected your thigh," the High King replied. "We are men of honour who must live by the laws, and the gods love men who live by them. Let me point out our ancient law on possession. The goldenhide bull grazes on my grass on my lands. Our law is water clear on the subject, and I can use the law to seize the beast if I so desire."

"Our laws were laid down long ago, and we must respect them, otherwise we cannot call ourselves honourable people," Maeve said. "We are willing to accept the terms and the duration of the truce. The swords and spears shall be put aside for nine days and nine nights, and Connaught shall not be the first to break the truce."

"I have sent fast messengers to Marbery and Cormac," Diarmuid informed the royal couple. "I have requested the kings to attend a peace conference in my palace. However, when they arrive I will take them to a place of tall oaks called Dowth, where no ears can listen at the door. There we can talk without interference from servants."

Diarmuid crossed the ford with his small band of warriors and sought out Connor. The servants roused the king from his slumber beneath a shady oak tree. Together the two kings walked through the camp. The warriors did not look up as the shadows passed; but concentrated on sharpening their words and spears, getting ready for the next battle. The two kings strolled past the burning funeral pyres, and walked against the wind.

"They remind me of the fires of my youth and the flames I made with autumn leaves," Diarmuid recalled. "I played with youthful friends around the bonfires with swords of wood, and we talked of wars and noble deeds. We did not realise back then that fire consumes the bodies of slain warriors, and that war is not noble but a consuming plague on the land. I stand here today under the request of Brigid who came to me in a dream last night and requested a treaty of peace."

"This war was not of my making, and Ulster has burnt many brave warriors," noble Connor said. "But when an immortal speaks, mortals must listen. I have no objection

162

to a treaty of peace, though I fear it will not be permanent. Neither do I impose conditions, except one. Ailill has unlawfully crossed the borders and seized my property. The beast must be returned before I agree."

"Lovely Brigid requested a treaty of peace to last nine days," replied Diarmuid. "I pray that common sense can prevail in the meantime and that the treaty will become permanent. As for the matter of the bull, the beast now grazes on my lands, and here is what I propose. I will instruct my smith to hammer a chain of unbreakable links. Then I will instruct my servants to tie the bull to the Stone of Destiny. Furthermore, I will place an armed guard to watch the beast day and night to ensure it remains and cannot be driven off. Perhaps we can sort out this sorry problem without further bloodshed. Morrigan has feasted enough, and the time has come to put a stop to her appetite."

Both sides accepted the terms of the treaty and the warring parties put away their swords and their spears. Throughout the day, warriors swam in the peaceful river, and washed the horses. They briefly forgot the business of killing. When night fell on the ford of the Boyne, the land was peaceful, and the funeral pyres were extinguished. Nothing remained of the pyres except the burnt patches of ground where the fires had burned.

Chapter Twelve

In a small copse of summering oak trees near a place called Dowth in the lands of Diarmuid, five kings sat on the mossy ground to talk peace. A servant of the king prepared the meal. He had been sworn to secrecy under the pain of death. The silent servant lit a fire and built a platform of stones on each side. He filled water from a nearby stream into a heavy bronze cauldron and placed it on the stones.

The bronze cauldron had two large handles, and its polished exterior was decorated with ornate heads of gods and armed warriors. The servant cut slices of venison and beef, and put them inside. He tipped a bowl of unripe blackberries and a bowl of sliced turnips into the cauldron, and let the stew simmer over the flames.

Now he placed ten bowls of carved oak on the mossy ground before the seated kings. He poured mead from a leather container into the bowls. Each king offered the first drink to the gods, and threw it over his left shoulder, uttering a prayer. Then each king drank the second bowl of mead. The kings were aware that the immortal gods were present at the meeting, though they could not see them.

Indeed, the immortal gods were present and unseen, and each god chose the king to sit beside. Brigid sat beside Diarmuid, and Ogma sat beside Connor. Manannan Mac Lir sat beside Marbery, and Morrigan sat beside Ailill. Finally, Lugh sat beside Cormac of Munster.

When the stew was cooked, the silent servant filled up the ten wooden bowls, and put down ten wooden spoons. The five kings repeated the same ritual as before, throwing the bowls of food over their left shoulder, offering the first food to the gods. They then ate their own food in the manner of kings, eating it slowly. The mute servant collected the wooden bowls and washed them in the stream. Then he took down the cauldron and cleaned it, and extinguished the fire.

In a small copse of summering oaks, the kings sat down to resolve the war. Since they were meeting in Meath, Diarmuid spoke first: "I decided to meet here because we can speak without servants listening at the door. Six summers ago there was a fire in the forests of my province. It started with a single spark, but the winds took hold and soon the whole forest was in flames. Were it not for Brigid who sent the rains to quell the flames, not only Meath but the whole island would have been destroyed. War is the same as that spark. If we do not act soon, the war could spread to every province in the land."

"Leinster does not intend to get involved in this struggle, but if our borders are breached we will respond," Marbery said. "I say let them fight it out until one side wins. It can only spread if neutral provinces take sides. If you ask me, I think the brazen queen will pay heavily for her venture. Cuchulainn has sent more than ninety of her finest warriors to the Isles of Otherworld. She cannot win against the son of Lugh."

Ailill exposed his thigh and showed the kings his wound. He spoke to them beneath the tall insect-flying oaks at Dowth, "I do not deny that we suffered at his hands, but he could not stop us achieving our objective. We seized the bull and took it across the bloody ford. The warriors stand there now ready to do battle if permanent peace is not declared. It is not denied by me that Cuchulainn slew some of our finest warriors, but none ran from his cutting sword or flying spear. The army of Ulster ran from us in the night."

"Night brings terror in its wake and some of our warriors heard the wails of the banshee calling their names," Connor said. "They believed the fairywoman was coming to take away their spirits. Yet these same men who ran away that night were in the foremost of the fight against the invaders. We are all of us mortal and we are all of us afraid of something. Yet men can fear the banshee and still be brave and courageous warriors. My warriors are not afraid of battle, but they would rather live in peace, as I would."

Not only did the kings argue amongst themselves, but the goddesses also got involved, though they were not heard by the kings. Brigid turned on Morrigan, and spoke harshly: "You are the cause of this war by sowing the seed of impossible ambition in the mind of a mad queen. The halls of the slain keen nightly with the voices of sisters and wives, yet you have no compassion. Epona was right to slam the gates in your face."

"First Epona and now Brigid!" exclaimed Morrigan. "Why do silly goddesses who know nothing of glorious war criticise my business? Do I interfere in your theatres of influence? No, I do not for I know my place. They can talk here all day and not solve the problem, but the war will solve it very fast. War achieves in days what peace cannot achieve in decades. How do you think the borders of the five provinces were fixed? Do you think they were fixed by kings seated beneath a copse of oaks? No, they were fixed by kings on the field of battle! How do you think the integrity of each province is maintained? By kings speaking words of peace, or by kings threatening total war if attacked? If you spent more time in this world you might learn the way of kings."

"They go to war because you have inflamed them with a love of war," lovely Brigid replied. "In comparison to war, peace is unexciting and dull. Yet I have no doubt that it is better to live a dull life of peace than live a bloody life of war. This is a concept that you can never grasp."

"That makes two of us! You can see your own point of view, but not mine. Your silly platitudes might draw applause in the Otherworld, but they make no impact on me. Wars have always been fought in this realm, and they are destined to rage until the end of time. I will tell you why, though your sensitive ears will no doubt reject my words. Warriors fight because warriors love fighting. Men go to war because men are war-mad. That is how they are, and that is how they will always be."

"What you say is untrue, and the five kings seated here under the talling oaks are proof of that," Brigid responded. "They have journeyed here to seek a formula for peace. Men are inclined more to peace than to war. If you were not roaming the land stirring up mischief, there would be no conflicts."

"Your problem is that you cannot face hard truth," Morrigan said. "I live with these people, and I know them better than anyone. They have no fear except the fear of base dishonour. They fear no calamity except the sky falling on their heads. Nothing else frightens them, except the banshee. They love warfare for that is how they gain glory. Do their bards sing about herders in the palaces of kings or do they sing about warriors? Come down from the clouds and face reality."

As the bitter war of words raged between Brigid and Morrigan, Cormac and Marbery detached themselves from the group, citing a call of nature. They walked beneath towering oaks until they came to a small clearing. Marbery stopped in the clearing and urinated, steam rising from his urine. Cormac stood at his side and urinated in the same place.

"My friend, we men have much more in common than women," Marbery commented. "We like to talk as we piss and that shared activity binds us in friendship. Women are loners in that matter, as in all matters! That is why they're not as convivial as men. Ah, wouldn't this be a better world without them! Is it my imagination, Cormac, or are they getting more angry day by day?"

"Yes, I have noticed that with my wife," said the King of Munster. "Some mornings I have to test the waters with her, if you get my meaning. One day she's as sweet as Munster honey, the next she's sourer than buttermilk in hot weather. She is past that time of life, but the change has not made her more mellow. Me, I am growing more mellow as I grow older."

"What is the matter with the wives of kings?" asked Marbery. "What do our queens want from life? The poor wives of herders never complain, or the wives of men who cut the crops. At least once a month I have to slap down my wife, otherwise she would rule in my palace! After all, that is why we are here, is it not? The ambition of a queen?"

"Marbery, sometimes my memory returns to the time I courted my wife," Cormac recounted, walking beneath the towering oaks. A startled deer ran across the path of the kings, briefly interrupting the conversation. "How young she looked back then, and so placid. Getting a word out of her was the same as pulling a hen's teeth, if you get my meaning. She was shy and demure, unlike some modern princesses! Now she never stops talking, whereas all I want at my age is a quiet life."

"My wife is the opposite," confided Marbery. "She doesn't talk, but she thinks a lot. That's most dangerous in a queen, thinking. What does she need to think for, eh? She's married to the most powerful king in the land. What more does she need?"

"Women change as they grow older," replied Cormac. "The beauty of my wife when I first saw her stopped my heart. She was more radiant than summer sunshine. Now she is wrinkled and old; but when I look upon my reflection, it has not changed. Thirty summers have passed since that time, and I have not aged at all."

"Know what I think?" Marbery said. "I think a queen with time on her hands is the most dangerous creature in the world. Such a woman broods and thinks up ways to cause mischief. If Maeve had cooked or herded sheep we would not be in this position."

"Do you think she believes the legend?" asked Cormac. "Do you think she regards it as prophecy, that sleeping in the hide of a dumb beast can render her invincible? She is my daughter, but I have never been able to see inside her head. She has always gone her own way in accordance to her own interests."

"Cormac, you and I know that is nonsense, but then we think as men," responded Marbery. "Women do not think as us, for they are devoid of logic. Ireland has never had a woman High King. We must work to ensure that never happens. Men can sort out their problems over a few goblets of mead, but they frown on such things. You should see the face of my wife when I get drunk and fall down!"

"We are cut from the same piece of linen," Cormac said. "My wife counts the number of goblets I drink, as if I were a child. Let us return to the reason why we are here. I have no intention of getting involved in this conflict. What is your position?"

"Same as you," said Marbery. "I say let them slug it out and exhaust their strength. Daily each side grows weaker at the bloody ford. That is good news for both of us. Tell me, Cormac, have you heard why the daughter of Maeve left Knocknashee?"

"Grainne?" said the King of Munster. "My grand-daughter? I heard she did not see eye to eye with her mother. Maeve was always headstrong, and mothers and daughters tend not to get on with each other at the best of times. Such is the way of the world. Why do you ask?"

"If Lugh had not intervened at the games to help his son, we would be talking here as two kings related by marriage," Marbery nodded. "Tagdah and Emer would be living happily in Leinster. But that is in the past, and we as kings must plan for the future. The king and queen of Connaught have no son. If they are killed in this war, Grainne becomes queen of that province, your grand-daughter. A queen must have a husband to rule by her side. My son Tagdah is a prince, and he is unwed. Would you raise an objection if he wed Grainne?"

"I see no cause to raise objection," responded Cormac.

"Good, good," nodded Marbery. "Before we return, there is a matter of some delicacy I must raise with you, my friend. My words are for your royal ears alone, and I trust they will remain there and not find escape. We spoke about the legend, and neither of us believes it, for it is nothing but foolishness. Having said that, there is one man who believes it, and that is Diarmuid."

"The High King?" said Cormac. "No, that is impossible!"

"Do not be fooled by his denials, my friend," said Marbery. "He is High King in name, but he burns to be High King in power. He is far too weak to rule the five provinces by force, so he seeks the authority of the Stone of Destiny. He is an ambitious fool, and that is the worst type of fool... Come, let us return to the conference, and keep my words in your heart."

When they returned to the group, the debate was still raging. Ailill was in hot debate with Connor, each king accusing the other of breaking the truce. Cormac sat and joined in the debate.

"I have a daughter in each warring camp, so I personally must be neutral in this conflict," Cormac began. "Two apples on the tree are seldom the same. Maeve is headstrong and her head rules her heart. Emer lets her heart rule her head. I do fear one of my daughters will be a widow soon, perhaps both of them. I stand here today to speak for Munster. My province is farthest from the fighting, and it is my intention to keep it that way! I do not intend to cause offence, but it seems to me that both sides are at fault. Ulster breached the sacred laws of hospitality, and Connaught breached the borders. How to resolve this problem is beyond me."

"This is not about a beast with four legs, but about a beast with two legs," Marbery said. "The wife of Ailill seeks to rule, and that is the kernel of this problem. She is not content with Connaught, but also desires to rule our provinces. Her husband knows this too, though he conceals it well."

Ailill exposed his thigh again, and spoke to Marbery: "The war is about honour and nothing else! Marbery cast insults in my face before, but I will not stand for them a second time. My courage in battle is proved by this deep wound. Who does he think he is talking to in that manner? Does he believe I am not his equal in the eyes of the kings gathered here? Or perhaps he thinks his large army can frighten me. He is in for a rude awakening if he believes that. One Connaughtman is more than a match for ten Leinstermen."

"My fellow kings, friends, let us not squabble between ourselves, and remember why we are here," Diarmuid said. "We are poking our fingers in the sky, as if that can solve anything. This problem can only be solved if both parties are willing to compromise. Ailill, are you willing to return the bull?"

"What we have, we hold," Ailill replied.

"There can be no possibility peace until the stolen property is returned," Connor said. "Furthermore, the kings who refuse to see that Ulster is right are truly blind."

Diarmuid spoke for the four kings seated under the tall and summering oaks at Dowth: "We are mere mortals, and we have not the knowledge to deal with this problem. I propose, therefore, that the immortal gods must decide the outcome. Let us therefore depart from here."

Chapter Thirteen

The day the peace expired began brightly and in windless calm. The sun emerged from the blue eastern sea and climbed lazily over the forests and rivers of Meath, sending shafts of sunlight across the land. It was a day for young men to walk in summer meadows bound in the hand of a young woman. It was a day for a father and mother to roll with their laughing children down grassy slopes. It was a day for walking in cool streams, and tickling trout from their lairs. It was not a day for dying. Yet on that haunting day many young men died at the ford of the Boyne.

Cuchulainn led the first charge, his brave charioteer Begmore whipping the yoked horses into the river, and charging at the enemy. Songs of battle erupted from the throats of the Ulstermen and they plunged into the quiet river. The chariot cut through the front ranks of warriors as a sickle mows down standing stalks of wheat. The army of Connaught reeled back from the onslaught. Cuchulainn was everywhere on the field of battle, killing men, and cutting a path to Ailill.

"So, you come to me again in the guise of a demon, like a lighted skull at Sowain," said Ailill. "Let me tell you that your battle-warp does not frighten me! I am

Ailill, King of Connaught, no less a warrior than my slain brother."

The king unleashed his spear. The weapon struck Begmore in the chest and killed him. Cuchulainn took the reins and urged the horses forward. Dust and heat swirled in clouds around the battlefield, and Ailill was lost from sight. Behind his chariot, Ferdia was fighting off three warriors. Cuchulainn wheeled the chariot and went to the rescue of his brother. He killed the three attacking warriors with his sword, and lifted Ferdia into the chariot.

"You are wounded in the shoulder, brother," he said. "Come, let me take you to safety."

Ferdia took his brother's hand, and spoke: "No, your place is here. I can make my way across the ford on foot."

Columns of dust coiled around the battlefield, kicked up the hooves of the horses. Warriors were caked in blood and grime, and some fell to the swords of their own tribe. The confusion of battle was heightened by the swirling storms of dust. As the battle raged, the dust cleared in a part of the field, and Cuchulainn came face to face with Maeve.

"What sort of demon are you?" asked Maeve. "Do you think your terrible features can drive me from the field? I can hurl a spear as straight as any man, and wield a sword with the strength of an ox. My spear lies buried in the heart of an Ulster chief, but my sword is ready for combat. We can step outside, or we can fight here in the midst of this mayhem. It is your choice."

"My name is Cuchulainn, and I do not fight women," he said. "They have no place on the field of battle. This is man's work."

"Before you were born I fought many battles," replied Maeve. "We women were as strong in battle as any man.

174

Then the kings met to lay down the rules for war. As if war needs rules! The kings decided that women should stay at home whilst they went to war. Men talk about rules, but women talk about winning. That is all that matters. If you do not wish to fight me now, very well, but the next time we meet one of us shall surely die."

As the battle raged fiercely in the heat and the dust of the morning, heavy reinforcements from Ulster arrived at the ford. The extra weight of numbers, added to the ferocity of Cuchulainn, pushed the army of Connaught back. Mile after mile the warriors retreated, fighting every step they took. Ailill fought beside his men, and offered a prayer to Lugh: "Oh, god of light, withdraw from here this day and send darkness!"

Night came in slowly falling dusk, and the armies disengaged. Both sides relished the break, and weary men fell on the grass and slept. Dara O'Brien sought out the royal couple, and he spoke to them, "The battle went badly for us today, and tomorrow offers no hope of a better day. We are badly outnumbered, and we have no warrior to match fearsome Cuchulainn in battle. As I see it, we have two options. Either we soon receive reinforcements, or we remove Cuchulainn from the field of battle. Maeve, we are doomed otherwise."

"Dara, your exploits today will be sung by praising bards in the halls of kings," Maeve said to her chief, looking directly into his blue eyes. "They who do not listen to good advice do not deserve to rule men. Reinforcements are out of the question, for our poor province is neither rich in soil or in men. That leaves the second option. Let me work to have that fearsome warrior removed."

Maeve called again on Morrigan for assistance in the war. The goddess took on the form of a raven and sped to the western ocean, and hovered over its dark waters. She called to the two sons of Manannan Mac Lir. One appeared on the surface of the dark waters, and swam to the shore. The raven changed and became Morrigan, and she walked with the son of Manannan Mac Lir on the shore.

"Peelo, why do you laze in the salty waters with the unknown creatures of the sea?" she asked. "Youths of your age should be out seeking glory. A battle rages near the ford of the Boyne, and there can be found great honour. Rise up now and go to war."

"My father treats me as a child, and I long to get away from his influence," complained Peelo. "He criticises everything I do, and has never once paid me a compliment, though I am his firstborn son. The last time he journeyed to the Otherworld he returned in a hurry because he did not trust me. Morrigan, I have my fill of that cruel tyrant."

"Your too-strict father does not appreciate your worth, but I do. I have watched your development with great admiration. Your mother was Caitlin, a mortal woman from Connaught. The men of Ulster are killing her cousins at the bloody ford."

"The news rips my heart, but what can I do?" Peelo said.

Morrigan produced a sword and a shield, and clashed them against each other. "The sword is the same as many others, but this bronze shield has magical powers," she said. "Bind it to your left arm so that it cannot be removed. No weapon can touch the bearer of this shield. No sword can touch his flesh, or no spear scars his body.

Take the shield and the sword, and break free from the control of your father."

Next morning the bone-weary warriors roused their tired and bloodied bodies from sleep, and readied their arms. They clashed again in a din of shouts and ringing swords. This day they fought on foot. Like dancers in ritual dance, they moved over the field, pausing momentarily, before moving again. Cuchulainn was in the thick of the action, and he came up against Peelo.

"The queen has pointed you out to me, and I have come to kill you," the son of the sea-god said. "My mother was lovely Caitlin of Connaught. She was born in the province you wage war upon. Therefore, you wage war upon me, for an insult to her is an insult to me. Come, let us do battle, for we are both sons of gods and mortal women. You have the experience of war lacking in me, but I have weapons to match. The shield I bear is made of the stuff of magic that no weapon can pierce."

"I fear the goddess of war has taken sides in our battle," Cuchulainn said. "It matters not to me, for skill and courage decide contests."

Peelo seized a spear from the grip of a dead warrior and unleashed it in fury. Cuchulainn ducked, feeling the rush of wind in his hair. He flung his spear at Peelo, and saw it bounce off the shield. They rushed into conflict, swinging swords and grappling. Peelo sliced through the shield of Cuchulainn. Holding his iron sword in two hands, Cuchulainn struck at Peelo, but his sword hit the shield and the blade snapped in smithereens. Peelo rushed in for the kill, swinging his sharp sword in whining arcs. Cuchulainn used his dexterity to back away from the advancing sword, using his dancing feet to evade the

177

blows. His retreat had an alarming effect on the army, and the warriors began to back away from the battle.

Sensing total victory, the warriors of Connaught fought with renewed vigour, and pushed their tired enemy back towards the ford. Cuchulainn retreated with Peelo in full pursuit. He reached the river and leaped into the waters. Peelo stood on the bank clanging his sword against the bronze shield. The clanging noise sounded out over the river and over the plain of fighting men.

The forces of Connor regrouped across the ford. Cuchulainn sought out Ferdia for advice, and bathed his brother's wound. The wound was poisoned, yellowing and swelling in the heat. "Depart to Emain Macha and have the wound treated, Ferdia, or the infection is certain to spread," he advised. "I met a warrior today I could not defeat, and that has not happened before. His name is Peelo, son of Manannan Mac Lir, and he has a magical shield. It is bound so tight to his arms that his flesh resembles the twisted torcs of gold worn by the chiefs. No weapon can touch him."

"I saw our warriors retreat," Ferdia replied. "This war is lost if you are killed. Yet how can you defeat him? No weapon can touch him, you say? Do you recall how you killed the hound that guarded my father's palace when you were young? You have not forgotten how to hit a ball with a hurley have you?"

From a grassy hill overlooking the fighting, Ferdia watched the army of Connaught trying to force the ford. Peelo was leading the charge. A hundred spears were thrown at him, and a hundred bounced off the magical shield. Swords had no effect on its powers, and were broken like saplings in a gale. Warrior after warrior fell at the watery feet of Peelo, and the ford ran red with blood.

Under the burning heat of the midday sun, Cuchulainn lifted Ferdia on a wagon and brushed away the flies from his wound. He smeared the wound with dark mud from the riverbank, and instructed the driver of the wagon to make all haste to Emain Macha. The two brothers embraced, and parted. Ferdia returned to the palace of his father, and Cuchulainn strode down the slope to the ford. He carried a hurley stick in his right hand and a hard ball of stone in his left.

"What has the boy in his hands?" Peelo enquired. "A hurley stick and a ball of stone! We are here to do battle, and he is here to play games! Stand aside, and let a man go about his work, for I have more killing to do. This ford is a place for warriors with swords, not for children with hurley sticks."

"You boast that no weapon can pierce your bronze shield," Cuchulainn said. "What I have in my hands are not weapons, but they bring your downfall."

Cuchulainn tossed the stone ball in the air and hit it with the hurley as it fell. The hard stone ball sped to its target faster than a hawk falling on a pigeon. It struck Peelo on the forehead and smashed his skull. He tottered on his heels for a moment, and plunged into the ford. At that moment a great surge of water swept over the dead body, and Peelo was returned to the sea.

Chapter Fourteen

Every wagon that rolled up the sandy road to Emain Macha was regarded with anxiety by the members of the royal family, and by their servants. They feared that the body of a loved one was coming home, as Lorcan had come home in a wagon.

Queen Rosheen and Princess Emer watched as the servants ran down to the road to the approaching wagon. They watched as the servants lifted a body from the wagon, not knowing if he was dead or alive. Emer held her breath. She saw the body move, and ran on swift feet to be at his side.

The servants took Ferdia to his room and removed his clothes. They washed and bathed him, and put him to bed. Emer made a bread poultice for the wound. She heated water on the fire and gathered up pieces of stale bread. Then she poured the boiling water on the stale bread and squeezed out the excess. She put the poultice on a clean linen cloth, and placed it on the wound. Ferdia was asleep, but his torn body reacted to the heat and sat up. She pushed him back in the bed.

The queen came into the room and watched Emer treating her son, pressing the poultice on the wound. "Last night in bed I was awakened by a cry in the night, and I went to your room," Rosheen said. "You were dreaming, and talking in your sleep. The name you uttered in your sleep was not the name of your husband. Is there some matter you wish to discuss with me?"

"Rosheen, who knows what dreams are made of, or why we dream our nightly dreams?" Emer replied to the queen. "No druid can explain their meaning."

"Remember, I too am a woman, and once was your age," said the queen. "I know how it feels to love a man to utter distraction. I know you love my son, but I fear it is not the son you married. Emer, your destiny is mapped out with your husband, and no wife can escape her destiny. Ferdia's destiny is mapped out too, for he is promised to the daughter of Maguire."

For three days and nights Emer cared for Ferdia, and changed his poultices. The poultices sucked out the yellow poison and the wound began the process of healing. Then she rubbed in heather honey and bound the wound in clean linen. On the morning of the fourth day she helped him from bed, and they walked to the rear of the palace to the field where the bull had grazed. Below them, in the green and gold fields around the palace, the ordinary ways of life had returned, and men and women worked as before. Peace had returned to the fields, and to the bending men and women working in the fields.

"I wish we could see how this war will end, but the gift of inner sight is not given to us," he said. "Many more brave men are destined to die before it is finished, that much is certain. None can be happy in these times except Morrigan. Your husband has shown remarkable courage and you should be very proud of him."

"When do you return to the ford?" she demanded. "Or why should you return? The bull has gone, but has the sky fallen down? It has not. Life goes on Ferdia, at least it does for some. The seasons still change, and the sky still turns blue; but I do not see the changes, and my eyes are blind to the sky."

He crooked an index finger and put it beneath her chin, lifting her head. He spoke to her, "Why so sad, princess? Summer is here at last, and the darting swallows have returned. Look how they feed on the wing. Listen to their voices raised in praise of the day. The cuckoo too sings a merry song, and speckled thrushes join in the chorus. Are they not happy?"

"Perhaps they are crying for their lost loves," she replied. "I wish this stupid war would stop! Each day that passes fills me with dread. I can foresee your death. Forgive me for speaking this way, but my mood refuses to match the sunshine. Let us ride to the sea on fast horses, and swim in the blue-salted waters. Your wound needs the healing waters."

"No, princess, tomorrow I return to the ford."

"If I had known you were going back to the war, I would not have healed you!" she replied. "Well, go and get yourself killed! See if I care! Go back to the slaughter and the burning pyres!"

He smiled at her, looking up at the darkening sky, and spoke: "The rains are coming, princess. Let us go inside. I must ready for departure tomorrow."

They walked back to the palace in the drifting rain, and she spoke, "Connor has betrothed you to Devlina, daughter of Art Maguire of Fermanagh, where the blue lakes are as plentiful as sands on the shore. I have been told she lives on an island in the middle of a lake. Does that not seem strange to you? Perhaps she has buckteeth, or a vile temper! Why else would she live on an island?"

"Her father has many enemies, and he uses the island for his defence," he explained. "It is a practice that goes back for many centuries. Princess, my father has made the match, and I will wed Devlina. Aengus played his mischief on us during the journey from Cashel to Emain Macha, but that was long ago. We both have our responsibilities now and we must live by them."

Manannan Mac Lir, grieving and angry over the death of his firstborn son, stirred the seas into a white frenzy of storms that lashed the shore. The white-tipped manes of his horses rolled across the sea and crashed on the shore. Huge waves rushed up the river to the ford and stopped the fighting. Both sides made sacrifices to the angry god of the sea. The army of Ulster killed a red deer and skinned it, and roasted its body on a spit. Six warriors carried it to the river and threw it in the waters. The army of Connaught killed a boar and sacrificed it to the angry god.

Still in an angry mood, he journeyed to the Otherworld. Epona would not unlock the gates until he brought his temper under control. He ranted and raved at the iron gates, but Epona refused to bend or be cowed by his fury. She said he could carry on as he wished in his own realm, but calm was required inside the gates. Finally, he cooled down and was admitted.

He spoke in anger to the gods and goddesses, "The son of Lugh has killed my firstborn son. I have come here to demand action against Cuchulainn. That warrior thinks he can do as he wishes just because he is the son of a god! We have to call a halt to his rampage. Who knows what more damage he might cause if we fail to act?"

"Did you not side with Morrigan at the meeting of the kings under the tall oaks of Dowth?" Brigid reminded him. "The god or the man who makes excuses for war condones it. We grieve for your son as we would grieve for a loss of our own children. Having said that, Peelo took up arms and went to war. Did he think he was going to gather berries? War is a very dangerous undertaking. Apparently you saw nothing wrong with the war before your son was killed, but now it's a different matter. Now it has come to your door, and suddenly you realise what the parents of the slain are feeling."

"It was with regret that I heard of the death of your son, and I am sorry for your troubles," Lugh said. "My son had no choice but to defend himself. It was warrior to warrior, and I certainly did not intervene on his behalf. I offered my son the gift of invincibility three times, and my son refused that gift three times. His honour would not permit his body to become invincible. It was either his death or Peelo's death."

"We are indeed sorry for your troubles, and our hearts are with you in your grief," Ogma said. "However, even in grief a god must be rational. It was agreed that each god be given his or her own area of authority. You were given the realm of the sea, and we do not interfere in your realm. Morrigan was given war, and we are unable to interfere in her realm."

"We are not talking about the death of a warrior, but about the death of the son of a god," Manannan said. "It is not denied that we must live by rules, but there must be an exception to every rule. We should not be bound in chains of rules so that we can never act. That is a foolish way to live."

"How can we expect mortals to live by rules if we suspend them every time it suits us?" Brigid asked. "If you interfere in the realm of Morrigan, what is to stop the

184

goddess of war interfering in your affairs? Do you want that disruptive goddess in your realm? The rules were laid down for that reason, and each one of us is responsible for our own affairs. That is how it is and that is how it remains."

As the gods discussed the death of Peelo in the Otherworld, the Queen of Connaught met in conference with her remaining chiefs to discuss the progress of the war. She had lost six chiefs during six savage days of fighting, and many brave warriors. The King of Ulster had recaptured the ford, and the army of Connaught was being pushed back towards the Shannon. O'Brien pointed out that they were losing too many men to sustain the war.

"Our experienced chiefs are getting killed, and their sons are being thrown raw into the battles," he pointed out. "We need a break from this hard fighting to regroup, to catch our breath, and to treat our wounded. Our warriors are drained of strength from six days of constant fighting. The son of Lugh roams the battlefield like a crazed bull. Some of our warriors lost heart at the sight of Peelo dying at the ford, killed by a stone ball. I make a suggestion now that could cause offence, but it has to be said. Send for Malachi Mac Carthy immediately. He is wise in war."

"That insolent chief insulted his queen once before and I do not intend to give him a second opportunity!" replied Maeve. "We have Morrigan on our side and she is doing everything to help. It is not denied that we need more. We need more warriors and we need to curb terrible Cuchulainn. We need more time too and we do not have that precious commodity. Tonight I pray to the gods to seek their guidance. Go now, Dara, for tomorrow brings more fighting."

Under the light of a full moon, Queen Maeve walked on silvery grass to the river. She removed her sandals and waded into the waters. About her neck she wore a gold lunula studded with precious gems. She removed the lunula and held it on the surface, and prayed to the goddess of the river. Then she released the lunula, and gave it to the goddess of the Boyne.

Connor woke from his fitful dreams, and under the moonlight examined his feet and hands that were dirty from a day of fighting. He decided to go to the river to bathe. He glanced across the flowing waters and saw Maeve, her eyes closed in prayer.

"Maeve," he called out, "our fleeting days grow short, and morning moves quickly into night so that we do not feel them passing. How did it come to this? Why do our warriors die at the ford? I did not want this war, and I do not enjoy fighting. At my stage of life, I should be watching the crops grow in the field, and playing with grandchildren on my knee. My warriors gather at the campfires by night and speak of noble deeds, as if killing were something to boast about. Today, after darkness ended the fighting, I took a walk in the woods, and I thought about the future of my province. Nothing appeared in my mind except darkness."

"This war was forced on me too, Connor, and I did not desire to pick up the sword against you," the queen replied. "If I am accused of ambition, it is not for my own personal glory, but for my province and my husband. Ailill was weak, but this war has tempered him as an iron slab in the white fire. Weakness in a man can be tolerated, though loathed; but weakness in a king is disastrous for any province. My husband has bloomed in this war as a flower blooms in the sun. He has recovered his lost honour, and he is a king in name and in deed."

They swam to the middle of the river and turned over on their backs, kicking their feet and paddling their hands. The moon bathed the river and the trees in pale silver light. Downstream, the campfires of the warriors glittered. Side by side, Maeve and Connor swam in the clear flowing waters of the Boyne.

"Maeve," noble Connor began, "can we as king and queen both not resolve this problem before more men are slain, and the keening of their widows replaces the birdsong of the larks? I would have gladly given you the three-horned bull, had not Bricriu threatened force. No king can bow before the threat of force, we both know that much. The bull now grazes at the Stone of Destiny. It has to be returned to Ulster before a permanent peace can be made. After our armies return to their homes, and the fever of war leaves their bodies, I promise to send you the bull."

"The offer is both good and wise, but I must refuse on behalf of my chiefs," she replied. "They came to bring the bull back to their province. If they return without the beast, their honour is flown. No warrior can live without honour. This war ends when it ends."

"What we need most is a time for reflection and wise council to prevail," he said. "In less than sixty days we celebrate the festival of Lughnasa at Royal Tara, the time of reaping harvest. I propose a truce until that time. Summer is upon us now, and we should return to our homes. Our fields have been neglected for too long, and the families of our warriors are in need of their presence."

"I accept the truce on behalf of my husband and my chiefs," said the queen. "Let us return to our homes, and meet again at the festival. Perhaps time can solve this problem. Let us talk again at the festival, Connor."

Next morning the two armies broke camp and readied for departure to the west and to the north. The wounded were lifted onto straw-filled wagons. The warriors went into the forests and gathered wood. They piled the bodies of the slain on the wood and lit the pyres. The armies departed, leaving columns of black smoke rising in the summer sky.

Chapter Fifteen

The summer solstice dawned on the burning plain of Meath, and the sun's rays appeared over the eastern horizon. The rays crept gently over the blackened land towards the royal burial tomb at Newgrange where the bones on Diarmuid's mother rested on a dish of stone. She had died of natural causes, and her body had been cremated. Then her bones had been placed in the royal tomb to await the coming of the summer solstice. Inside the royal passage tomb, King Diarmuid awaited the rays of the sun to lead his mother's spirit along the solar road to the Otherworld. However, the smoke was so dense that the rays could not enter the tomb. Coughing, Diarmuid pulled his cloak over his mouth and left the tomb.

Summer's end approached on balmy wings, and the truce was holding. The kings made preparations for the journey to Tara to celebrate the festival of Lughnasa. From every district in the land, bards and harpists and poets set out for Tara to take part in the competitions. Singers sang songs along the dusty roads, readying their voices, competing with the robins and ascending larks. Legal practitioners too set out, for laws and agreements were made during the festival, and signed in law by the High King. Disputes over land were settled, and arguments between husbands and wives resolved.

King Diarmuid inspected the tall chair his carpenters had manufactured for the visitation of Lugh, in whose honour the festival was held. The chair was from oak, and patterned with human heads and horses, carved in gold from Wicklow and ivory from Africa. The carpenters mounted the carved chair on an oak platform raised high, ready for the god of light. He would sit on the chair for three days to oversee the festival, though he would not reveal his presence to the throngs.

The king was very happy with the fine detailed work and congratulated his carpenters. Next, a servant placed a crown of intertwining wheat sheaves on his head, and held up a polished plate. The king nodded his approval to the crown he would wear for three days. Everything was ready for the festival.

On the first day of the festival, the five kings assembled at Tara with their queens to watch the parade of musicians pass by. They were dressed in their provincial colours, and like Diarmuid wore crowns of wheat. They bowed before the high chair and the unseen god, paying respects, and sat to watch the parade of musicians and storytellers.

Contests of song and storytelling and dancing were held over the sweeping mound of Tara, judged by the five druids. At the same time, traders and merchants were haggling over goods. They had journeyed from distant lands; from Gaul with weapons and wine, and from Britain with ingots of iron and tin. In exchange they sought wheat and hides of cattle, barley and yellow butter. Above all, they prized the crafted gold brooches and torcs made in Roscommon.

The raven hovered over the festivities looking down on the young men and women dancing on the grass before the kings and queens. The black bird viewed the warriors dancing, and the warring parties seated on each side of Diarmuid. After the dancing finished, the kings would retire to discuss peace terms. She was determined to give a demonstration of her powers, and to prove that war took precedence over every other event in the land.

The bird beat its black wings and flew west towards the sea. It descended and flew low over the white-tipped waves. It flew over a fleeting currach rolling over the sea waves in Galway Bay, its prow high. Fintan O'Malley pulled on two ashen oars and drove the currach into the waves. The raven descended and stood on the prow, and changed into Morrigan.

"Fintan, why do you pull oars with brown brawny arms in the white-tipped waves?" she asked. "Why are you not at Royal Tara celebrating the feast of Lughnasa?"

"I see no point," replied O'Malley. "I prefer to fish for fat eels than attend Lughnasa. Everyone knows that I can sing better than any bard, and compose more graceful poetry than any poet. As for dancing, I can toss my heels higher than any man. With me fishing for fat eels, others have a chance at Lughnasa!"

"There is one there who believes he is the best warrior in all the land, Fintan," Morrigan said. "As we speak, he is at Lughnasa with his wife."

"Cuchulainn is it? I went in search of him many times on the field of battle and could not find him. He must have heard of my prowess, and that is why he went missing."

"Your name is already sung by travelling bards in the rich palaces of kings, but you can gain immortality by killing him," said Morrigan. "Put away your oars and let me take you to the festival where the five kings watch the games with their queens. There are many young maidens there too in search of a husband. By killing him, you can have your pick of them."

"What of Lugh?" asked O'Malley. "That is the god's festival where he sits unseen on his high chair for three days and three nights. I fear no man, but only a fool insults a god, and I am no fool. Fintan O'Malley did not come down with the last rains!"

Morrigan took from her cloak an earthen jar of whiskey, and sipped from it. She passed it to O'Malley who took a great gulp, wiping his lips with the back of his hand. Now he was ready for her words of war. "It came from Ulster," she said. "There is many more where that came from. They have fine maidens there too. Is it not better to capture young maidens for your bed than fat eels?"

At Royal Tara, in the early rays of the afternoon, an armed warrior appeared in the midst of the jig and stopped the dancing. The young men and women formed an angry circle about him, not believing the evidence of their own eyes. They were visibly alarmed because weapons were strictly forbidden during the three days of the festival. A few dancers shouted at him, but the armed warrior took no notice of their calls. He sought out a dancing couple.

O'Malley spoke to Cuchulainn: "Go now, get your weapons, and let us step outside this dance. I vow that Epona shall garland your wispy spirit before this day ends. I promise she shall take your deathly spirit across the wide western ocean on Capall."

"Who are you that violates my father's festival?"

"Why do you ask the name of the most famous man in all the land?" he replied. "I am O'Malley."

"Why do you challenge me in the midst of a truce? Why do you come here armed when it is forbidden in law? Fighting breaks the truce, we both know that much. Perhaps you have drank too much whiskey, for I smell it on your lips! Sleep off the effects, and let us forget this incident."

"I can drink ten rivers of mead and not get drunk," O'Malley said. "Wine has no effect on me either. I have drank barrels of wine from Spain and had no headache afterwards. But now is not the time for talk of drinking, but of real fighting. There are weapons in the palace of the king. Go and ask for them."

"Why do you wish to stoke the consuming flames of war again?" asked Emer anxiously. "We have journeyed from Ulster to celebrate the festival in peace and with goodness in our hearts to all. Lughnasa is sacred to us, and Lugh looks down on us from his high perch with satisfaction. Fighting during the festival is an insult to the god, and no man dare do that, for a god does not readily forgive a human. We have many visitors from abroad here who came to enjoy the festival and to trade. How shall they regard us if we are unable to stop fighting for three days? No doubt they shall return home and tell their kings that the Irish made a show of themselves again! No doubt they shall consider us barbarians, and say that we are all war-mad! I beg of you, hold the truce."

"Does your husband hide behind the dancing gown of his wife?" challenged O'Malley. "We can fight here, or in a place of his choosing. Or perhaps he prefers dancing to fighting! Can it be that taming marriage has turned the brave warrior into the downtrodden husband who must seek the permission of his wife before he can put one foot before another?"

Cuchulainn flashed angrily, and replied to the armed warrior: "This is my father's festival, and the people came here in his honour. Having said that, I take no insults from anyone. Fighting breaks the truce, but that is your fault not mine. Your challenge is answered, and I go now to borrow weapons from Diarmuid."

Maeve watched the confrontation, and whispered words in the ear of her husband, cupping her hand. "Fintan O'Malley loves to boast, but he is seldom to the fore in fighting," she said. "Now he challenges that terrible warrior to single combat. He is drunk, for his legs are not steady. The goddess of war has sent him here to break the peace. We must in haste depart from this place and make ready to do war."

Now noble Connor rose and addressed the kings. "Our sad old eyes bear witness to the sacrilege of Fintan O'Malley," he said. "Not only has this armed warrior violated the festival, he has restarted the war by breaking the truce. There can be no doubt which side is in the right this time! We depart for Emain Macha to prepare for war."

Diarmuid attempted to stop the two kings leaving, but their minds were fixed. Ailill and Connor left him seated beside his queen, and walked away in opposite directions. The musicians drifted from the field, and from the impending violence. They were followed by the people returning to their homes, and drifting away in groups. The festival was over on the second day.

Cuchulainn sought out Diarmuid and requested arms to defend himself. The king, mindful that O'Malley was intent on fighting and violating the festival, supplied a sword, a spear, and a shield. The king asked him not to fight at Royal Tara, but to select another site.

"The armed warrior has broken the truce," Diarmuid said. "Lugh has departed because of the insult. These Connaught people cannot be trusted. They are war-mad."

The king embraced the warrior, and Cuchulainn departed the palace to fight the armed warrior. The king went to Emer and put an arm over her shoulder, and led her outside. He took her to a wagon and lifted her into the seat beside Connor and Rosheen. The Ulster king urged the horses forward, and the wagon rolled along the road to Emain Macha.

O'Malley and Cuchulainn walked side by side down the mound in the direction of the slow river. Their falling shadows preceded them, walking too in the direction of the river. Neither man spoke and their footfalls broke the silence between them. They walked through a field of golden wheat, leaving two tracks of flattened shoots. Emerging from the field, they approached the river, and found an open space to fight.

The two warriors circled, seeking an opening. Cuchulainn flung his spear at the heart of his foe. The whiskey affected O'Malley's movements. The spear found its mark, and he fell to the ground. The contest had not lasted long, but it ended the truce. Then Cuchulainn fell on his knees and begged forgiveness from his father for fighting on the sacred festival of Lughnasa.

As Cuchulainn wandered in the shaded forest praying to his father, the armies of Ulster and Connaught assembled to resume the war. There was not the enthusiasm of before in their ranks, and the warriors readied their weapons in quiet resignation and purpose. They kissed their wives and children goodbye, and walked in the fields and amongst the herds, as if saying goodbye to them also. Many of their friends had not returned from the first encounter, and they were aware that their own spirits might join the fallen in the Otherworld.

Beneath his stone hillfort at Loughrea, in a purple-tufted bog, Malachi Mac Carthy worked with a son and young daughter. He stood on a bank of turf holding a cutting tool. The tool had a wooden handle and a cutting head of bronze, two pieces joined at right angles. It was called a slean, used for clearing and cutting turf. He worked to clear away the heather, cutting at the roots and removing the heather, and exposing a large square of brown turf.

Working from right to left, he plunged the slean into the exposed turf and lifted a large sod. He flung it high over his shoulder as an offering to the gods. He lifted the second sod and threw it down to his son, Balor, who placed it on a wooden barrow. The barrow had two wide solid wheels and a pair of handles. When the barrow was filled with lines of wet turf, his daughter Aine wheeled it away, and replaced it with a second barrow. In this manner, the work was continuous. Aine removed the wet sods and put them on the heather to dry in the sun. She looked up, and seeing a lone figure walking swiftly across the heather, ran to her father.

Dara O'Brien, acting on behalf of the chiefs, walked over the purple-tufted bog to the cutting. He stepped between the rows of drying turf, and spoke to Mac Carthy, "What, a chief doing the work of servants! Cutting turf is surely beyond your dignity!"

Mac Carthy stopped working and grinned broadly at his friend. He replied to the harmless taunts of O'Brien: "Hard work serves to keep a man in good condition. That poisoned pup belly of yours could do with losing its fat.

Too much mead, I bet! Why are you here? Has the war ended?"

O'Brien removed his leather sandals and plunged his feet into a pool of bogwater, cooling them. He kicked at the brown water and related the events at the ford. The war had gone badly for Connaught, and many of his friends had been killed. They had fought as brave men of Connaught, but none had matched the sword of Cuchulainn. Only a truce agreed between Connor and Maeve had saved the army from total destruction. The truce had lasted for forty days, until broken at the feast of Lughnasa.

"It was brought to my ears that Fintan O'Malley broke the truce at the feast and insulted the god of light," Mac Carthy said. "That young chief is a boaster and a fool. Morrigan is at the back of this mischief. The kings behaved as she expected! What ignorant fools they are too! Kings should have more brains than that, and yet they fell for her guile."

"Aye, Malachi, two of my sons were at the festival, and they were witness to the sacrilege," replied O'Brien. "Indeed, they were surprised that O'Malley challenged the deadliest warrior in the land, for that young chief prefers to boast than to fight! He paid for his boasting with his death. However, the fight seemed to affect Cuchulainn also. He has gone missing. With Cuchulainn out of the way, I believe we can win when next we meet Ulster in battle."

Mac Carthy climbed down from the bank and sat beside his friend, plunging his bare feet into the brown water. "This needless war makes no sense or has no purpose," he said. "Why are you fighting it, Dara? Our province is not being invaded, and noble Connor poses no threat to our existence. There are many reasons to fight a war but they must have meaning."

"I grieved for Maol, and I offered sacrifices to Epona for his spirit," O'Brien said to his friend. "The kindly goddess sped his rose-garlanded spirit to the Otherworld on her white magical horse. Why did I cross the broad Shannon to fight, Malachi? I went because my queen needed me and because I owe allegiance to my born province. I could not watch my friends go to war whilst I remained at home. I felt a deep responsibility to join them for my honour. Why do I go a second time? The same reasons as before, the very same reasons."

"I told Maol not to go to war, but young men seldom listen to their fathers," Mac Carthy said. "I thank you for sending news to me that he was killed by Cuchulainn, and I bear that warrior no grudge. War kills men and that is its purpose. In my heart I know that Cuchulainn did not strike a cowardly blow, for no son of Connor could do such a base thing. My son died honourably at the hands of an honourable warrior. No father can ask for more."

"Pray that I can be as forgiving as you if my son meets his death at the hands of that terrible warrior!" replied the chief of the O'Briens. "I have come to seek your advice, though the queen does not know I came. Put yourself in the sandals of Ailill, and tell me how you would conduct the war."

"I would conduct it by ending it," Mac Carthy said, rising and taking the slean his hands. "I would bring my warriors home. What in the name of the gods is this bloody war all about, Dara? Does Maeve believe the legend that old men tell over campfires? Or did she start this pointless war to avenge Talteann? Or does she seek the booty of rich Ulster?"

"I know not, except that we fight it," replied O'Brien.

Mac Carthy climbed on the bank and thrust the slean into the soft turf, lifting a sod and throwing it high over his left shoulder, an offering to the gods. Then he leaned on the slean. "How long is it since we fought the battle on the plains of Emain Macha?"

"When Talteann was slain?" responded O'Brien. "That was fully twenty years ago. Why do you ask?"

"Twenty long years, Dara, and in all that time the spirit of our dead king has not returned to his ancestral home, except for this year. Then the spirit did not join us in a tankard, but stirred up trouble. Then there was a dispute between the king and the queen over a bull. It happened, as if by chance, that a bull blessed by Morrigan lived in the province of Ulster. Too many coincidences for my liking, Dara, too many. That scheming goddess of war is at the back of this dispute." He plunged the gleaming slean into the soft turf again and lifted a sod, tossing it to his son. Balor caught the slippery sod and placed it on the wooden barrow, his bare chest stained black from catching the slippery sods.

"Balor is but a year younger than Maol, but he is many years wiser," Mac Carthy said to his friend. "He becomes chief after my death."

"Let us hope he has to wait a hundred years," grinned O'Brien.

O'Brien said goodbye, and walked across the purple-topped heather to his horse. He mounted the horse and looked back at his friend. Mac Carthy was on the bank with the slean in his hands. He waved goodbye at the working chief, but his friend did not see him wave. Mac Carthy was lost in the shimmering heat, his manly profile broken up so that he became part of the bog, and part of the heather.

Chapter Sixteen

As the kings gathered at Tara to celebrate the sacred festival of Lughnasa, Ferdia rode to the fort of Art Maguire, located on an island in Lough Erne called Devenish. He arrived at the shore of the lake and dismounted, tying his horse to a tree. He picked up pieces of wood and dried mosses, and struck a flint, starting a fire. The grey smoke curled in the clear sky and aroused movement on the island. A black currach departed from the shore of the green tree-covered island. Two ashen oars plunged into the choppy blue waters, and the fast craft rowed over the white-topped waves. Ferdia stepped into the light currach, and two servants rowed to the green island nestling in the lake.

A winding path led from the shore through groves of green oak and holly, and low-hanging ash. The two servants led him to a rounded clearing in the forest where three buildings stood beneath the trees. The largest building, formed around a central thick pole, was conical in shape. From the top of the central pole, timbers radiated to beams buried in the ground, and roofed in thatch. The walls of the building were constructed in wattle and daub. The two adjoining buildings were of a round similar design, though smaller. Maguire lived in the large round house, and his servants in the smaller houses.

Art Maguire was a big burly man with bushy red hair and beard. He embraced Ferdia and spoke, "Welcome to my home. Last time I saw you was ten years ago. You were a skinny youth then, and not fully growed. Sit, and let us talk, and drink mead and eat fish."

Ferdia presented Maguire with a hollow gold torc, a gift from his father. They sat and drank mead and ate smoked trout. "My father has gone to Royal Tara to celebrate the festival of Lughnasa," Ferdia related. "Presently we are at peace, but it will not hold for long. Neither side is prepared to lose its honour. This problem can be solved only on the field of battle. My father respects you and your decision to remain at home."

Maguire replied to Ferdia, "Connor is a noble man and a good king. My heart said I should fight at his side, but my head ruled otherwise. Fermanagh is a land of opportunists seeking to profit from my absence, as foxes profit from the absence of a swan on its nest. I am surrounded on all sides by such men. Daily they come seeking the hand of Devlina in wedlock; not to love her as a husband loves his wife, but to get their greedy paws on my lands! The gods have not given me a son, and that is why these evil men prey on my daughter. I tell you, Ferdia, there is no district in all of Ireland where men covet land like they do in Fermanagh! That is why the request from Connor was music to my ears."

"May the immortal gods grant you long life and good health, Art," Ferdia replied in return. "Our lands lie side by side, and when I wed Devlina our lands will also be joined as one. Our sons, your grand-children, will inherit the combined lands. There is strength in such a venture. I wish to state that my father does not put you under any obligation because of the wedding."

"The future of my daughter is secure, and that lifts a great burden from my breast," Maguire said. "I would have put a torch to my lands rather than have them fall into the grasping hands of such greedy men! She is, as we speak, bathing in the lake. Her mother is dead, and I have raised her as best I could, though no father can be a mother. Five years ago I sent gold to Ingall the druid and he came to give her instructions. He remained here for a year and broadened her mind. Though she is not a princess, she has enough learning to be a queen."

Devlina entered the building drying the flame-red hair she had inherited from her father. Outdoor living had browned her skin, endowing her with a healthy glow. Freckles crowned the bridge of her upturned nose, blending into the browned skin. Ferdia presented her with a gold lunula studded with precious gems and red glass. She blushed and modestly thanked him for the gift, and greeted her father by kissing his cheek. Maguire asked her to show the visitor around the island, and she agreed to the request. Ferdia walked by her side down a dappled path of light and shade, beneath overhanging branches of nut-clustered hazel trees. She stopped briefly to pick nuts, cracked them between her teeth, and gave him the white kernels to eat. She picked ripe blackberries, her fingers staining purple with the juices, and put them in his mouth.

"This is a fruitful island where a man and a woman could live until the end of time and shut out the world," he said. "Fruit grows on trees and berries on bushes, and the lake throngs with fish. Your father does not have to sow or to reap. I could live here and be happy."

"Everything grows ripe here, all manner of fruits and nuts to sustain my father and myself," she replied. "Yet I long to leave here, though it is paradise. Faraway places call me in siren voices. Other places hold an attraction for me, places I have heard about but not seen. Tell me of Emain Macha."

"The palace of my father sits upon a hill and you can see for many miles in every direction," he related. "The changing seasons change the fields before your eyes. In spring the wheat grows green, and in autumn it changes to swaying gold. I live there with my parents, and with my brother, Cuchulainn. Lorcan, my other brother, was killed in the war. There are spacious rooms for us in the palace, but perhaps you would prefer to live elsewhere."

"I have the skills necessary to survive on this island, but not the skills needed for a palace," she confessed. "I would prefer to live at the palace to learn the skills. Do you wish to ask me about myself? My age is twenty summers, and I have a good knowledge of healing, and know the herbs to use. I can oar a currach and swim as fast as a man. I have a good knowledge of history and philosophy, taught by Ingall the druid. Do you wish to discuss philosophy?"

Ferdia picked hazel nuts, cracked them between his teeth, and fed the kernels to Devlina. "Yes, but only the question that matters," he replied. "Do we have free will? Could we have walked away from this war, or were we destined to fight it? Could we have turned deaf ears to Morrigan, or has she control over our minds?"

She ate the nuts and replied to him, "Men have free wills, but they also have honour. Men must seek peace, but they must not back away from war, especially a war that is just. A province that does loses all respect in the eyes of others. Does that answer your question?"

"Yes, that answers my question," he said. He remained quiet for a long time before speaking again.

"Ingall has taught you well. I pray for a lasting peace, but I expect Morrigan to stir up trouble again. I wish I could turn my back on it all and live here. No cares, no responsibilities, or no worries. I could gather nuts in the morning and fish in the evening."

"But you are a prince, Ferdia, firstborn of Connor and heir to his crown. You cannot walk away from your responsibilities. Your people need you in their hour of need, and your province needs you. A man could walk away, but not a royal prince."

"Yes, of course you are right, and also very perceptive. I was just thinking out loud, that is all, dreaming about how things might have been. This war will erupt again soon, Devlina, of that I am certain. We must face the possibility that I could be killed..."

She placed a stained forefinger on his lips, and spoke: "Please, do not use those words, Ferdia. Go to war with the stern resolve to come home alive. Do not even remotely consider the possibility of cold death. Fight the possibility of death as you fight the enemies of our province."

"Every warrior who goes to war believes he is destined to come back alive," Ferdia said solemnly. "He believes that the warrior to his left might be killed, or the warrior to his right, but not him. The fact remains that impartial death does not discriminate between the son of a king and the son of a herder. The wise man must make provisions for every eventuality. We were betrothed by our fathers, but the time is in our hands."

"I hear what you say, and your concern touches my heart," she said. "Do we postpone the wedding until the war is ended, or do we proceed? I say we proceed This war could last for many years. Let us return and make ready to depart."

"There is something you must know before we depart from here," he said. "Some time ago I journeyed to Cashel to fetch Princess Emer for my foster-brother. On the journey our lips met in embrace. I think I love her, though I am not certain. I tell you this because I believe in honesty between a man and a woman."

"The man who has not loved is the man who has not lived," she said. "Who has not heard of Emer and her startling beauty? The gods have not granted me beauty, but they have given me the ability to love one man until death. I believe that is more important in a woman than beauty. When we are wed, I will do everything in my power to replace her in your heart. Now, let us depart."

The black currach skipped over the white choppy waters and carried the couple to the waiting horse. Ferdia lifted her from the craft. For a brief time he held her in his arms, watching the black craft return to the island of plenty. Then he placed her on the horse, and turned his back on the island in the lake.

The king and queen warmly welcomed Devlina to the royal palace, and they instructed the servants to prepare a bath. They introduced her to Fidelma, widow of Lorcan. The children of Fidelma, sensing her open nature, rushed to Devlina, who picked up the little boy and girl and kissed them. But Emer was not in the palace, and the servants could not find her.

Nolan the druid of Ulster conducted the ceremony beneath a leafy oak tree near the royal palace. He invoked the presence of Brigid; and the lovely goddess journeyed from the Otherworld and stood unseen between Ferdia and Devlina. She gave them her blessing, and offered her guidance for the future. Nolan joined their hands of the couple, and proclaimed to the over-arching sky and to the visiting goddess that they were now wed. The king and queen kissed the new bride and expressed their happiness that she was part of their family. Fidelma warmly kissed her new sister, but Emer was nowhere to be seen.

Chapter Seventeen

Ogma was abroad at night, and teaching young bards the art of rhetoric. He saw Cuchulainn sitting beneath an oak tree staring at the full moon. Ogma detested Morrigan and loved those who opposed her. However, he concealed his hatred behind a broad smile whenever they met. He walked to the oak tree and sat beside Cuchulainn. Ogma explained that he could not help in the war because it was the realm of Morrigan, but he was willing to talk. In fact, Ogma was determined to oppose Morrigan in every way possible.

The god spoke softly to the man, keeping his voice low, out of range of the raven hovering above the forest: "My name is Ogma, god of rhetoric, and close friend of your father. Pour your troubles into my ears and they will receive an answer. I believe in justice and fair play, and the tricks that Morrigan is playing are worthy of nothing but contempt. That vile goddess has no sense of honour. She belongs to another era, to a darker age. She belongs to the past."

"I insulted my father," Cuchulainn replied. "I should have walked away, and yet I did not. I care not that the war has flared up again for I am a warrior. But the insult to Lugh is tearing at my guts."

"Your father is decent and fair, and gods such as Lugh see goodness in all," said Ogma. "For example, he does not withhold his light from men of evil, but bestows it on good and bad alike. Me, I am different. I do not bestow my gifts on evil men, but on bards and druids. Morrigan is evil. I can see that, but Lugh does not. He gave his word not to interfere in her realm, and he abides by that promise. I also gave my promise, but words to me are the same as coins, to be given or withheld according to the dictates of the occasion. Promises do not bind me in chains, for that would restrict my freedom of action!"

"He abandoned my mother," replied Cuchulainn. "Was that an act of goodness? The bond between mother and son is stronger than the bond between father and son. When she died I journeyed to Ulster, and Connor took me in. He was not my father, and yet he was more of a father to me than Lugh. Who is my real father, Ogma, the god who made me, or the man who reared me?"

"The god who made you, of course," replied Ogma. "Your mother was mortal, and Lugh is immortal. She was fated to die, and he is fated to live forever. He abandoned her because he did not wish to see her beauty change to old age, and her body wither and lose its supple movement. He remembers her as she was, in the full bloom of health and beauty, her flawless cheeks shaming the red roses. He remembers you too and carries you in his heart. He is very proud of you, though he is unable to form the words to tell you."

Cuchulainn stood up and walked in the night forest with Ogma at his side. They came to a clearing and gazed at twelve standing stones in a circle. Inside the circle they saw Morrigan clad in bronze armour.

"What are you doing here?" she demanded. "Of all the gods in the Otherworld, you are the one I trust least. Your soothing words are snares, and your smile is a trap. Begone, or I vow to bring my wrath down on your head!"

"We two are not natural enemies, you and I," Ogma replied. "When meek Epona slammed the iron gates in your face, I alone protested."

"No, you did not," Morrigan replied. "I am a god of truth, but you are a god of lies. None backed me up, and that is why the gates were slammed in my face. Go now."

"I do go now, but I will another demonstration that words have the sheer power to move mountains," Ogma said. He raised a finger and pointed it at a standing stone. The stone lifted from the ground, and fell with a loud crash.

Ogma vanished into the night leaving Cuchulainn alone with Morrigan. She lifted the fallen stone and replaced it in the hole. "That god has no honour," she said. "This is a sacred place that celebrates the solstices. He thinks words are better than honour or respect, but he is wrong. Honour is everything in life. Let us walk together."

Under a night canopy of shadowy trees, the warrior walked with the god of war. A full moon looked down on them, and changed the bronze armour of Morrigan to silver. Neither warrior nor goddess spoke for a long time, both thinking of the right words to say in the night. Morrigan spoke first. "We are indeed enemies, but I respect you," she said. "That we have chosen different sides is unfortunate. You and I understand war, but others do not. Men who die peacefully in their beds are not remembered, but you shall be remembered for all time."

"That is the wish of every warrior," he replied.

As they walked in the forest beneath the full moon, two lines of warriors moved toward the ford of the Boyne like moths drawn to a flame. Both sides were fully aware that where the lines met the war would resume, and both sides also sensed that it would be more savage than before. Yet the two lines marched without falter to the watery intersection at the ford.

From the north, Connor led his forces to the meeting place, and from the west Ailill and Maeve led the army. There was not the cheering of before in the ranks, or the good banter of men talking to friends and neighbours. They were going to end the war, to do it as quickly and efficiently as possible, and afterwards go home.

Ferdia rode in the chariot of his father, acting as his charioteer, and his protector. "We have not heard from Cuchulainn for three weeks," he said. "My mother weeps because she thinks he is dead where no women keen over his body. He is not, or I should have felt his loss in my heart. He is doing battle somewhere and there is none better in that field of endeavour than my brother. Father, the warrior that broke the truce at Lughnasa was goaded by Morrigan, of that I am certain. The provinces of Ulster and Connaught should have discussed peace there, and not stormed off in a huff."

"Was I not against this war from the beginning?" Connor said. "Did I not break my back to prevent it? And how were my efforts rewarded? By naked invasion and by theft! My kindness was regarded as weakness. That will not happen again, let me assure you."

"We outnumber them; but they are skilled in warfare, and O'Brien is an excellent warrior," advised Ferdia. "We do not have Cuchulainn in our ranks. I propose that we delay the fighting until he is found. Why not send scouts out for him to scour the forests and the fields before we do battle?"

"Wait for them to invade us as again?" said the king. "Would you have my people exposed to their raids and their herds driven off? How could I look my people in the eye if that happened? Ferdia, after my death the throne passes to you. The first duty of a king is to protect his people. Remember this when the crown is placed on your head."

To the shrill sounds of blaring trumpets, Dara O'Brien led the charge across the ford, hurling his spear and killing an Ulster chief. The warriors followed O'Brien and plunged into the massed ranks of Ulster. The men of Connor began to pull back under the onslaught, unable to withstand the ferocity of the charge. The king exhorted them not to give way, calling to them from his chariot. Bitter and bloody fighting spilled around the chariot of the king. The wounded were not left to recover from their wounds or to die, but were killed where they fell. Order fled from the field and was replaced by confused mayhem. O'Brien steered his chariot at Connor, sword raised high. Ferdia released the reins and engaged him in combat, flinging his spear at the chief. The weapon missed the chief but slew his charioteer. O'Brien leaped from the chariot, and grasping the wheel of the king's chariot, turned it over with a mighty heave. The chariot spilled over, tossing Connor and Ferdia on the field.

A mighty roar erupted from the throats of the Connaughtmen, and they swarmed over the fallen king and prince. Ferdia got to his feet and straddled his father, fighting them off. The warriors of Ulster, seeing Connor in distress, counter-attacked and rescued him. They righted his fallen chariot and lifted him inside, taking the reins and leading the frightened white-eyed horses away from the carnage.

The king leaving the field acted as a spur to the Connaughtmen, and they charged again. Ferdia was surrounded and knocked to the ground. Again the men of Ulster rushed to the rescue, and pulled him from the seething melee. In the blood-soaked field, littered with the corpses of the slain, as dusk fell on the land, Ferdia spoke to his father.

"We were lucky today. Tomorrow might not smile on us in the same way. We must withdraw to a better position that we can defend. They take courage from Dara O'Brien who slew many of our bravest warriors with spear and sword."

"My bones are old and tired and in need of sleep, my son," Connor said, breathing deeply. "Wake me early tomorrow morning and we will discuss this problem."

Ferdia pulled a cloak over his father and walked amongst the fallen warriors. The dead lay in each other's arms, enemies from both sides embracing in death, like brothers at sleep. Men moved in the moonlight, turning over bodies in search of their tribesmen. They lifted bodies over their shoulders and carried them to a pyre. They put the bodies on the pyre and went in search of more.

Chapter Eighteen

Unaware of its role in causing the war, the goldenhide bull grazed on the verdant slopes of Royal Tara, tied by a mighty triple-linked chain to the Stone of Destiny, guarded by sentries and free from the ravenous attacks of wolves. The great beast used the sacred stone as a scratching post, much to the annoyance of Ogma whose words were inscribed on the standing granite column to confer kingship. The constant scratching was erasing the words, rubbing them out, and making them difficult to read by the druids. Ogma was annoyed with the scratching bull. His words were meant to last for eternity, but a mere beast was obliterating them.

Every god was granted the authority to call a conference, and Ogma requested a meeting of the gods and goddesses to discuss his concerns. Since Morrigan was invited to attend the conference, they could not meet in the Otherworld. At midnight they gathered on the Hill of Tara, near the Stone of Destiny. Meek Epona did not attend because she was galloping over the western ocean with the spirits of the slain.

Ogma, voicing his concern, spoke to the gods, "Here am I trying to educate mortals by teaching them how to read words, and a beast of no understanding destroys my work. It is a disgrace, and I do not use that word lightly.

Some god has put the beast up to this mischief. The High King is proclaimed at the Stone of Destiny, and the sacred words spoken by the druid are inscribed on the granite column. How can the druid read the words if they are obliterated by a dull beast?"

"Do not read into this incident something that is not there," Lugh said. "When a bull itches, it scratches."

"It would not have scratched unless encouraged by some god who wishes to demean me," replied Ogma.

"See how this god reacts when he thinks we are interfering in his affairs!" Morrigan said. "He sees no conflict of interests when he criticises me behind my back. Well, some gods have very thin skins indeed. This from a hypocritical god who believes he is smarter than the rest of us? Well, now we see him in his true light."

The sharp words of the goddess of war wounded Ogma, and he forgot to smile when he replied, "As usual Morrigan tries to confuse the issue and to pour scorn on me for her own gratification. I did not call you here because my pride was hurt, for I am the most modest of gods. I called you here tonight because the words were rubbed out by the beast and I worry for the future of these people."

"Modest?" scoffed Morrigan. "How can he boast about modesty? The god of rhetoric appears not to understand the rules of speech! And he would dare look down on me?"

"We have reached a sorry state of affairs when we speak of a beast scratching its hide on a pillar and forget that a war is raging," lovely Brigid commented. "Warriors are dying daily, and the god of rhetoric is worried about the loss of his words. Has he no sense of right and wrong?"

"Stay out of this," warned Morrigan.

"I plainly see this war as a naked grab for power by the war goddess in the absence of Dagda" lovely Brigid said. "Do not forget that a people at peace offer no sacrifices to her. They forget her existence. In times of war she is elevated, and people pray to her and hold her in the highest esteem, seeking her favours. Her pride gets puffed up, and she actually believes she is more important than the rest of us."

"This lovely face conceals its true intent, which is to gain power," came the instant response from Morrigan. "She tries to be all things to all men, and all gods. The fools who listen to her call her wise, not able to distinguish wisdom from platitude. I have yet to meet a lovely face that is wise, and I will tell ye why that is. Everything comes too easy to the lovely face, and it does not have to seek because everything is given to its wearer. Wisdom comes only through constant seeking, and she has never sought anything in her life, except power, which she conceals behind her lovely face. She wears that like a crown, as if she had earned it, not capable of realising that all beauty is down to luck."

"We are here to discuss the complaint of Ogma which does not deserve consideration," Manannan said. "His words were erased by the beast. So what? It proves they were not worthy to last for eternity."

The arrival of Cuchulainn at the ford halted the retreat of the men of Ulster and turned them to face the enemy. The arrival had the opposite effect on the men of Connaught, filling them with dread. The certainty of victory dissipated at the sight of the terrible warrior appearing in the midst of the retreating army. Their confidence shrank and their steady advance faltered.

Every man looked to his comrade, unsure what to do, not wishing to be the first to die at the hands of the terrible warrior.

Dara O'Brien rose to the immediate challenge, and used his coarse tongue to chastise the faltering men. "Are ye men or women? Would ye rather be suckling bawling children? Why are ye not at home knitting wool or cooking food? I thought the hardy men of Connaught were the bravest warriors in the world, but it seems I was wrong! Ye are nothing but old women who should be milking mooing cows or grinding wheat. Why did ye come to war? Did ye think it would be easy? Or that immortal glory can be won as easily as picking apples? War is hard bloody work and that is why men win honour and glory through its pursuit. Go home to your hairy goats and woolly sheep if ye wish, but I go to fight the men of Ulster."

The harsh words of O'Brien acted as a spur to the faltering men, and they raised their shields and let out a mighty roar. The chief of Sligo led the charge in his chariot. His fast spear killed an Ulster chief. The dead warrior fell beneath the turning wheels of the chariot and stopped its progress. O'Brien dismounted and waded through the waters in search of Cuchulainn on the field of battle.

On the soil of Ulster, the two warriors advanced in deadly purpose, cutting through the melee, advancing face to face, their bodies spattered in blood and sweat. Only the whites of O'Brien's eyes were showing under the dust and the blood.

He spoke to Cuchulainn, "I care not how or why this war started, except that it did. Now it ends when it ends.

Your prowess has reached my ears, and I shall win much glory by killing you."

"You are too old and I am too young," replied Cuchulainn. "In matters of war, old warriors have an advantage over the young because of their experience. But this time it is different. My reputation is such that you are already thinking you cannot beat me. I have none of your doubts. I know in my heart that there is no warrior under the sun I cannot beat. If my own father, Lugh, transgressed the borders of Ulster, I would fight him, and I would beat him. Come, Epona waits to carry your spirit to the Otherworld."

The warriors hurled their bodies at each other, like two bulls in the same field. One only could survive the encounter. O'Brien drew first blood, his deflected sword opening a wound. The two armies revolved around the conflict of the two warriors. Each time Cuchulainn was pushed back, the warring men of Connaught steadily advanced. Each time O'Brien was pushed back, the warring men of Ulster steadily advanced. The two warriors fought without resting, their untiring arms swinging flashing swords. As the veil of evening fell on the bloody scene, Cuchulainn struck the killer blow, his sword piercing the chest of the Connaught chief. O'Brien fell dead, and the victor knelt to cut off his head.

The high-pitched voice of Maeve called out to her men in the thick of battle: "Do not let that terrible warrior take the head of Dara! He seeks to acquire the courage of the head! Do not permit him to dangle it from his bloody chariot! Go, rescue the body of my bravest chief! Let the gods curse any man who permits Dara's head to adorn his chariot."

Thirty fighting men attacked Cuchulainn, forcing him to abandon the body. The men of Connaught hoisted the body of the dead chief and carried him from the field. They retreated to the ford, pursued by Connor and his men. When night fell, the armies were divided by the ford.

Chapter Nineteen

Epona journeyed on fleet Capall from the Otherworld, washed and purified the spirit of the slain chief, garlanded it in red roses, and galloped over the western ocean. The men of Connaught prepared a funeral pyre and placed the body on a pyramid of dry wood. Maeve wept and tore her flaxen hair, and keened over the blazing funeral pyre of her dead chief. Her bravest warrior was dead, and his death had a profound effect on the men. Ailill and Maeve were aware that the men were disheartened. They were also aware, though neither said the words, that they could not win the war as long as Cuchulainn lived. Maeve walked into a nearby forest, and called to Morrigan, who was always present at the scene of battle.

In Connaught, Malachi Mac Carthy worked in the purpled bog beneath his hillfort at Loughrea. With his son and daughter working by his side, he loaded the dried turf on a cart pulled by an ass, and turned over the sods that had not dried. When the wagon was loaded, he told his son to take the load to the hillfort. Balor led the ass and cart through the bog, his young sister sitting on the load.

Mac Carty continued working, selecting the dried turf from the wet turf. His work was diverted by a swirling wind advancing over the bog. The spinning wind picked up pieces of heather and dried leaves, and churned the debris in its vortex. The wind ceased, and a white horse with silver hooves appeared. Seated on the horse was Epona, bearing in her arms a spirit garlanded in red roses.

Mac Carthy fell on his knees. "Kind-hearted goddess, is it my time?" he asked.

"The spirit in my arms desires to speak with you," the goddess said. "His message was so urgent that I turned Capall from the gates of the Otherworld and came here on fleet hooves."

"Do you not know me, my old friend?" asked the spirit. "My name was Dara O'Brien, your companion since childhood. Do you remember the promise we made long ago, when our muscled arms raced black high-riding currachs over the surfing waves? Do you remember the promise we made running through shadowed forests on sinewed legs in pursuit of a bounding stag?"

Mac Carthy slumped on his knees and wept, for he realised that his friend was dead. His body shook uncontrollably, and tears rolled down his sunburnt face. He struggled to his feet and wiped away the tears.

"Yes, I remember that promise, my old friend, though I do not for the life of me understand how a spirit can. When young, we promised each other with clasped embrace to bid our farewells before we departed this life. Do spirits remember such promises?"

"Yes, we remember the promises of youth before we depart this life, Malachi," said the spirit. "Allow me to draw down on our friendship once more before I depart, for I shall not visit this world again until the festival of Sowain. Lend assistance to my wife and to my children. Care for them as your own."

"I would have taken care of them, even had you not come to me in spirit form," replied Mac Carthy. "A fast horse will take me to them in less than a day after you depart. I will speak to your sons. I will tell them not to cross the broad Shannon and join the war."

"My thanks ring in your ears, my old friend," said the spirit. "Talk to them and try to persuade them not to go to war, though I doubt if they will listen. We are war-mad here! Help my wife, and bring turf to warm her nights for my ringfort is cold. I bid you farewell, for I long to go and live in my new home."

"Kind goddess, spare a mortal man some moments of your precious time," pleaded the chief. "My wife lives in your realm, and my son who was named Maol in this world. Is he happy?"

"In the midst of madness, Malachi, you alone remained sane, so I will answer your questions," replied the goddess. "Across the western ocean lies a broader ocean of blue and green calm waters. No storms ever touch the waters and no harsh or cold winds blow across them. All is calm and quiet serenity. Sprinkled in the calm waters are multitudes of diverse islands, more than a hundred thousand lying on the surface like water lilies in a pond. Every island is different. Your son Maol lives on one. It is called the Island of Apples."

"How is my lost son?" asked Mac Carthy. "This war has robbed me of his company, and of my grandchildren. Maol visits me in my dreams, but when I awake he is gone."

"Yes, the Otherworld is a delightful place for warriors and soon they forget about this world," said Epona. "Once a year, on the sacred festival of Sowain, they return to the land of the living for a day. On that sacred day I return their memories. Most of the spirits visit their former homes, though some choose not to return for their own reasons. Malachi, you are a decent man and I have no desire to garland your spirit in red roses. Do not go to war."

"The request of a goddess is a command to mortals. Before you depart, let me impose on your kindness again. How is my wife?"

"The Otherworld has many islands, and she lives on one which we call the Delightful Plain," replied Epona. "The spirits of the good can choose their own island. There is an Island of Snow for the spirits who love cold, and an Island of Silk for the spirits who love luxury."

"Goddess, your visit has warmed my heart," Mac Carthy said.

"Night approaches on silent wings and the silver hooves of Capall grow impatient," Epona said. "I leave you now, and wish you long life."

When the goddess departed with the garlanded spirit, Mac Carthy walked across the tufted heather in the descending darkness, picking his way over the rifts in the bog. Night fell on the walking chief, and stars glittered in the blue-dark sky. He walked up the pebbled road leading to the hillfort, and embraced his son and daughter.

Next day, in the fruitful and verdant province of Meath, two armies clashed again in bloody conflict. Days of savage fighting ensued, and the army of Connaught was hammered back towards the ford. Ailill and Maeve were aware, though neither mentioned it, that it was only a matter of time before the fast-dwindling army collapsed, and died. Relentless Cuchulainn led on the warriors of Ulster, and Connor ceded control to his son. Ferdia fought by his side and none could match the courage of the brothers.

Night fell on the army of Connaught resting near the ford of the Shannon. The summer had tamed the river and the ford was passable. Turnod the druid sought out the royal couple, and spoke to them, "My king and queen, the gods speak through me and when the gods speak mortals should listen. The ford of the Shannon is passable now, but in days the floods are due and we could be trapped here. A swollen river at our rear and Cuchulainn at our front is a nightmare vision too awful to contemplate. We must cross over tonight at the earliest, or tomorrow at the latest. Over there across the river are our lands and our homes. Do not hesitate or we are doomed."

"I hear your advice, Turnod, but I know not if you speak the words of the gods or the words of fear," Maeve replied. "Do you think I do not recognise the danger or that I care little for the lives of my men? I intend to cross soon and to muster our forces on the other side until the river rises. The war is not yet lost."

"Maeve, perhaps you should bury your pride in a bog and seek the help of Mac Carthy," suggested Ailill. "If there is one man who can defeat Cuchulainn, it is that chief. Bards still sing of his exploits, and the reputation he made in the battles of his past reflects well on the province of Connaught."

"Do you ask the Queen of Connaught to prostrate herself before a chief?" replied Maeve. "Has the world turned upside-down? That chief has no honour, or he would not have abandoned his queen. Well, let him seek help elsewhere if savage Cuchulainn crosses the broad Shannon and attacks his hillfort at Loughrea!"

Breaking dawn saw the army of Connaught crossing the ford at Athlone, the same ford the warriors had crossed to start of the war. The mood of the warriors was darker now, more sombre and less buoyant. Their heads and shoulders were stooped, and they crossed the ford with dragging legs. The honour and glory they had sought had eluded them. They were returning without their objective, the goldenhide bull. The beast was grazing on the Hill of Tara.

Cuchulainn led the pursuing army of Ulster to the ford and prepared to force the passage. The depleted army of Connaught opposed him on the other side. He expressed confidence that his men could sweep them aside and end the war. One more battle and Connaught would be forced to sue for peace.

Connor spoke to his two sons and to the chiefs at the ford: "We are at the border, and right remains on our side. Across the broad Shannon are the lands of Connaught. If we cross this river, we invade their lands, and in so doing put ourselves in the wrong. We must remain in the right."

"We have the chance to finish this war in one final blow," Cuchulainn said. "To postpone one battle is to invite many more. If we do not finish this war here and now, we shall be destined to fight it again under worse circumstances. That is the way of all wars. Connor, you are my beloved father and my king, but in this matter you are wrong."

"We must bow to the wise words of the king," Ferdia said. "We have right on our side and it is imperative we remain in the right. Let us return to our homes and our wives. The beaten men on the other side of the river too wish to go home. Perhaps sense can prevail in the meantime."

The chiefs were as divided as the royal family. Some desired to ford the river, invade Connaught, and finish the war. Others advised caution and the necessity to keep right on their side. Across the broad Shannon, pinpricks of camp-fires danced on the further shore where the army of Connaught rested. A scout reported to the king that there were no sentries on the bank, the men exhausted from fighting and cold after the crossing, warming themselves at the fires. Cuchulainn advised his father to attack immediately; but the king did not desire to be branded the aggressor in the war, and refused to give the order to advance.

Dawn found Connor still in debate with the chiefs, preaching caution under a cloudy grey sky. As they debated, the river decided the issue for them. The flowing waters rose steadily and flooded the ford, making passage impossible.

Chapter Twenty

Peace was not imposed, but the cessation of fighting brought peace to the warring provinces. No agreement to end the war was declared, but the warriors returned to their homes and their families. The returned men took up the ways of peace again and put the ways of war behind them.

The war had affected them, each man in his own way. The courage and valour of Cuchulainn had multiplied, and he wore the honour like a bright cloak. Ferdia too had excelled in the fighting, but he was more reflective and did not speak of the war. King Connor resolved to avoid a future war at all costs, having seen many of his chiefs slain in the fighting.

Ailill came out of the war with his honour restored, bearing on his thigh the proof of his valour. His voice now carried more weight, and ears were opened to his opinions. Maeve had come out of the war with the respect of her men. She had fought beside them and shown her courage. She had risen high in their esteem so that they forgot she was a woman and remembered she was a warrior. Soon they did not remember that they had retreated across the Shannon, remembering instead the sight of their queen in battle on her chariot.

At Emain Macha, Queen Rosheen viewed the returning men with relief, but also with trepidation. She was relieved that Connor and his sons had returned safely from the war. She watched as Devlina ran down the sandy road and embraced Ferdia, showering countless kisses on his cheeks. Princess Emer did not display the same affection for her returning hero. The queen issued orders to the servants, instructing them to prepare hot baths and a change of clothes for the men.

When they had bathed and eaten, Rosheen approached Ferdia, and spoke to him, "There are words I must say to your ears alone, my son. War has taken you away from your wife. Old wives say that absence makes the heart grow fonder, but that is not true. A young couple needs to spend time together, so that they can grow closer. The bunched mistletoe needs time to bind to the apple tree, and a woman needs time to bind to a man in wedlock. Take Devlina to the island of her father in the lake, and live there."

"I hear your words, but the war has not ended," Ferdia said.

"News has reached this palace that Goddess Shannon is angry," Rosheen replied. "The river has burst her banks and flooded the plains, though the season of winter has not arrived. The central plains are turned into an impassable sea. The armies cannot cross the river or the plains until the floods subside. The goddess of the river has imposed the peace that the kings could not, and young couples must take advantage. Go to the island in the lake with Devlina, and grow your love."

"Mother, I will go to the island in the lake," Ferdia said.

In the high stony hilltop fort at Knocknashee, thirty chiefs gathered to discuss the results of the war, and to plan for the future. Rory Guinan had been killed in the war, and the title of chief now passed to his younger brother, Grian. Dara O'Brien had also been killed in the war, and title of chief now passed to his son, Niall. Both young chiefs were eager for war. Grian desired to avenge the death of his brother, and Niall burned to avenge the death of his father.

Turnod the druid prepared the sacred brew, and drank it down. The crushed mistletoe berries and wine did not take long to act. His body trembled and he fell to the floor. When he spoke, his voice wailed like a banshee.

"Goddess Shannon speaks through me," he cried. "She has flooded the ford because the goddess has sided with Connaught. She has recognised that our cause is just. She will keep the river flooded until our strength has been recovered. We must use the time to our advantage, and prepare for war."

"Our druid has recovered his courage," Ailill said.

"It is not he who speaks, but Shannon," Maeve said.

The loud roar from the assembled chiefs rang out from the hillfort of Knocknashee and across the sleeping bogs and hills of Connaught. It echoed in the swollen rivers of the Shannon, and in the lakes and streams. It rang across the western ocean and reached the islands of the Otherworld. The unending war would resume when the waters subsided, and neither men nor gods could halt the conflict.

In the vast expanse of ocean, to the west of Connaught, Manannan Mac Lir planned to deter his second eager son from joining the war. Naylor was mumbling under his breath about his confinement, and threatening to join the fight. He burned to escape from his watery home and kill Cuchulainn. His father, aware of Morrigan's lures, was determined to keep his hot son beside him. To ensure Naylor could not run off to war, he went to his smith and instructed him to make an unbreakable chain of iron. The smith manufactured a triple-linked chain of unbreakable iron, and immune to the effects of the salty sea. Despite the loud and bitter protestations of Naylor, the god of the sea anchored one end of the chain to the seabed, and the other end to the ankle of his son. Naylor could move around the sea, but the strong chain prevented him leaving home.

When Morrigan came calling in the form of a raven and sang her sirensong of war overhead, Naylor rose to the surface. He swam towards the seashore, but the anchored chain held him fast. The raven landed on the seashore, and changed to Morrigan. Naylor tugged at the chain, and called out for help.

"See how my cruel father treats me!" he complained bitterly. "This is an outrage! I bet everyone is laughing at my discomfort! Ridicule is the worst form of insult! Morrigan, help me escape my watery prison!"

"Naylor," replied Morrigan, "I would dearly love to help you escape, but every god has his own ordained theatre of responsibility. Even gods must live by rules. Your domineering father has control of the seas and I dare not interfere. Looking at you, I can see that you are strong of body, and your eyes have the spark of intelligence. Find a way to escape your watery prison and earn eternal glory. The warrior who kills Cuchulainn attains eternal glory, and his name shall never die on the lips of men. I can make you invulnerable to weapons by chewing on white mistletoe berries and licking your naked body all over with my hot saliva. I can have my smith make magical weapons for your worthy hands. Escape and join the men of Connaught. Their fight is right."

"Let it be my name that the bards sing in the halls of kings," Naylor replied. "I will try to find a way out of this iron prison, either by entreaty or by force. Mark well my words, Morrigan, I will get out of here. Prepare your hot saliva for my naked body, and have your smith craft the magical weapons. I am going to the war and nothing can stop me."

On the tree-topped island of Devenish, Chief Art Maguire, father of Devlina, died in his bed, unlike thousands of young warriors that year, leaving his lands to his daughter. Ferdia now lived on the island with his wife, fishing and planting crops. The war was on hold because the central plains were flooded, and the warring armies were confined to their own provinces.

Devlina spoke to her husband in the home of her departed father, as she prepared food for the arrival of Cuchulainn and Emer, "I have been very happy here with you, but are you happy here with me, my husband? Often I find you down at the lakeshore alone in thought, gazing into the far distance, seeking something beyond the horizon. When I follow the line of your eyes, I see only the mainland across the lake, but I know you see what I do not. We have everything we need on this island, and yet you seek something else. What is it, my husband?"

"A dreamer sees dreams, Devlina, and that is how I am. Do not take any notice of my quiet moods. The fish traps are set, and I go there now to collect our dinner."

Ferdia walked beneath the hanging green boughs of oak and holly and ash to the lakeshore. He waded into the cold waters and lifted a fish trap, and carried it to the shore. Three flapping trout were trapped inside the hazel cage. Ferdia untied the knot at the rear of the hazel cage and removed the trout, killing them with a blow on the head. Using a river reed, he inserted it though the gills of the trout and carried them back to the dwelling.

He gutted and washed the rainbow trout and passed them over to his wife, who rolled them in ground wheaten flour. Then he returned to the lakeshore to bait the traps with bread and fat. He baited the traps and secured the ends, and waded into the water. The stones in the traps secured them on the bottom, and their open mouths gaped against the current. Kneeling to wash his hands, he heard the voice of Emer. She stood behind him, her shadow falling over his shoulders.

"I see you have become very skilled in fishing. Wedded life seems to agree with you too. This is a very beautiful island, moored away from the outside world. It is a place to dream, and to make wishes that cannot come true."

"Princess, how did you get here?" he asked. "I had a swift currach prepared for your arrival. Let us return to my home and eat the food my wife has readied. How long do you intend to remain on Devenish? Where is your husband?"

"Ferdia, one question at a time, please," she said. "Let us not hurry back to your home just yet for I wish to speak in private to you. Your wife rowed the fast currach and took us here and she is very skilled. My husband is at your home and your wife questions him about the war. We plan to stay for three days and nights, and then we return to Navan."

"How is the palace at Navan going, princess? This war does not help much, for the minds of the builders are on other matters. It is a race against time until the war begins again. You should have lived with my parents at Emain Macha until this war ended."

"Why is it that I find it much easier to talk with you than my own husband?" she mused. "Why do I not have to guard my words in your presence? No, they are questions that need no answers! Emain Macha was impossible. Women were swarming around the palace of your father like flies on a carcass, waiting to catch a glimpse of my husband. Or worse, if you get my real meaning! Some women have no shame or no modesty. Your father and mother decided to build us a palace at Navan, but the war has interrupted the work. Ferdia, I fear this war shall outlast us all."

"Princess, I feel you are circling around the point. I recall well your unbridled tongue on the road from Cashel! Speak to me, and I promise your words will not cause offence. I could never be angry with you, no matter what you do or say."

She removed her sandals and waded into the lake. "What is this thing called fame? Why are women attracted to its bearer? Cuchulainn was famous and handsome before this war started, but the glory has made him more handsome and more famous. Open your ears and listen to my woes. Not once or twice, but many times I have found women on his arm, though he is wed to me. Ferdia, I know he has not been always true to me, and when I challenge him he breaks into a smile. His wry smile is as strong as his sword-arm, but it is beginning to wear thin. There, I have poured out my heart to you, and I await your response."

"Princess, I am not a knowing druid, and I have not the knowledge why fame attracts many women, except that it does. Surely if women seek out your husband it is their fault, not his. Everyone knows that he is wed to you. Give him some time."

She walked from the lake and dried her feet on the grass.

"When I was a young girl growing in the palace of my father at Cashel, I dreamed of the man I would wed," she confessed, her voice low. "Young girls always dream of the future, and I was no different. I dreamed of wedding the most handsome man in the land, and I did. I dreamed of wedding the most courageous warrior in the land, and I did. Most of all, nightly I dreamed of wedding a man who would be true to me and to me alone. I did not marry that man."

"This war is at fault for all our sadness because it prevents us from living our normal lives," he said. His words were spoken to help her understand. "My brother is living on the edge and men in that position tend to live dangerously and for today. That is understandable because every day might be his last one on Earth. That explains the other women in his life, but I am certain they mean nothing to him"

"You too are living on the edge, yet you are true to your wife," she replied in a soft voice. "We should have married, Ferdia, because we were destined for each other."

"Enough of this sadness!" he grinned. "Let us return to my home and eat a meal of trout. All will be well, princess. This war cannot last much longer and when it ends your sadness will be no more. This year should end the madness, and then we can live in peace again, as the gods live in the Otherworld."

She took his arm and stopped his progress, and spoke softly to him, "Wait, Ferdia, for there is more, and this is the cruellest blow to my sense of womanhood, and to my pride. Your brother Lorcan was taken away by the war, the foster-brother of my husband. He left behind a young widow. Permit me to speak freely here, but keep the words I say in your heart alone. Fidelma and Cuchulainn are lovers."

Ferdia sank to his knees and held his head in his hands. He replied to Emer, his voice breaking under the sudden strain, "Is this needless war depriving us of everything that is good and noble? Have our minds become dulled by conflict? Have we become immune to everything that is proper? Do my parents know?"

"I think your mother suspects, for mothers are wiser in these matters than fathers. Oh, Ferdia, I do not blame Fidelma. She is attracted to the fearless warrior in him, as all women are. She is not shameless like the others, and yet she is without shame in his presence. They both exist in a sort of walking dreamworld, as if nothing matters except them. It seems to me that both have lost their senses and they do not care if they cause offence to the whole world. There is an aura of unreality about them that I can see, but that they are unable to see. They appear to belong to another world, not to this world."

He stood up and took her hand in his, and spoke. "Princess, let us return to my home and eat fish and drink mead. It is a passing thing with them, driven by this war. When it is over they will both recover their senses, and realise that they have done wrong. Princess, war makes men and women live in a dreamlike world; but when it is over they return to reality. Come, I can smell fish cooking."

Chapter Twenty-One

In the distant western province of Connaught, a young chief rode his grey horse through sleeting rain, a cloak pulled over his head. The young rider negotiated the stone defences around Knocknashee and guided his horse into the ringfort. The royal servants prepared a hot bath and a change of clothes for the young chief, but he refused to bathe. He had spiked and bleached his hair with lime so that is stood up like the horns of a dozen bulls. This made him fearsome to behold, and he wore the hair with pride.

The servants took him to the dining hall where Ailill and Maeve were seated at a table near a fire of blazing black turf. Seated opposite the royal couple was a woman, no older than the chief. She might have been beautiful except for her eyes, which had triple irises.

Maeve invited the chief to sit down near the turf fire. The young chief, Niall O'Brien, sat near the fire, warming his hands on the leaping flames. Meave told the chief that the young woman was Morrigan, the goddess of war. She was firmly on the side of Connaught, and had promised the province victory in the war.

"The war is destined to end this year and the hound of Ulster is fated to die," Morrigan assured the young chief. "Ulster will collapse without that terrible warrior in its ranks. I have come to the home of Ailill and Maeve to confirm that I am on their side, and consequently Connaught cannot lose. Soon Goddess Shannon will retreat from the central plains and the armies will take up arms again. I have come here to assure you all that I intend to remove Cuchulainn from the conflict."

Maeve spoke to Morrigan, and to the young chief. "We have lost many good chiefs and warriors, but that has hardened our resolve. We have been outnumbered but not outfought. They have the fierce son of a god in their ranks whilst we are mere mortals. Yet they could not defeat us and I will tell you why. Connaught is a poor province of bogs and soggy marshes. Such places produce hardy warriors who can endure hardship without complaint. Not once in the war did my chiefs come to me and exhort me to sue for peace. Once Connaught was treated like a beggar at the feast of kings. Not anymore. Now they do not look down their noses at us. Connaught will prevail in this war."

"The words you speak ring as twanging harp strings in my ears, sweet strains of plucked sounds," said Niall O'Brien. "My brave father fell to the swift sword-arm of terrible Cuchulainn. The son of O'Brien does not lack the courage of his father and he is also skilled in warfare. My hardy warriors are ready to follow me as their fathers followed my father."

"It gladdens the heart of the queen that courage has not died in my province and that the sons of the slain chiefs are made of the same stern stuff as their fathers and brothers," said the queen. "Talteann should be here to witness this scene! With brave men such as you, our province is guaranteed her freedom. None dares cross our borders. Now, Ailill desires to speak with you."

The king exposed his thigh and the healed scar for all to see, and spoke, "Ferdia the son of Connor inflicted this wound with his fast spear, but it was he who retreated from the field of battle. On three occasions I crossed swords with Cuchulainn himself in battle and he did not kill me, though he tried hard enough! Niall, I seek your advice as I sought it from your brave father. I believe Connor intends to attack us in our province when the Shannon recedes from the central plains. How would you react to an armed invasion of Connaught?"

Niall O'Brien leaped to his feet. "By killing that old northern king!" he exclaimed.

"The queen and I are thankful for your support, and with you on our side are confident of victory," Ailill replied. "Ulster looks down on us because we are poor. We cannot match them in gold or herds, but we can in valour. Yet a king must also consider all options open to him for the sake of his people. Should I send an envoy to Emain Macha to discuss terms of peace? What is your opinion?"

"My king, that would be a sign of weakness," said the young chief. "Let none doubt the resolve of Connaught in this matter. Does Connor think we are the same as the men of Ulster, grown fat and stupid from living off rich pastures? Listen to the wind howling outside the walls. If that same cold wind blew in Emain Macha, they would all hide under their beds and wail for their mothers!"

The king and queen laughed heartily at the warring words of O'Brien. Tears rolled down their cheeks to the floor, and even the formidable goddess of war smiled.

"How well you sum up the difference between them and us, Niall," Maeve said. "Do not fear, we do not intend going to Connor on our hands and knees. When we go, we

238

will go at the head of a conquering army. We will go as victors in glory and in spoils."

A lone rider reluctantly led his horse up the zigzagging path to the hillfort in the face of a sleeting gale. The servants bathed Malachi Mac Carthy and gave him a change of clothes. The old chief entered the dining hall, and balked at the sight of the goddess of war seated between O'Brien and the young couple.

Maeve rose from her seat, gave the chief a goblet of mulled mead, and spoke to him. "Malachi, my old friend, you are most welcome in my home. It gladdens my heart to see you looking so well. Come, sit here by the roaring turf fire. There is nothing better than looking at a black turf fire on a night like this, and smelling the burning peat. Does it not smell better than the reddest roses in summer bloom?"

Mac Carthy sat near the fire and sipped the goblet of mulled mead, warming his hands at the fire. "Maeve, I came under your command, for a chief should honour his queen though he might not agree with her," he began, sipping the hot mead. "But if I had known Morrigan was here, I would not have come. It is hard to understand why you allow her into your palace when the gods do not allow her into the Otherworld. Having said that, this is your palace to invite and to refuse as you please. Why have I been summoned here in this weather?"

Stung by the harsh words of the old chief, Morrigan departed from the royal residence, and flew into the night.

"Malachi, the war is destined to end this year, and I wish to put your mind at rest," Ailill said, patting the old chief on his bald and scarred head. "We did not invite you to our palace to request your help in the war. Morrigan is firmly on our side and the outcome is assured in our favour. We do not see eye to eye in this conflict, but I still value your opinion. Two provinces are engaged in this war. Do you foresee Diarmuid joining in?"

"There is no doubt that he desires to be High King in more than name," replied the old chief. "Perhaps that is no bad thing for the five provinces. We need a supreme ruler with the authority to knock heads together and to settle disputes. Having said that, I do not see him joining the war. He has too much to lose."

"What of Cormac of Munster" asked Ailill.

Eminent Mac Carthy pulled up the chair and sat closer to the turf fire, thinking about the question. "King Cormac is very secure in his rich province and he desires to remain so. He will not join the war because he could lose his lands, and his kingdom too. My king, in matters of war a king always looks first to the safety of his own kingdom. If he does not, then he does not do that, he does not deserve to be king. Besides, he has a daughter in both camps."

"What of Marbery of Leinster?" asked Ailill.

"He is the real threat," replied Mac Carthy. "That is why I urge you to end this war as soon as possible. He is like the lone wolf that watches two antlered stags clash in combat. The wolf waits until one stag is bloodied and weakened in battle, and then pounces."

"We are grateful for your sound advice," Ailill said. "Now, rest your weary bones here tonight for the storm is worsening."

Mac Carthy thanked the king for the offer, and then turned and spoke to the young chief, "What has the son of Dara done to his hair? Long ago when I fought in distant Gaul, warriors spent more time liming their hair than sharpening their swords! Such trifles are not for this

240

province. We are not as them and we should not adopt their ways."

O'Brien replied to the old chief: "The young are not bound by the old. We are of a different generation and we regard things in a different way. Spiked hair serves two purposes. It terrifies our enemies in battle, and it renders us attractive to women. Permit me to live life my way and do not criticize me for being young."

The storm grew in blowing intensity and the winds howled over the high ringfort. The cold rains sleeted across the stony walls and the outer defences. A lone raven moved across the dark sky, unmoved by the winds. The war was destined to resume soon, and there would be plenty of dead bodies littered over the fields and hills to feast upon.

Chapter Twenty-Two

Every society, whether mortal men or immortal gods, requires a leader, a figurehead of authority to give guidance and leadership. Lovely Brigid recognised this fundamental requirement, being the wisest of all the gods or goddesses. The Otherworld required a king or a queen to govern. She approached Lugh and explained that they had to resolve the problem of kingship, and set a good example for mortals to follow. The reason mortals were now losing respect for the gods, she explained, was because they had no single figure of authority, for Dagda was always missing. The gods and goddesses were all pulling in different directions, and they lacked a guiding principle and a figurehead. How were mere mortals expected to resolve their problems in the land of the living when the immortals could not resolve theirs? By selecting a king or a queen to rule and govern the Otherworld, they would send out a powerful message that every problem, no matter how intractable, can be resolved.

"We must consider the possibility that Dagda never returns," she said. "We must make plans for the future, for even gods must plan."

Lugh agreed with the wise words of Brigid and added that a king of the gods would have the authority to stop the war between the provinces. Morrigan did not listen to any god, but she would have to pay heed to a king of the gods. Turning a deaf ear to a fellow god was one thing, but turning a deaf ear to a king was unthinkable. He foresaw a basic problem however. The goddess of war would have to be permitted entry to the Otherworld for the selection of a ruler to replace absent Dagda, but Epona would undoubtedly object strenuously.

"Let us put our heads together and find a solution to the problem," advised Brigid.

The god and goddess came up with a plan to overcome the fears of kind-hearted Epona, and in a mood of high optimism they went to the rose-garlanded stables. She was brushing the white mane with a golden-tooth comb, and whispering words into the ears of the magical steed. Brigid addressed her, and spoke of the need for a king in the Otherworld.

"Mortals do not listen to dissenting voices of the powerless, but they do listen to the sole voice endowed with authority," she said. "Poor Capall is exhausted, and he needs a rest. It is obvious that only a cessation of the war can save him from total and utter collapse. Drastic times call for drastic actions."

Lugh took over and said that the curved rib-bones of the magical steed were showing beneath the wrinkled white hide. The thorny issue of kingship had to be sorted. A king would have the authority to end the war, and as a result Capall could regain his lost weight. Lugh went on to say that the consent of all the gods and goddesses was required to select a king and it followed therefore that Morrigan had to be allowed enter the Otherworld. Before Epona could raise an objection, Lugh added that her entry would be for a limited period only.

"After the selection of our new king, she will be banished again," he assured Epona. "The gates will be locked permanently against her and she will no longer be able to gain entry to the Isles of the Otherworld."

It was a good argument, presented well and in the high moral tones that always appealed to her intelligence. However, although Epona was meek and kind she was not simple-minded, and could think clearly for herself. Immediately she saw the contradiction in the argument of Lugh where others might not. She pointed out to the god of light that a king could permit Morrigan to live in the Otherworld, since the word of a king was law and universally recognised as such. She required, and indeed demanded, a prior guarantee from each god and goddess that, if elected, he or she would maintain the ban on Morrigan. Lugh gave his promise and his hand as a guarantee, and Brigid followed.

Epona unlocked the iron gates of the Otherworld and permitted the goddess of war to enter, accompanied by Manannan Mac Lir. The god of the sea had tested the anchored chain before departure, ensuring that his son could not escape. The gods and goddesses assembled in the temple on the Isle of the Gods. This was a circular building constructed in white granite and set on a green island.

Seated at a table in the temple were Bris the goddess of fertility; Bel, the god of fire whose feast day was Beltaine; Aine, the goddess of orchards who was also known as the Fairy Queen; and Danu who was known as Mother Earth. Taranis was not there, since he was a loner. Brigid said that the demonstration of their godly powers should be confined to the Isles of the Otherworld, and that it must not impinge on the world of mortals. She received their assent, and the contest began with Manannan Mac Lir.

The god of the sea gave a demonstration of his strength, and of his commanding power. The calm sea of the Otherworld had never known storms. Now he roused the blue-green sea into a frenzy of stormy waves. The huge waves rolled over the surface and battered the islands, sending the terrified spirits scurrying for cover. The white-topped waves uprooted trees and destroyed orchards. He looked at his fellow gods for approval, but they were not impressed by his destructive powers.

"Destruction is not the best method to prove you are fit to wear the crown," Brigid commented. "Creation is the standard we must strive to achieve. Let me give a simple demonstration of my powers. Look, and ascertain which of us is more worthy to wear the crown, the god of destruction, or the goddess of regeneration."

The lovely goddess smiled her charm on the sea, and the stormy waters calmed and came to rest. She waved a hand over the islands, and the soil sprang forth with new trees, and apples again grew on the boughs. When she was finished, the islands were restored, and the spirits came out of hiding. The spirits thanked the goddess for restoring their destroyed homes, and for making the islands fertile again.

Ogma relied on his powers of eloquence to make his bid, and spoke to the assembled gods and goddesses, looking down on the calm sea and islands. "We have changed from a society where might was right to a society where dialogue is seen to be not only right, but also the only proper way to conduct our affairs. For if mortals see that the gods do not resort to violence, perhaps they too will learn how to solve their differences by dialogue. The god of the sea has proved that he is strong enough to move vast oceans. So what does that prove, that physical strength alone is enough to place the crown on his head? The strongest wolf in the pack attains leadership that way, which proves that it is fit only for animals, which we are not! The true sign of an honourable society is the manner by which it elects its leader, and conducts its business. Let me pose you a question, and ponder before you reply. What is the greatest scourge known to gods or to men?"

"War is certainly the greatest scourge known to mankind, and they who promote it should be shunned," Epona replied.

Ogma nodded, and continued, "That is very true indeed, and consequently we must work to avoid the condition. The alternative to war is dialogue, and therefore he who promotes the tongue over the spear must be held in higher esteem. My good fellow gods and goddesses, personally I do not seek the crown. In fact, personally I would consider myself unworthy of the honour! What I want most for this society is for us all to live in peace and harmony. Let me add that my deep ears would be open to each god and goddess without favour if I am selected. Let me finish by stating that I do not desire the crown, but if the crown is forced on me, I will not shirk my duty."

Morrigan raised her triple-irises from the calm seas and islands, and spoke in an angry voice: "Never have I heard such hypocrisy! Of course we all burn to wear the crown and that is why we are gathered here! To say otherwise is to treat us as fools!" After the outburst she spoke more calmly. "The cloak of modesty does not hang well on Ogma. There is a great deal of difference between the god of rhetoric and the goddess of war. He speaks to deceive, whilst I speak the truth, although truth is unpalatable to both gods and men. Manannan and I talked as we journeyed here, and he explained that mortals do not admire weakness in a god. They admire the opposite, which is strength. When sickness strikes them down, or when a bolt of lightning destroys their abode, they pray fervently to the gods. War is the most important condition of mankind, and they who ignore that fact ignore reality. I represent war in all its glory, and consequently am more representative of mortals than anyone here. To put your minds at rest, I intend to confine my activities to the world of mortals, and war will remain a stranger here. You have my guarantee that it will not intrude on this kingdom."

"I see that some are already yawning when I rise to speak, yet they did not yawn when Morrigan spoke," Epona said softly. "Such actions speak for themselves, and require no interpretations from me. Why do all of ye ignore the quality of meekness? Do ye ignore me because I alone genuinely do not seek the crown? Very well, but that does not stop me having my say in who should wear the crown. They who seek it must be put under the closest scrutiny, for the crown is like a ship and its holder the captain of the ship. A good captain steers the vessel of state through the stormiest oceans, and brings the ship and all the people on board safely home. However, a bad captain steers the ship into the rocks, and destroys the vessel and its people. Therefore, we must always beware they who seek the crown for themselves and challenge their motives. Let me sound out a warning here, and though my voice is meek, my mind is strong. If the goddess of war is given the crown, I will remove Capall from his stables and ride away to the east, and dwell in the land of mortals."

"Morrigan states that war is the most important condition of mankind," Aengus said, pushing his own claim for the crown of the Otherworld. "She is, of course, wrong. Love is stronger than war. War is like a bout of sickness that afflicts men in the spring of their lives; but when the summer comes the sickness disappears, and they forget about the malady. Love, on the other hand, is never forgotten. It never dies in the soul of mankind, or in the heart. It endows the memory with fleeting wings that can wipe away the years and make old men young again. A plucked harp string can transport an old man with a staff back to his youth and he relives again the happy days. Sitting beside a still river, he can clearly see again the girl he swam with, and feel the water coursing over his flesh. Love is the magic elixir that grants eternal youth and eternal memories. That is why I should be selected, and why I deserve the crown."

Ogma replied to Aengus, and sought to destroy his bid for kingship, "A fine speech, long in cloudy nostalgic images, but quite short on practicality. Language should be concise, and it should convey what it says. Let us examine how the god of love has operated in his theatre of responsibility. Emer is married to Cuchulainn, but she loves Ferdia. Why did he cause that mischief on the road from Cashel to Emain Macha? It is all very well to speak nostalgic words; but actions speak louder, and they expose him for what he is. He has the power over human hearts and constantly abuses that power. He should use his considerable powers to ensure one man falls in love with one woman, and that one woman falls in love with one man. Then there would be no more broken hearts."

Ogma sat back, confident that his words had destroyed the bid of his rival. Lugh was last to speak, and he stood. "A king who does not resort to force must rule by widespread consent, and that fact speaks for itself. In other words, my friends, he must be a universal king, and not confined to one specific theatre of responsibility. Let us now examine the credentials of each of the candidates here. The god of the sea is undoubtedly very powerful, but his power does not extend over the land. How can he hope to govern where his sway does not extend? It is not possible. Let us now examine the bid of Morrigan. She represents war and as such the past. Her bid must be dismissed out of hand. Let us now consider Ogma. There is no doubt that his bid is genuine, and I acknowledge that dialogue is the future. But he should acknowledge that dialogue is not essential to life, for there are mortals who cannot speak, and yet they live. Aengus can be dismissed for the same reason. Love is not essential for life either. Let us now look at the bid of Brigid. It is true that she banishes the Winter Crone every year, but it is also true that life carries on during the cold winter months. Brigid is very important, but she is not essential. I am the god of light, essential to life. Without my powers, everything would die. I have the universal appeal lacking in every other bid. I am the only logical choice."

Lugh proceeded to give a swift demonstration of his power. He withdrew the light from the Otherworld and plunged the islands into darkness. The spirits clamoured for the return of the light, but Lugh closed his ears to their pleas. This was his chance to win the crown, and he was prepared to demonstrate that his power was greatest, and that he was by far the most important god in the realm of the Otherworld. He folded his arms and sat back.

The islands in the sea turned to darkness, and the trees and orchards began to die. The Otherworld took on the mantle of a wasteland, and the spirits clamoured louder. But Lugh would not relent. Epona complained that Capall was suffering, and that the magical steed did not know when to sleep. Still Lugh would not relent. In desperation, worried about the fate of Capall, Epona vowed to support Lugh. Slowly it became evident to them that the power of the god of light was like no other. Lugh held the power of life and death in his hands. He could destroy the Otherworld if he wished, and that fact brought them to their senses.

The selection of Lugh restored light to the Otherworld, and Brigid brought fresh growth to the islands. Lugh placed the golden crown on his own head, the symbol of supreme kingship. He spoke to them, "My reign will be benign but fair and firm. Neither do I intend to interfere in your individual theatres of responsibility, except where it is absolutely necessary. When I do speak, my words will carry the weight of my office. Let none question my decisions, or talk back. Let none doubt my ability either, or my importance. Morrigan, my first command as King of the Otherworld is directed to you, and hear well my words. Return to your realm and end this war."

The gates slammed behind Morrigan, much to her annoyance. The stinging words of Lugh rang in her ears. She took the form of a raven and sailed over the western ocean. Naylor swam to the surface and watched her progress across the sky, held in place by his chain. The goddess of war sailed over the land, and flew to Navan, where a palace was under construction for Cuchulainn and Emer. The dark bird hovered over the building, before flying silently across the land to the high hillfort of Knocknashee.

The raven changed into Morrigan, and spoke to the royal couple, "When flooded Goddess Shannon withdraws from the central plains, the war starts again. I have journeyed here to tell you that I have a plan to remove Cuchulainn from the field of battle. Ailill and Maeve, the advantage is with you."

Ogma too journeyed from the Otherworld, and he flew to the palace at Royal Tara. The god asked Diarmuid to take a walk to the Stone of Destiny where the goldenhide bull grazed on the verdant grass. The god and the king walked up the grassy mound beneath a cloudy sky. The guards saluted the king, unable to see the god walking at his side. The god and the king walked to the Stone of Destiny, and Ogma was very annoyed that his words were almost completely erased from the stone.

"Diarmuid, we have been too long without a king but at last we have resolved the problem of kingship in the Otherworld," Ogma said. "Lugh now rules there and we have agreed to abide by his decisions, though he has not tied our hands. There is a word that we use which has lost its true meaning and that word is anarchy, or literally without a king. Now, many people believe that anarchy equals bloodshed and fighting, but in fact this is not always the case. Anarchy can also equal indecision because there is no single person to take control in a crisis or make the final decision. The result is that nothing gets done. Diarmuid, you can become as Lugh, and rule all Ireland."

The ears of Diarmuid pricked up when he heard the words of the god and he sought to hear more. "How is it that the gods and goddesses are willing to listen to Lugh, but the kings and queens here refuse to listen to me? I am their High King, and they bow before my at the four festivals held at Royal Tara. Then they return to their own provinces and do as they please. They pay no attention to me, and if I dare make a suggestion they rattle their swords and shields. How can I become High King in more than name?"

"That triple-horned bull idly grazing there is the cause of the war," Ogma pointed out. "If you had a boil on your leg, would your physician not lance the lump? If you had a tooth that ached, would your physician not pull it? Remove the root cause of the problem and you remove the problem itself. The bull grazes on your grass on your lands. According to your laws the bull belongs to you to do with as you please. Do you wish to hear more?"

"Ogma, your rhetoric is sweet harp music to my ears and I long to hear more," replied Diarmuid. "Clearly it is wrong that two provinces can go to war and endanger the peace of the whole island, so that we are all in danger. How do I become as Lugh in this land of mortals? Speak, and my ears are listening."

"Kill the bull and sacrifice it to the gods," Ogma advised. "That act brings no disrespect down on your head. Quite the contrary, your action will be seen as just and right. You are not seizing the bull for your own use, but giving it to the gods. Also, by killing the bull you remove the cause for this war. How can the warring parties begin hostilities again when the cause is removed? Afterwards, you will be applauded as a peacemaker."

The king listened, and he decided to act. He gave instructions for wood to be gathered and piled into a pyramid, ready for the torch. Sixty strong warriors held the beast in ropes, and one cut off its head. It took three mighty blows from his strongest warrior to kill the beast. Then the smith broke the chain, and the warriors dragged the carcass to the pyre. Diarmuid issued instructions to skin the beast and clean the hide. When the servants had skinned the beast, they placed the body and head on the wooden pyramid, and set it on fire. Ingall uttered incantations over the burning pyramid, offering the beast to the gods. The black smoke drifted in rings to the clouded sky, watched by the druid. Ingall turned to the king and said the gods were pleased with his sacrifice.

Now King Diarmuid issued instructions to his servants and he ordered them to send messages to the four provinces, informing the kings that the reason for the war had been removed. He had sacrificed the bull to appease the angry gods, killing the beast and burning it in sacrifice. The servants sent out four fast riders to the kings of the four provinces. It was appropriate that the words were written in Ogham, because Ogma had been responsible for giving guidance to Diarmuid.

At Knocknashee, a servant brought the message to Turnod the druid, who read the words with unconcealed delight. He rushed to the royal couple, clutching the message in his hand, and excitedly spoke to Maeve and Ailill. "My lord and lady, great news from Diarmuid. The beast has been slain and offered to the gods. The immortals are pleased with the burnt sacrifice, for I hear Goddess Shannon is fast retreating from the lands. Their anger at the war has been demonstrated daily, for our province has suffered many deprivations. Now is the time for peace."

"How easily you forget the insult to your queen in this matter," Maeve responded. "Neither should you forget the insult to your province. Why has Diarmuid slain the beast? To appease the gods, or to become High King in more than name? How readily you are willing to bow the knee to foreign rule, Turnod."

The druid was taken aback by the harsh rebuke of the queen, and responded immediately, "Maeve, I value the independence of this province as much as you. The message in my hand is good and that is why I rushed here. We have drained our lands of men and everyone has suffered. The bogs lie idle and have not been cut. The wolves have multiplied and feast on our sheep, as Morrigan feasts on the flesh of our dead warriors. My queen, what do you require to put an end to this war?"

"Turnod, there is much wisdom in the words you say," Ailill said. "Let us dwell on them before we decide. We need more than that piece of parchment in your hand to satisfy us. We need assurances of our continued independence, and we need an apology for our province. Only then could we consider ending the war."

At Emain Macha, Connor discussed the message with his druid, Nolan. The king desired to end the war and spoke to the druid, "There is nothing I desire more than to end this war. The message you carry makes it clear that the gods want it ended too. Let us hastily arrange a meeting and talk terms of peace."

"My lord, it cannot be argued that peace is preferable to war," Nolan said. "If some concessions are required to end this war, then they should be given freely. I doubt if anyone recalls at this stage how or why it started. There is another matter that requires your urgent attention. Princess Emer has run away from the unfinished palace at Navan, and I believe Morrigan is to blame. I know not the reason why she has caused the princess to run away, but in my opinion the goddess of war is up to no good."

Chapter Twenty-Three

Goddess Shannon approached the iron gates by night and sought admittance to the Otherworld. Epona granted her wish, opening the iron gates with the key she kept on her graceful neck. Goddess Shannon sought out Lugh and asked him to accompany her to the land of mortals. Lugh joined with her in nightly flight, and side by side they flew to the broad Shannon, and to the middle lake on the river. The pair alighted on the shore of the broad lake, dark and silent in the night.

"This wide lake is called Lough Ree, the Lake of the King," the goddess said. "In this lake lies the supreme symbol of your power and authority. Dagda knew of its existence when he held the title, King of the Otherworld. Now that you have attained the title, I will demonstrate the terrible power at your command."

With these words, she waved her watery hand over the dark lake. In an instant, the waters began to boil and change from darkness to light. Steam hissed forth in a cauldron of light, and a fiery spear arose from the lake. The spear lit up the night sky, and Lugh watched as the trees around the lake burst into fire. Soon all the surrounding areas burned with the intensity of a forest fire whipped up by summer winds.

"What is it?" asked Lugh.

"The Spear of Light," replied the goddess. "It is the symbol of your power and majesty. The spear must be kept in water, for it burns everything when removed. It is invincible in battle, and no man or god can withstand its power. This spear has the capacity to destroy not only this world, but also your world. Therefore, the king who controls it must be wise and just. If you demand the spear from me once, I shall refuse you once. If you demand the spear from me a second time, I shall refuse you twice. However, if you demand the spear from me a third time, I cannot refuse you."

"From where did this terrible weapon come?" asked Lugh.

"It came from distant Persia," replied the goddess. "It was not taken here by warriors, but by three poets. They killed the King of Persia to obtain it, such was its lure. Then they regretted their actions because poets must respect life, not destroy it. In shame they sought to redeem their actions by making a present to me. The spear became my responsibility. I revealed it to Dagda, who has now gone missing. He demanded the spear once, but I refused. He demanded it twice, but I refused. Perhaps only then he realised it has the power to destroy the whole world. Now the spear is your responsibility, Lugh."

"Destroy it," commanded Lugh.

"I cannot," replied the goddess, "for the knowledge to build another exists. Lugh, you are King of the Otherworld, but even your great powers cannot destroy knowledge." She directed his eyes to three charred skeletons lying beside the lake. "These are the bones of the poets who brought the weapon to this lake. They took it here in the skin of a bull filled with water. They put the skin on the lake and watched it sail like a ship on the waves. But I snagged the skin on a rock and it burst open, revealing the spear. In an instant, they were consumed by fire."

"Return it to the lake," said Lugh. "Such a weapon must never be used, even against those we hate." When Goddess Shannon had returned the Spear of Light to its home, Lugh asked, "Is it your destiny to inform every King of the Otherworld of this weapon?"

"That is my destiny," replied the goddess.

"Even an evil king who would use it in anger?"

"That is my destiny, Lugh. We must therefore hope that the gods are wise enough not to select an evil king to rule over them."

In the rich province of Ulster, near wide Lough Neagh, two large panting wolfhounds chased a yellow-eyed grey wolf through a greening forest under a full moon. The forest rang to their deep baying and echoed in the ears of Cuchulainn and Fidelma. They ran naked after the two wolfhounds trying to keep up, calling out the names of the hounds. The names of Crom and Abu echoed in the haunted greening forest.

The two hounds halted temporarily, and then continued the chase. Fidelma stumbled and called out to Cuchulainn. He stopped running and returned to pick her up from the mossy earth, lifting her from the floor of the greening forest. Beneath the trees, in the echoes of the baying wolfhounds, the two lovers embraced and kissed.

"Guilt should overwhelm me because Emer has disappeared from sight, and yet I cannot help myself," she said. "A fairy or some other creature has taken control of my mind and taken it away from me. My husband is dead and I should be unhappy, but I have never been as happy in my life. You are wed to Emer, and I should not be here alone with you, but I wish to spend every hour of every day at your side."

Cuchulainn put her down and clasped his hands in the shape of a trumpet, calling out to the dogs, and commanding them to give up the chase. "Since this needy war started, I have become a different man," he said. "I know this forest well, and yet is different than before. War makes me look with new eyes on familiar scenes, and view them in a different light. Lorcan was my brother, and I loved him, and yet I feel no guilt loving his widow. Emer has run away from my rising palace at Navan and I should be searching for her, and yet I am in this shady forest with you. Fidelma, I have not the knowledge of a druid to explain such things, but I feel more alive in this time of war than I did in the times of peace. One day in war is more exciting than a hundred years in peace. I pray this war lasts for a thousand years."

"Your mother believes I should wear black and sprinkle ashes over my head," she said, embracing him. "She is of a different generation. I am young, and the fires of life burn in my breast. Does she expect me to end my life because Lorcan ended his?"

"No, life must be enjoyed for it is all too brief," he said. Fidelma took his hand in hers, and they walked beneath the green canopy, the baying of the hounds echoing in their ears.

"My love, what is to become of us, or dare we turn the page and glance at the future?" she mused. "I think not, I think it is better to live for the day, for the hour, for the moment. Let us enjoy the moment, for once gone it does not return. I should feel shame at my actions, but I do not. Look at the budding leaves on the trees, my love. They have never been as green or as bright as this since the dawn of time. Look, Crom and Abu return, their tongues licking the ground!"

Cuchulainn knelt on the mossy ground and softly muzzled the wolfhounds. Their tails wagged, and they licked his beaming face.

"We should not feel guilt because these things are beyond our control," he told her, his fingers tickling the dogs. "You could be miserable in the palace of my parents keening for lost Lorcan, and I could be miserable searching the fields and forests for Emer. Instead we have with eager hearts seized our chance of happiness, and now we are both happy. So let us enjoy this whilst it lasts, for it cannot last for ever."

Fidelma sat beside him on a fallen log, and made reply. "Your mother scolds me as a harlot, and the words roll off my mind like water from a duck's back. She says I am not a good mother, leaving my children to be with you. Am I not entitled to chase the rainbow of happiness as the dogs chase the wolf? I am young, and unable to contemplate a life of loneliness."

Cuchulainn played with the wolfhounds, and replied. "In the time of peace, when I attended your wedding to Lorcan at Emain Macha, I did not notice your beauty, or how the sun glinted on your auburn hair. Now, in this time of war I notice how it moves in the breeze, and the way it falls when your head tilts, like a breeze over summer wheat. Emer is my wife, but you are my love. See how the wolfhounds are eager to continue the chase. Come, let us run through the forest and chase the yellow-eyed wolf."

On the small tree-covered island of Devenish, Ferdia and Devlina made preparations to visit Emain Macha. A messenger of the king had informed them that Emer was missing. Devlina wished to remain on the island alone, but Ferdia persuaded her to accompany him because he feared for her safety. By fast currach they crossed the lake, trailing two horses in its watery wake. They pulled the currach from the water, mounted the horses, and rode to Emain Macha.

The king saw the couple riding up the sandy road and went out to greet them wearing an unhappy countenance. He kissed Devlina on both cheeks and told her he wished to speak with Ferdia alone. "Ferdia, Emer has gone missing," the king related when Devlina had entered the palace. "As we speak, every servant and every warrior is scouring the province for her. All that is except her husband."

"Father, I can see by the growing lines in your face that this war weighs heavy on your mind. It has gone on far too long and we must do everything we can to end the conflict. I need a change of horse, and your hounds, Crom and Abu. Where are they?"

"Shame hangs over my gloomy palace as a dark bird of doom," confessed the king. "Your brother, who should be out searching for his missing wife, is in the forests running wild with Fidelma. That pair have lost their wits and their sense of shame! Your poor mother cries herself to sleep every night. I have spoken to my son and to Fidelma, but my entreaties are ignored. Nightly beneath the stars I offer sacrifices of burnt stags to Aengus and beseech of him to break the spell, but he too ignores me."

Ferdia put an arm around the drooping shoulders of his father, and walked up the sandy road with him. "This endless war is to blame, not my brother or Fidelma," he said. "It has raised their senses, and dulled their understanding of what is right and what is wrong. Fidelma is human. She has lost her husband, and a grieving woman tends to seek solace anywhere she can find it. My brother is under stress caused by the war. It is understandable that the widow and the warrior were attracted to each other."

Princess Emer, on reaching the ford of the Shannon, crossed, and continued on the westward road to Knocknashee, stopping only when darkness fell on the land. After three days and three nights on the westward road she arrived at the outskirts of the hillfort, but was too overcome by cold and hunger to continue. She slipped from the horse and fell on the wooden road.

When the riderless horse arrived at Knocknashee, the servants went in search of the rider. They found her lying in the heather by the road, and carried her inside. The female servants of the queen removed her wet clothes, and bathed her body. Then they put her to bed and reported to the queen.

"We know not who she is, except that she appears to be of royal blood," a servant told the queen. "She is sick, for the cold has entered her bones. As we speak, Turnod is applying hot mead to her lips, though her lips do not move. I fear she will not recover."

Maeve hurried to the room, and recognised the young woman, for it was her youngest sister. "How is her health, Turnod?"

"My queen, she coughs in her sleep, but her eyes do not open. I have seen this sickness before and only they strong in body can survive. She is not strong, and it appears that she has not eaten for weeks."

"Tell the servants to remain with her day and night, never leaving her side" instructed Maeve. "Do not feed her mead, but pure heather honey. Pray to the gods too, Turnod. We need them now more than ever."

Emer did not recover, though heather honey was poured into her unwaking mouth. She did speak however, turning and tossing in the bed. The fever in her mind loosed her tongue, and words came out in torrents. The servants listened to her wild words, and reported back to the queen.

Maeve sent out fast riders and called a conference of the chiefs. The ford of the Shannon was passable, and plans were required for the new campaign. The chiefs responded to the messengers and journeyed to Knocknashee. They came and feasted, drinking mead and dark brown ale. During the feast, Ailill rose to speak at the head of the table. None made jokes about him now, for the wound had endowed him with much honour.

"My good friends," he began, "we have in our high ringfort the wife of Cuchulainn. She speaks not except in her fevers, but we have learned that she has run away from her husband. This is another sign from the gods that we are in the right." A loud cheer greeted his words. "My friends, the gods have given a sign that the house of Connor is a house of debauchery, for why else should she run away? Does such a house deserve to stand?"

The cheers gave Ailill the answer he required.

One chief did not cheer. "My king," Mac Carthy said, "the actions of an unhappy wife must not be used to tarnish a whole province, or a good king. Neither should such actions be used as a pretext for war. The goldenhide bull is dead. Let this war die with that accursed beast."

"Malachi," said Maeve, "the immortal gods give men signs to guide their way. The signs are there for all to see. The goddess of the Shannon has withdrawn the waters from the ford. My youngest sister has been treated with contempt at the palace of Connor. She has chosen to live here instead. What more signs do you need?"

"My queen," replied the old chief, "signs can be interpreted by each party to their own advantage. To reach the kernel of the hazel nut, the hard shell must be broken. Let us break the hard outer shell of this war to reach the kernel. The bull is dead, and therefore the alleged cause for this war removed. Yet you propose to continue the war. So there must be another reason. Can the kernel of this senseless war be the naked ambition of a queen?"

"The chief goes too far, criticizing the queen in her own palace!" Maeve replied, her eyes flashing in anger.

"We are here to debate, and this is not the time or place to curb our tongues," replied Mac Carthy. "Our queen should first listen and then give her opinion and her ruling. I suspect Morrigan has promised Connaught victory in this war. That cruel goddess cares not for our province, or any other for that matter. I suspect that this needless war began with her lying words. Neither can her promises be trusted. We must end the war now, and an agreement made so that both provinces can hold their heads high."

"The chief should be reminded of our punishment for insults to a king or queen," Maeve said, calmer now. "He is taken to a bog where his upper arms are pierced with hazel rods and bound to his body. His throat is cut and his body thrown into a boghole. Then the boghole is covered in clumps of heather to hide his shame. Malachi, you have high standing in our assembly and province, but I would advise you to choose your words carefully."

Two young chiefs were dismayed by the words of the old chief, and regarded him as a coward. They were high in dark brown ale, and strong drink moves the young to act. They rushed at the old chief and seized him violently, pushing him from the hall of feasting. Ailill called on them to stop, but the strong drink waxed their ears.

"Niall, I promised the spirit of your father that I would take care of his family," Mac Carthy said beneath a full moon. A chill wind blew over the ringfort from the western sea, whining in the stones. "I have fulfilled that promise by cutting turf for your mother and tending her flocks. I speak to you now as I spoke to my own son. This is a war that has no meaning. Get on your horse and return to your mother."

The advice of the old chief was lost on the young chiefs, for their ears were deaf to reason. Killing was in their hearts and swords in their hands. It was young Niall O'Brien who struck the first blow, plunging his sword into the breast of Mac Carthy. The blow did not kill the old chief. He staggered to the wall, clinging to the cold stones for support. Grian Guinan struck the second blow, and Mac Carthy fell dead beneath the high walls of Knocknashee. Overhead, the shrill winds blew cold like the keening of old women.

Epona mounted Cappall and galloped across the western sea and the land, sparks flying from the silver hooves of the horse. She plucked her golden harp, and the spirit of the dead chief departed his body. Then she washed and purified the spirit of the slain chief, and garlanded it in red roses. Holding the spirit in her tender arms, she sped on Capall to the iron gates of the Otherworld.

"Noble spirit," she said, inserting the rose-bound key in the iron gates and leading Capall inside, "warriors do not listen to truth in the palaces of war, and they who speak it put themselves in danger. Neither do they listen to wise words when their blood is up. Your words were brave in that palace, but they were also very foolish. Come, I take you to the isles of the spirits. There you can live in peace."

Darkest gloom stalked the wooden palace at Emain Macha with heavy and leaden feet. Queen Rosheen was in her bedroom and refusing to come out. The shame hung heavy on her shoulders. The mood of the palace affected the servants too, and they went about their duties with heavy hearts.

Devlina became a substitute mother for the children of Lorcan and Fidelma. Daily she bathed and fed the little boy and girl, and played with them in the orchard behind the palace. She took full responsibility for their education, teaching them in the orchard beneath hanging boughs. Soon they could identify the birds by sight, and the trees and flowers. The children slept in the same room as Devlina and Ferdia, so that if they awoke in the night she was there for them. In the darkness, Ferdia lay awake. Devlina too was awake by his side, listening to the gentle snoring of the children.

"Emer is in Connaught," Ferdia said.

"In the province of our enemy? How do you know?"

"Because her husband cannot go there, Devlina."

"Her husband is at fault not Emer, Ferdia."

"No, this unnecessary war is at fault."

In the early morning, as dawn was slowly breaking, they were awakened by the deep-throated baying of Crom and Abu. The dogs were returning from the hunt, barking as they approached the palace. Ripples of laughter replaced the baying hounds, the shared happiness of a man and a woman. Fidelma and Cuchulainn were dressed now to enter the palace. Their voices echoed the baying hounds, and the laughter rang out over the sleeping fields and over the royal palace.

Ferdia left the bed and pulled on his white woollen cloak, clasping it at the neck with a circular brooch. He went outside and watched the happy couple strolling up the sandy road, two panting hounds at their side. In contrast to the dark mood in the palace, their happiness glowed like a rainbow after rain. But Ferdia was visibly angry at their behaviour and it manifested in his voice.

"In times of war one side always seeks to exploit the weakness in the other side," he began. "Your disregard for the conventions of wedlock will be seized upon by Connaught. This is no time for flouting our sacred laws. This is a time to remain steadfast and true to our vows. Fidelma, your first duty is to care for your two young children. As for you, my young brother, your duty is to win back your wife, and to abide by the lawful vows of wedlock."

The sharp rebuke of Ferdia did not offend Cuchulainn, or remove his smile. "Brother, the man who finds happiness does not lightly give it up," he replied. "As for rules or conventions, in times of war they do not apply. In these times, we must live life to the full each day since we cannot plan for tomorrow. Can a man be with a wife he does not love or who does not love him? Is it not better to be with a woman he loves so that his days can be happy?"

"There is more to this affair than the happiness of one man and one woman," Ferdia said. "Our mother has taken to her room and refuses to come out. Our father is stooped from the burden of guilt he bears. Bad news travels faster than the swiftest hawk, and there is no doubt that in the palaces of the four provinces they are talking about your affair with the wife of your dead brother. Think of the harm you do to the reputation of Ulster."

"Have I not fought for Ulster, my brother, and driven her enemies from our sacred soil?" answered Cuchulainn. "Does Ulster also desire me to be unhappy? Or perhaps Ulster prefers hypocrisy to truth? Ferdia, I am unable to live a lie. I will not give up Fidelma."

"Then you must give up my brother," Ferdia said to Fidelma. "My wife cares for your children. They regard her as their mother, though they are not her flesh and blood. Do not further provoke the gods by neglecting your children."

"Was I not a good wife to Lorcan?" she said. "He died the death of a hero, but I am expected to live like a recluse, not seen or heard. In the palace of your father, everyone praises Lorcan though he is dead. None praises me though I am alive. Are the dead of more importance than the living? Why should my life end because his life has ended?"

"There are others you can wed," Ferdia said.

"I have made my choice and I care not what your father says," she answered. "My choice is the bravest warrior in the world, and I am the happiest woman. A million women would trade places with me if they had the chance. Neither do I care what the gods say, for mortals must choose their own way in life. Cuchulainn and I are more alive in this hour than we have ever been. Who else can say that?"

"Ferdia, you are my foster-brother, and yet I love you more than if we were natural brothers," Cuchulainn said. "But we are different, you and I. Your eyes see the future, but mine see only the present. I live for the moment, for tomorrow might never come."

Chapter Twenty-Four

King Ailill dispatched from Knocknashee four fast messengers to the kings, informing them that Emer was sick in his ringfort. Her eyes had not opened, and the servants were keeping her alive by pouring honey into her unfeeling mouth. Her flight from Ulster was a sign from the gods that Connaught was in the right. The king set out his terms for a permanent peace. He demanded an apology from Connor, to be read at Royal Tara. He demanded an annual tribute of ninety gold bars, nine chariots, and nine hundred sheep. He demanded the land of Donegal which he claimed had always been part of Connaught. If Connor submitted to his demands, the war would end. If Connor did not submit, the war would continue.

The message of the king was received at Emain Macha with mixed emotions. King Connor was indeed relieved that the princess was safe, though he was concerned for her state of health. However, the demands of Ailill alarmed and confused him. Over breakfast of boiled eggs and brown breads he consulted with his sons.

"We should have finished them at the Shannon," Cuchulainn said. "Now they grow bolder day by day. What is Ailill playing at? He makes demands from a position of weakness, not a position of strength. That is against all logic of warfare."

"He thinks we have lost the heart to fight, and that we will accept peace at any price," Ferdia said.

"Gladly would I give the gold and chariots and animals, but tearing Donegal from Ulster is out of the question," Connor said. "Where did that outrageous demand come from? Donegal has always been part of our province and his claim is false."

"Clearly we can see that Ailill sends conditions we cannot accept," Cuchulainn said. "He sets the wall too high for us to jump and that is an act of provocation. The king feels confident of victory, else he would have set the wall much lower. We must assemble our forces and march immediately. We must hit him such a blow that Connaught never recovers, not in a thousand years."

"Our most pressing concern must be the health of Emer," said Ferdia. "Our best physicians should be dispatched at once to Knocknashee to cure her sleeping sickness."

"We are in a state of war with Connaught," Cuchulainn said. "Our physicians are not welcome there. I say we strike first, and with sudden and overwhelming force of arms. Let us assemble our army and cross the Shannon ford. Better to fight them in their own province and let them feel the hot fires of war for a change."

"Let me go to Connaught under the brief aegis of truce and speak with Maeve and Ailill," suggested Ferdia. "Honour is not dead in that poor province yet, for the warring queen met me on the field of battle and treated me with courtesy. Messengers do not make decisions, but as the son of the king I have that power. Perhaps I can end this conflict by debating with them face to face."

Although Cuchulainn strongly objected, the king granted his assent and blessing, and Ferdia prepared to depart for Knocknashee. Before departing, he embraced and kissed his wife. "None but the immortal gods know what tomorrow holds, Devlina," he said. "I have no doubts of my good reception at Knocknashee, but I fear the mischief of Morrigan."

She placed her lips on his lips. "Fight her too, as you would the enemies of Ulster," she said.

As Ferdia departed to the west, a squat rider arrived from the east, riding up the sandy road on a white mule. His lined face was browned by the sun, and a slant scar ran from forehead to chin. He wore a black patch over his right eye, interrupting the running line of the scar. The servants offered to bathe him, but the visitor asked to be taken immediately to the king.

When the visitor entered the room where the king and his son were eating, Cuchulainn leaped up and embraced him.

"Scathnach," he said, "you are most welcome in Emain Macha. Come, be seated. Dine with us on boiled eggs and brown bread. What is ours is yours."

The visitor greeted Connor by kissing his cheeks, and replied to his son, "Mead is the best food after a long journey! You have growed, boy. Nine years have passed since I came to this palace from the land of the Danube. In the fields around this palace, I taught you and Ferdia the art of weapons, though your father did not agree with me back then. Noble Connor, I recall you tried to stop me teaching your sons, for you desired to live in peace. I think you realise now that the king who seeks to live in peace must be always prepared for hard war."

The royal servants brought the visitor a jug of mead. He drank a great gulp, wiping his chin. "Remember this, boy?" he asked, running his fingers over the scar. "It was in the winter when the snow lay thick on the ground. On that snowy day you and Ferdia were defending this palace in mock combat against my assault. I brushed Ferdia easily aside, but you challenged me. The pupil beat the teacher that day and I have the scar to prove it. No harm done, for you were under a solemn oath to defend Ulster."

"The oath remains," Cuchulainn replied. "As we speak here, Ferdia journeys to Connaught to discuss terms of peace."

"Yes, I have heard about the war," Scathnach nodded.

Connor took from his woollen tunic the parchment sent by Ailill. He read the terms demanded by the King of Connaught. Scathnach listened in silence to the demands, shaking his head from side to side. Connor finished reading and put the parchment inside his tunic.

Scathnach drank the mead, nodding his great head. "A guest should not cause offence in the home of his host, but I believe in straight talk. Noble Connor, it was a mistake sending Ferdia to talk terms of peace. The best response to an outrageous demand is an armed attack. If you pay once, Ailill shall soon be back for more. Next year his demands shall be higher again, and higher again the next year. No province can live like that, or no king."

"The words of Scathnach are wise, father," said Cuchulainn. "Not only is Ulster regarded as a weak province by talking peace with the aggressor, we are regarded as having no honour."

"Enough men have already died in this war," the king said. "If my son can come to an agreement with Connaught, I am willing to pay the price. Besides, Connaught is a poor province of bogs and marshes that needs our help."

271

"Most noble king, at your old and venerable age you should be living in a province at peace," said Scathnach. "But peace has a high price, and sometimes that price is the death of his subjects in battle. The province that sacrifices its warriors to defend its honour is held in high regard by friend and foe alike; but the province that is unwilling to fight, or to sign an unworthy treaty of peace, is regarded with disdain by all. That is a red stain of shame that no amount of water can wash away."

"I agree with him, father," Cuchulainn said. "If Connaught is poor, whose fault is that? Surely it is not the fault of Ulster that they live the way they do? They should look to themselves before blaming you for their poverty! Listen to the good sense of the warrior at your side, and send an army across the Shannon."

"Let us wait and see what Ferdia brings back," Connor said. "My old friend, you are welcome to remain in my home for as long as you desire."

"My ship departs in three days," Scathnach said, opening his bag. It was made of leather, finely stitched, and carved with intricate designs. From the bag he removed a circular iron object, shaped like a bowl. He placed it on the oak table, saying: "This weapon is called the *gae bolga*. It is a weapon of last resort, since no honour can be gained in its use. However, all types of weapons must be used to defeat an enemy that seeks to destroy you. Noble Connor, this weapon can save Ulster from destruction, and also save your family."

"My family is my most important possession," Connor said.

"This weapon can protect them," assured Scathnach.

Cuchulainn held the weapon in his hands, examined it, and asked, "How does it work? It has no cutting edges."

"It is thrown on the water as skimming a flat stone," said Scathnach. "The twisting movement releases the hidden barbs. They are as stings from a thousand bees. When the weapon touches the flesh of an adversary, the barbs enter his body and run through it as fish in a stream. Death comes in an instant."

In the high hilltop fort at Knocknashee, two goddesses stood unseen at the bedside of Emer, where the sick princess slept the sleep of fitful unrest. Her eyes had not opened, and daily she became weaker, her body wasting away. Lovely Brigid went on the offensive against Morrigan, and she did not conceal her hatred.

"Evil goddess of war," she said, "I have journeyed here out of pity to administer to the princess. I have the ability to cure her, but you have blocked my every effort. Is compassion not known to you, or do you delight in cold death?"

The goddess of war did not try to conceal her contempt for Brigid either. "I have told you many times not to interfere in earthly matters that you do not comprehend," she replied. "You are a goddess who sees the swan on the surface of the lake, but I am the goddess who sees below the surface. What do you know about important matters of war? You perform good deeds, not for their own sake but to gain esteem in the eyes of others. Begone, and leave me to do my work."

Brigid did not move, but folded her pale arms. "Your evil reputation is well known to all, but I cannot believe you can stand idly by and let this young girl die when I can cure her."

"I have been ordered by our new king to end this war and I shall do it in my own manner," Morrigan said. "Let me tell you what your problem is, and do not always have

273

your pretty, silly head in the clouds. You think men are tinted with beauty, but I see them as they really are. They are base creatures, redeemed only in the hot heat of war. They live briefly before they die, but they live forever on the tongues of bards when they die in noble conflict."

As the goddesses argued over the sleeping princess, Ferdia crossed the ford of the Boyne and journeyed to Royal Tara, paying his passing respects to the High King. He informed Diarmuid of his mission, and his host wished him well. As Ferdia talked with the High King inside the royal palace, a servant brushed the hide of the slain beast outside. The huge hide was stretched between two stone pillars, drying in the pale sun. In the afternoon sun, it appeared to be burnished in gold.

Chapter Twenty-Five

The sacred and universal laws of hospitality were extended to the prince on his arrival at Knocknashee though he was an enemy of Connaught. A woolly sheep was slain and skinned and prepared for the cauldron. As the stew was cooking, the servants heated water and bathed Ferdia and supplied fresh clothes. Before he sat down to eat, Ferdia asked to see the princess.

He stood over the sick princess and took her hand in his. Life was ebbing slowly from her body, her breathing quiet and uneven. Lifting her head gently, he said: "Where has the cheeky young princess gone?" He kissed her softly on the forehead, and left the room.

Night fell, and under the torches in the kitchen Ferdia dined with the royal couple. "We do not have much, but what we have, we share with our guests," Ailill said. "By Lugh, Ferdia, your arm is strong!" He exposed his thigh and revealed the wound. "Heather honey has made it small now, but I assure you that my thigh-bone was exposed by the blow. Such things happen in war however, and I bear no grudge."

"This sheep stew is good, Ailill," he said. "As for my spear, it was aimed at your heart! Let me assure you that I am happy now that my spear did not find its true target.

Let us forget about our differences for this night and discuss Emer, for her plight is more urgent."

"My sister is on the road to the Otherworld," Maeve said. "Our best physicians can find no cure for her condition. They believe it is a disease of the body, though they have cured such diseases in the past. I instructed Turnod to drink the sacred brew, and he visited Brigid in his vision. The goddess informed him that Emer suffers a disease of the heart."

"Of the heart?" asked Ferdia.

"Yes, she loves a man who is not her husband."

"Have you offered burnt sacrifice to Brigid?" he asked. "The lovely goddess can cure any malady. She knitted my brother's wrist at Royal Tara and it is stronger than ever."

"Yes, we have sacrificed a ram to summon the goddess from the Otherworld but she did not come," said Ailill. "Ferdia, our provinces are at war; but we do not make war on women though she is the wife of our most implacable enemy. She is protected in Knocknashee by the sacred laws of hospitality and she is welcome to remain here. Her father is sending his best physicians and they are due here tomorrow bearing healing herbs. That is all can be done for the moment. Now, let us talk of our conflict."

"Time is most important so I shall come straight to the point," said Ferdia, finishing the stew. "Now is not the occasion to pin blame on anyone as a brooch is pinned to a cloak. My noble father has no objections to gold or sheep for he believes a rich province must help its poor neighbour. He sends his apologies that he has not helped Connaught in the past and raised it up to the same level of good living as Ulster. For when all provinces are equal, there is no envy and the causes for war are removed. But the demand for the land of Donegal he cannot meet. That has always been part of Ulster, and no king can split his kingdom and hope to survive."

The queen clapped her ringed hands, and Turnod entered the kitchen bearing a rolled scroll in his hands. Maeve cleared the eating vessels and the old druid spread the scroll on the table, unfurling the parchment. It was a map of the country, old and battered with age. The five provinces were clearly marked out and bordered, and within them the counties. Ferdia studied the map, and to his utter dismay saw that the land of Donegal was within the boundary of Connaught.

"Where did this map come from?" he asked.

"It has been in our family for generations," Ailill replied.

"Why has it not been brought to our attention before now?" Ferdia asked, glancing from Maeve to Ailill. "Yearly our men of law visit Royal Tara on the feast of Lughnasa, and resolve disputes over property. The records of the lands and who owns the lands are kept there. The records clearly show that Donegal is part of our province and always has been."

"This map is older than the maps at Royal Tara," Turnod said. "Indeed, it was drawn in the time of the Milesians. They came from Spain many centuries ago and conquered the native inhabitants. They divided the island into five provinces and this is their map."

Ferdia rubbed his chin, his head shaking, his mind struggling against this new development. The map appeared genuine. The parchment was old and worn, and the words on the map were written in an unknown language. Ferdia understood Oghham, but he did not understand the words on the map. Yet there was no doubt in his mind that Donegal was inside the boundary line of Connaught.

"The night has aged and I am tired," he said. "Let me think on this map and give my answer in the morning."

A servant led him to his room in the hilltop fort. Before going to bed, he visited the room where Emer slept. Two servants were seated at her bedside. One was bathing her forehead in cold water, and the second was feeding honey into her unfeeling mouth.

Ferdia could not nor did not sleep, tossing and turning in his bed, trying to solve the riddle of the ancient map. He rose from the bed and slipped on his cloak and sandals. Walking outside, he shivered in the cold wind blowing from the sea, pulling his cloak over his head. Standing in the ringfort illuminated by shafts of pale moonlight, he experienced a sense of sympathy for Ailill and Maeve.

Unlike Emain Macha, Knocknashee was heavily fortified, indicating that the royal couple existed in a state of fear. The land outside the walls was poor, unable to sustain crops. The ringfort reflected the poverty of the land for the floors of the royal residence were covered in hard earth, unlike the waxed wooden floors of his father's palace. Emain Macha nestled in groves of oak trees and holly trees, but no trees grew in Knocknashee, and the land only supported stones.

Next morning he dined with the king and queen. A servant reheated stew and ladled it into three bowls. Ferdia ate the stew with a wooden spoon and talked about the weather. Summer's end was in the air, the nights turning cooler. Soon they would celebrate the festival of Sowain.

"Ailill," he began, forsaking the weather, "kings live in the present, but they should live in the future. That is why they are much more concerned with today than with tomorrow. We must consider the future of our provinces if this war is not ended soon. Have you heard Lugh is now king of the Otherworld?"

"Yes, Turnod has been informed by Brigid," said Ailill.

"We must take a page from the book of the gods and learn from them," explained Ferdia. "We should recognise what our problems are. The five provinces are each far too independent. No king recognises any authority but his own. As a result, we exist in a state of constant tension. Once a year we journey to Royal Tara to resolve our differences, and even then there is squabbling over minor issues."

"As king, you would cede independence?" asked Ailill.

"Yes, part of it for better security," replied Ferdia. "We need a High King with the authority to knock heads together. Each province must cede part of its power to a single authority. That single authority must be given the power to end disputes by dialogue, not by conflict. We need a High King in authority, not in name."

"We will never agree to such an arrangement," Ailill said.

"We must look at better ways of resolving our differences," Ferdia said. "However, let us deal with the present. Ulster is prepared to help Connaught with gifts of gold and sheep; but not as an annual tribute, and that is what you are demanding. Tributes are given to overlords, and you are not overlord of Ulster."

"You are well skilled in the ways of diplomacy," Ailill said. "Words are of little importance to me. If Connor sends sheep and gold and chariots, I will gladly accept them as gifts. Yet I see there is something troubling you. What is it?"

"Bring me the map," Ferdia said.

Turnod brought the ancient map and unrolled it on the table. Ferdia enquired about the princess, and the druid replied that the physicians of her father were administering to her.

"I do not dispute the authenticity of this document, but I do question its time in the present scheme of things," Ferdia began. "The Milesians arrived here from Spain and took the land by force of arms. Then they divided it up between themselves. That was in their time, but time does not stand still for kings. We have moved on, and in this time the boundaries of the five provinces are fixed, and they are recorded at Royal Tara. We who live in the present cannot return to the past, and neither can we use old maps to redraw new boundaries. That would cause chaos and present insurmountable problems for all our peoples. Let me give ye an example. Let us suppose that the Milesians returned and claimed back this land. Would we not fight them? Of course we would because we now occupy this land. Therefore, we must always see how things stand in the present, not how we perceive them in the past. As matters now stand, Donegal is part of Ulster, and this map does not change that fact. Ulster has right on her side, and that right is backed up by legal documents at Royal Tara."

Ailill and Maeve pondered on the speech of Ferdia, and could find no faults in his argument. "Good prince," Ailill replied, "your words make sense, but we have a map. We require more land, for we find it difficult to survive here. Ulster is rich in land and Connor does not need Donegal. We are poor, and we do."

"Ailill, you talk about land without mentioning the people living on the land," replied Ferdia. "Donegal is peopled by men and women of Ulster. They are a proud people and they pay full allegiance to their king. They are like sons to my father and no father gives away his sons. Therefore, your unlawful demand is denied."

"Then the war resumes," said Maeve.

"Good queen," replied Ferdia, "peace should always be made when possible, for war is the throw of the dice. None can know how the dice turn up. War is a gamble conceived by a deceitful goddess. Peace with honour is far better than war with uncertainty. The queen must also remember that Ulster has my brother to defend her, and he is by far the greatest warrior in the land."

"The prince plays a hard game," Ailill said. "We do not intend to push our claim to Donegal. In diplomacy, there must be give and take. No side gets all its demands in negotiations, and that is a fact. We are prepared to leave the current boundaries as they stand, and as they are recorded in the books at Royal Tara. However, we do seek an apology from Ulster for starting this war."

"Ailill, Ulster did not start this war," the prince replied. "To apologise for a crime we have not committed is not only foolish, but also a sign of weakness. Ulster is always reluctant to fight, but Ulster has never shirked a fight. The king should not doubt the resolve of my province."

The negotiations continued until noon, but the parties could reach no conclusion. The apology proved the stumbling block. Neither side was prepared to give ground, though they talked until noon. A word from the prince could have resolved the matter, but he was not prepared to issue an apology because the honour of his province was at stake.

In the late afternoon, Ferdia mounted his horse, and rode down the wooden road beneath a sky of driving rain. As night fell on the lone rider, he dismounted and struck a flint, succeeding after many attempts in making a fire. He pulled a cloak over his shoulders and sat down at the fire. Wolves howled in the falling darkness, and Ferdia comforted the nervous horse. The flat marshy landscape danced with yellow eyes, wolves on the prowl, and the dark night resounded with their piercing howls. On the wings of darkness, a raven flew over man and horse, and hovered over the land.

At Emain Macha, King Connor listened to his firstborn in silence, his white head shaking. The news that Ferdia brought from Connaught grew progressively more serious in the telling. Princess Emer was dying in Knocknashee and he feared the physicians of her father could not save her life. Ailill and Maeve were inflexible in their war-demands. Not satisfied with rich gifts, they were also demanding an apology. This was a step too far, and Ferdia reported that he was forced to choose war rather than betray Ulster.

"Evil comes in many different guises, but war has no equal," Connor said. "How I wish we could turn back time and start all over again. We should have explored every possibility for peace, but we left it in the lap of the gods. We should have used our own brains to prevent this war, and not relied on them!"

"Father, the health of the sick princess is our most pressing concern," Ferdia said. "We must make sacrifice to Brigid. We must kill our finest bulls and rams. Meanwhile, I need to return to the island of Devenish, and in the peace of that island find a solution. Let us hope that the physicians of her father can keep her alive until I return."

Chapter Twenty-Six

Summer's end approached the browning island of Devenish and painted the trees in gold and mottled hues. Leaves drifted in crispy falls to the ground, lying in soft hills at the feet of the trees. The days declined and the sun lost its heat. The course of the winds changed, and now they bore in their breath a foretaste of winter. Devlina swam in the chilled lake in the evenings, and Ferdia set fish traps. Briefly they both forgot about the distant war and lived in harmony with the island in the lake, and with each other.

In the westward province of Connaught, Princess Emer slept the sleep of unwaking life, her strength waning daily as the late summer sun waned over the purpled mountains of Knocknarea, and over the calm lakes. Men and women gathered dried turf from the bogs, taking it to their homes in carts for the coming winter. They stacked it in layered pyramid reeks and covered it with blankets of moss tied on top by ropes. The warriors prepared their weapons and readied their bodies. One more battle before winter flooded the fords and the war was theirs the chiefs assured them, one more battle.

In the northern province of Ulster, ripened harvests of tall wheat were already reaped and stored in barns for the winter. Apples and pears were packed in baskets of straw and stacked indoors in rows. Cattle and geese were rounded up and herded in pens, and keen hunters prowled the forest in search of wolves to kill. In the thick forests of falling gold, the deep baying of bloodhounds resounded as their masters hunted down elusive grey wolves.

Noble Connor, old and increasingly fragile, having lost all heart for the final battle he knew was coming, handed control of his army to his foster son. One more battle and the war was theirs the warrior assured them, one more battle.

In the verdant middle province of Meath the grass ceased to grow, and early frosts whitened the hills and valleys. Beehive stacks appeared on the landscape, fodder for the cattle to sustain them over winter. The men of Meath covered the beehive stacks with cattle hides to protect the fodder from the coming rains and snows. Cattle were the source of the province's wealth and every effort was employed to keep them safe over the winter. The men of Meath trained wolfhounds to remain with the cattle, sleeping with them and watching over them. Gentle with cattle, the wolfhounds were fierce against wolves, attacking and killing them on sight.

Diarmuid also realised that a final battle was necessary to end the war, and it would be fought at Royal Tara. He inspected the hide of the bull which he held in the palace, believing it would grant him the authority that his high title deserved. He hoped by cunning to acquire the authority he could not impose by force of arms.

Eighteen days before the sacred festival of Sowain, Ailill led the army of Connaught, moving eastward to the ford of the Shannon. The day was calm, the last mild remnants of summer lingering in the rising sun. The army crossed the ford, the waters low, and moved to the site of conflict. On the same morning, Cuchulainn led the army of Ulster, moving southward to the ford of the Boyne. The brown forests they passed through were unmoving, no breezes stirring, and the leaves that fell beneath their feet came down under the command of the season. The armies crossed the land, converged at Royal Tara, and prepared for the final battle.

The armies met at the Stone of Destiny, standing tall and grey on the grassy hill near the palace of Diarmuid. Cuchulainn dismounted from his chariot and approached Ailill on foot, issuing a challenge to step outside the ranks, to fight man against man. The king immediately accepted the challenge to step outside, but demanded that Cuchulainn fight as a warrior, not as a monster.

"There is a time for talking and there is a time for killing," Cuchulainn said. "This is a time for killing. I fight as always in my battle-warp for I have no control over my body. The barbs rise when I take up my sword in anger, and they decline when the fighting is done. Do not ask me why this happens, ask the eternal gods."

The king exposed his upper thigh. "This wound proves that the King of Connaught is not afraid of combat," Ailill declared. "There are foolish men who accused the king of cowardice on the field of battle when his brother was killed. The spirit of his dead brother too came to Knocknashee and made that charge. The first duty of every king is to protect his people, and he did that day. In retreat, he saved the army from utter destruction. Men who would have died that day lived to father more sons for Connaught. Yet his wise decision was regarded as the act of a coward, and even his own chiefs treated him with contempt. A wise decision was seen as a base act, such was the king judged by his chiefs."

At that moment, before Ailill dismounted from his chariot, Epona appeared in the sky riding on Capall. Sparks flashed from the silvered hooves of the white horse as it galloped on high between the two armies. The horse descended at the ford, and Epona took up her golden harp and a ringlet of red roses. Both Ailill and Cuchulainn realised by the presence of the goddess that one of them was destined to die that day.

Ailill dismounted from his chariot and approached his queen, his head held high though he feared death. "The king was prepared to live with the stain on cowardice on his head to save his people from the curse of Morrigan," he said. "That day, on the bloody field of Emain Macha when he saw his brother killed, formed him for life. The king was brave that day, the last man to leave the field, not the first. He had a choice to make between saving the head of his dead brother or saving the men of Connaught from utter destruction. He chose to save the men, and he fought a hard rear-guard action all the way to the ford of the Boyne. But who remembered the king standing alone against the forces of Ulster, his body cut to shreds and his sword red with gore? All chose to remember the retreat but none the courage of the king, though he was but a stripling boy. And when the queen desired war and the king did not, she regarded him as a coward. Did he have to explain to his queen that his reluctance was borne out of concern for his people, not for his own safety? Does he now have to prove his courage to his queen on this bloody field against the best and mightiest warrior in the land? Very well, if that is the price a king must pay for the respect of his queen."

Maeve took hold of his arm before he went into battle, and spoke to her husband in soft tones, "The king has no doubt heard the rumours in drunken company that he is not the father of Grainne. This rumour is false, spun by idle servants as a spider spins a web to catch foolish flies in its web. The king is the father of his daughter and no other. Go to face that terrible warrior as a father and as a husband. Go to face him with the courage of the King of Connaught."

At noon they clashed in ringing iron under a breaking cloud. Their clanging iron swords met in anger, silencing the birdsong and scattering birds in high flight from the forest. The sharp blades cut the shields to pieces and both men fought without protection. Pride glowed in the eyes of Maeve as she watched her husband trade strong blows with the terrible warrior, not giving up a foot of ground. The iron sword of Ailill was torn from his grasp by the ferocity of Cuchulainn's blows, yet he did not yield ground. He danced as they had danced in the blossoming days of their early marriage, his feet moving swiftly, his body evading the cutting sword of the Ulster warrior. Ailill dodged the raining blows on nimble legs, awaiting his opportunity.

Seizing the Ulster warrior by his long hair, the king threw him on the grassy mound. The blow temporarily winded Cuchulainn. Ailill picked up his sword and fell on the fallen warrior. Hands clasped wrists as both men sought to gain the advantage. In silence, the armies watched the pair struggle on the ground. They rolled down the mound, locked together in mortal combat. Now Cuchulainn was on top, seeking to thrust his sword into the breast of the king. Then Ailill rolled on top, his sword aimed at the throat of Cuchulainn, the tip cutting his flesh.

A mighty cheer erupted in the throats of the Connaught ranks when they saw Ailill rising from the ground. He stood up and faced the army of Ulster, his arms raised aloft. The din from the men of Connaught grew louder, and they banged spears on shields. Then the king turned to them, and the din subsided and became mute.

In mounting horror, they saw the sword lodged in the belly of their king, and Cuchulainn rising from the ground unhurt. Ailill stumbled across the field to his chiefs, his bloody hands trying to pull the weapon from his body. His lips moved in seeking help to remove the sword, but they could form no words. He sought to tell them that he had died as a Connaught king in battle, but his voice was silent. The queen leaped from the chariot and rushed to her husband, who fell dead in her arms.

"Terrible warrior, we require three days to mourn our dead king," she said. "He lived as a man unsure, but he died as a king. Who on this bloody field can dispute his courage in battle? Ten thousand years from this day his bold name will still be sung by bards."

"We have already granted Connaught too many concessions in this conflict," replied the warrior. "My noble father has bent over backwards to meet your unlawful demands. My beloved older brother journeyed to your hillfort with generous offerings of peace. It is Cuchulainn you deal with now, not my father or brother. We fight this war on my conditions."

"May the gods never forgive this sacrilege!" replied Maeve.

"Good queen, the gods always forgive the victor," he replied.

Epona plucked her golden harp and the spirit of the king rose from his dead body. She purified the spirit in the waters of the ford and bound it in a garland of red roses.

Then she mounted Capall and galloped across the western ocean to the Isles of the Otherworld. After unlocking the iron gates, she galloped over the islands, calling out their names as she passed over. The spirit requested the Island of Silks, and the horse descended on a white land. The goddess told the spirit that she would return on the eve of Sowain, when it could return for a day to the land of the living.

Now Cuchulainn strode across the ground to the queen, who was clutching the dead body of her husband to her breast. He told her to stand aside, for he wished to cut off the head of Ailill and tie it to his chariot. The angry queen leaped to her feet and drew her sword. The ferocity of her attack drove the warrior back thirty paces.

"Steal the courage of my dead king and husband, would you?" she stormed. "Never, as long as a breath stays in my body! I vowed the next time we met one of us would surely die! That time is now!"

It was against his honour to fight a woman, and his sword was raised in defence, not attack. He backed away from the maddened queen into the ranks of Ulster. The men of Connaught now joined the fight. The battle that followed was raw in intensity and red savagery. Neither side was prepared to yield a foot of ground and no quarter was asked or given. The body of the dead king was taken from the field intact. Cuchulainn would not be permitted to steal his courage. Night alone stopped the tireless carnage, and the armies rested on the grassless plain, the grey granite Stone of Destiny separating them.

Maeve issued instructions to her servants in the lull of night. They put the body of the slain king in a wagon and turned the horses west. Turnod left in the wagon and promised the queen to give her husband a royal burial in the passage tomb at Carrowmore.

"I did not love him in life, but I love him dearly in death," she told the druid. "He did not live as a king but he died as one to the eternal glory of Connaught. The bards will sing his praises in the halls of kings until the end of time, and his name will inspire men who are not yet born. Spare no expense on his burial. Gather ninety women to keen over his body, and store his goods in the royal tomb at Carrowmore so that he can enjoy the afterlife."

At dawn, in the swirling smoke of burning funeral pyres, the two armies clashed bloodily again. The savage fighting cascaded over the stripped mound where the bull had grazed. The warriors were as sunburnt men cutting black turf in a bog, or reaping golden wheat in a field. There was not the emotion of before in their work. They killed without feeling or joy, without pity or remorse. They were as hungry wolves in a forest, killing because they had to kill.

As the battle swayed and moved in ringing iron around the Stone of Destiny, another conflict brewed at Emain Macha. Queen Rosheen left her room after many days of shame to confront Fidelma. She found the young widow in the kitchen preparing food for her children. The queen instructed the children to go outside and play, and closed the door.

Rosheen spoke to Fidelma, "What unfit shame you bring down on us with your immoral behaviour! My son is a married man, and yet you flaunt with him before the servants! A widow should wear ashen rags to mourn for her husband; but no, not you! You wear shining clothes like sprinkled flowers in the spring meadow!"

"Do you, as a mother, wish to deny your son happiness?" replied Fidelma. "A good mother should rejoice in the laughter of her son, not turn her back on him. Daily he puts his life at risk for his family and for his province in the knowledge it could be his last day to see the sun rising or hear the birds singing. It seems to me that the queen is more concerned with what people think than with the welfare of her son."

The queen was stung by the words of Fidelma, and replied, "In this palace we live by rules! We set an example for others to follow! We do not flout the laws but obey them! If you do not live by our laws, you are free to leave Emain Macha!"

"The queen has no sense of proportion," Fidelma responded in a forceful voice. "Why do you not mention the brave warriors of Ulster dying at Royal Tara? Or the keening of broken widows in homes of desolation? Why are you more concerned with my happy love than with their grievous paining loss? May I suggest you examine your own warped views of life and immorality before confronting me."

The old queen, unable to overcome her daughter-in-law by words, or force her from the palace, called Nolan to her side. The queen spoke to her druid. "I have no control over that young strong-willed widow who brings shame on our palace, but I utterly refuse to let her corrupt the children of Lorcan also. Nolan, have the servants prepare a wagon, and take the children to Devlina. They hold her in high esteem and regard her as their lawful mother. Indeed, she is more a mother to them than their own, for she lavishes love on them. That is what children need most in the growing bones of their young years.

Keep them at Devenish until the gods bring that shameless widow to her senses."

"I will go immediately," promised the druid.

"Nolan," said the old queen sadly, "there are many types of women in the world, just are there are many types of men. There are women like Emer who love a man to distraction regardless of everything else. There are women like Maeve who love power and regard it as the highest possible achievement. Then there are women like Fidelma who are obsessed by the cult of the warrior. She did not love her husband for himself, but for the warrior in him. Neither does she love Cuchulainn for himself, but because he is the mightiest warrior in the land. And should he fall on the field of battle, she is not the type to grieve. If she sheds tears, they shall be tears of joy that he died the death of a warrior. Afterwards she shall seek out another warrior to lie down with."

Chapter Twenty-Seven

The wagon reached the lake on the second day, and the druid called out. Ferdia rowed a high-riding black currach over the waves of the lake, his oars breaking the image of the declining sun in the waters. He lifted the little boy and girl into the boat, and Nolan joined them. Then he turned the boat and rowed to the island, where Devlina greeted them with open arms and carried them to her home.

Night fell on the island, and under a burning torch the druid dined on roast trout and chestnuts with Devlina and Ferdia as the children slept. He informed his hosts why Queen Rosheen had sent the children away from the palace. The queen and her daughter-in-law were in conflict, in the way of women living under the same roof. The druid could not take sides in the conflict, commenting only that they were of different eras.

"This war is the cause of all our woes," Ferdia said. "Fidelma and my brother would not behave as they do if we were not at war. In times of peace, men and women think of tomorrow; but in times of war they think only of today. How is Emer?"

"Brigid appeared in my dreams and spoke to me," Nolan said. "She journeyed to Knocknashee to cure the princess, but the goddess of war intervened. Brigid could not act because war is the realm of Morrigan. As we speak, Emer grows weaker."

"I do not understand why the gods give Morrigan free rein," said Devlina. "Do they not know the difference between right and wrong? How can they allow Emer die if Brigid can save her? If they do not give good example, why should mortals honour them? When this war has ended, they will have lost all authority."

"Morrigan is up to no good, of that I am certain," Ferdia said.

Nolan opened a leather pouch he carried about his waist. He took a goblet, and put three toadstools and a clump of mistletoe berries into the vessel. Then he poured in red wine and stirred it in his hand.

"I intend to find out what Morrigan is scheming," he said, grinding the toadstools and berries. "Let my live spirit journey to the Otherworld and consult with wise Brigid. She is the patron goddess of druids, and bestows wisdom on us."

"How can you divide spirit from body?" Devlina asked.

"None but a druid can perform the act," replied Nolan. "My spirit rises so high that everything appears small below. The spirit sees the body it has left, and to which it will return. It hovers as a lark in the meadows of summer and flies to the Otherworld."

Nolan swirled the brew in the goblet, and drank it down. In a few seconds his body convulsed, and his eyes closed. He fell on the earthen floor, his body trembling. Soon the trembling ceased and the body lay still.

Early shafts of dawn's light entered the abode, and gently crept along the earthen floor. The rays passed over the sleeping druid, and wakened him. Ferdia helped him to his feet and offered a goblet of water. Nolan drank the water, and spoke, "Brigid informed me of Morrigan's plan. Emer can be saved, but it requires the greatest sacrifice. The price is so high that none can pay it. Morrigan desires a sacrifice to save the princess."

"A sacrifice of death?" asked Devlina. "Does she desire the offer of a bull, or an antlered stag?"

Nolan shook his head slowly. "No, she requires a man to fight Cuchulainn for the princess. As that terrible warrior is invincible, the man who fights him is certain to die. Men fight for many reasons, for their province, and to find glory. This is different, Devlina. How can a man be found to fight the husband of the princess?" The druid yawned, and said, "Now, let me go to bed for tiredness closes my old eyes."

After the druid went to bed, Devlina took the children to the lake to bathe them. Ferdia walked beneath the bare branches, his sandalled feet kicking the leaves, the children's laughter ringing in his ears. The prince was deep in thought. He spent a day and a night in the forest, before coming up with a solution. He had balanced the life of one woman against the life of a province.

After the contemplation in the forest, he retraced his steps home, where Devlina was drying the children's hair. They dined on smoked trout, and having eaten she put the children to bed, kissing them and pulling hides of sheep over their bodies. She waited until they had fallen asleep before leaving them. Then she washed the copper plates and sat beside her husband.

"I sense you have made your decision," she said, pulling back his hair and kissing his cheek. "I sense it is a decision that shall not please me. So, you are going to fight your brother. I read it in your eyes for they speak as words."

"Yes," he nodded.

"Even though you have no chance of beating him?"

"The outcome matters not a bit, Devlina," he said. "This is something I must do. I have thought much on this matter and see no other way to save her. I must fight my brother."

"Are you fighting because you love Emer?"

"No, I love you, my wife," he replied. "I did love her once, but the spell of Aengus has been broken by my happy life here with you. I could never be happy with Emer for we are complete opposites. With you I have discovered that love is not a ship on a stormy sea, but a steady ship sailing in calm waters. The reason why I must fight for Emer is simple. If we allow her to die when I can save her by fighting, then we cannot call ourselves people of honour, and no man can live without honour. The future fate of Ulster pales in comparison to her life, and likewise the fate of kings. They can call me a traitor if they wish, but I will not stand by and let that happen. Nothing matters in this life except doing what is right."

"Yes, I understand, my love," she answered. "But Cuchulainn will not raise a sword against his own brother."

"I have already solved that problem," he said. "My plan is to wear a mask."

She was silent for a few moments, her freckled brow deep in thought. "Morrigan demands that a warrior must fight invincible Cuchulainn for the life of the princess," she said quietly, having thought out the problem. "She neglected to demand that the warrior must fight to the death. The druid interpreted it that way, but it is not a condition. Therefore, fight Cuchulainn until Emer is restored to blooming health. Fight not in attack but in defence, and keep your shield raised. When she turns up at the bloody ford, remove your mask and embrace your brother."

Next morning Ferdia went into the forest and hacked a thick bough from an oak tree. He sat beneath the tree and carved a mask. His blade shaped and formed the wood, working the knife to cut out slits for his eyes and nose and mouth. Piece by piece the wood fell in chippings until the mask took shape, and it resembled a bull.

As Ferdia carved the mask, warriors fought and died at Royal Tara. Maeve was in the thick of the battle, fighting as a chief and urging her men forward. She promised her daughter in marriage to the chief or warrior who killed Cuchulainn, the fair Grainne. Maeve had sent news to her daughter that her father was dead, requesting her to come home. Many warriors flung themselves against Cuchulainn to win her hand, and many died. Dark night fell, and the business of burning the bodies began again. Prayers were raised on high to the gods, and Epona was offered sacrifice. The weary warriors rested on the grass, exhausted by the fighting.

At the same time that Ferdia rowed the black high-riding currach over the waves, with Devlina and the children of Lorcan waving him farewell, Brigid took matters into her own hands. She flew to Knocknashee and confronted Morrigan in the hilltop fort.

"The chiefs and warriors of Connaught and Ulster who die on the field of battle are men of free will," she said, her strong determination displayed in her voice. "They went to war knowing the dangers and they died in that knowledge. War kills men, and they were aware that they might not return to see their homes again or their families. However, Emer has no part in this bloody conflict, and she should not have been involved. I have journeyed to this hilltop fort with a single mission in mind, and that is to cure her. You stopped me before when I came to heal her, but that was then and this is now. I warn you that I shall not depart from Knocknashee until she is fully restored to health. Do not attempt to stand in my way or you will feel my powers on your back. I can defeat you too as I defeat the Winter Crone each spring."

"Such fighting talk, especially from a foolish goddess who does not understand how to fight, or indeed when to fight," replied the god of war harshly. "Stick to your usual platitudes and leave the business of fighting in the hands of those who know the business. Having said that, I do not intend to stand in your way. But do not for a moment consider this small concession a victory of any kind, moral or otherwise. In this realm I reign supreme, and do not forget it. I stand aside because my plan has been fulfilled."

With these words, Morrigan took flight and flew from the fort to Royal Tara. The dark raven hovered over the standing Stone of Destiny, the scene of the forthcoming final battle, and descended.

When Brigid entered the room where the princess lay, she found the servants weeping. One held a mirror to the mouth of the princess. She held up the mirror and checked for signs of Emer's breath. The mirror was clear, indicating that the princess was dead. Another servant held her head at the bosom of Emer, listening for a heartbeat. The bosom was still, with no rising or falling.

Unseen in the midst of wailing, Brigid draped her cloak of three hues over the dead princess. Then she stooped and kissed Emer lightly on the closed eyes and on the white lips. Life entered the dead princess, and her heart began to beat again. Her eyes opened, and the wailing of the servants ceased. Then Brigid returned to the Isles of the Otherworld, and no mortal was aware she had restored the princess to life.

Emer sat up, much to the joy of the watching servants, who sank to their knees in joy and relief. They informed the princess that the king was dead and that Queen Maeve was fighting in the ranks of the army at Tara. Emer demanded food and a horse. The servants reheated stew, which she ate greedily; but were loath to give her a horse because of her weak condition. She reminded them that the wish of a princess was the command of servants, and they bowed to her wish.

When Ferdia arrived at the trampled and muddied ford of the Boyne and viewed the scene across the river, he beheld the Tara battleground, and was appalled at the number of burning pyres. The fires were turning dark night into bright day, and the lands around Tara burned like a forest in flames. He removed the halter rope from his horse and slapped its flanks, setting the animal free. Then he settled down to rest for the night, prayed to the gods for courage, and waited for morning to dawn.

Dawn frosted the scene of battle in shades of white, and dawned on the dying pyre embers and on the living warriors in pale light. They stood as one with clanking weapons, ready to face another day, ready to do battle again, each man unsure if he would see another dawn. Before the armies could engage, a lone armed warrior strode between them, bearing an oak mask to cover his face. The mask covered his features making him unrecognisable, and it was shaped in the form of a bull.

"I challenge Cuchulainn to step outside," Ferdia said.

"Are you another foolish Peelo, lured by the false promises of the deceitful goddess of war?" asked Cuchulainn, leaving the ranks of the men of Ulster and standing alone. "Have you not heard that the warrior you challenge has no match in the land? Depart from here with your life intact. Do not clash swords with me."

"I am a mortal man, not the son of a god," Ferdia said. "I fight for my own reason, but not because I seek glory."

Cuchulainn walked across the frosted mound to the masked warrior. The ground was bare now, the grass worn away by the feet of warriors.

"Your voice is familiar to me, and your gait," said Cuchulainn. "Who are you, and why do you wear the mask of a bull? Do you not know that the warrior who kills me is destined to become immortal, and his name sung in the halls of kings?"

"This is not a time for talk, but a time for fight," Ferdia said.

"Your death is of your own making," warned Cuchulainn.

The two warriors circled, testing each other. Ferdia's fast spear was brushed aside by the shield of Cuchulainn. The warrior raised his spear and flung it at Ferdia. The prince anticipated the flight and stepped aside. Now they advanced against each other with swords drawn and shields held high. Swords hacked at shields until their protection disappeared. The two warriors locked swords and arms, fighting with iron and with bodies. They fought until noon, until exhaustion filled their arms with lead.

Cuchulainn took water in the ranks of his men, asking if any knew who the masked warrior was. None knew him, though some said he was familiar. "He seemed to anticipate your every move," Desmond Mac Neill said, the brother of slain Hugh. "His walk is like that of your brother, Ferdia, though he is with his wife on Devenish."

"His voice too sounded like my brother," replied Cuchulainn. "He is a shape-shifter who resembles Ferdia, Desmond. He is a trick played on me by Morrigan. He is not my brother, for why should Ferdia come here to fight me?"

Maeve carried a leather bag of cool water to Ferdia who drank without removing the mask. She poured water into the mouth-slit, and it dribbled beneath the mask.

"We have met before, though I know not where or when that was," the queen said, pouring more water into the slit. "Why do you fight that terrible warrior? Is it to wed my daughter, Grainne? For why else would a man fight Cuchulainn, unless to gain a fair wife and a province?"

"There are many reasons why men fight," he replied.

"Be assured that he is destined to die," Maeve said. "Let it be your sharp sword that ends his life. The province of Connaught awaits the warrior who kills him, and the quills of the bards are poised ready to write his name in glory."

The contest resumed in the afternoon, and both armies looked on, grateful for the respite. The combatants were evenly matched. There was no doubt that Cuchulainn was the superior fighter, but the masked warrior knew his every move. When night fell, both were bloodied, but neither was beaten.

Ferdia retired across the ford, to recover on the soil of Ulster. His left arm bled profusely, and he pinched the wound to stop the flow. Hearing footfalls in the ford, he reached for his sword.

"I do not come to break the truce of night," Cuchulainn said, crossing the ford. "I bring a fist of moss to clean the wound, and honey to heal the cut. I have also brought you bread and meat, for food helps the body to regain its strength."

He applied the wet fist of moss to the wound and bound it in linen. Then he cleaned the body of Ferdia, and held a bowl of water to the mask. "Brave warrior, you remind me much of my brother," he said. "As young children we fought with wooden swords in the glens of Ulster and he knew my way of fighting. Now he lives with his wife on an island, and he lives in happiness. He is the future king of Ulster and our province is in good hands. The future is bright under his leadership."

Chapter Twenty-Eight

Dawn dulled cloudily over the silent battlefield. Armed Ferdia crossed the ford, the water brushing his thighs. Cuchulainn left the ranks of his men and went to confront the masked warrior. Their swords raised and saluted before joining. Then they clashed again, and the ringing iron sang out across the fields, and across the river.

Darkness ended the fighting, and the warriors retired from the field. Ferdia ate bread and cold meat, and then crossed the ford and entered the ranks of Ulster. He told the resting warriors that he came in peace. Desmond Mac Neill spoke to him: "Have we met before? A man can wear a mask, but he always walks the same way."

"Yes, we have met before, Desmond," Ferdia said.

"Then you are not a shape-shifter?"

"No, I am a man just like you."

Exhausted Cuchulainn was resting by his chariot, his head leading on the wooden wheel, a physician attending to his wounds. Ferdia knelt at the side of his resting brother, and said, "I have brought mead to help you sleep. One goblet is sufficient."

Cuchulainn thanked the masked warrior, and replied: "You fought well today, and your sword inflicted a deep wound to my shoulder. Yet instead of pushing home the advantage and killing me, you hesitated and drew back. I do not understand why, except that you did. My way of waging war does not permit hesitation or indecision. If there is advantage in combat, I exploit it."

"Sleep," Ferdia said. "We meet again tomorrow morning."

Rain bathed the third day of combat, sweeping in from the sea and turning the ford into a quagmire. The two warriors fought against each other and against the conditions. They sank to their knees in water and mud, slowing their movements. The mud clung to their upper bodies and weapons, turning them into men of clay. At noon they halted to rest, and to eat.

Two great roars greeted Emer's arrival on the battleground. Both sides were united in the happiness that the princess had recovered. The cheers turned to groans, however, when she fell from her horse between the opposing forces. Desmond Mac Neill rushed from the ranks and lifted her in his arms, carrying her to Cuchulainn.

"She is weak," he said, "but I think the sleeping sickness has left her body. Otherwise she could not have ridden here. It is a good sign from the gods. They are on our side."

"Men decide war, Desmond, not gods," Cuchulainn said.

Meanwhile, having slept in the hide of the bull for two days and two nights, King Diarmuid awakened on the morning of the third day, and instructed his servants to carry it to the Stone of Destiny. For the king believed the legend, and thought the stone would proclaim his supreme authority over the five provinces. The king, not wishing to be recognised, dressed as a servant, a cloak concealing his features. The servants placed the hide beneath the Stone of Destiny, and the king crept inside. From the hide he could watch the battle unfolding.

In the afternoon, the rains ceased and the sun emerged from the moving clouds. Steam rose in wispy mists from the ground, rising like ghostly wraiths. Warriors leaned on their spears and watched the fight. The masked warrior was getting the upper hand, pushing Cuchulainn from the ford towards the ranks of Ulster. The fight spilled onto the trodden grass, two men locked in mortal combat. Darkness halted the fighting, Ferdia retiring behind the Boyne, and Cuchulainn returning to the ranks of his men.

Desmond Mac Neill spoke to him: "Cuchulainn, the many wounds you suffered are taking their toll. The strength has drained from your body. Your limbs are hacked and weary from constant fray and loss of blood. Perhaps the masked warrior you fight is a god in disguise, or the son of a god as you are. There is but one way to defeat such a strong adversary, by using the ultimate weapon."

"Where is the honour in that?" he said. "How is Emer?"

"Sleeping in a wagon. She is weak and exhausted from her sickness and from her long ride. I have covered her in woolly hides, and a strong fire burns beside the wagon. Cuchulainn, the future of our province is at stake. We must win this battle or Ulster is lost and our civilisation turned to ashes. We must resort to the ultimate weapon. That masked warrior must be destroyed."

For a long time he pondered about using the weapon of last resort. He was torn between his honour and his oath to protect Ulster against its enemies. In the light of a flickering turf torch held by the chief, he walked to the ford and called out to the masked warrior. His voice echoed across the watery ford. In a few moments, Ferdia appeared, standing on the riverbank.

"Peerless masked warrior," Cuchulainn began, "you have matched me in arms for three days and I could not better you. Perhaps you are a god, or assisted by a god, for no mortal man has withstood me before. I slew Peelo in battle, the son of Manannan Mac Lir, though he bore invincible arms. Fearless masked warrior, this is a contest I dare not lose, for that would signal the defeat of my province. I cannot allow that to happen for I have sworn an oath to defend it with my life. That oath cannot be broken, for it was made to Connor who adopted me as his son. I have in my left hand a weapon called the *gae bolga*. It was given to me by a demigod called Scathnach who trained me in arms. He came from a distant land near the Danube, from the distant land of Bohemia where weapons of consternation are made. This is a dread weapon of last resort that I do not desire to use, but will if I have to. Therefore, depart from here with your honour and your life intact."

"Here I am, and here I remain," Ferdia replied.

"Masked warrior, this weapon does not wound, but kills. It skims over the water like a boy throwing a flat stone. When it touches the flesh, it splits into a thousand pieces as the stings of a thousand angry bees. The barbs burrow into the flesh as worms. Therefore, depart from here with your honour and your life intact."

"Here I am, and here I remain," Ferdia replied.

"Then let us finish this combat by night in the light of the burning torch," Cuchulainn said, taking sword in hand. "If you better me with your sword, I will use the *gae bolga*. I will not use it in honour since it has none, but to protect my province. I am bound by a sacred oath made when I was a boy to protect Ulster."

In the flickering light of the burning torch, Cuchulainn and Ferdia advanced into the watery ford, swords glinting in the torch-light. They clashed once more, the hound of Ulster striving to end the contest by the invincible strength of his sword. But his bloodied body would not respond, sapped by his many wounds and loss of blood, and soon Ferdia began to push him back towards the bank.

Under a relentless attack, Cuchulainn fell on the slippery bank and plunged beneath the water. Ferdia backed away from his submerged brother to take up a defensive position once more. But now Morrigan intervened. She had the power of transformation, the ability to change shapes, and she had not forgotten the insult at Emain Macha when Cuchulainn had rejected her amorous advances. She changed into an eel, large and slippery, and curled into a circle, lying in the path of Ferdia's retreat. The prince's feet trod on the eel, slipped, and he stumbled forward in the ford unable to control his movements.

When Cuchulainn surfaced gasping for breath, he saw the masked warrior flinging his body at him. In the belief that his life was in danger, he released the fearful *gae bolga* from his left hand, the weapon of last resort. It skimmed over the waters and struck Ferdia's upper thigh. The barbs shot out in a thousand jagged pieces and coursed through his body. Ferdia fell headlong into the ford, killed by the weapon of consternation.

A loud piercing scream rent the fabric of night sky, a banshee cry of utter grief. It was not the death-cry of the masked warrior, for he died in silence. It was the wail of

Emer as she ran across the battlefield to the ford, tearing her hair. She fell into the waters on her knees and clasped the dead warrior to her breast.

"I will never forgive you for this!" she screamed. "Never, though you live a thousand years!"

"Who is he?" her husband asked. "Take off his mask."

Emer removed wooden bull mask, and demanded: "How does the greatest warrior in the land now feel that he has killed his own brother?"

Cuchulainn sank to his waist in the ford waters, his pain too great to bear. He took his sword and broke it in two pieces. Then he sought to clasp Ferdia in his arms; but Emer pushed him away, clinging to the body. A struggle followed over Ferdia until Emer, weakened by grief and despair, relented and released her hold.

He carried the body past the ranks of Connaught. The tearful men bowed their heads as he passed in a gesture of respect, and prayed to Epona. As he approached the ranks of Ulster, the men backed away, displaying their horror at the killing. They regarded him as a demon, though his battle-warp had subsided.

Cuchulainn looked each man in the eye, and spoke, "I did not know it was Ferdia." He paused as tears rolled down his youthful cheeks. "Had I known, I would have bared my breast to his sword. I would gladly trade places with him if the gods permitted. Take his body to my father and mother at Emain Macha with every honour and respect due to a prince and a beloved brother. Go home to your lonely wives and families. I remain her on this bloody field to end the war alone."

Dusk fell on the departing army crossing the ford. Emer sat on the wagon beside the body, her keening echoing in the falling dusk. In the ranks of Connaught, many hardened and bloodied warriors were moved to tears. Cuchulainn took up Ferdia's sword, and prepared to fight the final battle.

In the falling dusk, Maeve urged her horses across the field, and the chariot ascended the hill. She dismounted and walked up the remaining few paces, carrying a lighted sod of turf on a pole, the flames dancing on the Stone of Destiny. The flickering flames fell on the hide of the bull. Maeve kicked the hide and Diarmuid emerged.

"Lily-livered cur!" she stormed. "You are as the cunning fox in waiting, seeking to profit from the misfortunes of others!" She took up her sword and banged it on the Stone of Destiny. "Get out of here before you feel my cutting sword on your scrawny neck, you dirty swine! A cur such as you does not deserve the honour of High King or the title! You bring nothing but shame on a noble title! My husband was a far better king than you, and a better man!"

King Diarmuid, fearful of the queen's anger, vacated the hide and scurried back to his palace. The queen took up position inside the hide, rested her head on her arm, and slept. When dewy morning arrived on the hill, Cuchulainn stood alone in the field armed with the sword of his brother, and ready for combat. Honour prevented the Connaughtmen from attacking a lone warrior. They were reluctant to move forward, though urged on by their chiefs. They murmured about going home, as the Ulstermen had gone home, and the haranguing of the chiefs fell on deaf ears, and the men refused to move.

Two young Connaught chiefs, in the expectation of glory and the hand of the fair Grainne in wedlock, split from the ranks. The men shouted insults at the young chiefs, saying they were not true men of Connaught by attacking a lone and wounded man. But Grian Guinan and Niall O'Brien ignored the taunts of their men, for they longed to hear their names on the lips of bards.

"My name is Niall O'Brien and you killed my father," The young chief called out. My name will ring in the halls of kings when I kill you."

"I am already dead, Niall," he replied weakly. "For when I killed my beloved brother with the *gae bolga*, I killed myself too. I welcome death, though I intend to sell my life dearly."

They clashed in bouts of ringing iron, and O'Brien proved that he was as skilled in battle as his father. Cuchulainn had been wounded by Ferdia and was not agile. He laboured to escape the cutting blows of the young Connaught chief. O'Brien's sword pierced his lower leg and slowed him further. O'Brien moved in for the kill, but was killed by a swift thrust of Cuchulainn's sword.

Now Grian Guinan engaged the wounded hound of Ulster. His swift sword struck Cuchulainn in the chest. The hard blow further weakened his body, but not his will to fight. He summoned up his remaining strength, and killed the young Connaught chief as the clouds cleared from the sun. In shafts of emerging bright light, he struggled up the hill to the Stone of Destiny, leaving a trail of blood in his wake. Removing his bloodied cloak, he tore it into strips, and tied his body to the stone.

Morning dawned in frost on the ranks of Connaught, standing in the ragged field, looking up at the Stone of Destiny. The war-weary men saw Cuchulainn standing upright, sword in hand. His body was torn, and his skin reddened with blood. The bodies of two young chiefs lay dead nearby, a raven feasting on one of them. The men did not move to remove the bodies, for they feared Cuchulainn was still alive.

Morrigan appeared in the ranks of the watching warriors and spoke in a harsh voice, "Why do you hesitate? Did I not promise Connaught victory in this war? Did I not promise the death of Cuchulainn? He is dead. Go up there and cut off his head, for the man who does acquires his courage."

No warrior moved to advance in the ranks. No man believed Cuchulainn was dead. He was standing at the stone, sword in raised hand, and they feared his vengeance. Even the harsh words of the goddess of war did not stir them to move.

The goddess transformed into a black raven and flew over the field of battle and over the two dead chiefs. It alighted on the left shoulder of the dead warrior, and plucked out his eyes. Its harsh call resonated over the ford and over the watching men. Cuchulainn was dead.

The ranks of Connaught did not rejoice over the death of their most implacable enemy. Wearily they trudged over the bloody field, their heavy legs dragging in the muck, their hearts low. Twelve men removed the bodies of the dead chiefs and placed them in wagons. They turned the wagons and headed to the ford of the Shannon.

A group of men worked to untie the body of Cuchulainn from the stone. As they untied the strips holding his arm aloft, the sword fell from his dead grasp. The sword bounced and struck the stone three times, its ringing sound echoing in the still morning. It sounded over the hill and over the river, ringing out like a bell on a clear day. The sound rang out and echoed back to their ears, three times. Beneath the stone the queen slept in the hide of the bull, and the ringing did not waken her. The falling sword pierced the hide, and the heart of the sleeping queen. A low cry came from the hide, the dying breath of Maeve. In a moment the cry passed, and the land returned to quietness.

It was Balor Mac Carthy, son of Malachi, who heard the groan of the dying queen. This young man had joined the war after the death of his father; not with a sword, but with a quill. He desired to record the events for the men of the future. He pulled the sword of Ferdia from the hide and revealed the dead queen, her blood turning the goldenhide red. Then he broke the sword on the Stone of Destiny, saying, "Let us return home."

Morrigan appeared in their midst, bronzed and armed, and in full fury spoke: "The road to Ulster is open! Seize the opportunity now and make haste to Emain Macha! Occupy that rich province and sack its towns! There is much booty up there!"

The men of Connaught, their king and queen dead along with most of their chiefs, hesitated to act. They could turn their faces north, or they could turn their faces west. It was Balor Mac Carthy who stepped out from their midst and spoke to them.

"Warriors, ye know that my father was Malachi, chief of the Mac Carthy clan," he began. "He was wise in council though he did not read or write. He taught me the ways of the world as I caught slippery turf from his slean. He said men must heed the gods, but only if they are right. He said men were given free will and can choose their own paths in life. Morrigan urges ye to strike north and sack Ulster. Is this not the same goddess who destroyed the horses with her spell? Is this not the same goddess who did not raise her hand to help them when wolves tore the flesh from their bones? Is this not the same goddess who watched and did nothing when the horses drank the water she poisoned? Are not horses sacred to us? Warriors of Connaught, heed not her cries of war. Let us return to our homes and to our families."

The words of Balor sent Morrigan into a frenzy. "Warriors, do not listen to him!" she shrieked. "He is a coward and the son of a coward!"

"We do not listen to you now, Morrigan," Balor said. "As for they who do listen, they are the worst fools."

Now the young chief issued instructions to the men, and ordered a wagon for the lifeless bodies of Ferdia and Cuchulainn. He told the men to treat the bodies with due reverence and respect. The men put the bodies of the brothers in the wagon, and took it to the ford. There Desmond Mac Neill accepted the intact bodies. He put away his sword and held out his hand. Balor shook his hand, a sign that the war was over. Then the young chief of the Mac Neills urged the horses into the ford, and the wagon crossed into the territory of Ulster, and set out on the road to Emain Macha.

Another wagon brought the body of the dead queen home to her people, who grieved openly at the loss of Queen Maeve. The news of her death spread quickly by word of mouth across the land. Thus when the rolling wagon carrying her body crossed the ford of the Shannon, it was met by thousands of them bearing turf torches. Bonfires lit the road to Knocknashee, lighting up the bleak land.

For three days and three nights the body of the queen rested in the hilltop fort so that people could pay their last respects. On the morning of the fourth day, Turnod gave instructions to move the body to the passage tomb at Carrowmore. The queen's chariot followed behind carrying her crown and jewellery, and her bolts of fine cloth. After the body was burned on a funeral pyre, the bones were placed on a stone dish. Then the dish was placed in the passage tomb at Carrowmore with the possessions.

After the solemn funeral ceremony at Emain Macha, the bones of Ferdia and Cuchulainn were placed in the long passage tomb at Navan, near the unfinished palace of Emer and Cuchulainn on the hill. Three hundred women keened over the tomb of the brothers, their mournful cries drowning out the geese flying overhead. As darkness fell on the land, the mourners drifted slowly from the passage tomb and returned to the palace of King Connor.

Emer did not return, but mounted her horse. She rode to the unfinished palace and set it alight. As the palace blazed, she urged the horse on the long road to Cashel.

On the eve of the festival of Sowain, Epona summoned the spirits of slain warriors to the iron gates of the Otherworld. At midnight she opened the iron gates with a key she kept on a twig of white roses around her slim neck. Then she opened a silver casket in which she hoarded the memories of the spirits. As each spirit fled from the Otherworld to the land of the living, Epona returned their memories, warning them that memory could be used for good or for evil.

She also warned them they had but one day in the land of the living and they must return before the last echo of the midnight bell. If they failed to return before the echo faded away, the iron gates would be closed permanently against them. Then they would roam for eternity over lonely hills and valleys seeking another home, but destined never to find one.

The spirits found no welcome in the palace at Emain Macha. There was no feast for them, or no fires burning to welcome them. The king and queen were mourning their dead sons. No laughter rang in the halls of the palace, or no torches burned.

Neither did the roaming spirits find a warm welcome at the hilltop fort of Knocknashee. No chiefs were gathered to celebrate the festival, and no games were played. The servants were in deep mourning for their lost king and queen. They went about their duties silently, and prayed to Manannan Mac Lir for the safe passage of Grainne.

The god of the sea heard the prayers and did not hinder the passage of the ship bringing Grainne to her home in Connaught. A single-masted craft sailed into Galway Bay loaded with ingots of iron and jars of red wine. A lone woman stood on the prow of the ship, watching the land she had left five years previously as a girl. She had flaxen hair, inherited from her mother, and she wore a green dress and cloak. When the craft berthed, she disembarked, and was greeted by the new chiefs of Connaught. Grainne was now queen.

The declining sun cast its dying rays over the island in the lake where Devlina was heavy with child. The declining rays moved over the western province of Connaught. It burnished the bogs and the small worked fields surrounded by stones. Its rays fell on the farmers returning to their homes, and on the herders of skinny sheep calling to their prowling dogs. Shafts of golden light fell on the mound of Carrowmore where the bones of Queen Maeve lay resting beside the bones of King Ailill, before descending into a copper sea.

Chapter Twenty-Nine

The war ended because it had run its course. Neither gods nor men had brought it to a close, but its own lack of momentum, its own weariness. Since there was no victor in the war, there was no vanquished. Both sides retired behind their watery borders, the Shannon in the west and the Boyne in the north. The cessation of fighting brought relief to both provinces, to the neglected fields, and to the families of fighting men. But Morrigan secretly resolved to start the war again because men of peace did not make offerings at her altars. Meanwhile, bards were busy sharpening their quills to compose the heroic deeds of warriors.

The last casualty of the war was its greatest warrior, who was killed by thirty wounds to his body. Epona journeyed to the Stone of Destiny, removed the spirit of Cuchulainn by playing her golden harp, and purified it in the waters of the river before garlanding it in sprigs of red roses. Then she mounted Capall with the spirit in her arms and galloped over the western ocean to the Isles of the Otherworld. Sparks flew from the silver hooves of the horse like a shower of falling stars.

The kind-hearted goddess called out the names of the islands below as Capall galloped across the sunless sky. The wispy spirit responded and asked to be set down on the green island called the Delightful Plain. Capall descended on the island and the spirit dismounted. Before departing, Epona told the spirit that she would summon it on the eve of Sowain.

Under a yellow sunless sky, two wispy spirits chased a large purple bull across bogs of emerald heather and through forests of sapphire spreading trees. The fleeting spirit of the bull skimmed over the land followed by the happy spirits. Bright yellow light streamed from a sunless sky on the land where no darkness existed. It was a green island of continuous day, and no approaching dusk interrupted the hunts, and no curtain of night came down on the land. The light held sway, beaming down endlessly on the hunters and on the hunted.

"Have we pursued a bull before?" asked Ferdia.

"Perhaps, in another life," replied Cuchulainn.

"I sense we have known each other before."

"I sense the same. Perhaps it was our destiny to be friends."

"Perhaps we were closer than friends."

"Yes, I sense the same."

They chased the purple bull from the sapphire forest and the beast fled on wispy hooves towards a place of boulders, a dolmen of three standing stones and a flat capstone. Trapped at the dolmen, it bellowed and tore at the orange grass with its hoof, kicking it towards the sky. Cautiously, Cuchulainn and Ferdia approached the trapped beast.

"The beast has three horns," Cuchulainn said.

"Watch out for the middle horn when you leap on its back," Ferdia warned. "I know not why it has three horns, except that it has. It must be a magical beast."

318

Cuchulainn slowly approached the spirit bull, its wide nostrils emitting plumes of green smoke. The beast pawed the ground again, watching the grey spirit advancing. It charged, lowering its great head, and thundering at the spirit. Cuchulainn stood his ground, waiting for his opportunity. At the last moment, he leaped over the horns, and flipped onto the back of the beast.

"Hold tight!" Ferdia said.

The bull bucked and twisted, trying to throw the rider, kicking out in a desperate attempt to dislodge the spirit. Unable to throw off the rider, it sped from the place of stones. Ferdia pursued the beast over emerald-topped heather and through sapphire forests to a lake of still golden waters. The beast skimmed over the waters, like a flat stone thrown by a young boy. Ferdia chased the galloping beast and rider across the surface of the golden lake. The beast stopped, and in plumes of green smoke turned to challenge Ferdia. Cuchulainn dismounted and walked on the lake to Ferdia.

"Watch out for the third horn," advised Cuchulainn.

Ferdia approached the bull carefully, walking with wispy feet on the surface of the golden lake. The beast bellowed and tore at the calm waters with its hoof. Droplets of water erupted and cascaded as falling coins, golden in the light. It charged at Ferdia who prepared to grab the spearing horns. The beast proved too quick for his hands, its horns goring into his belly and flipping him into the sky. He fell with a splash on the surface of the lake, and returned to Cuchulainn.

"Tomorrow, perhaps," Ferdia said.

"Tomorrow?" queried Cuchulainn. "I know not that word."

"The word slipped out," Ferdia said. "Why do I use a word that has no meaning? That is a problem I am unable to answer. Why do I use words when I know not their origin?"

"Perhaps we shall find the answers to our questions on another island," said Cuchulainn. "There are a hundred thousand here. Do you think we have always lived here, or do you think we were taken here? I seem to recall a journey on a steed, but perhaps it was a dream."

"I have no memory of a past existence, but I sense that I have been in another place in another world," Ferdia replied. "Spirit, to my way of thinking this is a place of reward. We can hunt, and we can sip wine, and we can visit the Isle of Women if we wish. Yet for some reason I have no desire to visit that place. I must therefore conclude that there was a special woman in my past, that is if I had a past. But I am unable to remember her, or my former life."

"Perhaps there was no past," suggested Cuchulainn. "However, I too believe that we are being rewarded for mighty deeds that we both performed in another life. But who is to say that everywhere is not like this? Perhaps this is how it is meant to be, a place of pleasure for all."

"Let us think about Epona and she will come," Ferdia said.

The two spirits thought about the meek goddess, and in an instant Capall appeared above them in the sunless sky, its silver hooves sparkling. Epona descended on the horse and asked what they required, for the request of a spirit was her command. She listened as they explained, and then responded. "This is indeed a place of pleasure, but there can be no pleasure without pain," she told them. "In the furthest part of the western sea lies an island, alone and isolated from all others. It is called the Isle of Wolves. That island is a place of punishment. I can take ye there, but heed well my warning. Do not dismount from Capall, or do not let your wispy feet touch the soil of that island. If that happens, ye are doomed to remain there for ever. They who inhabit that island cannot leave, not even for the sacred festival of Sowain."

The two spirits mounted the magical horse, Ferdia clinging to the white mane and Cuchulainn to the white tail. The horse galloped over the western sea, its hooves trailing bright sparks. As it galloped, the sunless sky grew darker until there was no light except the sparks. Then the horse descended and stood on an island of darkness. The deep baying of wolves filled the darkness, and Capall neighed fearful of the howls.

The spirit of a running man darted from jagged rocks, pursued by a pack of howling wolves biting at his wispy heels. The spirit emitted an unearthly cry, calling out in the darkness for help. Ferdia was about to dismount, but Cuchulainn held his arm. They could offer no help to the persecuted spirit.

"What was his crime?" asked Cuchulainn.

"He fought for a dishonourable cause," replied Epona.

Capall ascended and galloped into the east, and into the light. The horse descended on the island called the Delightful Plain, and Ferdia spoke, "How can a kind goddess allow a spirit to suffer that torture?"

"Noble spirit, the gods do not punish men," she replied. "Men punish themselves by their own deeds."

They walked side by side through a forest of purple oaks and holly trees, and came to a clearing. Under beams of yellow light they rested, sipping mead beneath arching boughs. As they sipped the sweet mead, two spirits approached, and Ferdia offered them a drink. The spirit of Dara O'Brien thanked him for the offer, sipped the mead, and gave the goblet to the spirit of Rory Guinan.

"I was on the distant Isle of Snow but I was not happy there," O Brien said. "Epona grants every wish and she took me here. I asked her what my name was, but she said spirits have no name. I seem to recall I had a name in a past life, but perhaps it was a dream."

"Do you give much thought to that, or to whether you lived before in another world or in another place?" asked Ferdia.

"Yes, I do," said O'Brien. "I know not this spirit at my side, and yet feel strongly that we have known each other before. I have the same strong feeling about the spirit at your side. Is it possible that we were friends in another life before now?"

"Epona grants every wish but that one," said Cuchulainn. "She turns a deaf ear to the question of another life before this life. Since the kind-hearted goddess has our best interests at heart, we must conclude that she knows what is good for us. I like to believe that we were friends in another life, and that we sipped mead together and spoke of our friendship."

O'Brien returned the goblet and said: "Is this the only life we have known, or have we known another somewhere in our past?"

"No, this is all we know or all we have ever known," said Rory Guinan, his flowing hair now grey like his features. "What is the use of asking questions which have no answer? We must make the best of this life and enjoy it while we can. Tell me, good spirits, does a bull of three horns roam this island?"

"Yes, and we pursue it now," answered Ferdia.

"To what purpose?" asked O'Brien.

"To ride the wild beast and to tame it, of course," said Cuchulainn. "That is what we must do."

"What then?" asked O'Brien. "A tame bull is of no use."

"Do not bother thinking about the future, good spirits," said Rory Guinan. "There is no future here or no past. There is but the present. We who dwell here must live in the present for the days are ceaseless. Just learn to enjoy the present."

"There is no tomorrow?" asked Cuchulainn.

"I know not that word," Guinan replied.

In the yellowed forest on the Isle of Apples, under the sapphire spreading trees, the spirit of Malachi Mac Carthy strolled with the spirits of two young chiefs, Niall O'Brien, and Grian Guinan. They picked wispy apples, eating as they walked. "Perhaps we were friends in another life," said Mac Carthy.

"Everything is possible," said Niall.

"Perhaps you were my sons too," said Mac Carthy.

"Perhaps," said Grian.

On the Island of Silks, the spirit of King Ailill approached a tall castle of many turrets. He walked through fields of purples and greens. In a window, he saw the spirit of Queen Maeve. Although she too was grey, Ailill saw her in different hues. Something from his past lingered yet.

"Your hair is the colour of ripened wheat in the broad meadows of fruitful Meath under the celestial August sun at the sacred festival of Lughnasa before the cutting arched scythe reaps the sunbursting harvest," he said. "And your bluebell eyes are as the precious lapis lazuli mined by giants that come from strange and distant lands to the east on the backs of humped and thirsty camels across boundless seas and impassable continents. And your face is as a pool of crystal water set in an endless desert of hot sands that weary travellers long to behold beneath a scorching sun hotter than the fires of Sowain to welcome the gods. Come with me and be my only love until the stars cease to shine and the heavens tumble about our feet as falling sleet on the windswept mountains of Connaught. I shall build for you a royal palace of gold and ivory and silks to shame the fabled palace at Persepolis where the Kings of Persia looked down on the world from thrones of gold. I shall command for your dainty feet a thousand rugs of closely woven threads and rose petals to garland your craning neck. We shall be happy in our castle, and have many sons."

The End